THE BROKER

THE BROKER

Harold Q. Masur

ST. MARTIN'S PRESS • NEW YORK

Copyright © 1981 by Harold Q. Masur
For information, write: St. Martin's Press,
175 Fifth Avenue, New York, N.Y. 10010
Manufactured in the United States of America

Library of Congress Cataloging in Publication Data

Masur, Harold Q., 1909-
  The broker.

  I. Title.
PS3525.A835B7   813'.54   81-8756
ISBN 0-312-10589-4   AACR2

THE BROKER

When Frank Hanna, the Wall Street
Wizard, tries to take over Arcardia
Films, broker Mike Ryan and his partner Liz Harwood are caught up in a web
of financial conspiracy and murder.

1

At precisely 3 : 59, with sixty seconds remaining before the closing bell, two red bars flashed across the digital clock high above the floor of the New York Stock Exchange, and six hours of tumultuous activity flared into a final scene of Breughe-lesque bedlam. Brokers, specialists, and clerks in their powder-blue jackets broke into cheers and tossed computer cards into the air. The trader from Gregorius & Company, normally phlegmatic, performed a small spontaneous gavotte.

By some rare coincidence that only chartists or astrologers might find significant, sixty-four million shares had changed hands and the Dow Jones Index had soared exactly half that amount. Finally, decisively, after weeks of relentless erosion, the market had turned. In a single session pervasive gloom changed to buoyant optimism.

Wall Street. The denizens working this command post of American capitalism devoutly believe that money is the root of all happiness. It occupies less than one square mile of Manhat-tan's lower extremity, with the graceful spire of Trinity Church visible at its western border. The church ministers to the spirit of its parishioners while not endorsing their sentiments.

One block east, in a high corner office of a glass-panelled skyscraper, Mike Ryan, chief executive of Gregorius & Com-pany, waited for the late tape to post its closing figures. When the Dow Jones industrial average appeared he smiled with satisfaction. Almost, he thought, as if Fred Hanna himself had engineered the reversal. His own information credited institutional investors and foreign capital, suddenly aware of bargains. And tomorrow morning the public would be swarm-

7

ing aboard to further fuel a suddenly rampant bull.

He leaned toward his desktop Videomaster and punched out the UMI symbol of Universal Media Industries. His smile stretched wider. Up two and a quarter for the day. Hanna would be pleased. He tapped the keys again. Arcadia Films unchanged, one of the few issues that had failed to respond to the buying surge. Better and better.

"Renews one's confidence in capitalism, doesn't it, Mike?"

He glanced up and saw Elizabeth Harmon, the firm's chief security analyst, framed in the doorway. He beckoned her in and pointed. "Sit."

"I recognise that voice," she said. "What am I being accused of now?" She crossed her legs, eyes speculative and faintly mocking, a slender woman in her early thirties with dark tousled hair and a pert face. Resourceful, subtly intuitive, she had a sense of style and purpose and a graduate degree from the Harvard School of Business Administration. "I take it there's a problem."

"There is. What the hell have you been smoking, Liz?"

"Never touch the stuff."

He held up the current issue of the Gregorius Market Survey and waved it in the air. She saw that he had used a heavy felt-tipped pen to slash red ovals around a dozen phrases.

"Let me read,' he said. "Quote: 'In view of the above, equity postures at this time are exceedingly viable'." He dropped the sheet with distaste. "Geezus, Liz! Where in hell did that one come from? If you mean common stocks are in a buying range, why in Christ's name don't you say so?"

"That fancy locution is not mine, friend. Nor any of the others you've underscored."

"They all appear over your name."

"I admit only to the basic ideas. I simply said there were bargains all over the board. And today's activity bears me out. But my copy was edited."

"By whom?"

"The grey eminence himself."

"Anson?"

8

" Mr. Anson Gregorius. Correct. I sent you a memo last week. What happened to it?"

He indicated a mass of documents on his desk. " Who has time for memos? I'm snowed under. I apologize."

" Accepted. May I offer a comment?"

" You'll make it anyway. Go ahead."

" These last few weeks you seem to be concentrating all your efforts on one single project, promoting Mr. Fred Hanna's insatiable appetite to swallow the world."

" Not the world, Liz. Just one small slice of Hollywood. Arcadia Films would fit very nicely into Hanna's Universal Media. I know your opinion of the man. But Gregorius & Company is now his investment banker and you'll have to adjust."

" Why did you hire me, Mike?"

" Two reasons. You're decorative and you're smart, not necessarily in that order." He grinned. " Your opinions are valuable and appreciated. Hold the advice until solicited. On those terms you're worth every nickel the firm pays you. Probably more."

" Then how about a raise?"

" You had a raise last month."

" Inflation is killing me."

" You and everyone else. Let's get back to Anson. When did he start tampering with your deathless prose?"

" This is a first. I think he has too much time on his hands now that you're in charge. God help us if he intends to read all the copy headed for the printer and starts editing. I know I can't turn a phrase as elegantly as Galbraith, but my prose is generally serviceable and our customers understand what I write. Please, Mike, can't you find something else to keep him busy?"

" Like what?"

" I don't know. A concubine, maybe."

" At his age? After that last coronary? You want to kill the old boy? It's a harmless pastime, Liz. Let him enjoy it."

' No, sir. Not at my expense. Our market surveys get a fairly

9

wide distribution. My colleagues would laugh me out of the profession."

"Your colleagues, dear heart, dish out some of the most flatulent claptrap I ever read."

"You think so? Wait until you see next week's report on Universal Media."

Mike clapped palm to his forehead. "Oh, no! Anson doctored that one too?"

"It's at the printer now. Without troubling my conscience too much, I characterized Fred Hanna as an aggressive and innovative executive. Which indeed he is. Too aggressive and too innovative. Guess what Anson changed it to?"

"I'm afraid to ask."

"Entrepreneurial dynamism."

Mike laughed. "Jesus! The old man has a flair."

"Not really. I think he collects that stuff and files it away so he can torture me later."

The intercom buzzed and Mike answered. "All right," he said. "I'm on my way." He stood up. "We'll talk about it later, Liz. Our salesmen—excuse me—our account executives are waiting. Dinner tonight?"

"If you like."

"What I'd like is a little more enthusiasm. Pick you up at seven."

*   *   *

Some twenty-odd registered representatives, a varied assortment, had assembled in the board room. Some of the older men were still brooding over the loss of customers who had fled the market in the early seventies. They recalled those years as a traumatic experience. Marginal producers had been forced to abandon Wall Street for other jobs. Many brokerage firms had folded or merged to survive.

From the front of the large room Mike's gaze encompassed the group. He cleared his throat and the murmuring stopped. "Have I got your undivided attention, gentlemen? Thank you. As you all know, Gregorius & Company has in the past participated in various financing projects for Universal Media Industries. I am pleased to say that we are now acting as syndicate manager for a new issue of UMI convertible bonds. Gregorius is anxious to show UMI how effectively we can handle this financing.

" First, a brief profile on the company. Fred Hanna founded the business as a small electronics outfit manufacturing transmitter components. It was an instant success. Over the years, through a series of acquisitions and mergers it has become a communications conglomerate that controls a network of radio and television stations. The Universal Broadcasting System. UBS. Recent acquisitions include a publishing division with a trade-book list and several magazines.

" Share earnings of the parent company have increased in each of the past twelve years. Debt structure is sound. Unlike other conglomerates, Mr. Hanna has limited acquisitions to his principal area of operations—communications and entertainment." He paused. " Why a new equity issue at this time?"

Ryan was finely tuned to the wavelength of his people and he sensed a quickening of interest.

" First, to raise money for an earlier bond that matures next month. Second, to increase the amount of securities held by the company itself. Some of you probably know that Universal Media has been accumulating a substantial position in the shares of Arcadia Films. Objective, a merger or a possible takeover. A preliminary approach to Arcadia's management has been unproductive. So on Friday, UMI will announce a tender offer to Arcadia stockholders. As payment for their shares, Fred Hanna is offering a package of securities worth substantially more than Arcadia's current quote.

" As a consequence, only half of the new bond issue will be available for sale. So each of you will receive only a limited allotment. A registration statement has been filed and is now in effect. Copies of the prospectus are now in the supply room. A tombstone ad appears in tomorrow's papers. I would like to see your entire allotment sold out within forty-eight hours. Any questions?"

11

" I'm a bit confused, Mr. Ryan. Arcadia Films hasn't turned a profit in years. The studio is sick. In fact it's terminal. Universal Media needs it like I need a case of hemorrhoids."

There was restrained laughter.

Mike shook his head. " Your diagnosis is premature, Murray. Mr. Hanna believes he can turn Arcadia around. Under any circumstances it would be a valuable acquisition for UMI. It has an extensive film library which could be used for exhibition over the television network, saving UBS from having to bid for pictures on the open market. Consider, too, Arcadia's potential for additional TV programmes through its production facilities. And last, but not least, the studio's important real estate properties."

" If it's so attractive, Mr. Ryan, how come NBC or CBS haven't tried to grab it?"

" Because the Justice Department would block any such move as a violation of the anti-trust statutes. UMI, however, is not in the same league and poses no threat of monopoly."

" Has an acquisition been cleared with Justice?"

" Yes. UMI already has a favorable ruling." His eyes swept the room. " Any other questions? No? Okay then. Now listen to me and listen good. One important caveat. A warning. Until news of UMI's tender offer to Arcadia's stockholders is made public, no employee of this firm will buy for his own account, for his relatives, for any of his customers, through us or any other brokerage house, one single share of Arcadia Films in anticipation of a possible merger. Noncompliance of this prohibition puts you in violation of SEC regulations. You do so at your own peril. Gregorius will not come to your rescue. Am I clear?"

Heads bobbed in acknowledgement.

" In fact, gentlemen, I would take pleasure in personally booting any malefactor out on his ass, whether he's caught by the law or not." He glanced apologetically at the three female account executives. " Excuse the language, ladies. You would of course be treated more gently, simply escorted to the door with no severance pay and no letter of recommendation. At this

12

particular time Gregorius wants no problem with any government agency. Do you read me?"

" Loud and clear," Murray sang out.

" Good. I won't mention it again. Please take home a copy of the UMI's prospectus on the new convertibles and read it tonight. Now one additional item. Next week's market report by Elizabeth Harmon examines the company's operations. I want you to study it carefully in preparation for our move to acquire Arcadia Films. That's it for today."

He turned abruptly and headed for his office.

2

The huge corner room with its hand-carved desk, its thin Bokhara rug, and its commanding view of New York harbour, had been vacated by Anson Gregorius and ceded to Mike Ryan when the old man had finally and reluctantly decided to relinquish management of the firm to his administrative assistant. The office was peaceful now, largely deserted except for a few of the backroom people. Thank God, Mike thought, for computerized procedures. Fifty clerks working through the night would not have been able to cope with today's hectic session on the floor of the Exchange.

He leaned back, fingers laced behind his neck, relishing the perquisites of rank. His recent primacy at Gregorius & Company was a long long haul from those early years of apprenticeship on Montreal's St. James Street where he'd first learned the art of hawking securities. Although what he'd sold in those days could hardly be called securities. Engravings, perhaps, printed in wholesale lots.

As a schoolboy, Mike recalled, money problems had been

incessant and pervasive, his father constantly complaining about the cost of milk to feed his ulcer and his four children. Mike had been forced to wear his older brother's hand-me-downs. The experience had matured him early. Upon graduation from high school he had accepted an offer to learn about stocks and bonds from an uncle who had settled in Canada.

It was a boiler-room operation, shady and somewhat distasteful. As always, Mike had been an apt and diligent pupil. The timbre of his voice belied his age. He found that he had an unusual talent for salesmanship, a line smooth enough, as his uncle put it, to charm the drawers off a nun. Within a single year, pursuing various leads, relentlessly persevering on the telephone, he was selling more paper than both older salesmen combined. His victims ranged from bus drivers to brain surgeons, all with little or no business experience.

Memory leapfrogged back through the years in a spinning kaleidoscope that sat him once again at the rickety desk, telephone in hand, a ring of sincerity in his voice. He could remember almost verbatim the high-powered hustle.

" Let me tell you something, Mr. Adams. I earn my livelihood as a security dealer. If I steer you wrong, I lose you as a customer and I'm out of business, right? I can't afford to do that. So I've been waiting for a special opportunity. And I'm delighted to tell you that today, right now, we're in luck. This one is gilt-edged, a sure thing. We recently managed to accumulate a sizeable block of Alberta Mining Ltd. at eighty cents a share. That was Tuesday. Today it's being quoted at one dollar. A profit of twenty-five per cent in just forty-eight hours. Now listen to this, Mr. Adams. In order to generate good will, and to win new customers for this firm, we are prepared to sacrifice our own profit. So if you place an order now, this morning, you can have a limited number of Alberta Mining at our original cost. Without blinking an eye, you already have a profit. All I ask is that you hang onto your shares until I give you the word. God alone knows where this stock is headed."

Mike remembered lowering his voice to a confidential whisper.

14

"I am going to let you in on a secret, Mr. Adams. I have this in strict confidence from one of the company's geologists. An incredibly rich vein of uranium ore was discovered only last week less than one mile from the Alberta property. Please keep this under your hat. We don't want to drive the price up into the stratosphere before all our customers have completed their buying. That's all I have to say. Except don't let this one pass or you'll never forgive yourself. I'm not even sure I can handle your order at this time, but I promise I'll do my best. All right, sir. I have an order blank in front of me. What is your pleasure?"

Mike stirred. It had been raw but effective. He was not proud of those years, not proud of the merchandise he had peddled, nor of pandering to naked cupidity. But at that time, and in that place, only a pitchman unencumbered by scruples could survive.

But making money in that fashion had failed to satisfy him. He began to take courses at night school and spent much of his spare time in the Economics Room at the public library. And as he grew more sophisticated, as his horizons expanded, he hungered for more legitimate challenges.

He had visited New York on several occasions, vectoring in on Wall Street like a homing pigeon, standing on the Visitors' Balcony of the Stock Exchange and watching the frenetic activity below. Here was the trading heart of a great nation and he could not resist its call. He discussed it with his uncle, who, although reluctant to see Mike leave, knew that sooner or later it was inevitable.

So on a cold and blustery November morning he shook his uncle's hand and boarded an Air Canada flight to La Guardia.

His timing was perfect.

In the superheated economy of the late Sixties there was an illusion of endless prosperity. On Wall Street, the bulls were rampant. Private companies were going public at arbitrary prices that generated huge profits for the promoters. Mutual funds were plunging recklessly into new untested issues. Glamor stocks soared to premiums that discounted not only the future

15

but the next millennium. Money, it seemed, was spermatic. Properly invested in the womb of Wall Street, it would produce wildly proliferating offspring. Thousands of newcomers opened accounts. Brokerage firms were expanding with quixotic optimism.

In this atmosphere, Mike Ryan quickly found an opening. A large retail house took him on, provided the necessary training, and in due course he breezed easily through the examination that qualified him as a registered representative. A stranger in the city, he needed customers in order to generate commissions. He joined organizations, made friends, cultivated likely prospects. Although his manner was easy and disarming, he nevertheless exuded an air of uncompromising integrity. There was a flinty quality to his blunt-featured face that inspired trust and his clientele grew rapidly. By the end of his second year, he had become one of the firm's top producers.

Nor was he idle in other areas during this time. Several evenings a week he attended courses at Columbia in finance and management, and then, just before the market collapse at the end of the decade, he decided to move on again.

An executive recruitment agency, having evaluated his résumé, suggested an opening at Gregorius & Company. The head of the firm, it seemed, needed an administrative assistant. What appealed to Mike was the opportunity for rapid advancement.

He checked it out and learned that Gregorius was a modest but substantial house with a fair amount of retail trade and decent participation in underwritings. Anson Gregorius, well into his seventieth year, had recently suffered his second coronary, and had been ordered by his doctor to curtail his activities. Or else. So the firm Anson had founded almost half a century earlier would soon need a new pilot.

During his initial interview with the old man, Mike instinctively sensed that his future would henceforth be inextricably linked to the affairs of Gregorius & Company. Despite a disparity in age, the two men found themselves instantly compatible. Anson recognised in Mike much of himself as he had been years ago. And he agreed with Mike's inclination to emphasise the firm's investment banking activities.

From the beginning, Ryan knew that Anson's son posed no threat to his ultimate coronation. Floyd Gregorius was a pallid and lackluster shadow of his progenitor. Indecisive and uncertain, he lacked executive drive. Anson himself had reached the reluctant conclusion that Gregorius would never survive with Floyd at the helm. He knew his son's limitations and had regretfully relegated him to a job as manager of back-office procedures. In this slot, free of competitive pressures, Floyd seemed to function with acceptable competence.

So both the timing and the situation were felicitous. Mike joined the firm as Anson's administrative assistant. His old customers, without exception, transferred their accounts to Gregorius. Before long, Anson knew that he had the right man in the right job. And almost at once he began delegating authority and increasing Mike's responsibilities.

During the second half of the sixties Mike had observed with concern the excesses of mindless speculation, the injudicious expansion of his competitors, and the reckless transactions of mutual fund " gunslingers ". At Gregorius he began to retrench, tightening operations. He courted with messianic zeal modest participations in new underwritings, first assuring himself that the enterprise was viable.

Subsequent events justified his misgivings. The market collapsed as the decade ended. By May of 1970 stocks had lost half their value in a single year. High flyers traded over-the-counter plummeted eighty and ninety per cent. It was a disaster. But it provided Mike with the opportunity to buy for himself a seat on the New York Stock Exchange at a cost less than one-fifth its value during the boom years.

Gregorius & Company weathered the storm. More important, Mike derived a deep sense of satisfaction from the firm's investment banking activity. Raising fresh capital for business expansion created jobs and brought new products into the market place. Starting on a small scale, he took the firm into equity financing as syndicate manager. In time, a respectable group of

17

brokers seldom refused participation in these underwritings.

So Gregorius & Company was prepared to seize the opportunity when it came.

Mike had met Fred Hanna of Universal Media Industries on several occasions, both socially and professionally. And he became aware that Hanna had been taking his measure for some time. Then, after a number of exploratory conversations, Hanna made his decision. Gregorius would head the syndicate for UMI's new financing, and would also act as dealer-manager in its attempt to acquire control of Arcadia Films.

It was, by far, the most important coup of Mike's career.

3

A T the opposite end of the suite, Anson Gregorius slouched behind his desk, dozing fitfully. Behind him an oil portrait, painted in his prime, showed a bulky, heavy-shouldered man with a great cleaving nose. The years had dwindled his hulking frame. His face now was seamed and parched. Liver spots stained the hairless dome of skull and the backs of his gnarled hands.

He stirred restlessly. Hypertension pills had filled his bladder and he pushed himself erect and maneuvered stiffly to his private lavatory. Goddam prostate, he thought. Keeps me awake half the night, but I'll be damned if I'll let the butchers have a go at me. The afflictions of age irritated him, especially his failing powers of concentration.

After his morning conference with Ryan, he hadn't followed a single word of Mike's report on the UMI situation. Mike, he knew, was maintaining the fiction of the old man's sovereignty by discussing important developments and asking for advice.

Anson made a face. The steely acuity that had once marked his intelligence was now sadly flawed.

Everyone except Mike kept pressing him to retire. His daughter Julie, Floyd, his doctor, all of them trying to keep him from coming down to the office. And do what instead? Take up golf? Too strenuous and too late. Julie had suggested the house at Palm Beach. He shook his head. No way. He could not see himself as one of those sun-baked old farts stretched out on a beach chair, chewing a dead cigar and ogling the bikini-clad dollies. Leaving his desk here at the office would be the ultimate surrender.

Anson Gregorius had started on Wall Street as a runner. And he had learned the business in much the same way as Mike Ryan half a century later. Then, with a loan from his immigrant father, who ran a hash joint under the old elevated railroad on Third Avenue, he had opened a small over-the counter operation. Unrelentingly ambitious, a tough, cantankerous man with a sulphuric vocabulary, often incongruous in its mixture of profanity and self-learned classical reference, he had been and still was a source of frequent discomfort to his establishment colleagues. Over the years he had built the original business into a substantial brokerage house, the present Gregorius & Company, a member of the New York Stock Exchange.

Retirement might have been more acceptable, he reflected, if only Floyd had been more competent. Transferring power to his own son would have made a difference. That dream had died long ago. He had not pumped his life's blood into the firm, wheeling and dealing and conniving and hanging on through all the bad years, just to see it go down the drain through ineptitude.

Anson sighed. There had been a time when it looked as if Ryan might solve the problem, back when he'd been courting Julie. But it did not last. And that, too, Anson thought, was inevitable. And probably his own fault. He had been too indulgent. He had spoiled his daughter. She was beautiful yes, and desirable, but she had misjudged Mike. No one could run a ring through Mike's nose. At first Anson had wondered whether opportunism was the motivation behind Mike's court-

19

ship, but had rejected the notion as unfair. He himself had brought them together, encouraging the relationship.

The romance, of course, was doomed, foreclosing Anson's dream of dynasty. Floyd, in his forties, was a bachelor and likely to remain one. Julie, ten years younger, a late arrival, was still single.

But hardly a virgin.

That much Anson knew from personal observation. Now, as it often did, the hateful memory surfaced unbidden.

He had leased the Italian villa that summer at Forte dei Marmi on the Mediterranean coast. Martha had been alive then, two years away from her malignancy. Anson had joined the family for one week in August, the only time he could spare.

The villa came with a servant, a Fiat, a motor launch with docking privileges at Viareggio, and a darkly handsome young boatman named Marco. On the fourth morning of his stay, with a forecast of rain, Anson had informed Marco that he would not be using the launch that day. By early forenoon the weather had unexpectedly cleared and Anson had changed his mind.

He had driven to Viareggio and made his way along the pier to the polished deck of the launch, soundless in his rubber-soled topsiders. The cabin door was open and he saw them and heard them before he could back away.

They lay on the tumbled bunk. A beam of light slanted through the porthole, illuminating Julie's young face, her eyes blind with passion, her mouth contorted, her body leaping and bucking under the goddamned swarthy-faced greaseball. He saw the lurid mermaid tattooed on Marco's left arm, saw the muscular buttocks grinding feverishly, both of them unaware, lost in an obliterating fog of carnality.

Sudden rage bloated the veins in Anson's temples. His first impulse was to grab a butcher's knife in the galley and emasculate the sonovabitch. Instinct held him in check. Julie's shame at being caught like this could alter their relationship forever.

Ten seconds passed, burning the picture into his brain, and he silently retreated. He had lumbered frozen-faced to the car, marooned in some private hell, driving aimlessly for hours.

The next day he had discharged Marco. Something in his face warned the boatman not to ask for an explantion.

Julie was only seventeen then and he hoped that she had taken precautions. He would not permit her to carry the greaseball's kid. Nor would he permit any damned abortionist to tamper with the girl. He remembered his vast sense of relief when several months had passed and Julie remained slim.

Over the years there had been a steady procession of men in Julie's life. Mostly playmates. She had a modest income from her mother's estate, generously augmented by Anson. He leaned back now, wondering about her new attachment. This fellow Bendiner—Ward Bendiner. He seemed a decent enough chap. Personable, intelligent, and apparently well-heeled, a recent Gregorius customer, with Mike Ryan personally handling his account. Anson knew little about Bendiner's background except that he seemed to have inherited a very considerable estate, mostly securities, which he was in the process of liquidating.

Julie had met the man one afternoon while visiting the office. She had paused at Mike's door to say hello. Bendiner was there, signing some stock certificates, and Mike had introduced them. Later, spotting Julie trying to flag a cab, Bendiner had offered her a lift. It led to dinner that same evening and they had been seeing each other ever since.

Anson remembered a very pleasant evening. Julie had brought Bendiner over to the apartment. Anson found that they talked the same language. Bendiner was articulate, financially informed, and politically conservative, a welcome change from that soft-headed liberal she had been dating a year ago. Over brandy snifters Anson had questioned him on the advisability of selling his securities.

"Losing confidence in the American economy, Mr. Bendiner?"

"Yes, sir. For some time now, I've had the uneasy feeling that our way of life here is vulnerable."

"In what way?"

"Limited resources, energy problems, foreign competition, labor demands, to name a few."

21

" So you're pulling out. And what other haven have you in mind for the proceeds?"

" Some more stable currency. Swiss francs, perhaps."

" Does our friend Mike Ryan agree with you?"

" Not entirely. He tells me the oil sheiks are investing *their* money in this country."

" He's right, you know."

Bendiner shrugged. " They can afford it, sir. They have dollar bills coming out of their nostrils and an inexhaustible supply rolling in with every breath. I gather they're buying farmland and urban skyscrapers, rather than stocks and bonds. Ryan is a broker, Mr. Gregorius, and with all due respect, sir, you brokers have a vested interest in being bullish on securities."

Anson chuckled. " You have a point, Mr. Bendiner."

" Ward, sir. Please call me Ward."

" This conversation isn't getting to me at all," Julie broke in. " Time to leave, Ward. I have a certain disco in mind."

After they were gone, Anson allowed himself to hope that this one was serious. Bendiner seemed genuinely fond of the girl. It was time Julie settled down and gave him a grandson.

A knock on the door brought him back to the present.

The mail clerk deposited some papers on his desk. Anson shuffled through them and abruptly his dentures glistened in a wide anticipatory grin. He had found proofs of next week's market letter by Elizabeth Harmon.

He read the four pages with shrewd appraisal. Not bad, he thought grudgingly, not bad at all. But Jesus Christ! A woman analyst? He remembered his reaction when Ryan had hired her, believing it a momentary aberration. His comments were cutting and abrasive.

" Give the lady a chance, Anson."

" Let somebody else give her a chance. What the hell do women know about finance?"

" Depends on the woman. You think bankers have a monopoly? Look at the record, the bonehead mistakes in handling trust funds. And remember, women control some of the biggest fortunes in the country."

22

" Through inheritance, Mike. Only through inheritance. Who the hell made all that money in the first place?"

" Maybe we never gave women the chance, Anson. Maybe we kept them in the kitchen too long. You're out of touch. I know Liz Harmon's credentials. For the past few years the lady's been head of research for both of Pete Sternbach's mutual funds. Top performers this year and last year. I'm impressed."

" Impressed by her brains or the size of her jugs?"

" Anson, Anson, since when do I mix business with pleasure. You're a dirty old man."

" I was a dirty young man too. All right, Mike. You're calling the signals and she's your responsibility."

To himself, Anson now admitted that Harmon had indeed lived up to her billing. She was bright and intuitive, a whiz at figures. And she had a keen nose for snake oil. She could spot a doctored report through all the juggled numbers of creative accounting. Even so, he reached for his red pencil and went to work on her market letter. Simple language turned flamboyant. " Fringe benefits " became " peripheral entitlements ". Anson wondered where the devil that one came from, suspecting that some of these implausible locutions had become part of his normal vocabulary through half a century of absorbing the convoluted prose of security analysts and government bureaucrats.

He knew the pride Harmon took in her work and he guessed that his syntactical improvizations might be driving her up a wall. Well, she could always complain to Mike.

Now, by some odd quirk of telepathy, Mike came striding through Anson's door, waving one of Harmon's prose masterpieces. Anson reverted instantly to his old strategy of deflecting complaints by attacking on a different front.

" Goddamnit, Mike! What the hell is wrong with our sales people?"

" How do you mean?"

" Those Global Airline bonds. Forty per cent of our participation is still in inventory. Can't they move that stuff?"

" They're trying, Anson. The coupon is too low."

23

" Then knock the price down and make the bonds more attractive."

" We can't. They're still in syndicate."

Anson glared. " Why in hell did we accept this deal in the first place?"

" A favor to Stoufer, Wingate. We talked about it, remember? You reminded me that Ernie Stoufer is a friend of yours. And I went along because they're reciprocating by taking a large slice of the Universal Media issue."

" Lousy way to do business. First chance we get, cut the price and unload."

" Liz Harmon suggests we keep the Global bonds in inventory."

" What the hell for?"

" She thinks interest rates are peaking. If she's right we may be able to mark the bonds up a couple of points and turn a profit."

" And when does she say this happy event will take place?"

" She has no crystal ball, Anson. If she could pinpoint predictions, we'd be twice the size of Merrill Lynch."

Anson gave a short barking laugh. " Too many imponderables, eh, Michael? Who knows what the oil sheiks have in mind, or the boys in the Kremlin?" He sighed. " In the old days we controlled the market ourselves."

" And gave us the Great Crash of '29. People jumping out of windows, selling apples on street corners, breadlines, depression. Those old freebooters had a gay time cornering stocks, sandbagging competitors, and shafting the public. We need government regulation, Anson. You wouldn't want those days back again."

" Ah, well, Michael, you're right, of course. What's that you're waving in my face?"

" Elizabeth Harmon's market letter."

" She's unhappy with my editing?"

" You're driving her bananas, Anson."

" And you want me to cease and desist?"

" It would certainly improve morale at Research."

24

The old man raised his hands. "All I get these days are orders. My doctor says don't do this, don't do that, lay off the booze, cut out tobacco, no red meat, no salt. Now you tell me to stop amusing myself at Harmon's expense. So what's left? You know what Julie says?"

"What does Julie say?"

"She says if I like it down here so much, I should make a deal with Trinity Church. A substantial contribution in exchange for a plot in the church graveyard. So I can spend all of eternity here in the financial area." He was chuckling when the intercom buzzed. He answered and his face brightened. "Speak of the devil."

"Julie?"

"On one of her surprise visits."

"Then you'll want to be alone," Mike said, heading for the door.

4

Old family tintypes revealed few physical attractions among women in the Gregorius lineage. So the brittle beauty of his daughter was a source of constant wonder and pride to Anson. Julie was a woman of fugitive moods, restless, mercurial, and given to theatrical gestures. She had dark hair, a flawless, almost translucent skin, and her mother's enormous eyes.

She swooped down on Anson and planted a kiss alongside his left ear. Even as a child she had known instinctively how to win over this formidable and autocratic figure, using the knowledge on numerous occasions to gain a variety of concessions.

Anson beamed. "Now tell me you were down here on some

25

kind of errand and couldn't resist dropping in because you missed me."

" Did I ever lie to you, lover?"

" Frequently. Whenever you want something. What is it this time?"

" Guess."

" That's easy. Money."

" Well, isn't that what Wall Street's all about?"

" Not quite, Julie. How much?"

" Are you in a generous mood?"

" Misers are never generous."

" How about a thousand, pocket money, maybe two."

Anson looked up in mock despair. "Dear God, where did I go wrong? I raised a daughter who wants to put me on welfare."

" Why don't you retire? You'd be eligible for Social Security."

" At my age, I'm eligible anyway. And I'm collecting. Not enough to keep you in panty hose. My bank transfers money to your checking account every month. Tell me where it goes."

" Everything is so expensive these days."

" So I hear. What you need is a rich husband. Doesn't Bendiner pick up the tab once in a while?"

" Only for food and entertainment. We're not married; you can't expect him to buy my clothes."

" You have enough clothes to stock a boutique."

" Fashions change, darling. And how about my analyst?"

" I thought you were finished with that joker."

" Almost. Now it's supportive therapy."

" It sure is. It supports him in pretty good style. How many times a week?"

" Three."

" At fifty bucks a crack?"

" Sixty-five now. He's a victim of inflation too."

" No wonder he doesn't cut you loose. That's more than a dollar a minute. Just for listening."

" Sometimes he makes suggestions."

" Except the one suggestion that could settle your problems."

" You mean get married."

" Is it such a bad idea?"

" Would you sacrifice your only daughter for the sake of a grandson?"

" Sacrifice is not the word. I would be grateful if some member of the family could come in here and run this business."

" How about Floyd?"

" Julie, please."

" You never gave Floyd a chance."

" Your brother can't cut the mustard, girl. We'd be filing a Chapter Ten in less than a year."

" Chapter Ten?"

" Bankruptcy."

" I have an idea," she said brightly. " Why don't you adopt Mike Ryan?"

Anson laughed. " It wouldn't be the same. Not my own flesh and blood."

" Suppose I did get married and presented you with a grandson. And suppose he hated Wall Street and wanted to be a poet."

" Julie, there's no money in poetry."

" Daddy, there's no poetry in money."

" Ah, but you're wrong. Money sings. It resonates. It's a form of power. What kind of life would you have without it?"

She smiled, conceding the argument. " All right, Daddy. But you'll have to convince my son, if I have one. And I promise I'll work on it."

" Bendiner?"

" Soon as he gets a divorce. He hasn't asked me yet, but I think he's close." She patted his face affectionately. " Let's make a deal."

" In your deals I always lose."

" Not this time. I've heard of a very clever doctor, an expert on hormones and fertility drugs. If you're kind to me, I'll go to him for treatment. Think of it, lover, you might wind up with a whole litter of descendants, maybe even quintuplets, all

27

boys, trained as economists, bankers, and brokers. They could run Gregorius & Company from top to bottom."

Anson threw his head back and laughed, eyes watering. He wiped them with a handkerchief. Easy badinage had always been a part of their relationship. "You're impossible," he said. "Still, it's an idea that appeals to me. I'll make a down payment." He reached into his desk for a checkbook, scrawled, tore out a draft, and handed it to Julie.

She folded it into her purse without looking at it. "You're the nicest daddy a girl ever had." She brushed a quick kiss against his cheek. "I'll bring him to the apartment for dinner next week."

"Let's make it definite. Tuesday. I'll expect you at seven."

"It's a date, lover."

In the corridor, she started for the exit, changed her mind and headed for Ryan's office. She had seen him only once since their breakup. As an afterthought she was willing to concede that it was probably more her fault than Mike's. She had not handled the incident well and now it returned in a rueful flashback.

They were in a cab at two-thirty in the morning, returning from a large bash thrown by one of Julie's friends. She had moved away from him, distant and wintry, tight-lipped, when Mike sighed and said patiently, "All right, Julie, what is it this time?"

"You ignored me. I saw the way you were eyeing that ghastly blonde."

"You disappeared."

"Why didn't you come looking for me?"

"I'm not a lap dog, Julie."

"I saw you writing her address."

"It was business. I promised to evaluate her portfolio."

"With that cleavage, her portfolio was in full view and your appraisal was already made."

"I forgot her the minute she was out of sight."

"Will you stay over at my apartment tonight?"

"I can't, Julie. I'm tired."

" Of me?"

" Just plain physically tired, exhausted. I need some sleep. I have to be at the office early tomorrow morning. I'm a working man, Julie. I can't play all night and sleep all day."

" You had plenty of energy when we first met."

" The supply is not inexhaustible."

For a moment she sat in tense silence. " You want to call it quits, Mike, is that it?"

He sighed with long-suffering patience and she had taken it as an affirmative response. She leaned forward and rapped sharply against the glass partition. " Cabby! Stop right here. You're losing a passenger." When the taxi pulled up, she said in a muffled voice, not looking at him, " All right, Mike, go home. Get your beauty sleep."

" Your choice, Julie." He opened the door, climbed out, and disappeared into the darkness.

He had not called her after that and her own pride would not permit her to call him. So the relationship had simply expired from lack of nourishment. And just as well, she now reflected. If she were still seeing Mike she would never have gotten involved with Ward Bendiner. But she should, she felt, try to ease some of the tension between them. That had been her intention when she had stopped by his office some weeks ago, but he had been occupied with Ward.

She paused now at Ryan's open door, took a tentative step across the threshold, and waited for him to look up. He was totally absorbed in a mass of documents, so she gave a polite cough.

He looked up. " Julie!"

" Congratulations, Mike. I hear you're running the joint now."

" So they tell me. How are you?"

" Fine. I saw you hurrying away from Dad's office. Are you still angry?"

" I was never angry. How's Ward?"

" Ward is a very gallant gentleman. I want to thank you for introducing us."

" I like your taste."

" I'm meeting him in about an hour. Any messages?"

" Yes. Ask him to call me for lunch next week. Something important I want to discuss."

" Business, always business."

" I have to make a living, Julie."

" I wish you well. Mike—" She hesitated.

" Yes?"

" Be patient with Floyd."

" I always am."

She wiggled her fingers. " 'Bye now."

It was done and she felt better. Mike, after all, had taken a tremendous load off Anson's shoulders. She headed uptown. Her cab crawled fitfully through the clogged Manhattan traffic.

5

Whatever genes evolve into prepossessing characteristics, none seem to have been available when Floyd Gregorius was conceived. Considering the ultimate product, that a single sperm managed its struggle toward fertilisation was achievement enough.

At forty-one, Floyd was a thin balding man with neat precise features somewhat blurred by a hangdog air, the result of long parental bullying. Anson's attitude had always been one of intolerance, irascibility, impatience. As a consequence, Floyd tried to avoid paternal encounters whenever possible.

At various private schools he had worked his way through the educational process without distinction. When, ultimately, Anson had taken him into the firm, Floyd's early attempt to sell securities was aborted by a lack of customers. A shy man, he made few social contacts. Anson had put him through an apprenticeship in various departments: Registration, Compliance, Transfer, Bonds, and eventually had settled him in the back office with a vice-president's title and the tacit understanding that Floyd's assistant, a computer expert, would handle most of the department's day-to-day operations.

While Floyd recognized Mike Ryan's skills, his drive, his unfailing courtesy, he was nevertheless unable to dismiss a feeling of injustice. At home, Julie took precedence; at the office, it was Ryan. With an almost paranoid need for acknowledgement, the fiction of injustice helped to preserve his fragile ego.

When he encountered Anson at all, it was generally an abrasive experience. Like that incident in the early seventies. With the market dropping to new lows every day, Floyd, as everyone else before computerization, had been snowed under by an avalanche of paperwork. Then his margin clerk had quit for another job. Back office procedures were in turmoil. As a result, he had failed to follow through on a margin call to one of the firm's heavy traders.

The man was a plunger, an indiscriminate gambler, his position rapidly deteriorating. Simple prudence demanded the call. Stock Exchange regulations made it mandatory. Gregorius itself had a bundle riding on the account. And when, ultimately, a new margin clerk sold the man out, it was too late. The firm was in the hole for eighty thousand dollars and forced to absorb the loss because the customer had filed for bankruptcy.

Anson hit the ceiling. He was furious. With Ryan in attendance, he had chewed Floyd out unmercifully. "Imbecile! Sitting on your ass and playing with your yo-yo while that crook keeps trading an illegal margin account with our money. How many times do I have to tell you that we don't violate rules at Gregorius, especially if it costs us eighty thousand dollars and maybe a suspension? Some goddamn gypsy must have kidnapped my son from the maternity ward and left you instead. Tell me, sonny. Help me to understand. How did it happen?"

Floyd, dismantled by the outburst, had begun to stammer. Mike was embarrassed by the man's distress.

31

Anson's voice was shot with contempt. "No defense? No excuse? Just the usual incompetence?" He faced Mike. "Well, Mr. Ryan, what do you think? Can we afford to keep him? Should we turn him out into the street? Or maybe find him another job here, vice-president on latrine duty?"

"Anson," Mike said quietly, "every house on the Street has back-office problems these days. One of Floyd's key men had quit. He was under too much pressure. We're all to blame. We should have seen this coming. We should have modernized our equipment two years ago. Look at it this way—a large chunk of that eighty grand is a tax write-off. So let's swallow the loss and get on with the job. We learn from experience. We need a completely new computer setup. I don't think Floyd is going to let anything like this happen again."

Anson sat brooding, a man whose patience had been tried beyond human endurance. He leveled a finger at his son. "You heard him, Floyd. You have a soft head; Ryan has a soft heart. For my sake, he tolerates nepotism." His fingers drummed on the desk. "How much did you inherit from your mother's estate? Maybe a hundred thousand? We ought to hold you personally responsible." He gestured helplessly. "What happens after I retire? How long will you last? All right, leave us alone. I want to speak to Ryan privately. And try to remember one thing, sonny. A head is not a hatrack."

Floyd trotted from the room.

*   *   *

He wondered now if he would ever be able to erase that humiliation from his memory. His hands were clenched. Anson should not have demeaned his own son like that in front of a stranger. Some day, perhaps, he would gather the courage to walk into his father's office and tell the old man to take his job and shove it. But where would he go? What would he do? How would he support himself?

A sizeable piece of his inheritance was now gone. Lost in the last bear market. For privacy, he had opened a personal trading account at Stoufer, Wingate. And for a while every-

32

thing seemed to be coming up roses. Those were the wild crazy years of the mid-sixties. Junk stocks going through the roof. At one time his account had showed a very respectable profit. And then, inevitably, came the blow-off. Like many others, he'd hung on, watching his position deteriorate, until he had decided to take his loss and run.

He was, he knew, not alone. Security selling had turned into a tidal wave. Even the blue chips were being ferociously mauled. Nothing could stem the tide. The Federal Reserve manipulated its money levers, to no effect. At Gregorius, as elsewhere, record keeping was chaotic, with the transfer of securities late or nonexistent.

Largely through the heroic efforts of Anson and Mike Ryan, Gregorius had weathered the storm. To himself, Floyd had made a solemn vow. One day he would pick a winner. He would recoup. He would beat them all—Mike Ryan, his father, everyone.

He sat motionless now, feeling a vague sense of growing excitement. The opportunity, it seemed, was at hand. For weeks he had been collecting information, putting together bits and pieces of intelligence, monitoring transactions. There had been a steady accumulation of shares in Arcadia Films for the Universal Media account. He had learned, before it became general knowledge, that Ryan had been holding secret meetings with Fred Hanna. From all indications, he guessed, a takeover or a merger was in the works.

Floyd knew that the shares of a target company generally soared on such prospects when the news became public.

He had seventy thousand dollars in cash available. If he bought Arcadia shares on full margin, and the deal was successfully negotiated, he could turn a handsome profit. It occured to him fleetingly that he might be operating on inside information. Would it come back to haunt him? Was it worth the risk?

Floyd moistened his lips. He couldn't let this one pass. It was the chance of a lifetime. He couldn't possibly lose. He got to his feet and closed the door. He went back to his desk and dialed Stoufer, Wingate and asked for Robinson. The account executive was surprised at the size of Floyd's transaction.

"Hey, friend," he said, "anything going on there I ought to know about?"

"Nothing. Just a hunch."

When he hung up, he felt a bit queasy. He wondered if Robinson suspected anything. Probably not. Floyd's past record at picking winners had been somewhat dismal. He smiled minimally, and sat back, experiencing a keen sense of anticipation. Later this evening, when he saw Janey Spacek, he would tell her of his coup and bask in the glow of her warm admiration.

6

The Universal Media building vaulted high above Madison Avenue, presenting a facade of tinted glass, typical mid-century architecture. Although the corporation did not own the property, a twenty-five-lease on eight full floors put the UMI logo above the marble entrance.

Pete Sternbach crossed the plaza and frowned at a convoluted mass of bronze flanked by twin fountains of recirculated water. Sternbach, the ultimate pragmatist, had little appreciation for abstract art. By squinting his eyes and distorting his vision, he was able to imagine a double-jointed Amazon eight and a half months into labour.

Sternbach was short and chubby, with a sunlamp tan and the pale flat eyes of a gambler. His hair was long, his garb casual. He held a majority interest in a management company that operated two hugely successful mutual funds, one conservative, the Empire Fund, and one speculative, the Croesus

Fund. Although Sternbach Management maintained a skilled research staff, Pete himself as portfolio manager made all major investment decisions.

He was sharp and flexible, moving decisively from one investment vehicle to another. This agility had in the past saved both funds from serious erosion during falling markets. Confidence in his own judgement insulated him against panic and had enabled him to survive the random vicissitudes of Wall Street with uncommon success.

Entering the lobby, he went directly to a single elevator reserved exclusively for passengers to the UMI executive floor. The car already had one occupant.

"Hello, Pete," Mike Ryan said. "On time, as usual."

"Can't keep his majesty waiting. Congratulations, Mike. I hear Gregorius is now UMI's investment banker."

For some time Ryan had been vigorously promoting both of Sternbach's mutual funds, the funds reciprocating by often trading through the Gregorius firm. Even with negotiated commissions, Sternbach Management was an important client.

As the elevator lofted them upward, Mike said, "Did Fred Hanna give you any clue about this meeting when he called?"

"He didn't call. I called him. A fishing expedition. Heard some rumors about another acquisition. He sounded cagey, wouldn't talk. Instead, he made an appointment for today and said you'd be here too. I tried to reach you. No luck. And this morning I heard the announcement. So Hanna's got his eye on Arcadia Films. Okay. Fair enough. He didn't want me acting on confidential information. I guess I should have suspected something when I learned he'd been accumulating shares in Arcadia." Sternbach shook his head. "It's a dog. What the hell does he want it for?"

"Have you checked it out?"

"Not lately." Sternbach gave Ryan an aggrieved look. "I thought you were my friend, Mike. You might have tipped me off."

"Sorry, Pete. The SEC is taking a close look at this one. We can't afford embarrassing questions."

" Everything by the numbers?"

" Always by the numbers with Gregorius."

" Well that's one way for Hanna to gain respectability."

" You do the man an injustice, Pete."

" Maybe. I don't think so. How about Liz? What does she think?"

" Fred Hanna doesn't turn her on either. But the man's our client now and she's trying to be fair. You still sore that we stole her away from you?"

" Unforgiving. She's one of the best. And decorative too."

" You should have offered her more money."

" I did."

" The lady needed a change."

" Well, whatever she needed, it sure affected her prose style. Jesus, Mike! Those Gregorius Market Letters! What cooks?"

" Don't blame Liz. Anson's been fiddling with her syntax."

" She ticked off?"

" To put it mildly. I'd like to humor the old boy, but not at her expense."

The elevator discharged them into a reception area on the twenty-third floor. On a wall behind the receptionist's desk there were Kodachrome photographs of network broadcasters and television personalities. Another wall carried a display of current periodicals and books produced by UMI's publishing subsidiary. The receptionist herself was a British import, tall, cool, blonde, with a dazzling smile and an almost genuine Oxonian accent.

She recognised Mike. " How do you do, Mr. Ryan." And lifted an inquiring eyebrow. " Mr Sternbach?"

" In person."

" Mr. Hanna is expecting you." She whispered into a telephone and looked up. " Someone will be out directly. Please be seated."

They sat in leather chairs and Sternbach offered Mike a cigarette. Mike shook his head.

" Gave them up two years ago."

"You gonna give me a lecture."

"Not today."

Sternbach sighed. " I catch a lot of flak about Big C when nobody really gives a shit. What they all really want is a tip on the market."

"Wouldn't mind a good tip myself."

"You've got Liz Harmon. What's her outlook?"

"Probably the same as yours."

"Mine is bleak, Mike, bleak. Warning flares all over the landscape. Tight money, runaway inflation, overpriced energy, negative trade balance, et cetera, et cetera, et cetera, the whole depressing potful. We're in trouble, friend."

"Both your funds are still loaded with common stocks."

"Only solid merchandise. We've cleaned out the crap. Sitting on a lot of cash these days. Money instruments, Treasury Bills."

"You could be wrong, Pete."

"Not often, though." He grinned. " Hell, nobody's infallible."

"How about that new computer you're advertizing, the one that analyzes stock values?"

"Bullshit gadgetry, boy. A sales gimmick. Worthless. Show me the machine that can predict mass fear and greed—" He paused to watch a high-hipped beauty heading in their direction.

She spoke their names and conducted them along a carpeted corridor to a vast corner office with a garden terrace visible through the picture window. Fred Hanna rose from behind his desk and greeted them.

"Mike. Pete. Thanks for coming." His voice was strong and resonant. He indicated the man seated alongside his desk. " Have you met Bob Egan, Pete?"

"Not personally."

Robert Egan, UMI's general counsel, was a thin-lipped clerical-looking man, American Gothic, immaculate, square-jawed, brush-cut. He was Fred Hanna's resident expert on government regulations. And considerably more, his right hand, his corporate head hunter. He had collaborated with Mike on the registration statement for the new UMI bond issue. Mike had found him to be a sharp tough lawyer, but had been unable to get a fix on the man as an individual. Egan was a closed book, inhospitable to any personal approach.

Hanna seated his visitors and looked at Sternbach. "You heard our announcement this morning, Pete? About a possible acquisition of Arcadia Films?"

"Sure. It was on the tape. But you refused to confirm when I called you last week."

"Against regulations. Had you acted on the rumor, you'd be ahead of the game today. We made our tender offer to Arcadia stockholders this morning and the stock is up sharply. Are you still interested?"

Sternbach was noncommittal. "I'm interested in knowing what you wanted to see me about."

Hanna smiled. "Your Croesus Fund once held a substantial block of UMI. Did you lose any money on that investment?"

"It was not an investment. It was a speculation. We cleaned up." Sternbach matched Hanna's smile.

"I prefer the first description, Pete. And I believe I understand the Croesus pattern. You prefer to lock in your profit and use the money elsewhere. Some other vehicle that's just beginning its climb. At this stage I believe UMI still has a considerable upside potential."

"And you want me to buy it again?"

"Have you seen our last quarterly report."

"I have. And it looks enticing. How accurate are your auditors?"

"Pete, your own research team was in here looking at our books before you ever invested in UMI. They must have seen something that appealed to them."

"That was more than a year ago. And I'm not at all sure that acquiring Arcadia Films is going to improve your bottom line."

"We've taken a long hard look at Arcadia. For our purposes, it has enormous potential. We think the company's a sleeper. I don't want to go into the specifics at this time. But like yourself, UMI hasn't made many mistakes. And we don't intend to make any in future. We have some interesting plans on the drawing board. And there's one particular item that should interest you."

" I'm all ears."

" Our board meets next week and the UMI directors intend to increase the dividend. Sharply."

Sternbach lifted an eyebrow. " Is that wise? Your new bond issue is still in syndicate. I understand the SEC frowns on dividend increases during a public offering."

Hanna addressed Egan. " Tell him, Bob."

" Let me quote from an SEC ruling, Mr. Sternbach. Verbatim." Egan spoke from memory. " ' The declaration of a dividend increase not warranted by the business conditions of the issuer contemplating a public financing is characteristic of manipulative schemes '." Egan spread his fingers. " Not applicable to UMI. Our profit margins are up in all divisions. We could have raised the dividend six months ago."

Hanna resumed. " So you see, Pete, our prospects are even better today than when your people originally looked us over."

Sternbach frowned. He sat back and pinched his bottom lip, concentrating. He knew the terms of the tender, a package of UMI securities worth almost twenty per cent more than the current market price of Arcadia. Very attractive. In fact, almost irresistible. And he knew exactly what Hanna was trying to accomplish. If for any reason the UMI securities moved down, then the inducement to accept UMI's offer would vanish. So it was imperative for Hanna to maintain the value of his company's shares. A dividend increase would serve that purpose. And if, in addition, Croesus started buying again, the securities would rise.

He said, " I'll give it some serious thought."

" And I'd like to make one further suggestion, Pete. I just read your annual report. The Croesus Fund is sitting on some very heavy reserves. It might be wise to commit some of that money to a speculation in Arcadia."

Sternbach gave him a sleepy look. " The run-up this morning, after your tender announcement, may have squeezed some of the juice out of it."

"There's a lot more juice left. I guarantee it."

"Guarantee? Sure things appeal to me. Elaborate, please."

"In strict confidence, Pete."

"Of course."

"At the right moment UMI intends to increase its tender offer."

Sternbach's sleepy eyes opened wide, crinkling. "Well now, Mr. Hanna, that's nice to know. And not bad for a stock like Arcadia that's been heading south on every graph in the business for a long, long time. I appreciate the tip. And in all probability I will act on it."

"You know of course what I'd like in return."

"Certainly. If I buy the stock, and your takeover attempt boils down to a proxy fight, you'd expect me to vote my Arcadia shares in favour of UMI. Fair enough."

The two men were grinning broadly.

Pete said, "You really think you can make Arcadia healthy again?"

"Yes. There's too much fat. Nonutilization of facilities. No vision. Arcadia needs an infusion of fresh blood, fresh capital, tighter controls. An area in which UMI shines."

"How about their new chief executive officer, this fellow Dan Hedrik? I hear he's a good man."

"Good men are in short supply. If Hedrik is willing to implement our programs, he stays."

Sternbach nodded, studying the man behind the desk. He knew that during the early sixties, with the market for new issues flourishing, Hanna's privately owned electronics company had gone public. Over the years, using the inflated value of his shares, he had been able to acquire a number of other corporations, some of them considerably larger than his own, until he had forged a communications conglomerate of impressive dimensions.

Sternbach remembered that his researchers had not been able to penetrate UMI's Byzantine web of interlocking enterprises. Hanna reminded him of those legendary robber barons, the pathologically acquisitive predators. And the man looked the part too, iron-haired, heavy-shouldered, with a blunt emphatic face weathered to a look of austere distinction, projecting an implacable aura of command.

"Before I buy into Arcadia," Sternbach said, "I would have to know the answer to an important question."

"Ask it, Pete."

"The trust busters in Washington, would they hold still for this acquisition?"

"It's all settled. We discussed it with the people at Justice before making our decision. They gave us a green light and, I might add, their blessing. Why? Because we'd be offering increased competition to the three major networks."

"All right," Sternbach said shortly. "I'm satisfied." He glanced at his watch and got to his feet. "I think we understand each other, Mr. Hanna."

"Thanks again for coming, Pete. Mike, I'd like you stay for a few minutes, please."

Sternbach, smiling affably, shook everyone's hand and left.

Egan said, "You know the man better than we do, Ryan. Can we trust him?"

Mike shrugged. "Up to a point. I think he'll buy Arcadia on the basis of an increased tender."

"Will he vote those shares for us in a proxy fight?"

"Providing he still owns them at that time. His prime consideration will be the Croesus Fund. If it suits his purpose, he'll sell before we need them."

Hanna looked grim. "I took him into our confidence. There is a moral obligation."

"Owed primarily to his own shareholders. On the other hand I've already taken steps to compensate."

"What steps?"

"We do business with a number of other mutual funds. And after this morning's announcement, I gave Arcadia a very strong recommendation. A substantial number of shares are now in friendly hands."

Hanna consulted the UMI counsel. "Bob, what do you think?"

Egan nodded. "I agree with Ryan. It would help to offset shares of Arcadia held by banks in trust accounts. We've seen it happen before. Banks traditionally vote for management and they will probably support Hedrik."

Hanna said, "Anything else, Mike?"

"Yes. We've given Arcadia stockholders ten days to accept our offer. That puts them under pressure. We will, of course, extend the time, if necessary. Meanwhile, we can expect some reaction from Hedrik. Probably an announcement attacking your motives, attacking UMI, promising a dramatic turnaround in Arcadia's affairs, and strongly urging his shareholders to reject our tender. I have several maneuvers in mind."

"For example?"

"We know that Kate Rennie is the studio's largest individual stockholder. Her support is vital. I'm going to visit her personally and try to win her over. I'll leave for the Coast early tomorrow morning."

"Kate Rennie," Hanna said. "The founder's widow. How old is she now, Mike?"

"In her eighties, probably. According to rumor, she was at least thirty years younger than Max Klemmer when he married her."

"Is she a Hedrik loyalist?"

"Probably. But it's worth a try."

"Persuade her to throw in with us, Mike, and you'll be a hero. Why not take another crack at Dan Hedrik, too, while you're out there?"

"I intend to. But I don't expect the man to welcome me with open arms. Corporate officers are usually prejudiced by self-interest, and a successful takeover might cost him his job."

"Let him know we intend to retain key personnel. Especially the top man."

"You'll put that in writing?"

"Yes."

Mike sat back, looking complacent. "Now for an interesting

piece of news. Gregorius has a new client, a man named Ward Bendiner, with some very extensive holdings. I'm handling his account."

Hanna bent forward, eyes suddenly bright. " The same Ward Bendiner listed in Arcadia's records as a stockholder?"

" That's right."

Egan exhaled softly. " Jesus, Ryan! He's a big one."

" He is indeed."

" How did he manage to accumulate a position that size?"

" Inheritance. The stock was bought many years ago, when Arcadia went public, and it's been split at least six times since."

Hanna bent forward intently. " This Bendiner, Mike, have you got him in your pocket?"

" So far, he seems to have unbounded confidence in my judgement."

Hanna's palm cracked hard against the top of his desk. " Good. Excellent. Can you get him to accept your offer?"

" I'm going to make one hell of a good try."

Fred Hanna got impulsively to his feet and reached across to pump Mike's hand.

7

The guard at the studio gate recognized the company limousine and waved it through. The chauffeur pulled into a reserved slot alongside Arcadia's executive building and Dan Hedrik alighted. He headed for his office, pausing at his secretary's desk.

" Morning, Sara. Ross Landry. Is he in yet?"

" Any minute."

" On the double. Soon as he arrives."

"Yes, sir. Coffee?"

"Please."

Dan Hedrik was a direct, self-assured man, broad-beamed, slightly rumpled, with a wide expanse of sun-baked forehead, still quizzically amused at the perquisites of rank and his present tenancy behind old Max Klemmer's desk in the ornately-paneled office. In the space of a single month he had adjusted comfortably to his sudden elevation as president and chief executive officer of Arcadia Films.

Almost half my life, he thought. An investment of twenty-five years. In a job now which he had never anticipated. Far removed from his years on the Lower East Side of Manhattan as a struggling writer of short stories. And the abrupt change in fortune when he had published his first novel. Arcadia had bought the film rights. And better still, from Hedrik's point of view, the studio had brought him to Hollywood to work on the screenplay.

Hedrik could not remember a time when he had not been a movie buff. As a small boy, bewitched by his first picture show, he had made Saturday matinees a ritual, coins tightly clutched and eagerly surrendered at the box office. When, hours later, he finally managed to tear himself away from the darkened theatre, he would swagger home, a chunky boy, his imagination fired, identifying with implausible heroes—tall, invincible, irresistibly handsome.

The industry fascinated him. In his teens, on holidays, he often patronized two double features in a single afternoon. He knew the names of stars and bit players. He devoured fan magazines. He knew the backgrounds of Laemmle, Zukor, Lasky, and Max Klemmer. He developed a loathing for the Motion Picture Patent Company that had driven these early pioneers westward, not in search of eternal sunlight, as legend had it, but to avoid lawsuits for patent infringements.

Later, after he had become a successful screen writer, he had acquired, at considerable cost, for sentimental reasons, one of the ancient kinetoscopes used in the penny arcades.

He remembered his first arrival at the studio. Before starting

44

the adaptation of his own novel, he had carefully studied several screenplays by Ben Hecht, whom he admired. He found that he had an instinctive flair for the medium. His dialogue was crisp and colloquial. In a comparatively short time, to the consternation of other contract writers, he had fashioned a workmanlike scenario. The producer and the director were pleased. When the film was released, it earned enough critical and box-office approval so that Arcadia quickly exercized its option for his services.

Hedrik took the work seriously. Unlike many of his colleagues, he had never deluded himself into believing that he was merely marking time until he could write the Great American Novel. He was aware of his own limitations. He knew that he had no special insights, no burning messages, no solutions for mankind's enduring dilemmas. He was, quite simply, a storyteller, a spinner of dreams. He was adroit and inventive. He had an innate sense of plot, character, conflict, and atmosphere. And it pleased him to be handsomely compensated for doing what he enjoyed. As a consequence, he suffered few frustrations.

In the ensuing years he had authored a procession of potboilers that always turned a profit. And then, quite unexpectedly, one of his screenplays evolved into a film that caught the public imagination. Long lines queued up for admission everywhere. It earned Hedrik an Oscar nomination and a summons to the front office.

In those days Max Klemmer had resembled a smiling Buddha. But Hedrik knew that the placid smile concealed a vision and an inner force that had driven the man across a continent to start the small underfinanced venture that ultimately developed into Arcadia Films.

Max Klemmer had offered him a chair and a cigar. " Brandy, Daniel? Scotch? Name your pleasure."

" Coffee, if it's available."

" Gertrude," the old man bellowed. " Two coffees. And make sure the cups are clean." He beamed. " You're a credit to the studio, my boy."

During his tenure at Arcadia, this was the first time Hedrik had been called into the great man's presence with no one else in attendance. Always, on previous visits, a group had gathered for story conferences. Max Klemmer was no studio tyrant. The most benevolent of monarchs, he mingled freely. At the executive commissary, any middle-level administrator could sit at Klemmer's table, first come, first served. Atypically, he was generous in delegating artistic authority to his creative people.

Klemmer's history was common knowledge. He had quit his job as a fabric salesman to rent and convert a small store into a nickelodeon shortly after the first films and projectors were available. It was an instant success. The public was intrigued by images moving on a screen. The small improvized theatre did capacity business. Klemmer expanded. By the end of his second year, three additional nickelodeons were in operation.

Still, Klemmer was not satisfied. His vision and his energies extended far beyond this limited scope. In time, he branched out into production, opening a small studio in Brooklyn, grinding out a procession of one-reelers. Like other independent entrepreneurs, he ran into trouble. Patents on this infant industry's equipment were held by a so-called Film Trust whose resident tyrant was a man named Jeremiah Kennedy. Early one morning Kennedy's goon squads attacked Klemmer's studio and sacked the building. The Trust was ruthless. It would tolerate no encroachment upon its vested interests.

So Klemmer had joined the other pioneers in their flight to California, bringing with him a supply of film and a skeleton staff of technicians. Arcadia Films was born.

Demand for motion picture entertainment had burgeoned insatiably and the new company prospered. Never as large as MGM or Paramount, it nevertheless acquired some one hundred acres in the Valley, complete with scene docks, carpentry shops, street sets, film labs, and recording studios, with a ready market always available from importuning exhibitors.

Early in his career at the studio, Dan Hedrik had become aware of the old man's innate decency and sense of fair play. If a contract had years to run with inadequate compensation,

46

Klemmer himself would initiate talks to renegotiate. It brought him loyalty, even affection. So Hedrik was not surprised when Kate Rennie, one of the studio's rising stars, less than half the old man's age, accepted his proposal of marriage. Industry people snickered, predicting a quick divorce. They were wrong. The marriage endured.

*　　*　　*

Klemmer's secretary, a brisk middle-aged woman, appeared with a coffee tray.

Klemmer said, " Help yourself, Daniel. I like mine black, strong enough to walk on." He poured and settled back. " So. It's time we had a talk, face to face. I've been watching you, Dan Hedrik. I like the way you work. Never a problem. We need a story. You cook one up. We buy a property, you adapt, no complaints, not like some of the prima donnas around here, screaming it's junk. Tell me, at the end of your first year at Arcadia, who called your agent and arranged for more money?"

" You did, Mr. Klemmer."

The old man tapped his temple. " Smart, no? So you stayed with the studio and now you gave us a big one. Earned your salary for the next ten years, several times over."

" A lot of people contributed to the success of that film, Mr. Klemmer. It was a team effort."

The old man raised his eyebrows. " I like that. Modesty in a business filled with egomaniacs. Well, Daniel, I have a proposition to make. Ross Landry tells me you often come up with valuable suggestions during shooting. How would you like to produce? Maybe one of your own screenplays."

" Full artistic control?"

" Why not? Who's better qualified?"

" I'd like it fine."

" Here's what I have in mind. Work with Landry as assistant on his next picture. Get the feel. Learn the details. Then pick your story, pick the actors, the director, everything but the budget. That's my department. You'll find I'm not a stingy man. Okay?"

"Better than okay. It's perfect."

"You have a story in mind?"

"Yes, sir. Something I've been thinking about for a long time."

"Good. How about a director?"

"Can you get me Ernst Lubitsch?"

"Don't talk crazy. We got our own people on contract."

"Then I'd like Hank Bruno."

"You got him. And your leading lady?"

"Kate Rennie."

"Kate has script approval. She likes your story, she's in."

"Thank you, Mr. Klemmer."

"Thank yourself, Daniel. You earned it. Tell your agent to call me about financial arrangements." His brow crimped. "Can I ask you a personal question?"

"Sure."

"How come you're not married?"

"Always too busy, I guess. Never gave it much thought."

"Think about it. Settles a man down. You know how I feel about casting couches?"

"I've heard."

"Okay. I won't interfere in your private life. Are you free Saturday night?"

"Yes, sir."

"Kate's having some people for dinner. You're invited."

"I'd like that."

"Seven o'clock."

The dinner invitation certified Dan Hedrik's acceptance as a member of Arcadia's upper echelon.

In time, he justified Max Klemmer's confidence by completing his own production eight days ahead of schedule and well within budget. He had discovered an unsuspected talent for management. His facility for mediating between the conflicting temperaments of inflated egos kept things moving. In an industry traditionally administered with prodigal extravagance, he succeeded in operating on a rare level of restraint.

Two years later he was supervizing several units simul-

48

taneously. He made relatively few clinkers. A Dan Hedrik Production was synonymous with sophisticated yet popular entertainment. For another decade Arcadia prospered. But there were serious problems ahead.

Principally, television. People stayed home and watched the box. Profits dwindled. Then, working behind his desk, Max Klemmer suffered a massive coronary and was dead before the ambulance arrived. The men who succeeded Klemmer seemed impotent. The decline accelerated. Banks tightened their purse strings, and production fell to a new low.

Close to default on its debt, the company's directors had appealed to Dan Hedrik. He understood the problems. He was willing to accept the challenge, demanding total autonomy. He got it. His rescue plan was uncompromising. It called for ruthless surgery. He terminated the Eastern headquarters and severed its acolytes, consolidating operations. He axed deadwood at the studio, and discontinued most executive perks.

Then, with an extended line of credit, Hedrik turned his attention to actual making of pictures. There was, he knew, one way in which considerable solvency might be achieved; acquiring and filming one hugely successful blockbuster.

He had studied the industry figures. He knew that Paramount had grossed over three hundred million on *The Godfather*. *Star Wars* had done even better for Fox. And several others were now racking up astronomical profits.

That, Hedrik, believed, was the way to go. But he needed a property. Then, one of his contacts in publishing sent him advance galleys of Logan Stern's new novel, *The Romanoff File*. He took it home and read it over the weekend—read it with a growing sense of excitement. His own experience as an author, his eye for story values and background that could be richly translated into cinematic terms, convinced him unshakably that Arcadia had to film this novel, whatever the cost.

He did not wait until Monday morning. Late Sunday afternoon he called his contact and learned that Miles Foreman was the literary agent involved. They had dealt with each other on previous occasions. He got through to Foreman in New York.

49

"Miles? Dan Hedrik of Arcadia Films."

Foreman was not surprised at the Sunday call. Picture deals were negotiated at all times and in every conceivable place. "Yes, Mr. Hedrik."

"I just read the new Logan Stern."

"Publication is still a month away. Haven't seen a finished copy myself."

"These were galleys. I like the book, Miles, and I'm prepared to make an offer."

"It'll cost you. We think we have a big one here."

"So do I. Look, Miles, when and if bidding starts, you may be offered more elsewhere. Then again, you may not. My directors will go into shock when they hear this. Half a million, Miles, no haggling, take it or leave it. With another hundred and fifty thousand if Stern writes the screenplay."

"You're right. We may do better elsewhere. Especially when the book hits the best-seller lists."

"That's a gamble you'd be taking."

There was a moment's silence. "Tell me, what are you planning for this one?"

"We'll budget it at ten million and go as high as necessary. I'll pull the plug, Miles. Best available stars, director, the works."

"We'd want a participation interest."

"Agreed. Ten per cent of net earnings."

"No way, Mr. Hedrik. A percentage of net, we usually wind up with zip. Nada. I think you know the gonifs I'm talking about. They hassled us to death on the break-even point, deducted set construction, equipment, utilities, salaries, legal, clerical, photographic, foreign taxes, domestic taxes, advertizing, and then, to top it off, they tacked on a thirty per cent distribution fee. The picture was released two years ago. A smash, worldwide, and we still haven't seen dime one of our participation. Tell you what, we'll settle for five points of gross income. If Stern agrees, we're in business."

"You're bleeding me to death, Miles."

"Sure. But we're talking about a hell of a property. You

know Logan Stern's track record. I think *The Romanoff File* is the best thing he's ever done."

" Five per cent of gross. It's yours. When can you let me know Stern's answer?"

" I'll call him right now."

" He lives out here, doesn't he?"

" Santa Barbara."

" And tell him our own publicity people will help to promote the book."

" We'll get back to you."

Twenty minutes later the phone rang and Logan Stern was on the line.

" I just had a call from Miles Foreman, Mr. Hedrik. He told me about your offer. We should wait until publication date and the majors start bidding. But I know your work and I know your reputation. I told Foreman to accept."

Hedrik's spirits lifted. " You'll do the screenplay?"

" I'd hate to see it loused up by someone else."

" Mr. Stern, I'm delighted. I'll iron out the details with Foreman tomorrow and put our lawyers to work on the contract. Have you had any reception from the book clubs?"

" Both the Guild and Book-of-the-Month are interested."

" How about paperback?"

" They're clamoring, Mr. Hedrik. It goes on the block for open bidding as soon as we have a firm commitment from the book clubs. Gives us added leverage."

" So does a picture deal. Can you have lunch with me at the studio next week?"

" I'm free on Wednesday."

" It's a date. Some people here I'd like you to meet."

Hedrik stood up and flexed his fingers. He paced his living room, planning strategy. If his line of credit was insufficient for a budget this size, he'd ask the board for approval to sell off a piece of Arcadia's real estate. At today's bloated prices for California acreage, a dozen developers would leap at the opportunity, waving their checkbooks.

Now, on Monday morning, in his office, Hedrik's secretary

opened the door for Ross Landry. Landry was a slight, frail-looking man with pale quizzical eyes. He headed for the coffee tray, poured a cup, and holding it with both hands, lowered himself into a chair.

"So, Dan? They said it was urgent. What's on the menu?"

"Something special, Ross. How long will it take you to finish *Piece of Cake*?"

"We're editing now. Another day or two and it's in the can. *Piece of Crap* would be a better title. I hope to Christ we can recover negative costs."

Since the picture had been scheduled by Hedrik's predecessor, he was not offended. He said, "I just closed a deal for the new Logan Stern."

Landry sat up, grinning. "Hey, I've heard rumors, Dan. Fellow over at Universal saw uncorrected proofs and flipped. He says it's a blockbuster and he'd give his right arm for a crack at it. Are you telling me true, Dan? Have we really got it? Signed, sealed, and delivered?"

"I spoke to Stern and his agent yesterday. *The Romanoff File.* Got a verbal commitment. Espionage-adventure. But with extra ingredients. And Stern himself will do the adaptation."

"How much?"

"Half a million. Plus an additional one-fifty for the screenplay. Plus five per cent of gross. And I'm thinking of a preliminary budget of ten million."

Landry whistled softly. "Jesus, Dan! You're into one hell of a crapshoot here. You may have to double that before you're finished."

"I know. But you can't buy class merchandise without paying the ticket. I have a gut feeling about this one, Ross. If we pull it off, the picture will pack 'em to the chandeliers. It can make Arcadia healthy again. God, how I'd love to film it on location!"

"Not a chance. Yugoslavia, maybe. We can use stock shots of the Winter Palace, the Kremlin, KGB Headquarters, Moscow street scenes." Landry looked wistful. "Who's producing?"

"You are."

The grin returned. " I love you, boss. When can I see those galleys?"

" I brought them for you." Hendrik slapped a package on his desk. " Stern is coming to lunch next Wednesday and we'll kick it around."

" Logan Stern. Who tagged him with a combination like that?"

" Irish mother. Logan is her family name. Jewish father. Stern himself is an agnostic, according to a recent *New Yorker* profile."

" Got anybody in mind for the leading role?"

" Clyde Elliott. Custom-tailored for the part. Read the book and let me know if you agree. We'll have to offer him a piece of the action. And I'm thinking of Kate Rennie as the Grand Duchess."

" Will she come out of retirement?"

" For Arcadia, probably yes. She's still the biggest individual stockholder, with a strong attachment to the company."

Landry studied Hedrik over the rim of his cup. He said quietly, " There's a lot more than just a successful film riding on this production, isn't there, Dan?"

Hedrik nodded. " Ross, I don't have to spell out our problems. Too many years of loose management and red ink, which makes us fair game for a takeover by corporate scavengers."

" Something like that shaping up?"

" Didn't you hear the announcement?"

" I've been isolated in the cutting room. What announcement?"

" Universal Media Industries made a tender offer to our shareholders."

Landry made a face. " That's Fred Hanna's outfit." He sounded bitter. " At a handsome premium, I suppose."

" Naturally."

" Cash?"

" Hell, no. That's not Hanna's method. He'd like to swallow us without the trouble of chewing."

" That prick doesn't know the first goddamn thing about

making pictures. He'd turn the studio over to TV soaps."

" Probably."

" Are we fighting back?"

" I've already retained counsel. Lawyer named Slater—Paul Slater, in New York. Specialist in proxy fights. Law professor, too. If we lose, we go down kicking and screaming. Too bad we don't have *The Romanoff File* ready right now for immediate release. It would be oil in the ground."

8

Julie Gregorius's gaze swept the Palm Court at the Plaza, searching for Ward Bendiner. He beckoned from a corner table and she felt her pulse quicken. As she approached, she could not resist comparing him once again with Mike Ryan. Both men projected an impressive masculinity, but Ward was more responsive, easier to manage.

" Sorry I'm late," she said.

He smiled. " Worth waiting for. The usual?"

" Please."

He flagged a waiter and ordered Martinis. " Sitting here is no hardship, Julie. This is a pleasant room, a little baroque perhaps, but pleasant. Besides, I've adjusted. I expect you to be late."

" Always?"

" Inevitably. As a natural order of things."

" Ryan says it's a kind of arrogance."

" Is Ryan also an expert on human behaviour?"

" That's one of his problems. Always analyzing. He says it's an occupational hazard. What do you think? Am I arrogant?"

" Most beautiful women are arrogant. Men spoil them at an early age. When did your father begin?"

" You noticed? The day I was born."

" Well, he couldn't help himself. And neither can I."

The waiter brought their drinks. Julie suspected that Ward's amiability masked a considerable purpose, even though he seemed untroubled by the fact that he had never held a job. She understood that he had inherited a sizable fortune. Preserving his inheritance in a capricious economy, he had told her with a rueful smile, was challenge enough, adding that it would be uncharitable to deprive someone of a job who really needed it for survival.

She nibbled her olive, wondering aloud why his deep tan never seemed to fade.

" Try baking yourself in Mexico," he said, " and then finish the job in Florida."

" Mexico. Isn't that where you met your wife?"

" Yes. In La Paz."

" I'm curious. Tell me about her."

" What do you want to know?"

" Her name."

" Cora."

" Is she attractive?"

" Spectacular. Once, crossing the street in Mexico City, wearing a miniskirt, she started a chain reaction that totaled twenty cars."

" So why are you divorcing such a prize?"

" Because of her libido."

" Ha! Since when would that particular trait turn you off?"

" It didn't. The trouble started when it turned other men on. Marriage, apparently, did not entitle me to an exclusive."

" And that wounded your male ego?"

" My pride mostly."

' 'Do you think of her occasionally?"

" Not with any pleasure."

" Do you hate her?"

" Hate, Miss Gregorius, is a destructive emotion. I prefer tranquility."

" Is she still living in Florida?"

55

He nodded. " Ocala Beach. In a place my family built years ago. Kind of isolated. I doubt if she'll stay there after the final decree. Not her style at all."

" Alimony?"

" My lawyer suggested a cash settlement. That way it's over, finished, and we have no more contact. I have a very smart young lawyer down there. Chap named Bogart. He really doesn't belong in a small community. He could probably make it big here in the east, with one of those top Wall Street shops."

" Mexico," Julie said musingly. " I've been all over the world, but never Mexico. What's the attraction?"

" It's warm, peaceful, secluded. I never really enjoyed big cities, Julie. Too many people, too much activity, an undercurrent of hostility. Cora catered to me and even suggested the town, San Miguel Allende, with a small foreign colony."

Resting her elbow on the table, she propped her chin on a closed fist. " I'm fascinated. Tell me all about it."

9

Cora Bendiner lay on a mat alongside the swimming pool, basting in fragrant oils under a Florida sun, trying to erase all thoughts of her husband. It wasn't easy. It was, in fact, impossible. Perversely, he kept intruding, and her conscience, she knew, had very little to do with it.

She had met Ward through a random encounter. A microsecond of time either way, and she would not be here in this place on the Gulf Coast, almost insulated from the world.

Ward had been wandering across Central America and had worked his way north into Mexico for a look at the Mayan ruins. Neither she nor Ward had been alert at the time of the accident. In La Paz, in the early-afternoon heat, she had absent-mindedly stepped off the curb into the path of a rental Fiat driven by Ward and he had bunted her a good one, tumbling her to the ground and spilling the contents of her shopping bag. A group of passive-eyed onlookers had gathered instantly.

Ward had leaped out of the car to bend over her in anxious solicitation. " Don't move," he cautioned. " I'll call for help."

She sat up, wincing, rubbing her hip. " You'd better get me out of here fast." She took his helping hand and limped to the passenger side of the Fiat. " Hey!" she said. " Forget the shopping bag. Let's roll."

He slid behind the wheel. " I'm a stranger here. Where to?"

" Any place. For your own sake, my friend. And *mucho pronto*, unless you're willing to serve time in the local slammer. These Mexican jails are not run by Señor Hilton."

Prodded by the urgency in her voice, he released the clutch and scattered bystanders. She told him to turn at the corner, and again at the next, glancing back over her shoulder.

" Okay," she said. " I think we made it. Nobody's following. An accident down here and they clap you behind bars, no discussion, no excuses, until everything's ironed out, liability, insurance, doctor's fees, which may take days or even weeks."

Cora was accustomed to men staring at her. This one was no exception. Her flawless complexion, burnished hair, green eyes, generous mouth, and all the richly wrought components of her slender figure had been attracting males from the moment she had first attained puberty. She knew instinctively that this stranger had been totally unprepared for a physical impact so tangible.

She smiled brightly and said, " I'm Cora McElroy."

" Ward Bendiner."

" Hello, Ward. Your first trip to Mexico?"

He nodded. " Just drove up through Guatemala and Panama. So far, I like this country. I like the natives. I'd stay for a while if I could find the right place. And you?"

" Been here about a month now. Though I've been to Mexico

57

several times before." She did not tell him that the man she was traveling with on this trip had suffered a stroke and was in a critical condition at the local hospital.

" About that accident, Cora, I'd like—"

" Please. Don't give it another thought. It was my fault. I was daydreaming. Contributory negligence, as the lawyers say. But I would like to stop at a *botica*."

" Translate."

" Pharmacy. A couple of aspirins might help. Do you have any Spanish at all?"

" About three words."

" Would you like to hire a guide?"

" Is there a good one available?"

" The best. Me. Cora McElroy. I know the country and my Spanish is adequate. What sort of place are you looking for?"

" Something with a few civilized amenities. And not too many people."

" You don't like people?"

" I like them in small select numbers."

" I'll drink to that."

" Sold. Where can we find a bar?"

She glanced about to find her bearings. " Slow down at the next corner and turn left. You'll see a sign. *Cantina*. I happen to know for a fact that their ice cubes are made of purified water."

It was a cool dim oasis. A young boy came through, selling newspapers, and Cora sent him out for aspirin, handing him a bill and promising a handsome reward when he returned. She suggested Mexican beer and ordered for the two of them.

Ward tasted it and nodded approval. " What you said about Mexican jails, was all that true?"

" You better believe it," Cora told him. " Mexico does not observe the subtleties of Anglo-Saxon law. They presume guilt until one proves his innocence. Maximilian's legacy, the old *Code Napoleon*. Anyone involved in an accident gets tossed into the jug until everything is settled. So it's hit-and-run. If nobody is hurt, you take flight before the constabulary arrives."

58

Cora saw that he was impressed by her concern over his welfare rather than the extent of her own injuries. His interest and his curiosity grew. She guessed that he had been alone for a long time and was deliberately prolonging this interlude.

He said, "Tell me about yourself, Cora."

"It's a fascinating story, Ward. Settle back and make yourself comfortable."

*   *   *

Cora McElroy had been born and raised in Wichita, Kansas, one sister preceding her. Her father, now dead, had been a widower and a dentist. She attended local schools and ultimately had married an aeronautical engineer employed at the Cessna plant. During the courtship her suitor had kept himself under control. Within weeks she knew it was not going to work. Her husband was a heavy drinker, emotionally unstable, a rancorous man with a low flashpoint that often erupted into bursts of violent temper. Toward the end of their first year, driving alone at night, speeding along a rain-slick highway, he had missed a curve in the road and smashed into a concrete abutment. He was dead before the ambulance arrived.

After a brief period of griefless mourning, Cora had collected the insurance, sold the house, and departed forever from Kansas. She had never been especially close to her sister, who still lived in Wichita. Like many Midwesterners, she had been drawn to coastal areas. In Puerto Vallarta she had found a quality of life that appealed to her. Someone told her about a school, the Instituto, in San Miguel Allende, where she could brush up on Spanish, and she studied there for several months.

In her recital, Cora omitted a number of episodes that would have left Ward Bendiner's jaw sagging.

Encouraged by the belief that they had much in common, two people who had abandoned their native land to find a more compatible haven elsewhere—Bendiner unburdened himself. Cora was an avid listener, manifesting all the appropriate reactions.

He described his lonely boyhood in Vermont, in the old

59

mansion overlooking the Bendiner Mills. His mother had died when he was four and his father was deeply preoccupied in a long struggle to keep the family business operating. Most of the textile factories had departed from New England for non-union labor markets in the South. Emil Bendiner stayed, feeling an obligation to his workers. Finally, realising that his son had no particular disposition for the world of business, he had accepted defeat and closed his doors.

Over the years, starting with Ward's great-grandfather, Bendiner profits had been carefully invested in equities. During a period of unparalleled industrial expansion, the family's fortune had multiplied tenfold.

Emil Bendiner and his son moved south. A place was waiting for them. In the early twenties Emil's own father had acquired a hideaway in a remote section of Florida's west coast, and reached only by a private road. They called it The Lodge, and it had been a family tradition to spend at least one winter month there, trawling the Gulf of Mexico for game fish.

The Lodge was isolated, ten miles from the nearest town, Ocala Beach, but neither Emil nor Ward minded the seclusion. They had their books, and Emil kept in touch with his investments through subscriptions to a number of financial journals. He introduced his son to the stock tables and enlisted his help in watching the progress of the Bendiner portfolio. After all, the boy one day would have to manage the estate himself.

Ward was most intrigued by the extraordinarily large position in Arcadia Films, the only holding that lacked blue-chip quality. "Your grandfather bought it," Emil Bendiner explained. "When the movie companies first went public. He saw it as a growing industry and for many years he was right. The stock split five times. I suppose it should have been sold long ago. And that's a lesson you'll have to learn, my boy. It seems harder to sell an investment than to buy it in the first place."

Father and son spent most of their time together until Ward went off to Gainesville to finish his schooling. At the State University he was a loner. He rented a small apartment and made few friends. Two weeks before graduation, his father

60

became ill. Ward was at his bedside when Emil Bendiner died. He felt desolate, deserted. He did not return to school for his degree.

When the estate was finally settled Ward paid off the housekeeper, closed The Lodge, then drove across the state, and arranged for a custodial account at a Miami bank to handle dividends and income.

He had registered for the draft because of a police action in Korea. Within a month, no longer a student, he was inducted into the army. But he saw no action. A treaty was signed before he had completed basic training, and ultimately he was separated from the service.

Long-held travel plans now materialised. He settled in London for two years, then Paris, and finally Rome. Although he was presentable and articulate, he cultivated no close attachments. And he'd been wondering on this present trip to Mexico if there was some quirk in his personality that had influenced his choice of privacy.

And so, Cora McElroy gathered, the accident that had brought them together found him now in an unusually receptive mood.

*   *   *

She reached a decision. This appealing man, not normally gregarious, was obviously attracted to her. And just as obviously seemed loaded. Her own funds were running low. Taking the initiative, she elicited a dinner invitation. Her own hotel was not convenient, she told him, smiling, wondering if it would be possible to use the shower at his place. The request seemed to blur his vision.

At Bendiner's motel she left the bathroom slightly ajar. She hung her clothes on a hook and stepped into the shower. She had examined herself often, knew the perfection of her body, and knew, too, that her effect on men had always been irresistible.

She dried herself, donned a thin robe that belonged to Ward, rolled up the sleeves, belted it loosely, then walked into the bedroom and smiled shyly. Without a word she moved into his arms. Oh, he was human all right. She knew that from his instant tumescence, the importuning pelvic thrust. She tumbled him backward onto the bed, tugging at his clothes.

Cora wanted this man to be emotionally involved. She wanted him to see her face, the contours of breasts and slender waist. She straddled him, heard him groan, and rocked gently, murmuring his name. Sensing his rhythms, she slowed intuitively, prolonging his transport. And then clued by his urgent tumult, she quickly brought him to a climax of such blinding intensity that he cried out and pulled her flat against him, holding her tightly while his blood cooled.

They stayed coupled, luxuriating in postcoital ennui. Then she rolled to one side and met his eyes and saw that he was staring at her in wonder.

" Was it good for you, darling?" she asked.

" Words fail me."

" Serendipity, no?"

" Yes, indeed. Finding each other by accident. Like an art dealer running across a Rembrandt among the junk contents of an abandoned attic."

And suddenly they were ravenously hungry. They went out for a leisurely dinner. Afterward they came back to the motel and made love until dawn. Ward was insatiable—he could not get enough of her.

He told Cora that he would not leave La Paz without her. He asked her to plan an itinerary, places she had enjoyed and would enjoy again. New places they could explore together. After breakfast he drove to Cora's hotel and waited in the Fiat until she packed her bags. She left without calling the hospital where Ward's predecessor lay dying.

They managed a reservation for the car aboard the ferry for Mazátlan. Crossing the Gulf of California, they huddled at the rail, holding hands.

Ashore, they journeyed south along the coastal road, pausing at fishing villages, and blending at night into the single greedy creature of an ancient ritual. They drifted inland to Taxco, then Cuernavaca, climbing northward onto the colonial highlands, heading for San Miguel, which Cora assured him was just the kind of place he would like.

She was right. Bendiner's initial view of the town pleased him, the way it nestled peacefully in the hills, its homes isolated behind thick walls. They checked into a small *posada*, and the next morning they toured the cobblestoned streets seeking more permanent quarters.

They found a place located atop a sparsely settled hill, a comfortable villa surrounded by high sienna walls, its courtyard ablaze with tropical plantings, complete with a tiny swimming pool and a maid, a diminutive *mestiza* of inexhaustible energy. It was available on a long-term lease, and Bendiner signed the papers with no quibbling.

Cora discouraged any overtures from their neighbors, making it an idyllic time for Ward. He preferred to loll in the sun, reading omnivorously, while Cora took courses at the Instituto. During the long languid afternoons they took siestas, coupling frequently, Cora always humid and receptive, working under him and above him with sinewy diligence.

On one occasion he quoted from a book he'd been reading, about a married couple involved in a venomous divorce, fighting bitterly over alimony and a division of property. She sensed his determination to preserve the inherited fortune and perceived that it had made him overly cautious about making any permanent commitment. So she planned her campaign carefully. Later, she made a casual remark about her sister in Kansas, struggling to support an invalid husband, telling Ward that if she were ever to get married again, she would insist on a prenuptial agreement, with each party surrendering all claims to the other's estate, so that she could leave her own money to her sister.

Two days later, he proposed.

It was almost time to cross back into the states in order to renew their Mexican tourist permits. They drove to Laredo and visited a lawyer, who drew the necessary papers. Cora repressed a smile. She had supreme confidence in herself. She felt that in time he would ignore the prenuptial agreement and would ultimately draw a will making her his sole legatee.

They found a Justice of the Peace, and in a brief ceremony Cora changed her name to Mrs. Ward Bendiner. They returned to the villa in San Miguel and settled easily into domestic tranquillity.

Before the year was out, Ward became aware of disturbing symptoms. When he infrequently ventured outside the walls, a climb back up the hill winded him to the point of breathlessness. There was a heaviness in his chest. He did not worry about it, attributing the discomfort to San Miguel's high altitude. Nor did he mention it to Cora.

She discovered the problem one morning as he swam in the pool. He stopped suddenly, clearly in distress, sucking air. She dove in and helped him out.

" Nothing important," he said in a gravely voice, his face ash-grey.

" How long has this been going on?" she demanded.

" Couple of weeks. It's the altitude."

" You're going to see a doctor. I understand there's a fairly competent man here."

She called and made an appointment for that afternoon.

Dr. Emilio Hernandez had a small unpretentious office above a pharmacy operated by his wife. Since he treated most members of the American community, his English was adequate. He asked questions, made notes, used his stethoscope, and after taking Ward's blood pressure, he sat back, frowned, and pinched his lip. He used the pressure cuff a second time and said, " Too high, too high."

" What's the prognosis, Doctor?"

" There is medication. We can reduce the blood pressure. How long are you staying in San Miguel?"

" I've rented a house here."

" I see. Well, Señor Bendiner, high blood pressure is not unusual, but it must be controlled. I would like to see a complete workup. Perhaps you can arrange for an EKG at the hospital in Querétaro."

64

Ward nodded. " Any other suggestions?"

" Only this. If my own reading was elevated—at your level, for example—I would move to some other area, closer to sea level." He smiled. " It is not an emergency. Let us see how the medication works."

Cora was waiting, looking solicitous. " Nothing serious," he told her. " Blood pressure is a little high. Hernandez says I can expect some discomfort at these altitudes."

" I won't have it," she said. " We're leaving here as soon as possible."

" We have a lease."

" Break it. Pay them off and break it. My God, darling. Let's get our priorities straight. I know you have a place in Florida. You can get better medical attention there."

Two days later they were in Mexico City, with reservations for a flight to Miami.

10

Liz Harmon reached the restaurant before Mike Ryan. He had called, asking her to meet him there. A table had been reserved and she ordered a drink.

Sipping her Martini, she recalled their first meeting. Mike had been a speaker at one of the lunches sponsored by the New York Society of Security Analysts, discussing problems involved in the underwriting of new securities. She had listened to him extol Wall Street as a vital conduit for the flow of capital from investors to industry, an essential ingredient in the American economy. Platitudes, she remembered thinking. Warmed-over cabbage. But then, how often had she heard anyone come up with a truly fresh concept? Not ever in this forum.

After Ryan's talk, the questions had been polite and inoffensive until Liz, out of a whimsical sense of perversity, had chimed in with a barbed comment about the incomprehensible prose in underwriting prospectuses. Surprisingly, Ryan agreed with her, attributing those convoluted semantics to the legal profession.

Afterwards he invited her to join him for a drink. As they sat at the bar he looked at her appraisingly. " So," he said, " you're the formidable Elizabeth Harmon."

She arched an eyebrow. " I thought we analysts were anonymous."

" Generally, yes. But I've heard about you from Pete Sternbach. I'm curious. How the devil did you ever get into this racket?"

" That's a question you men usually ask hookers."

Ryan threw his head back and laughed.

Liz said, " You mean because I'm a woman. My father got me interested. You may have heard of Dr. Anthony Harmon."

" *The* Anthony Harmon? Economics professor at Columbia? Him? My God, yes. I've read his books and sat in on his seminars. I'm a disciple. If those clowns in Washington would only adopt some of his ideas, it might solve a few of our problems."

She was pleased. Admiration of her father always pleased her. They moved from the bar to a table. Ryan forgot that he was due back at the office. She seconded his views about the fatuity of Presidential advisors, about the proliferation of alphabet agencies. He queried her about her investment philosophy.

" I'm sure of only one thing," she told him. " Security bargains are available during times of extreme pessimism. Trouble is, when the so-called experts are wringing their hands, nobody has the courage to buy."

" Pete Sternbach had the courage."

" As a speculation, for the Croesus Fund. But Pete's an exception. He's a born maverick."

Mike put his glass down. " Do you enjoy working for Sternbach?"

"Why do you ask?"

"I'd like to offer you a job. With Gregorius & Company. Chief of Research."

She studied him. "Just like that?"

"Yes, ma'am."

"But I already have a job."

"Whatever Sternbach Management is paying you, we'll increase it five thousand."

"A week?"

He grinned. "Five thousand a year, to start. We also have a profit-sharing plan, and at your level you'd be entitled to participate at a pretty good percentage. And if your vanity requires, you can pick a title."

"How about chairman of the board? Or rather chairperson."

"Sorry. Anson Gregorius is still with us. If it works out, you could be offered a general partnership."

"No, thanks. If the firm goes bust, general partners are responsible for its debts. I might settle for a spot on the policy committee."

"Next year maybe. All we need is twenty-four hours to find you a suitable office."

"Not so fast, Mr. Ryan. I thought Pete Sternbach is a friend of yours."

"So?"

"You're raiding his talent."

"Why not? I understand he stole you away from Stoufer, Wingate."

"You're not worried?"

"Of what?"

"The risk. Sternbach generates a lot of commission business for Gregorius. He may get angry and pull his account."

"I doubt it. Pete would never concede that anyone but himself is important to his operation."

"When do you want an answer?"

"Take your time. This evening will do."

She cocked her head. "Why all this sudden urgency?"

"I'll be frank, Miss Harmon. We've been expanding our

asset management services. Last week our top researcher was ordered to leave New York. Lung trouble. So he's moving to Arizona. We've been interviewing candidates, so far without success."

" How much were you paying the man?"

Mike rubbed his jaw quizzically. " Okay. Equal pay for equal work. You'll get the same contract."

" When would I have to start?"

" Day after tomorrow."

" Impossible. Pete's entitled to fair notice."

" Two weeks, then."

" Suppose he raises the ante."

" I doubt it. Anyway, working for a mutual fund can never offer the same challenges you'll meet in investment banking."

She nodded. " I'd expect an employment contract with a two-year guarantee."

" No problem."

She smiled and reached across the table to shake his hand. She was not quite certain why she had made this decision without more time for reflection. The opportunity of working with Ryan might have been a factor.

Within a month she was functioning smoothly at Gregorius & Company, aware of old Anson's initial opposition. Ryan, always under pressure, with little time for office conferences, had begun taking her to lunch, ostensibly for business discussions. Then, one evening, working late, she had looked up to see Mike watching her from the doorway. He suggested dinner and she had accepted. When he brought her home, she had invited him in for a nightcap. Once inside, he had reached out and taken her roughly into his arms. She had submitted passively for a moment and then responded. Instantly his hands had cupped her rump, pulling her close. She wrenched free, and her open palm had caught him across the side of his jaw with such stinging ferocity it left his face numb.

" Jesus Christ, Liz!"

She smiled sweetly. " A friendly kiss, my friend, is no invitation to uninhibited license."

He rubbed his jaw ruefully. " Outraged virginity?"

" Hardly."

" Then what?"

" You came on too strong and too fast."

" So let's try it again. This time slowly and gently."

" I'm afraid not, Mike. It takes some affection too."

" Couldn't you tell? I was feeling very affectionate."

" You were feeling lecherous. It's not the same thing. Please don't get me wrong. Lechery may be a perfectly acceptable form of recreation."

" So?"

" So you've got the wrong customer. A casual romp in the sack is not my idea of sport, and I believe that's what you had in mind."

He hung his head contritely. " Well, excuse me all to hell, Liz. I humbly apologize."

" Apology accepted."

He worked his jaw tentatively. " And I'm deeply grateful."

" For what?"

" For not closing your hand and using your fist. It probably saved me from some expensive dental repair. You pack a very wicked wallop, Miss Harmon."

" A matter of survival, Mr. Ryan. Living alone in this town, a girl learns how to protect herself. I know some karate too. My dad taught me. He's very good at it."

" My God!" Mike said. " A black-belt economics professor." He mimicked a hand chop, grunting savagely. Then he grinned. " Truce, Liz? Can we go back to square one?"

" Of course."

" Then I'll take the nightcap now. A double, if you please. For its anesthetic effect, naturally."

*　　*　　*

She saw him now, entering the restaurant, checking his coat, striding tall and briskly toward their table. " Sorry," he said. " Sudden conference with our client Fred Hanna." He sighed. " Unexpected little crises always cropping up."

"Is he pleased with the way Gregorius handled the new bond issue?"

"He should be. All sold out. I handed him a check this afternoon. Your face shows mild disapproval. What's the beef now, Liz?"

"I'm wondering what he has in mind for Arcadia Films."

"The company is sick. He plans on restoring it to good health."

"How? And for whose benefit?"

"Ah, Liz, we've been through all this before. You know the man's track record."

"I do indeed. And I seem to recall several companies that welcomed Hanna's embrace and are no longer in business."

"And that bugs you?"

"Yes, it bugs me, Mike. Because a lot of good people were suddenly out on the street looking for jobs. Your Mr. Hanna decided those companies were worth more dead than alive. So he gutted them. He liquidated the assets and buried the remains."

"Come off it, Liz. Sentiment has no place in business. You just don't like the man."

"True. And I'm not crazy about his bookkeeping either. Don't forget, when you first bagged this account, I took a hard look at UMI, and it was my opinion that Hanna employs a team of very creative auditors. I don't usually have trouble understanding corporate setups. But UMI is a lulu. Holding companies, subsidiaries, interlocking directorates, and figures I couldn't cut through with a linoleum knife. Like trying to untangle a knot with my toes. Oh, sure, the bottom line is a lovely sight, with increased profits every year. But how those numbers were reached is something else. Granted, I don't have a degree in accounting, but I can read a balance sheet as well as anyone, which is why Gregorius hired me."

"Give me one concrete example."

"I can't. It's intuition, Mike. When I don't understand something, it makes me suspicious. UMI uses mathematical formulas that would have stumped Einstein. You're convinced that

Hanna is some kind of executive genius. Okay. You're entitled. A difference of opinion is what makes Wall Street work."

"Would you at least agree that Hanna, starting almost from scratch, has built himself a nice little empire?"

"So did Attila the Hun. It's the method that counts. Look, Hanna wants Arcadia Films. Does he know anything about making pictures?"

"Not essential. And irrelevant. Paramount, Universal, Twentieth Century-Fox, all now comfortably tucked into conglomerate setups and thriving nicely, while Arcadia is still flat on its corporate ass. Movies are popular entertainment. So is TV. And UBC, Hanna's network, has increased its viewer percentage in each of the past five years. Nielson's figures, not mine. That's one message I can read. So you've lost me somewhere. You feel Arcadia should preserve its independence. Tell me why."

"Well, some time back, when I was still working for Pete Sternbach, he had a hunch the picture business could be making a comeback. He thought a flier for the Croesus Fund might prove profitable. I flew out to the Coast for an in-depth work-up of the industry. At Arcadia, they turned me over to Dan Hedrik. He was still producing then, but he'd been with the company for a long time. I had lunch with him. I was impressed. He understood the business from A to Z. From inception of an idea to the finished product. He never once bad-mouthed management, although I sensed that he was unhappy with the overall policy. He had ideas. He made predictions. And most of them came true. Well, Dan Hedrik is in charge now, and I have a feeling that he has a better than an outside chance of putting it all together."

"Intuition again?"

"I know you prefer facts, Mike. But facts are never the sole criteria on Wall Street. Otherwise we could program facts into a computer and wind up with googol."

"Googol?"

"It's in the dictionary. Number one followed by a hundred zeros. And that, my friend, is enough tickets to run all the governments in the world. Even so, I am not indulging in intuition alone."

" So give me something I can chew on."

" Hedrik spotted the trend before it developed. He wanted to make the big film, something unusual. He was certain it could turn Arcadia around. But he could not persuade the faint-hearted boys in the front office. They were afraid to risk the money. So look what happened. *Jaws, Star Wars*, grossing hundreds of millions. Box-office blockbusters. All right, I heard a rumor that Hedrik had found a property with enormous potential, and that he's going to make that kind of picture. He deserves the chance."

" What makes you think Hanna would disapprove?"

" I believe Hanna has other plans for Arcadia. And I doubt if he would spring for the kind of budget Hedrik has in mind."

" You could be wrong."

" Mike, if Fred Hanna wins control of Arcadia, I have a feeling Hedrik would quit and go independent."

Ryan considered it. " I'll know more about the man after I talk to him."

" Talk to Hedrik? Is he coming to New York?"

" No. I'm flying out to the Coast."

" When?"

" Tomorrow morning. Very early. Let's order dinner right now so I can get to bed at a reasonable hour."

11

Cruising at eighteen thousand feet in his executive jet, destination O'Hare in Chicago, Fred Hanna gazed down at the geometric pattern of farmland visible off the port wing.

After a moment he turned and studied Robert Egan's impassive profile.

The UMI lawyer was sipping tomato juice. A strange one, Hanna reflected. In the twelve years of their association he could not recall ever having seen his adjutant indulge in alcoholic spirits or cast a speculative eye at any woman. Egan seemed to exist in some emotional vacuum that excluded personal indulgence. The ultimate organization man, dedicated to the affairs of Universal Media Industries.

Once, in Zurich, on a business trip, partly out of curiosity and partly as reward for unearthing an obscure tax shelter, Hanna had tested him. He had sent a gift to Egan's hotel room —one of those long-legged bosomy Scandinavian professionals, with instructions to perform and report back.

The woman did not report back, and when Hanna called her the following morning she uttered an obscenity and hung up on him. At breakfast, Egan made no mention of the episode.

Hanna could not resist inquiring. "That merchandise last night, did you find it satisfactory?"

"Adequate."

"Shall I keep it accessible during our stay here?"

"No."

The terse response invited no further discussion. Now, in the plane, watching the lawyer's dime-thin lips sip the tomato juice, he wondered if Egan was heterosexual. Abruptly the speaker system crackled and the pilot's voice spoke.

"We'll be running into a spot of turbulence, Mr. Hanna. Please fasten your seat belt."

The *Citation* was his favorite plane. He had personally selected its furnishings. Under his standing instructions, it had been swept for electronic bugs before takeoff. Having resorted to corporate espionage himself, he accepted it as a fact of business life.

Egan removed a headset and said, "Arcadia Films is up another point and a half."

"We expected that. The target company always jumps on a tender announcement."

73

" Hedrik's acquisition of that new Logan Stern novel may be partly responsible. They're hyping the goddamn book as if it were written by Jesus himself. He paid half a million for the film rights."

" Insanity. Is the man playing with a full deck?"

Egan shrugged. " Book-of-the-Month is taking it, and paperback bidding is out of sight. Arcadia's publicity is touting it as the picture coup of the year and predicting a huge success. Makes management look good, as if Hedrik is the new company messiah."

Hanna said harshly, " I don't like it, Bob. Not with a proxy fight shaping up."

" I agree. Arcadia stock is beginning to look attractive. We should knock the price down."

" How?"

" Sell it short."

" What the hell are you talking about? Sooner or later we'd have to cover and kick it back up again."

" Not necessarily. We already hold a big position in Arcadia. So we sell short against the box, putting up our own shares. And the selling pressure drives the prices down. In the meantime, we circulate pessimistic rumours. Hedrik is gambling on an unknown quantity. Stern's book lacks cinematic possibilities. Things happen. Production delays, accidents, strikes. Costs skyrocket. So the stock heads for the cellar. And shareholders panic. Speculators who bought on our takeover announcement start running for the hills. Selling pressure increases. Margin accounts are sold out. Ultimately we cover our short position, buying more at depressed prices."

Hanna threw his arms up. " And just what the hell do you think the SEC is doing all this time? The Exchange itself is programmed to detect unusual activity. They'll start tapping broker records to find out who's shorting Arcadia. And they find that UMI keeps popping into the picture. And don't forget Mr. Gary George Pressman, that crusading prick from the SEC's Enforcement Division, the one who gave us all that trouble last year. He would dearly love to stick it to me. And

74

he's got some three hundred fucking lawyers policing corporate activities. So they'd nail us for insider trading without making the obligatory reports. To say nothing about stock manipulation. Especially during a proxy fight."

His hand shot up, forestalling comment. " Hear me out. I'm not finished yet." His voice was thick. " I know Pressman. He'll build a file and he'll turn it over to Justice. Then some tough young sonovabitch U.S. Attorney eager to make a score hits us with an indictment. Have you forgotten that our broadcast stations operate under a licence? You want the FCC to challenge us when we come up for renewal." He paused and took a breath. " So? Are you still holding to your suggestion?"

Egan's gaze did not waver. " Yes. Because we do not short any stock held in our own name, or in the name of any brokerage house here in the United States. We work through nominees outside the country, mostly through our bankers in Zurich. We'd be home free, protected by Swiss secrecy laws."

" You told me the Swiss were beginning to co-operate with Uncle Sam."

" Only in the case of criminal activity. Even then, U.S. authorities must prove that similar actions are illegal in Switzerland. And so far the Swiss have no laws requiring disclosure of stock transactions."

" For a moment Hanna sat motionless, eyes narrowed. Then he nodded shortly and said, " All right, Bob. Let's do it. Instruct our people in Zurich as soon as we're settled at the hotel."

The *Citation* trembled in sudden turbulence and clouds fogged the portholes. Minutes later they were again flying in thin clear air. Hanna unfastened his seat belt.

" That chap you told me about, the one publishes *Investor's Newsbeat—*"

" Mark Ruskin."

" What kind of circulation does he have?"

" Very broad. Individuals, banks, pension funds, brokerage houses. By subscription only."

75

"Would he plant an unfavorable report on Arcadia?"

"For the right price, yes."

"Is it worth the expense?"

Egan shrugged. "Probably."

"Okay. Let's spring for it. Use your special account."

"It needs replenishing."

"How much?"

"For now, fifty thousand."

"That's a pretty big number, Bob."

"I'm working on several projects. You want details."

"No."

"An itemized accounting?"

"Dammit, no!" Hanna was emphatic. "Do what has to be done. The cash will be available as soon as we get back to New York." He shot his cuff and glanced at his watch. "Ryan must be in L.A. now. I hope to Christ he can win over the Rennie woman. Corraling her proxy might even persuade Hedrik to throw in the towel." He regarded Egan in silence. "You hinted last night you had another angle."

"It's in the works."

"About this one I'm curious."

"Kate Rennie has a nephew, her only living relative. Young fellow named Kiser—David Kiser. Doesn't quite have his head together, one of the former Haight-Ashbury flower children. But the old lady is devoted to him. More important, he's the sole legatee of her estate."

Hanna sat erect. "You know that for a fact?"

"I have a xeroxed copy of the old lady's will."

A conspiratorial smile wreathed Hanna's face. "How in hell did you— No, don't tell me. Let me guess. One of your mercenaries got into the lawyer's secretary, or into his files."

"Something like that."

"This nephew, Kiser, are you in touch with him?"

Egan's face was inscrutable. "I suggest we drop the subject."

Hanna turned away, still smiling. "I had a talk with Ryan before he left. He told me there are rumors on the Street that Hedrik might be looking for some other merger prospect. An outfit he could live with, some conglomerate he'd find more compatible."

Egan's thin lips twitched into the semblance of a smile. " In that event, we immediately notify his prospect about the extent of our holdings in Arcadia."

Hanna frowned, then gave a short barking laugh. " So the prospect drops merger talks like a hot potato. Because who the hell would want Mr. Fred Hanna as one of his major stockholders, maybe even demanding a seat on the board."

The two men grinned at each other. The pilot's voice said, " Seat belts, please. We're coming into O'Hare now, Mr. Hanna."

The plane circled and dipped a wing into the terminal leg of its landing pattern. They heard the thump of lowered flaps and felt the drag of diminished airspeed. Then the runway came up and tires bumped onto concrete. The *Citation* decelerated sharply with reverse engine thrust.

*　　*　　*

The following morning, a Wednesday, at the opening bell, five thousand shares of Arcadia Films hit the floor of the New York Stock Exchange in a single block. Most of them found customers. Within minutes, another five thousand were offered for sale. These shares were mostly absorbed by the specialist who made the market in Arcadia. Selling pressure continued and by the end of the first hour the stock had fallen two and a half points.

On Thursday Arcadia shares were out of hand. The decline accelerated following a highly negative report in *Investor's Newsbeat*. Boardroom speculators who had bought on the takeover announcement were unloading and licking their wounds. At the end of the week the worried specialist, having dipped heavily into reserves, appealed to the Board of Governors for relief. At one o'clock, trading was suspended until a new price could be established.

Dan Hedrik was inaccessible to financial reporters for comment.

On Monday morning the stock opened again three points below its previous trade. At the same time, when senior staff members of the New York Stock Exchange gathered in Room 602 for their regular weekly meeting, they heard a report by the head of the Stock Watch group, and directed him to personally conduct an investigation of member firms in an effort to determine what had caused the unprecedented activity in Arcadia shares.

12

Wearing denims, a wide-brimmed straw hat, and a pair of disreputable sneakers, Kate Rennie knelt at a flowerbed and pruned shrubs of yellow and crimson hibiscus. Behind her loomed the massive showplace that had been Max Klemmer's wedding present more years ago than she cared to remember.

A Spanish conquistador, she thought with wry amusement, would have relished its baronial excesses. It was uneconomical, a nuisance to maintain. Should have sold the damn place after Max died.

His earlier home, the Bel Air house, would have been more suitable. But Max had put it on the market after he lost his first wife and he moved into a large hotel suite at the Beverly Hills. Several years later, when Max had started courting Arcadia's rising young star Kate Rennie, the film community had lifted its collective eyebrows. Incredulous and cynical when she'd accepted his proposal. But Kate had been genuinely attached to Max Klemmer and not in the least awed by his sovereignty at the studio.

Willie Hearst had thrown a wedding party for the couple at San Simeon, and two weeks later Max retained an architect to build his version of the Hearst showplace. Although considerably smaller than San Simeon, it nevertheless dwarfed other homes in the area.

Max Klemmer managed to enjoy the place for fifteen good years before a massive coronary dropped him like a bag of sand on Sound Stage C. Kate had mourned for two months and then immersed herself in work. She had hung on to the house out of sentiment.

Now, long retired, she lived quite comfortably with one maid and a professional service that sent a crew of men once a week to care for the grounds.

She heard tires crunch on the driveway, and straightened to watch a car pull up under the south portico. She peeled off the canvas gloves as Mike Ryan alighted and came striding toward her.

"Miss Rennie," he said with a smile. "Thank you for letting me come. I'd recognise you anywhere."

"Don't snow me, young man. My mirror doesn't lie. I no longer resemble what you see on the Late-Late Show. This way, please. We'll be comfortable inside."

The diction, the warm vibrant voice had not changed, and she carried herself well. Ryan paused at the door of the vaulted living room, staring.

"A sense of *déjà vu*, Mr. Ryan?"

"You're clairvoyant, Miss Rennie."

"Not really. The studio used this background in over a dozen pictures. They still do, as a matter of fact. And pay me a rental besides, which helps with taxes."

"Then you're lucky. You make it both ways."

"How do you mean?"

"Should the picture be successful, you'd also collect dividends on your Arcadia stock."

"Not recently, Mr. Ryan. Not recently at all."

"Doesn't that trouble you, Miss Rennie? Or should I call you Mrs. Klemmer?"

"Whichever makes you comfortable. Yes, it troubles me. I know you're here to talk about a merger with Universal

Media. And I suppose the studio's fortunes—or misfortunes—will be one of your arguments."

" A plausible argument, wouldn't you say? The studio hasn't turned a profit in some time."

She smiled. " It's a dog, right? Arcadia is a loser. Then why is Universal Media interested?"

" Several reasons. Taxes, for example. By acquiring the studio UMI can utilize past losses. For another, Fred Hanna is confident he can rehabilitate Arcadia, turn it around, revitalize its finances."

" Confident? Surely he must know that picture-making these days is a gamble, a high-rolling crap game." She sighed. " It wasn't like that when my husband was alive. In those days anything on film made money."

" Perhaps in those days the public was less discriminating."

" Do you watch television?" she inquired with mild irony.

" On occasion."

" Then you must have seen some of the inane pap designed exclusively for cretins. Less discriminating? Good Lord, the worst of our B-pictures were intellectual and artistic monuments compared to television."

He smiled. " At least television is free."

" Where are you staying, Mr. Ryan?"

" At the Beverly Hilton."

" Open your window and take a deep breath." She sighed ruefully. " We pay a price for everything, including industrial pollution. Oh, dear, I'm echoing that Fonda girl again. Would you like a cup of tea? It's on the stove. Ginseng. It doesn't do what they say it's supposed to do, at least for me, but it has an interesting flavor."

" Yes, thank you." Sharing refreshments, Mike thought, usually enhances sociability.

She left the room and returned with a tray. " Poppy-seed cookies. I bake them myself." There was pride in her voice. She poured from a silver teapot.

Mike munched a cookie and said, " Perfection."

" Good," she said. " Always compliment the pastry chef."

She studied him over the rim of her cup. "When you first called from New York, I asked my attorney to check out Gregorius & Company. He tells me it's a very reputable firm. He's not quite so sure about Universal Media. On the face of it, their offer sounds quite generous. Such magnanimity troubles me."

"Simple arithmetic, Miss Rennie. A merger of the two companies would be mutually beneficial. Fresh operating capital for Arcadia. A substantial film library for UMI's television network." He smiled. "Which would upgrade the quality of their programs, even the B-pictures. As it stands now, Arcadia cannot utilize its own tax losses because it doesn't have any profits. UMI habitually makes money. Hence, the studio's losses would reduce our tax liability."

"Could you be more specific? How would a merger benefit Arcadia stockholders?"

"They would benefit from a broader diversification of their investment. From more efficient management. By receiving more for their shares than the going price. It must have been difficult, Miss Rennie, watching your own Arcadia stock move in only one direction, down."

"It has not been pleasant."

"A decline over the years of some sixty per cent from its highs."

She tilted her head. "And currently quoted at less than book value, Mr. Ryan."

"Your shares are worth only what you can sell them for."

"I disagree. We'd probably get more if we went out of business and liquidated our assets."

"Possibly. But it would mean the end of a company which has the potential of becoming a viable money-making operation, especially under the aegis of UMI."

"Can you offer any guarantees, Mr. Ryan?"

"About what?"

"That Mr. Hanna really intends to run Arcadia as a studio producing decent films. Or will he cannibalize the company and concentrate on TV junk? You see, Mr. Ryan, my interest in Arcadia goes beyond just realizing a fair price for my shares. I think I owe it to the memory of Max Klemmer."

"Miss Rennie, I can only rely on Fred Hanna's record in the past. He's absorbed a number of companies and nursed them back to health."

"But not all of them, I understand."

"True. Because some of them were terminal, too sick to survive. Those companies were phased out. There was no other sensible alternative. But remember this, the stockholders who accepted Mr. Hanna's tender received shares in Universal Media, shares which subsequently appreciated in value."

She reached for a tin of Dutch cigars and removed one, thin as a pencil. "Do you smoke, Mr. Ryan?"

"Not any more."

She snapped a lighter. "Schimmelpennincks," she said, exhaling. "I permit myself two of these a day. It used to amuse Max. Tell me, Mr. Ryan, what exactly are you asking of me?"

"I'm asking you to consider our tender offer with an open mind."

She rolled the cigar thoughtfully between her fingers. "Arcadia Films was and is a part of my life. It has problems, yes. Who doesn't? As you know, I'm a member of the board. For a long time we agonized over the selection of a new chief executive, until we realised we had the ideal candidate right in our backyard. Dan Hedrik. He's an efficient administrator and he understands film-making in all its aspects. If Arcadia can be restored at all, I think Hedrik is the man to do it."

"And I believe Mr. Hanna shares your opinion. It has always been his policy to keep able men at their posts."

She tapped ash into a tray. "Let me tell you something. When I first inherited Max Klemmer's estate, I knew nothing about investments. I had to rely on so-called experts. First my banker, with less than commendable results. Then a highly touted financial genius. I won't bore you with the details, but I fired the imbecile before he left me penniless. I made up my mind to handle my own affairs. God knows, I'm no expert, but at least I managed to preserve my capital. And I learned something, too, about takeovers. I learned that a parent company usually interferes in the operation of its subsidiaries. It simply cannot keep its bookkeeping mentality out of the front office. I am not sure that Dan Hedrik would choose to function under any kind of outside meddling."

"I would hardly label UMI's management skills as a bookkeeping mentality, Miss Rennie. And those skills have certainly been lacking at Arcadia."

"How about artistic control? Would Mr. Hanna defer to Dan Hedrik's judgement?"

"As long as Hedrik avoids costly blunders, yes. Not even the present Arcadia board would tolerate continued incompetence."

"Would the studio start producing soap operas for television?"

"That, I admit, is a distinct possibility."

"At least you're honest."

"Look, Miss Rennie, television production would provide writers and actors with work. And profits for the studio. Profits which in turn could be employed for more ambitious projects. Nothing wrong in that, is there?"

She gave him an admiring look. "You're a fine salesman, Mr. Ryan."

"I deal in an excellent product."

"Which is?"

"A share in the American dream. Every man a capitalist."

She laughed. "I already have a share in the American dream. Trouble is, the dream sometimes turns into a nightmare. Look what happened to my Arcadia stock these last few days. It's being slaughtered. Dan Hedrik is just as puzzled as I am. Do you have any idea what's happening?"

"Only this. The stock rose sharply on Hanna's tender announcement. One can always expect some kind of reaction."

"Even a reaction so severe and so persistent?" She sighed. "Brokers always have answers, and seldom any solutions."

"Sad, but true, Miss Rennie. One finds incompetence in every field, from shoemakers to brain surgeons."

"One does indeed. But incompetence in brain surgeons should be outlawed by a constitutional amendment. How about *your* investment advice, Mr. Ryan? Is it generally reliable?"

"I do what I can. I study the available information and I make an educated guess. On balance, it works out often enough to keep me in business."

"I like that answer. I rather like you too, Mr. Ryan. Well, obviously I am not going to make a decision right this minute. I want to discuss with Dan Hedrik and with my colleagues on the board. Whatever the outcome, I've enjoyed talking with you."

"Then let's do it again, without discussing business. I'll be here till the end of the week."

She arched an eyebrow. "Are you free Friday evening?"

"Yes. Let's paint the town."

"Young man, that's the best offer I've had in years."

*　　*　　*

She went upstairs to her bedroom. An afternoon nap was not only part of the ritual, it was mandatory. She examined herself in the mirror and wondered again about visiting one of those Swiss sanatoriums that were reputed to reverse the inevitable. Ah, vanity, she thought. Her age was on record. Everyone knew she was somewhere between estrogen and the mausoleum. Her arms and thighs, though, were still relatively firm, and for that she could thank her daily regimen of six laps in the pool. Every single day, weather permitting. Good for the circulation, her doctor had said. Opens the arteries, preventive maintenance, sort of. Well, it hadn't prevented a thickening of her knuckle joints, and she'd been so proud of her hands.

As she stretched out on her bed, she saw the framed photograph of her nephew. Poor dear Davy. With his father's irresolute face and sallow complexion. Still, if she concentrated hard, she fancied a faint resemblance to her sister Marcie. Kate had never been able to understand why Marcie had married Harve Kiser. Perhaps a more discriminating woman would have recognized the man's limitations. A traveling salesman

84

for a marginal publisher of second-rate encyclopedias, with headquarters in Cincinnati. It was twenty years before Marcie gave birth to her first and only child.

By then, Kate was an established film star. She had sent Marcie enough money for the down payment on a small house and asked for snapshots of her nephew. The boy was only three when Harve Kiser died, as he had lived, prosaically and undramatically in his sleep, leaving a total estate of one six-year-old Chevrolet and a life insurance policy of $5,000 on which he had already borrowed $4,200. So every month, regularly. Kate's business manager had sent Marcie a check.

They had spoken on the phone at least once a week. Marcie had visited Hollywood with Davy a few times, never complaining about her illness. I should have noticed, Kate thought, the loss of weight, the pallor, and finally it was out in the open when Marcie was hospitalized with renal failure. So now they were all gone, all except Davy and herself. She had outlived even her kid sister.

After flying to Cincinnati for the funeral, Kate had brought the boy back to California. Max had been very understanding about taking Davy in. When Davy was old enough, Kate had registered him in a private boarding school and had visited him often.

Davy did not adjust well. Academic standards were high and his attention span was limited. Then, after Max died, Kate took Davy out of school and brought him back to the house. At seventeen he told her he wanted to be out on his own, to try to find himself. She gave him an allowance and saw him off to San Francisco. He was all she had left now and she was thankful for his occasional visits. He was strange and remote. He never went out with girls and she suspected homosexual tendencies, but she did not have the courage to suggest analysis.

When he left he seemed perfectly content with a backpack, a pair of jeans, and a few T-shirts. He'd been gone now for over a year and she was worried about him.

Kate Rennie fell into a troubled sleep.

85

13

As Arcadia stock continued its decline under selling pressure, Floyd Gregorius suffered a growing sense of dismay. His shares had now fallen twenty per cent below his initial purchase. Because he was fully margined, the downside leverage was murderous, and he had already lost forty per cent of his investment.

Distracted by his rapid eroding position, he found it increasingly difficult to concentrate on even the most routine task. When addressed, he was vague and unresponsive. He frequented the board room, looking for a temporarily deserted desk so he could tap out the Arcadia symbol on a Videomaster, a form of self-torture. The news was always bad, and growing worse.

Returning now to his office he heard the phone ring. He reached for it and recognised the voice of his account executive at Stoufer, Wingate. " Floyd?"

" Speaking."

" Have you been watching the tape on Arcadia, pal?"

" Yes, Murray." Floyd had an unsettling premonition.

" They keep hammering it down. So the margin clerk here is riding my tail. I'm afraid I have some bad news. You'll have to come up with additional margin."

Floyd felt physically ill. His resources were already committed. " I . . . I'm a little short at this time."

There was silence for a moment. The account exec's voice hardened. " Well, look, pal, you're not leaving us any alternative. Our office manager is a stickler for regulations. Hell, you're in the business. I don't have to spell it out. We can't carry the account. We'll have to sell you out."

Floyd groaned audibly. " No, please. How much time can you give me?"

" I can stall until Monday, at the latest." Murray paused. " If you can't raise any cash, how about posting some additional securities? That should cover you for a while. What the hell, Arcadia has to stabilize pretty soon. It can't keep going down." His voice brightened. " Maybe your old man can help you out. The temporary loan of some paper. He'd hardly miss it."

" I'll talk to him and let you know."

They broke the connection. Floyd bent over the desk, resting his face in his hands. Nothing, not even impending disaster, could induce him to appeal to Anson. In his position, presumably in possession of inside information, he had no business buying the stock in the first place. Anson's anger might erupt into apoplexy. And there was no chance the old man would bail him out.

The full impact of his predicament suddenly engulfed him in a wave of nausea. He rose hastily and went off at a stumbling trot to the men's room. He caught a glimpse of Janey Spacek frowning at him, but he deliberately avoided direct eye contact. He locked himself into a cubicle and emptied himself in wrenching spasms. He flushed the bowl and lowered the lid and sat down, his eyes watering, feeling miserable.

He felt oddly difused, wondering what had gone wrong. How could it happen? Merger candidates seldom collapsed unless the deal had been canceled. Had UMI abandoned takeover plans without his knowledge? He shook his head. Even now Mike Ryan was in California, working on the deal, confering with stockholders and management. So the price drop made no sense. His Arcadia shares would go up again. They had to. All he needed was time, and the resources to maintain his position.

He stirred, brow furrowed, trying to recall something he had read. A piece clipped from a magazine to show Janey because it had amused him. Suddenly it flooded back, striking a spark, electrifying him. In a quick flash, he had a solution.

It started his pulse racing. Oh, my God, he thought, it can work, yes, yes . . .

He left the cubicle and went to the washbasin. He rinsed his mouth and splashed cold water on his face. He felt better now, almost as good as those first few days when Arcadia shares had been climbing with every trade.

Passing Janey on his way back to the office, he gave her a quick, covert smile. She looked relieved. Janey, too, had been worried.

Speculating heavily in Arcadia had been an act of faith in himself, an affirmation of his independence. He had been confident. He had even borrowed from his bank, extending his credit to the limit. It seemed inconceivable that he might lose.

And on the third day, showing a handsome profit, unable to contain himself, he had confided in Janey. So she, too, had been following the tape. And now her anxiety and dismay seemed to match his own.

He had left his door open so he could see her desk. She was round and chunky, with blond hair and a Slavic tilt to her eyes. She had been hired as a filing clerk in the bond department. He had first noticed her when she brought him some bearer certificates for an inventory check. She had placed the bonds on his desk, smiled shyly, and left. His eyes followed the neatly symmetrical rump, a sight that lingered as an after image even with the door closed. Twenty minutes later he had invented an excuse to leave his office, stealing surreptitious looks at the girl. Twice she had met his eyes, color rising in her face.

Something about Janey Spacek appealed to him. He had thought about her that first night, conjuring erotic fantasies. He was angry at himself. It offended him to find his imagination sinking to a level of such coarse and grubby details about this particular girl. Even in his sleep she flitted in and out of his dreams.

Late the following afternoon he had invented some chores to keep her busy past closing time. After the other employees had left he told her it was company policy to supply meals for late workers and he invited her to dine with him. She accepted gravely.

He took her uptown to a small unpretentious restaurant. At first they were both reserved, but half a bottle of wine later they were conversing freely. She told him that she lived alone. Her parents were still alive, her father employed as a machinist in Stamford. She was not happy working as a filing clerk and had recently completed a secretarial course at night school to upgrade her job. She found New York, despite its huge population and frenetic pace, a lonely place.

Floyd surprised himself. He had never been so talkative with a woman. He was completely at ease with Janey. By the time they finished the wine they were on a first-name basis. Later, at the door to her small apartment, she thanked him, told him she'd had a wonderful time, and then, impulsively, she stood on her toes and brushed a fleeting kiss across his lips. The artless sincerity, the warm flavor of her mouth, almost bent Floyd out of shape. He asked if he could see her again over the weekend and she readily agreed.

He took her out regularly after that and by the end of their second week together he stayed over and slept with her on the narrow daybed. Their love-making had none of the frenzied license of his earlier fantasies. Janey Spacek was a young woman of limited experience but considerable instinct. She cradled him between her chunky thighs and held him gently and rocked him into a state of almost unbearable transport.

Just before he fell into a deep and blissful sleep, with her arms still clasped around him, he vowed to himself that nothing on this earth could ever induce him to surrender the solace of this warm and extraordinary creature.

14

It was generally conceded that no administration would deliberately court Congressional outrage by separating Mr. Gary George Pressman from his job as head of the Enforcement Division of the Securities and Exchange Commission. Pressman was a solid meaty man invariably garbed in rumpled attire, oblivious of the dictates of fashion. He had a broad nose, penetrating eyes, and a full head of closely cropped hair. Not since the days of J. Edgar Hoover had the tenure of any bureaucrat been so solidly entrenched.

After graduating from Harvard Law, he had served for one year as law clerk to Supreme Court Justice Hugo L. Black. From that lofty perch he could easily have moved into one of the major Washington firms. Instead he opted for an appointment as an Assistant U.S. Attorney for the Southern District of New York, where, in a comparatively short time he became one of the Justice Department's star litigators, specializing in corporate transgressions.

Although successful as a prosecutor, he found himself even more intrigued by the investigative aspects of high finance and white-collar chicanery. In due course he resigned from Justice and moved over to the Securities and Exchange Commission. Here, his ability and drive quickly brought him to the attention of the commissioners. He was allowed to serve in each of the five operating divisions, and eventually, at his own request, wound up in the Enforcement Branch.

Pressman's relentless pursuit of corporate legerdemain brought him a rapid succession of promotions. And when approaching senility forced the resignation of his chief, he was immediately appointed as head of the division. Unintimidated by politicians or corporate Brahmins, he administered his office with integrity and fairness. He was mildly amused by the veneration of his staff and used it to promote a total dedication to the work at hand.

Now, leaning back, feet on his desk, he listened to his prize acolyte, an implausibly handsome young man named Kevin Anthony Duke III. Duke shuffled some notes and said, "The first large block of Arcadia Films to hit the market on short selling, near as we can judge, came from a Zurich bank. Stock Exchange firms handling the transactions say they don't know the names of any principals. There's no point trying to pump the Swiss because we always end up with a nice fat zero. Those babies disgorge information with all the prodigality of a slot machine."

"Neatly phrased, my boy."

"Thank you, sir. Speculators who bought on the takeover announcement don't know what hit them. They got out fast. Then there were margin calls, and that started the rout. Now, every time there's an uptick, more short sales. It's killing the specialist, so he's knocking the price down as fast as the Exchange will allow."

"What's your guess, son? A little flimflam here?"

"Sure looks like it."

"Engineered by whom?"

Duke shrugged. "Universal Media, maybe. But I can't get a handle on it. Can't seem to find a motive."

Gary George Pressman sighed and massaged the side of his jaw. "I've been a student of Mr. Fred Hanna's operations for a long time. When he wants something, he pulls out all the stops. And UMI's counsel, that Robert Egan, he knows all the tricks and then some. That is some kind of Machiavelli, that Egan. So what I think they're trying to do is create a bit of panic and scare Arcadia stockholders into accepting their tender."

"I see," Duke said, nodding. "And because the price of Arcadia is way down, while Hanna's original offer still stands

91

at a fat premium, he can expect a lot of stockholders to embrace his tender."

" And what else?"

" If it comes down to a proxy fight, this poor market performance makes Arcadia management look bad."

" Correct on both counts, son."

" You want us to go all out on this one?"

" Every man we can spare." Pressman bared square teeth in a Teddy Roosevelt grin. " I would dearly love to whittle that pair of jackals down to size." He glanced again at the list of brokers most heavily involved in the short selling of Arcadia. " Gregorius & Company is UMI's investment banker. I don't see it listed here."

" Gregorius never showed up on the computer."

" Screw the computer. I want their records checked six ways from Sunday. Put Buchwald and Zachary on it."

" Yes, sir. Incidentally, we ran across a transaction at Stoufer, Wingate that might interest you."

" Let's have it."

" They handled a substantial purchase of Arcadia shares, fully margined, in an account under the name of Floyd Gregorius."

" Before the public announcement of a tender?"

" Yes, sir."

" Jesus! The silly ass! I'd heard Floyd was short on brains. What's he trying to do? Hang himself? The schmuck is right there in the Gregorius office, so he has to know their plans. And he decides to make a killing, trading through another house." Pressman gave a short humourless laugh. " So it backfired and he got mousetrapped. Serves him right. Okay, Kevin, keep an eye on that one for me too, will you?"

" Yes, sir. You think old Anson Gregorius knows what Junior is up to?"

" Probably not. The old boy always ran a clean shop. And near as I can judge, Ryan seems to be a cut of the same cloth. But you never know. All right, son, let's get back to UMI."

Duke said, " I think we have the classic situation here.

92

Arcadia Films is a fading company with some valuable assets. So Fred Hanna targets in, and management turns him down. He appeals to the stockholders with an attractive tender. Arcadia takes off. Then it's goosed even higher by news that Dan Hedrik has bagged a hot literary property and a bankable star. All of a sudden, out of the blue, heavy selling pressure, mostly on the short side, and the stock is in a tailspin."

"Your conclusion?"

"Whoever's responsible has to be sure he's in control of a ticklish situation."

"And the likely candidate?"

"Mr. Fred Hanna."

"You'll outrank me yet, Kevin me boy. I want you back in New York tomorrow morning. Cut through the smoke. Bring me something we can take to the U.S. Attorney."

Kevin Anthony Duke III snapped to attention and saluted smartly. "Yes, sir." He wheeled and marched out like a marine bearing the regimental colours.

G. G. Pressman smiled indulgently. He was bringing young Duke along nicely. Nothing wrong with the furnishings in that boy's attic. And he had elected public service at a modest government salary in preference to the prestigious firm of Hughs, Duke, Morgan & Russell, whose managing partner was Kevin A. Duke II.

Pressman had studied the young man's résumé. Yale undergraduate, magna cum laude, his father serving on the University's Board of Trustees. Then to Yale Law School. Assistant editor of the *Law Review*. From there, straight to the Securities and Exchange Commission. Pressman knew that several of Duke's more cynical classmates claimed he had chosen this course in order to acquire a more intimate knowledge of the government agency so that one day he might be more valuable to his father's firm. G.G. had long since dismissed this canard as sour grapes.

He had found that Duke had a natural affinity for the Enforcement Branch. He was quick to grasp the labyrinthine complexity of trading vehicles. He had a keen eye for the many

93

ways in which a gullible public can be flimflammed. And better still, like his mentor, Duke had a sense of mission. Although not yet quite as unsparingly draconian with malefactors as the boss himself.

A psychiatrist friend, speculating aloud, had once attributed the severity of Pressman's professional verdicts to the venality of a Wall Street largely responsible for the excesses that brought the market down in the great crash of '29. It had bankrupted Pressman's grandfather and lowered the family's lifestyle from middle-class to near-penury. G.G.'s comment to his psychiatrist friend had been characteristically blunt: " You're full of shit, pal."

Still, as a student of those events, he readily admitted his outrage at the rapacity of manipulators that had made the final blowoff inevitable, causing a collapse of the nation's economy and the worst depression in its history. And yet there had been one beneficial result—the Congressional hearings that had brought into existence the Securities and Exchange Commission. To the extent that he was in a position to police the market, he had vowed that it would never happen again.

The financial community quite naturally had little affection for Gary George Pressman. They did, however, respect him. On the other hand, it was rumored that his wife and two small daughters considered him a marshmallow.

15

Alex Bogart awakened with a start, bathed in perspiration. The dream that had started his heart thudding dissolved at the moment of consciousness, its details lost. He groped for the night lamp and sat up. For a moment he was disoriented.

These were not his accustomed surroundings. He was in a hotel room, a very luxurious hotel room, part of a suite.

He got off the bed and shuffled into the bathroom, white tiles, floor to ceiling. He drew a glass of ice water, found his barbiturates and swallowed one. He examined himself in the mirror. Smudges under his eyes were barely visible against the tan. Too much night life, he thought. To say nothing about those strenuous calisthenics between the sheets.

He left the bathroom and went to the window and looked out at the city landscape, at the towering silhouettes limned against the nighttime sky. After a while he got back into bed and lay in the dark, waiting for the anticipated drowsiness. It did not come. Instead, Cora Bendiner's face materialized above him. He smiled, remembering the first time she had called on the telephone.

He had been in his office when the bell rang. The voice said, " May I speak to Judge Bogart, please."

It would have to be a stranger, he thought, someone unfamiliar with events in Ocala Beach. " May I ask who's calling?"

" The name is Bendiner—Mrs. Ward Bendiner. I'm calling for my husband."

He had visualized her instantly. One-half of that reclusive couple who had reopened The Lodge about ten miles outside of town. Only the day before, at the counter of Mindy's Luncheonette, over a cup of coffee with Sheriff Ben Nestor, he'd seen her through the window, crossing the street.

" Down, boy, down," Nestor said. " Your mouth is watering. Can't say I blame you."

He had explained over the telephone. " I'm sorry, Mrs. Bendiner. Judge Bogart passed away in '75. I'm Alex Bogart, the judge's son. Perhaps I can help you."

" Are you a lawyer, Mr. Bogart?"

" Yes, ma'am. I've taken over the judge's practice."

He heard a murmuring of voices in brief consultation, and then she was back on the line again. " It's a simple matter, really. We called your number because my husband remembered that Judge Bogart handled the original purchase of this property."

" I see. Would you like to make an appointment for your husband?"

" That's our problem, Mr. Bogart. A visit to your office isn't possible. My husband sprained his ankle and it's badly swollen. The doctor says he'll be immobilized for at least a week. Would it be possible for you to drive out to The Lodge with the necessary papers?"

" What kind of papers, Mrs. Bendiner?"

" He needs a power of attorney that would permit me to handle some business matters for him."

" A limited or general power?"

" Aren't there printed forms for these things?"

" Yes, there are."

" Then suppose you bring both kinds. You can explain the difference and my husband will decide which one best suits his needs. I have a typewriter and we can fill in the blanks here. Does it have to be notarized?"

" No problem. I have a notary's commission."

" Would three o'clock this afternoon be convenient?"

He had made a pretense of consulting his appointment book. " I'll be free at four."

" Do you need instructions?"

" I know the place well, Mrs Bendiner. I've lived in this area all my life."

" Then we'll expect you."

He hung up and settled back. At least this one's voice matched its owner's appearance. Warm and sultry in tone, precise in diction. Only last week he'd had a call from a tourist with a voice so enchanting it had conjured angelic visions. And yet she had turned out to be a scarecrow of such unappetizing homeliness, he remembered thinking that nature had no right to short-change any human being so cruelly.

Alex Bogart felt comfortable in this old-fashioned office that occupied the upper floor of a white frame building, above the Ocala Beach Hardware Emporium. The judge had practised law in these surroundings for fifty-three years and it was a conceit of his son's to maintain it intact. He kept the roll-top desk, the scarred wooden filing cabinets, the fading prints, and on occasion he even assumed the liquid drawl of Southern speech for selected clients, although he had long since erased all traces of any regional accent.

Initially, he had intended to abandon the area for some more cosmopolitan center but devotion to his father precluded such a move while the judge was still alive. His mother, childless until after her fortieth birthday, had passed on into the next world at the same time that she had brought Alex into this one. The judge, startled by the sudden proof of fecundity, had mourned, and then had reared his son with affection and extravagance.

After Alex graduated from law school, he had accepted a partnership which lasted until the elder Bogart joined his wife three years later. Pending litigation had kept Alex in Ocala Beach until its ultimate disposal. In the meantime, new matters materialized. Nothing exciting—real estate closings, probate, domestic relations. The town would never amount to much. But the practise threw off a reasonable income, and a combination of inertia and familiar surroundings inhibited any change.

There were compensations and, of course, the usual diversions. During the tourist season a few vacationing secretaries and lonely widows were generally available, always in more abundance than eligible males. He had never tried to rationalize these brief and meaningless episodes, accepting them as a simple biological release. Some day, perhaps, there would be a more permanent commitment.

*   *   *

Shortly after four o'clock he had driven through a gate that held a warning sign to trespassers. The Lodge, a rambling redwood structure, was visible beyond a stand of pines along the private road. He parked and rang the bell. Mrs. Bendiner opened the door. Up close, her smile was so bright, so vivid, her impact so overwhelming, he felt awkward as a schoolboy.

" Mr. Bogart?"

" Yes, ma'am."

" Do come in, please. I'm Cora Bendiner."

She led the way, carrying herself like a dancer. In a large bedroom Ward Bendiner was propped up against the headboard, his right leg immobilized by a tightly wound bandage around the ankle.

Cora said, " This is Alex Bogart, darling. My husband."

Bendiner offered his hand. " Sorry to inconvenience you, Counselor. I have a vague recollection of meeting your father many years ago. Didn't he have an old roll-top desk with several hundred drawers?"

" He did and it's still there. In fact, the whole office hasn't changed at all."

" Too bad we can't say that about the rest of this world. Too many changes and almost none of them an improvement. Has my wife explained what we need in the way of documentation?"

" A power of attorney. Either limited or general. Tell me what you need it for."

" I've sold some securities and I need the certificates for delivery to a broker in Miami. They're in my safe-deposit box at the First Florida Trust."

" The Ocala Beach branch?"

" Yes. I'd like my wife to have access so that she can remove the certificates and forward them." He glanced at Cora. " Don't forget, registered mail, return receipt requested. I'd attend to it myself, Counselor, but the slightest movement is quite painful."

" How did it happen?"

" Carelessness. Moss at the edge of the pool. About the certificates, what do you suggest?"

" A limited power for the specific purpose of providing access to your box would do the job nicely. I have a form in my briefcase. Mrs. Bendiner mentioned something about a typewriter. After we complete the form, I'll notarize your signature." Alex smiled at the woman. " If you have any problem at the bank, ask for Mr. Kinaston and have him call me."

" This way, Mr. Bogart."

" It was a comfortable den, overlooking the pool area. Alex handed her the form and explained the technicalities. She listened, standing close and fragrant, the pupils of her dark eyes enormously large, and Alex suddenly felt his mouth go dry.

She sat at the desk and uncovered a portable Olivetti. She was a competent typist, tapping the keys rapidly. When she handed him the completed paper, he could not find a single error.

" Were you trained as a secretary?" he asked.

" I learned typing in high school. They gave us all sorts of practical courses—home economics, shorthand, things that were supposed to teach young ladies how to be useful citizens. Not the movers and shakers of this world. Just useful. I kept my typing in practice simply because my handwriting is so illegible it would confuse the most expert cryptographer."

" And shorthand too? Well now, Mrs. Bendiner, would you like a part-time job?"

She smiled. " No, sir. Not now, or ever." She ran her tongue slowly over her upper lip. " I have to be at the bank tomorrow morning for those stock certificates. Then back here so Ward can endorse them. And then back again to Ocala Beach for delivery to the post office. Which would just about make it time for lunch." She paused, her eyes direct.

" I know an acceptable place," Alex said.

" Secluded?"

" That's why it's acceptable."

" Where shall we meet?"

" Park your car at the Flamingo Shopping Center and look for a green Mustang."

" Perfect. About twelve, Mr. Bogart."

" The name is Alex."

" I won't forget." She touched his cheek with a fingertip, and it felt like a live wire. " You have your little notary stamp,

I hope, that gizmo with all the numbers. My husband is waiting."

*　　*　　*

Nothing in Alex Bogart's past experience had quite prepared him for Cora Bendiner. Not his years at college and law school, nor all the eagerly amenable tourist ladies. As one clandestine meeting followed another, he had found himself under an increasingly hypnotic spell. She was volcanic and addictive.

Ocala Beach was a small, fairly intimate community, and to function secretly had required maximum discretion. Even so, she would occasionally appear at his office, ostensibly as a client, always in the afternoon, when she knew he would be alone. She would close the door, snap the latch, and turn quickly into his arms, the message of her body so urgent it would bring him instantly to a point of savage physical need. He would take her violently on the old leather sofa, driven almost beyond reason.

More frequently, they had patronized a motel that catered chiefly to trysting couples, located well up the coast between Ocala Beach and Naples. The rooms were reasonably clean, the beds sturdy, and in the antiseptic chill of air conditioning, with harsh sunlight muted through drawn curtains, Cora would practise her unique brand of sorcery with such Saturnalian abandon that she became for him a consuming obsession.

Once, lying alongside her in exhausted lethargy, watching the protagonist in an old film of Somerset Maugham's *Of Human Bondage* on television, he had thought, with sudden recognition: My God, that's me! Enslaved, hopelessly, and I love every minute of it.

16

Al Clinton lounged inconspicuously against a lamppost halfway down the block from San Francisco's methadone center. Clinton, at thirty-three, was a pale sandy-haired man, lean and muscular, wearing shapeless denims and an old campaign jacket. He had longish hair and a benign face. His hooded eyes were bracketed with smile wrinkles that masked a total amorality.

Mr. Egan, he knew, would be pleased. Clinton had finally located and befriended Kate Rennie's nephew. Posing as Davy's friend, a polite telephone call to the old crow had elicited the information that Davy's postcard had been mailed from Frisco. And if he found Davy, would he please, please, ask him to keep in touch.

After prowling the streets for a week, he had finally spotted an item in the *Chronicle*. David Kiser, along with several others, had been picked up and charged with possession. Clinton noted the details and attended the court hearing. A charitable judge, deeming Kiser no imminent threat to society, had suspended sentence, with one proviso—the accused would have to submit to voluntary treatment.

With the genial fellowship of a practised con artist, Clinton had contrived a meeting, sympathizing with Davy's plight and suggesting a few beers. They sat in a saloon and rapped for hours, seemingly kindred spirits, exchanging confidences.

Kiser was an easy mark. Slightly built, unprepossessing, manipulative, he was highly flattered by the attentions of his new companion. Clinton learned that Davy was an indiscriminate pill popper, anything from barbiturates to speed. He

101

discovered, too, that lack of funds and an incapacity to victimize by mugging had so far limited Kiser's debut into hard drugs. By nightfall Davy had accepted an invitation to share Al Clinton's pad and his generous cache of Acapulco Gold.

The younger man, scarcely able to credit his good fortune in teaming up with the macho and resourceful Al Clinton, had from very beginning of their relationship developed an almost puppylike dependence.

Five years earlier, using forged papers, Al Clinton had been hired as a security guard by the Universal Broadcasting System. During the first eleven months some twenty thousand dollars' worth of electronic gear had disappeared. A careful check yielded no clues until Robert Egan had retained a private investigator.

The investigator learned that some of the equipment had been sold by a man resembling Clinton's description. He placed the security guard under round-the-clock surveillance, with negative results. Instinct and long experience convinced him that Clinton suspected he was being shadowed and was mocking his pursuers by leading them on long and ultimately futile chases.

Egan studied the report and personally probed into Clinton's background. He discovered that the man's original recommendations were forged and that his past history seemed untraceable. After surmising that the suspect had changed his identity and that the deception was vital to Clinton's survival, he managed to accumulate enough evidence to support this belief.

One night, unannounced, Egan appeared at Clinton's apartment. Behind closed doors, he laid it out and they had a long and revealing talk. At its conclusion Al Clinton resigned his job as a security guard for the broadcasting subsidiary. The next morning he went to work for Robert Egan at triple his former salary, paid out of the UMI special fund at Egan's disposal.

The lawyer's instructions were invariably oral, and carefully repeated by Clinton for accuracy. Payment was tendered in cash. When a task was assigned, no explanations were offered, and Clinton demanded none. He received only that background information which Egan deemed appropriate.

102

In the intervening years Al Clinton had faithfully discharged a variety of assignments. He was always notified if danger was involved. And he always received a bonus at the conclusion of each job, a sum commensurate with the risk. He kept his money tucked away in a lockbox under an assumed name, paying the rental fee well in advance to avoid the mailing of an invoice.

His loyalty to Robert Egan was not unlike that which the lawyer himself felt toward Fred Hanna.

When David Kiser emerged from the methadone center, Clinton draped a comforting arm around his shoulder and steered him back to the apartment. His instructions had been to keep Davy under wraps until further orders.

17

As a boy, Pete Sternbach had never been highly esteemed by his youthful peers. Whenever teams were chosen, he invariably languished on the sidelines. Realising that any distinction he achieved would be through the exercise of his wits, he had applied himself at school with single-minded diligence.

While his intellectual range was fairly broad, he had a special aptitude for mathematics. Numbers appealed to him. He enjoyed solving complicated problems. In an ever-changing world, he had found a reassuring immutability in numbers, a beautiful logic, a sense of order.

So the declining numbers on the ticker tape were sending him an urgent message about Arcadia Films. It was accepted dogma in the market that pessimism feeds on itself. Heavy selling usually triggers additional selling by the faint-hearted. The laws of momentum applied to psychology as well as to physics.

But the havoc in Arcadia stock made no sense, not with a merger in the works. He had studied the action, he had made discreet inquiries, and he was now convinced that the avalanche of selling was being professionally orchestrated. His cheek bulged thoughtfully behind his tongue. So who was responsible for all this manipulation? His mouth pursed into an odd little smile. He did not for a single instant doubt the identity of the man behind the scenes.

Sternbach's success was based in some measure on his ability to take decisive action. To swim against the tide. When he saw prices at bargain levels, he moved, regardless of the tape.

By accumulating Arcadia shares now, he could sell them later at a profit, probably to UMI. Even if the takeover failed, the stock was cheap. Investments for the Croesus Fund were geared to capital gains. His shareholders understood the risk. They were betting on Sternbach's ability to pick winners. The Fund always kept large reserves on hand for just such an opportunity.

Several large purchases would, of course, halt Arcadia's downward trend. Undoubtedly it would put Fred Hanna's nose out of joint. And since mutualfund transactions were a matter of public record, Hanna would know who was crossing him.

Tough shit, he thought. It's a dog-eat-dog world. Another big win for the Croesus Fund would make it the top performer for the year, with fresh investments pouring in and management fees skyrocketing. A fellow has to look out for number one.

He reached for the phone and dialed and got a woman's voice. " Lilian? Pete Sternbach."

" How are you, Mr. Sternbach?"

" Fine. I have an order for you. Buy five thousand shares of Arcadia Films for Croesus."

" At the market?"

" Yes."

Lilian, the registered rep, was a small, attractive redhead with a large ambition, and in appreciation for the commission business, she might one day bestow her favours on the author of this unexpected largesse. He knew that her firm would execute his order at the best possible price or risk losing Sternbach Management as an account.

" Shall I use my discretion?" she asked. " Throw it at them in thousand-share lots?"

" Not this time, Lilian. Just buy and call me back with the details."

" Thank you, Peter."

" You're welcome. Lunch next week?"

" I'd be delighted."

He spent the rest of the afternoon buying Arcadia through half a dozen houses, distributing his orders judiciously among those firms that had been active in promoting his funds to their customers, carefully watching the reaction on his desktop Telequote. By the closing bell he had, at least temporarily, halted the decline and goosed Arcadia's price up almost a full point. He would continue buying on the following day.

He sat back and stretched until his shoulders creaked. With tension ebbing, he felt that he was entitled to a small celebration. He reached for the phone again and called the massage parlour.

" Sternbach," he told the man. " Listen, that blond Norwegian, Elke, the one with the jugs, is she available at seven? . . . Good. No substitutes, hear?"

What the hell, he could afford the ticket and he wanted the best.

18

Immediately after Mike Ryan's request for an appointment, Dan Hedrik phoned long distance to Paul Slater, his New York lawyer. He had known Slater back East, admired his legal acumen, and had retained him at the first hint of UMI's interest in Arcadia to superintend the opposition to a takeover.

"Guess who's on his way here to see me, Counselor."

"Michael Ryan, the man from Gregorius & Company."

"What the hell!"

"Simple logic, Dan. I heard he was on the Coast. A little dialogue can't do us any harm. Hear the man out. You know the drill. Smile a lot and tell him nothing."

"He's already spoken to Kate Rennie."

"And?"

"She's a bright old lady, Paul. She made no commitment. I'm hoping she'll stick with us right down to the wire."

"She'd better. We'll need her votes in a proxy fight. They may be crucial."

"How goes it at your end?"

"Working our butts off, Daniel. Spent half the night framing a new letter to Arcadia stockholders. It goes out today over your signature. A short history of Universal Media and its president, not a little unsavory, analyzing his offer and stressing the pitfalls. It appears tomorrow in a full-page ad in the *Wall Street Journal* and the *Times* financial section. I hope your budget can handle it."

"Whatever it takes, Paul. I have a green light from the board to fight this thing to the bitter end."

"Good. Because we just hired one of the best proxy solicitation outfits in the business. And my man in Washington is trying to find out if a takeover would be in violation of the anti-trust laws."

"Any likelihood?"

"Remote. I imagine Fred Hanna already has an opinion from Justice. And I would dearly love to know how much cash found its way under the table from UMI to this administration's reelection committee."

"You are a cynical man, Counsellor."

"To say the least."

Hedrik said, with a light touch of irony, "You think the Oval Office would try to exert influence on the Attorney General?"

"Don't confuse our republic with Utopia, my friend. By the way, did you discuss my proposal with your board?"

"Which proposal? You made so many."

"Finding some more compatible candidate for a possible merger. Some flourishing conglomerate you could live with."

"No chance, Counselor. I need the autonomy. I can't have outside nitpickers challenging every nickel in a picture's budget."

Slater sighed. "I understand. We'll have to resist UMI's bear hug some other way. And you can help, Dan."

"How?"

"Go out and buy a radio station. Buy two."

"Say again?"

"Find a radio station that shows a decent profit and buy it. Make the deal so attractive the owner can't resist. And the sooner the better. Yesterday, if possible."

"What the hell are you talking about?"

"I'm talking about a broadcasting subsidiary. It would put you in the same business as Universal Media. Hanna is limited by FCC regulations to the number of stations he's allowed to control. So an attempted takeover of Arcadia would create one hell of a big problem for him."

Hedrik sat erect, feeling a quick surge of optimism. "Would it checkmate the bastards?"

"Maybe yes, maybe no."

"So where's the loophole?"

"He might weasel out by agreeing to divest himself of several other broadcasting subsidiaries."

"He might do just that, Paul. Hanna is a very determined man."

"Conceded. Nevertheless, we have to throw up roadblocks. We have to slow him down. Sometimes, when there are too many obstacles, they get discouraged and walk away. You want to draw some blood, don't you?"

"In buckets, Counselor."

"Then call a special meeting of the board. Throw your weight behind it. In the meantime, contact a broker who specializes in broadcasting properties and see what's available. Confront your board with a concrete recommendation."

" I'll work on it as soon as you hang up."

" And, Dan . . ."

" Yes?"

" Don't look for bargains. I don't want Hanna claiming you bought some crappy money-loser to the disadvantage of your own stockholders just to block his plans."

" Clear enough."

" And talking about stockholders, Dan—in checking the records we find that a man named Ward Bendiner holds a very substantial block of Arcadia shares. The name familiar to you?"

" No."

" We have an address near Ocala Beach, Florida, a jerkwater whistle stop on the Gulf Coast. I don't think this one should be approached by our proxy solicitors. Too impersonal. One of your own people perhaps, someone with a title, familiar with the company's plans, a sincere type with industry credentials. Got anyone who fits the bill?"

Hedrik did not have to search his mind. " Yes. Ross Landry. My producer on *The Romanoff File*. He's been with the company for years."

" Trustworthy?"

" I'd trust Ross with my bride, if I had a bride."

" Can you spare him for a couple of days?"

" If necessary, yes."

" It's necessary, Dan, believe me. This Bendiner's proxy would be an invaluable trophy."

" Ross is no superslick salesman."

" Fine. A superslick salesman is the last thing we want. Any investor smart enough to accumulate Bendiner's kind of money isn't likely to be impressed by a con artist. Put him on a plane tomorrow morning."

" Consider it done."

Twenty minutes after he broke the connection, Hedrik's secretary announced the arrival of Mike Ryan. His visitor was not what Hedrik expected. He found Ryan to be an agreeable,

108

unaffected character with an attractive air of candor, although he suspected there were other less visible aspects.

When he was seated, Ryan said, " I'm sure you've heard stories about Fred Hanna. Let me tell you how we, at Gregorius & Company, see the man." There followed a remarkably able tribute to Hanna's executive skills in directing the various enterprises under Universal Media's aegis.

" Now, Mr. Hedrik," Ryan continued, " of all the people in this world, I don't have to tell you about problems confronting the film industry. You know them far better than I do. And in the area of problems, finding solutions, overcoming obstacles, that's where Fred Hanna shines."

" Does he have any specific plans in mind?"

" Specific plans, Mr. Hedrik, can emerge only after he's thoroughly familiar with Arcadia's problems from an insider's point of view."

" Your confidence in the man seems unqualified."

" With considerable justification. I know his record."

" I've heard contrary opinions. Shall I name several companies that Hanna acquired and no longer exist?"

Ryan smiled. " Not necessary. I'm aware of the facts. Only companies no longer viable were phased out."

" Then why did he want them in the first place?"

" Good question. Let me be perfectly frank, Mr. Hedrik. The rehabilitation of a sick company is not the only purpose for an acquisition."

" I'm a simple movie-maker, Mr. Ryan. Name me another."

" Eliminating competition within a certain market area, for one."

" And what happens to the defunct company's personnel?"

" Able executives are generally absorbed into the parent company or one of its subsidiaries. The others would have lost their jobs in any event."

" Does Mr. Hanna have something like that in mind for Arcadia?"

" Oh, no. Arcadia doesn't compete with any current UMI enterprise. It would, in fact, complement Hanna's operations."

" And how would it benefit Arcadia?"

" You'd benefit from proven management techniques. And, of course, the infusion of fresh capital. Arcadia could move into television production, a highly profitable area. You could increase your budget on *The Romanoff File*. Mr. Hanna believes you made the right move, whatever it costs. He's prepared to back your project with all his resources. After all, his own success in large measure was built on an appreciation of popular entertainment. And it goes without saying that he's familiar with your work in films. I know for a fact that he's eager for you to stay at Arcadia as chief operating officer."

" He said that in so many words?"

" In my hearing, Mr. Hedrik."

" And he'll put it in writing?"

" You'd have an iron-clad contract, approved by your own attorney, specifying salary, duration of employment, stock options, profit sharing, pension and health benefits, a liberal expense account, and all perquisites appropriate for a top executive."

" Sounds attractive."

" Why not, Mr. Hedrik?" Ryan smiled, fingers spread apart. " It wouldn't cost UMI a cent. Mr. Hanna expects you to generate enough profit over the term of your contract to more than compensate the company for any expenditure."

" My present company already grants me most of those benefits."

" Profit sharing?" Ryan shook his head sympathetically. " The fact is, as you well know, Arcadia hasn't turned a decent profit in years. And if the company folds, you can tear up your contract. But as a member of the UMI family, with all its diversified interests, your financial security would be assured."

Hedrik studied him, pinching the bridge of his nose. His voice altered subtly. " Suppose we open our hands, Mr. Ryan. To put it bluntly, you're asking me to throw my support behind a merger in return for certain inducements."

" Not quite. Stated in those terms, the offer has an unpleasant connotation."

110

" Make it more palatable."

Ryan smiled. " Mr. Hanna would simply be making a fair bid for your services, for your acknowledged expertise in this business. As a matter of fact, he might not even be interested in Arcadia if the deal failed to include you."

Hedrik smiled back. " Ah, no, Mr. Ryan, that one does both of us an injustice. Don't snow me, please."

" Put it this way, then. Finding an equivalent replacement would be time-consuming and uncertain."

" Does Mr. Hanna know that I'm not a rubber stamp?"

" What makes you think he's looking for one?"

" I've heard rumors."

" Hearsay. You don't build an organisation like UMI with knee-jerk yes-men."

" How soon does he want an answer?"

" As soon as possible."

" Like within the next few minutes?"

Ryan laughed. " It would help."

" How much time do I have?"

" How much do you need?"

" I need enough time for Logan Stern to complete a shooting script for *The Romanoff File*. Enough time to get that picture into the can, to distribute it for worldwide exhibition, and to evaluate its success. Just to see if Arcadia can survive without interference. I take it Mr. Hanna would consider that an unreasonable request."

" I'm afraid so. Mr. Hanna is a man of action. The tender offer has already been made and papers are on file with the SEC. A number of stockholders have accepted. It's too late to turn back. And let me point out, as you probably know, UMI has previously acquired a heavy position in Arcadia, possibly enough to demand representation on your board."

Hedrik said evenly, " We don't know that for a fact, not yet. Right now we have no way of knowing how many shares are held in Street names or by foreign nominees."

" Are you willing to risk a proxy fight?"

" Mr. Ryan, prudence and self-interest suggest that I court

111

Mr. Hanna's good will in order to protect my flanks. On the other hand, there's a matter of pride and personal integrity. I took this job with one goal in mind. To rebuild Arcadia, not to acquiesce in its seduction and possible dismemberment. Even if Fred Hanna wins control, I don't think I want to be associated with him in any capacity whatever. You wanted an answer as soon as possible. You can have it right now. Arcadia Films will not fall into Hanna's arms. He wants the company, he'll have to fight for it."

Ryan shrugged. "You know, of course, the odds are against you."

"The odds were against David too, and he knocked Goliath on his ass. If you had persuaded Kate Rennie to throw in with you, then we'd be in trouble. As it stands, I believe she'll support the company's management."

Ryan sighed and stood up. "Sorry we have to square off, Mr. Hedrik. I would have enjoyed working on merger terms with you."

"Good-bye, Mr. Ryan. I expect we haven't seen the last of each other."

They shook hands without enthusiasm.

19

Anson Gregorius lumbered out to the reception room to greet his visitors and escort them back to his office. The call for an appointment had surprised him. Egan yes; Egan had been there before. But Fred Hanna himself, in person, deigning to leave his eyrie, instead of summoning retainers to his presence—something was in the wind.

Hanna accepted a cigar and crossed his legs. "Well, Anson, you're looking fit."

"Why not? I just finished two hours on my trampoline."

Hanna chuckled. Alongside him, Robert Egan sat stony-faced. "And Julie? Is she well?"

Anson was puzzled by all these amenities. The UMI chief had never before evinced the slightest interest in any member of his family. "Julie's fine," he said.

"She has a new suitor, I understand."

"Julie's an attractive woman. She has several."

"One in particular. Chap named Ward Bendiner."

"Yes. I've met him."

"Anything serious?"

"With Julie, who knows?" Anson half closed one eye. "You making a point of some kind, Fred?"

"I am. This Bendiner is an Arcadia stockholder. A very large stockholder."

"So?"

"Mike Ryan tells me he's a Gregorius customer."

"That's right. Mike personally handles the account."

"Then perhaps you can tell me why these Bendiner shares have not been committed to UMI."

"I really can't say, Fred. That's Ryan's province. And Ryan is in California, on UMI business, as a matter of fact. We expect him back tomorrow. I'll ask him about it. I imagine he's waiting for the right moment."

"The right moment is now. Dammit, man, I want those shares locked up."

"I understand your impatience, Fred. I'll discuss with Ryan."

"Why not discuss it with Bendiner himself?"

"Because Mike wouldn't like it."

"And that bothers you?" A muscle rippled in Hanna's jaw. "Have you been in touch with him?"

"In California? Not yet."

"Then let me enlighten you. Egan got through to him last night. Ryan struck out with both Hedrik and Kate Rennie. So

113

we're heading straight into a bare-knuckles proxy fight. Something I wanted to avoid."

"That's not Ryan's fault. You never expected Arcadia to fall into your lap. I think we have the muscle to win. What are you worried about?"

"We're worried about Arcadia's lawyer."

"Paul Slater?"

"Yes. That sonovabitch spells trouble. Did you see his ad in the papers this morning?"

"The letter to Arcadia stockholders." Anson made a face. "How many of them read the *Wall Street Journal?*"

"It'll be mailed out to them too." Hanna compressed his lips. "Our P.R. people spend five years building an image and these bastards try to tear it apart in one day."

Anson drummed his fingers on the desk. He was not intimidated by this man. Gregorius & Company had made it through a lot of tough years without UMI's business. Ernie Stoufer had mentioned some troublesome situations when Stoufer, Wingate had been Hanna's investment banker. From the very first he had been dubious about handling UMI's affairs. But Mike had won him over. Mike wanted the account.

He said quietly, "I don't quite get the point you're making, Fred. Are you holding Mike responsible? Because if you are, that's a crock and you know it. UMI approached Hedrik long before Gregorius took over. Egan here, for example. And he got exactly nowhere. There was no way Hedrik would consent to a friendly merger, not with UMI, or anyone else, for that matter. Ryan is damned good, but he doesn't perform miracles. You want miracles, hire one of the geniuses at Lazard or Salomon. Because it is not too late to turn your problems over to another house. No hard feelings. We'll part friends."

Fred Hanna was momentarily taken aback by the old man's reaction. He recovered at once, smiling, offering a conciliatory gesture. "Anson, Anson, settle down. I meant no offense. The last thing we need is friction among ourselves. I came here merely in search of clarification."

Egan spoke up. "And to suggest, Mr. Gregorius, that you

114

sound out Bendiner. During a social visit perhaps. No harm in that. It would help us to plan our strategy if we had some inkling of his intent. Mr. Hanna recognises Ryan's ability. That's why we retained Gregorius in the first place. And we think he did a splendid job on the convertible preferreds. I should imagine Gregorius & Company turned a handsome profit on that underwriting. And there should be more of the same in the future. We have large plans."

Anson nodded, slightly mollified. " All right, Fred. Tell me this—which would you prefer, Bendiner's proxy or his acceptance of your tender?"

" Either one."

" I'll speak to him. Julie is bringing him to dinner Tuesday evening."

" Let me know the result."

" Of course."

Both men stood up. Hanna said, " It was good to see you again, Anson." He grinned. " Don't overdo it on that trampoline."

*　　*　　*

Cora Bendiner had shed her bikini. Her skin glistened with perspiration. Flame vine and yucca screened the pool area. She felt the strain of abdominal muscles as she slowly lowered her legs to the exercise mat in the strenuous regimen that kept her body supple as a dancer's.

Once, through several weeks of indolence, she had allowed herself to gain a few pounds. She remembered glaring at the scale and vowing never to let it happen again. Her body was money in the bank. Judiciously exploited, it had served her most profitably.

She rested for a moment. Above the soft whisper of the pool's filtration system, she heard the silvery note of a mockingbird. She took a breath, laced fingers behind her neck and did twenty sit-ups. She stood and walked to the edge of the board. She dived and was instantly refreshed by the engulfing water.

115

She left the pool, entered the house, and filled her bathtub with warm water. Bath oils followed. She climbed into the tub and settled back, luxuriating, gently lathering herself. The warm water had a hypnotic effect. Ward's face flickered unbidden and she blanked it out instantly, imagining instead Alex Bogart's white smile, feeling a quick rush of desire.

Alex is really something, she thought. One of the rare ones. Always capable of bringing her to a tumultuous release, matching her passion with his own insatiable demands. She had found most men to be selfishly quick, leading to a sinful deprivation suffered by too many women with resignation. She remembered her initial experience.

She had been in her second year in high school, her young body already in full bloom. The boy was a football jock, vectoring in at a school dance, tapping her partner on the shoulder, smiling fatuously. She felt complimented. By adolescent standards, the jock was a status symbol. Even then, in her teens, she had been aware of her effect on boys, secretly amused by their embarrassment at the involuntary bulge of tumescence. She let the jock hold her close, and Jesus, he was really endowed.

He had offered to drive her home in his garishly painted jalopy. She did not object when he swung off the blacktop and parked under a dense spread of willows. Impulsively, without preliminaries, he was suddenly all over her, snorting and groping. She permitted him a few liberties, finding it pleasant in a mildly detached way. But when he reached under her skirt, she stiffened and rocked a knee into his groin. He jackknifed away, gasping with shock.

"That's enough, superman," she told him. "Take me home."

"Aw, hey, Cora, please—"

"*No.*"

"You're driving me crazy."

"You're driving yourself crazy. Go take a shower."

She knew from schoolgirl gossip that he usually scored. It was hard for him to believe the rejection. He thought she was playing coy, teasing him. He bulled her into a corner of the jalopy, and quite calmly she raked her fingernails across his face. He backed away and touched his cheek. The feel of his own blood subdued him instantly.

"What cooks with you, Cora?" he asked plaintively.

"You don't listen. I told you to lay off." She was oddly calm, not in the least frightened.

"You a virgin or something?"

"None of your business."

He took it rightly as an affirmative answer. "Listen, I could teach you a lot of things."

"Yeah. I know. And it'll cure my pimples, only I don't have any pimples."

"Aw, it's not that at all."

"What is it then?"

"Well, sex is more fun than anything. You remember that TV commercial?"

"What commercial?"

"Try it, you'll like it."

"I'll think about it. Start the engine."

In aggrieved silence he drove her home to the white frame house. He looked so crestfallen she allowed him to kiss her goodnight, but she pulled sharply away when he began having respiratory problems again.

"Can I see you another time, Cora?" he pleaded.

"Maybe. My number's in the book."

She had kept her promise. She did think about it. She thought about it a lot, and the subject fascinated her. Two of her friends had already gone all the way and had given it their enthusiastic endorsement. The time had come, she decided, to find out what all the commotion was about.

And the jock seemed a suitable enough partner. He was physically attractive, tall, clean, healthy. He'd had more than his share of experience. She had gathered information, asking explicit questions. She read some of the more lurid paperback manuals. She knew that her first experience might be painful, perhaps even messy. She wished it were possible to have her maidenhead surgically pierced. But where could she go in this stupid town without having to answer embarrassing questions.

117

She remembered rummaging one rainy afternoon through her sister's bureau. Lila was seven years older than Cora, seemingly the product of different genes, bony and somewhat graceless, with no boyfriends, working part time at the public library. Cora had found the device wrapped in a pair of pantyhose and hidden away in the bottom of a drawer.

One of those tubular vibrators, shaped like a man's thing, battery-operated. She had examined it curiously, amused and intrigued. Good Lord! she thought. Who would have believed it? A secret vice for the prim and spinsterish Lila. A substitute lover. Cora turned the switch and felt the vibrator tickling her palm.

When the time came, she decided that it could solve her problem. Lila was away, visiting Grandma. Her father was downstairs in his office, drilling molars. Cora retrieved the instrument and locked herself in the bathroom. She remembered that dark overcast afternoon, astride the commode, wincing against anticipated discomfort. But there had been very little discomfort and almost no pain at all.

My God, she had thought, maybe I lost it that time I went riding bareback on old Katie, Grandma's mare. She turned the switch and within moments her mouth went slack. Her haunches flexed in response to sensations that unfocused her eyes and left her lolling boneless against the backrest.

She had realised instinctively that a shared experience would be immeasurably more satisfying. And even then she knew with absolute certainty that some day, employing her considerable enticements, she would be able to capitalize on a male craving for erotic fulfilment. She vowed to learn through actual experience all the various techniques and artifices she'd read about.

Four days later, in the back seat of the jalopy, at a drive-in theatre, she opened herself to the jock. It was a total disappointment. A farce. In two frenzied thrusts, whinnying her name, he spent himself. When he caught his breath, he apologized abjectly and promised to improve the next time.

And he did. With the recuperative powers of youth, he was soon ready. This time he had better control.

By the end of the week he was constantly dogging her heels, a humble supplicant, a lovesick puppy. The affair lasted to the end of the month, and then, abruptly, Cora ended it, seeking wider horizons. College youths home on vacation, an older man who operated the local boutique and who provided her with several expensive outfits at a one-hundred-per cent discount, plus a few items of technique he had picked up on a trip to Japan.

Cora was an apt pupil. She soon learned how to push the right buttons for maximum response and how to feign ecstasy. Suitors coveted her favors, often to the point of irrationality.

*   *   *

Now, in Ocala Beach, in this odd redwood building called The Lodge, she stepped out of the tub, dried and anointed herself with lotions. She stretched out for a nap. It did not come. Relaxation these days was elusive. Recent events keep materializing, flickering erratically, like some ineptly edited film.

The phone rang. She answered, and a man's voice said, "May I talk to Mr. Ward Bendiner, please?"

"This is Mrs. Bendiner. Who's calling?"

"The name is Landry—Ross Landry."

"Does my husband know you, Mr. Landry?"

"Probably not. I'm from California and I just arrived in Ocala Beach. I'd be obliged if your husband could spare me a little time. I'd like to discuss a matter of some importance with him."

"Important to you or to my husband?"

"To both of us."

"Would you care to tell me what you wish to see him about?"

"I'm here on behalf of Arcadia Films. Mr. Bendiner is a large stockholder in the company. We are resisting a takeover attempt by Universal Media Industries. I believe your husband would want to know the advantages of voting his proxy against the takeover."

"I believe he's already received some correspondence about

119

the matter. However, I'm afraid you're going to be disappointed, Mr. Landry. My husband is not available at the moment."

"Tomorrow, then. Any time at his convenience."

"You don't understand. He's not here. He's in New York on business."

"Oh-oh!" There was a note of frustration in the voice. "When do you expect him back?"

"I'm not sure. I can try to reach him and let you know."

"I'd be most grateful, Mrs. Bendiner."

"Where are you staying?

"At the Everglades."

Cora knew the motel. "How long do you expect to be there?"

"That would depend on Mr. Bendiner's plans."

"I'll be in touch with you as soon as I have any information."

She hung up and sat on the edge of the bed, eyes narrowed, bottom lip caught between her teeth. "Damn!" she said. "*Damn, damn, damn!*"

After careful consideration, she decided that she had better call New York to discuss Landry's arrival. She reached for the phone again, even though she had promised not to call.

20

Floyd Gregorius watched the recovery of Arcadia with lifting spirits. He felt an almost irresistible urge to rush out of his office, grab Janey Spacek, and waltz her around the bond room.

But his deliverance was short-lived. Less than forty-eight

hours later, after the Croesus Fund had completed its buying, the stock began to lose ground again. He read the tape with blurred vision, his face convulsed like a baby's in torment. He knew now that he would have to proceed with his rescue plan. Bracing himself, he reached for the phone and dialed a number.

When he had identified the voice, he said, " Me again, the party you spoke to on Wednesday. I'd like to use the machine this evening."

" Seven-thirty. You must come alone."

" I understand."

" With cash."

" The money is ready."

" Knock three times."

He sat for a long moment, his mouth dry as dust, fingertips stroking his closed eyelids.

*   *   *

Ten minutes after seven Floyd left the deserted office, a manila envelope clutched tightly under his arm. The financial district was now dark and abandoned. He walked north along Nassau Street to Fulton. The stationery store was closed, a shade pulled down over its glass door. He rapped three times. The shade moved aside to reveal a narrow, incurious face. Floyd signaled and the door opened to admit him.

" I gotta be outta here by eight o'clock," the man said. He was the assistant manager of the store, which for several decades had been printing letterheads and business forms for brokerage firms in the area. " How much time do you need?"

" Not long. Just show me how the machine works."

" Look," the man said, " anything goes wrong, you were never here. I don't know you, right?"

" I give you my word."

Floyd followed the man down the aisle, past heavily stocked shelves, to a glass-enclosed cubicle in the rear. An overhead light illuminated the Model 6500 Xerox copier.

" How many copies you need?"

" Five."

121

"All right, Mac, I don't know what you're up to and I don't give a shit. Where's the money?"

Floyd handed him a packet of bills. "Five hundred dollars, as agreed."

The man fielded the bills, made a penciled notation of the number on the copier's register, and flipped the switch. "Okay, pal, here's what you do." He demonstrated the machine's operation, turned, and left the cubicle.

Floyd had learned about the 6500 from a magazine article. It was a highly versatile piece of equipment that could reproduce documents on both sides in full colour. It was capable of accepting various types of paper. Its copies were remarkably accurate. It had, in the past, been used to duplicate everything from diplomas to bank drafts, including currency that had deceived a number of merchants.

There was, however, one shortcoming: a tendency to sharpen colors. Floyd had shrugged off this flaw as inconsequential to his purpose. He had observed some color dissimilarities on stock certificates because of ink variations at the time of printing. More important, his own copies were being offered by a seemingly irreproachable source. So there would be no reason to suspect their authenticity.

He had given it careful thought. Margin clerks were under constant pressure, handling stacks of securities with indifferent scrutiny. In addition, he felt that he was borrowing these certificates on a temporary basis. Once his investment in Arcadia stabilized, there would be no need to maintain his margin at its present level. Stoufer, Wingate would return the copies and he would destroy them. There would be no evidence of wrongdoing.

He removed five bond certificates from the manila envelope. Issued by Universal Media Industries, paying nine and a quarter per cent, due in the year 2001. There had been rumors around the office that Fred Hanna might be responsible for the erosion of Arcadia stock. Floyd smiled minimally. There was a kind of justifiable irony in employing UMI paper to support his own speculation in Arcadia.

122

The bonds were registered in his father's name. They were part of Anson's personal holdings, locked away in the firm's vault, available for easy access and liquidation should Gregorius & Company need additional capital. Only Floyd and Mike Ryan held keys to the vault. In the morning Floyd would return the originals and deliver his copies to Stoufer, Wingate. It would, he hoped, satisfy all margin requirements for now and in the future.

He placed his own paper in the machine, paper of suitable weight and quality which he had carefully selected. The machine hummed and clicked. When the first copy came through, he held it up for inspection. The color did indeed seem a shade brighter. Beyond that, he detected no flaws.

An idea suddenly struck him. It made his heart lurch and his palms sweat. Good God! he thought. With my name, with my access to the Gregorius vault, I could bring off one of the biggest swindles that ever hit Wall Street. I could liquidate millions in fake stock certificates before anyone realized what had happened. He had a momentary vision of himself living in one of the banana republics in baronial splendour, one of those countries with no extradition treaty. Dizziness closed in and he had trouble breathing.

Then it passed and he brought himself back to reality. He was oddly conscious of the capacity for dishonesty that lurked in the human psyche, how even the most circumspect of citizens might be tempted except for the fear of punishment and disgrace.

He continued working. He made single copies of all the bond certificates, carefully separating them from the originals, then identifying each one on the reverse side with a barely visible pencil mark.

He left the store with no further conversation, and went home. Sleep was elusive. His mind was too active. It occured to him that he could not be certain of avoiding detection at Stoufer, Wingate. But he could escape that risk by tendering the originals. The copies would go into the Gregorius vault. The replacement was, after all, only temporary. It was unlikel that anyone would disturb his father's papers. And before long the originals would be returned and he could make the substitution. He would burn the copies, destroying all trace of their existence.

Having reached that decision, he fell into a fitful sleep.

*　　*　　*

Anson's co-op was far too large for a widower whose children had long since deserted the nest. Nine rooms on the uppermost floor of a limestone fortress, constructed long before skyrocketing costs mandated the sterile caves sprouting all across the city. Anson realised that sooner or later he would have to put it on the market, another admission of his ultimate retirement.

His housekeeper, a middle-aged woman, was indisposed, so Julie had arrived early to supervize dinner arrangements. On those evenings when Anson entertained, meals were delivered by a local catering service.

At seven-twenty the doorman phoned from the lobby. " A Mr. Ward Bendiner, sir."

" Yes," Anson said. " Send him up."

In the drawing room, over cocktails, Julie was a garrulous source of inconsequential but amusing trivia. At precisely eight o'clock the caterer arrived with smoked salmon, filet mignon Rossini, and chocolate mousse, all carefully packaged to preserve temperature and texture. They dined leisurely, lingered over dessert and coffee, and then returned to the drawing-room for brandy.

" Julie," Anson said, " would you mind if I discussed some business matters with Ward?"

" Of course I mind."

" Ward?"

" Not at all, sir."

Julie made a face. " Anyway, I have some phone calls to make." With an expression of mock indignation she headed toward her old bedroom.

Anson offered his guest a cigar, selected one for himself,

and clicked a lighter. " Tell me, Ward," Anson said, " I trust you're satisfied with the way Gregorius is handling your account."

" More than satisfied. Mike Ryan is solid. I have no complaints."

" Your portfolio, I gather, holds a very substantial position in Arcadia Films."

" Yes, sir. It's been in the family a long time. Ever since the company went public. My father had great confidence in the industry. Movies were the only source of entertainment in our town."

" Where was that?"

" Vermont. More people were reading fan magazines than the *Saturday Evening Post*."

" Why Arcadia? Why not Paramount or MGM?"

" My father liked what he read about Max Klemmer. And he was more than adequately rewarded, at least for a time. The company grew and the stock split a number of times. It would have been wise, I suppose, to sell it years ago."

" Why didn't you, after your father died?"

" Sentiment, I guess. Perhaps stubbornness. I was hoping the situation would improve."

" Hardly a valid reason for an investment decision."

" I agree. But then, after I reached that conclusion, the stock was down so far, I figured it had finally reached the bottom, so I hung on."

" Well, Ward, you're not the first. How do you feel about it now?"

" I expect to unload one of these days."

" You are, no doubt, aware of UMI's offer."

" All Arcadia stockholders know about it. We've been bombarded with letters and publicity from both sides."

" And I take it you also know that Gregorius & Company is acting as dealer-manager for UMI in its efforts."

" That, too, is common knowledge."

" Considering Arcadia's recent performance, the tender appears most generous. Don't you agree?"

125

" I do, sir. In fact, I'd call it magnanimous."

" Are you considering the offer, Ward? Would you be receptive?"

" I think not, sir."

" May I know why?"

" As you know, I've been a seller on balance. I am no longer interested in acquiring corporate equities. So the offer of UMI securities in exchange for my Arcadia stock doesn't really interest me."

" But you might be interested in an outright sale."

" Definitely. For cash. But not at the present market, Mr. Gregorius. Some massive selling has driven it too low. Perhaps when it recovers, the stock will be available to the highest bidder."

" Have you discussed it with Ryan?"

" Yes. About a month ago I was anxious to sell. Ryan told me that a merger was in the works. He suggested that I wait awhile. I did, and sure enough the stock went up. Now it's down again, drastically, and it's costing me money. But I can't hold that against Ryan. He was acting in my best interest. And I really appreciate that, because he also had a responsibility for UMI's acquisition plans."

Anson studied his cigar. " If you haven't sold your stock, and it comes down to a proxy fight, would you consider voting your shares for our client Universal Media?"

" That depends, sir."

" On what?"

" My conclusions after I've studied all the arguments on both sides."

Julie appeared in the doorway, arms folded. " All right, gentlemen. Enough is enough. Whose date is Ward anyway, yours or mine, Daddy?"

" We're finished," Anson said.

She surveyed him critically. " You look tired."

" It's been a long day."

" Then we're leaving right now." She advanced and kisse her father. Ward rose and shook his hand.

126

Alone, Anson sat back to consider his report of the evening's outcome to Fred Hanna. Hanna, he expected, would be less than pleased, but it could not be helped. Bendiner knew what he wanted and he was determined to get it.

21

When Mike Ryan returned from the Coast, Liz Harmon tried unsuccessfully to buttonhole him. Under the pressure of accumulated responsibilities he had put her off and suggested dinner.

Now, in the restaurant, she said, " I have some news for you."

" Good news?"

" Hardly."

" Then save it. I'm still suffering from jet lag and I want to relax. Enjoy. And don't look at the prices on this menu. Nobody in his right mind eats in this beanery unless he's on an expense account. Whenever I waste time accomplishing nothing, I like to indulge myself. California was a bust."

" Tell me about it."

He shrugged. " Lovely climate."

" And the people?"

" They seem a little bent."

" Everyone? Including Kate Rennie?"

" Kate Rennie is special." He leered lecherously. " First movie star ever made a pass at me."

" You're joking. The lady must be over eighty."

" At least."

" How did you make out?"

He looked down his nose. " A gentleman never talks."

127

"I am referring, Mr. Ryan, to your efforts on behalf of UMI."

"No luck. Rennie is backing Dan Hedrik all the way. She told me so at dinner." He paused. "That pleases you, doesn't it?"

"No comment."

Between courses Mike painted word caricatures of the people he'd met. Liz surprised him with flashes of insight on various aspects of film-making, explaining her interest as a long-time enthusiasm. Finally, over coffee, she said, "Okay. You've had your relaxation. Are you ready now?"

He sighed. "Shoot."

"We had visitors while you were away."

"Who?"

"A very sharp young chap named Kevin Anthony Duke III."

"Should I know the name?"

"Not unless you've been been up to your eyeballs in skulduggery. He works for G. G. Pressman."

"The SEC? Enforcement Branch?"

"Yes, sir. And young Mr. Duke was accompanied by a pair of Market Surveillance investigators from their New York office. They're trying to smoke out the people responsible for the sharp drop in Arcadia."

"Why us? Very little selling cleared through Gregorius."

"That, my friend, is precisely what troubles them. They figure Arcadia is being manipulated, possibly by Fred Hanna, and because of our connection with UMI, they're taking a hard look at all Gregorius transactions."

"So? Are they happy now? We haven't been selling and we haven't been buying."

"Exactly. They probably feel that at these prices, we should be eating the stuff. Hanna wants control, this is a good time to buy. Mr. Duke was very skeptical. He intimated that Hanna had ordered us to sit tight, no further accumulation at this time that might support the price, while he's trying to knock it down."

"Why the hell should Hanna pay cash if he can get the stock through an exchange of paper?"...

128

" Just what I told him."

" And?"

" More skepticism. These characters know all the dodges ever invented and maybe a few nobody ever thought of. But they have a problem. They can't cut through the fog on this one. Too much selling by foreign nominees. They're frustrated, and determined, gnawing at it like bulldogs."

Mike stared at her, eyes narrowed. His palm slapped the table. " Damnit, Liz! Hanna's got to be clean on this. The risk is too great."

"The man is a gambler. He's taken risks all his life."

" But why jeopardize his position? He's riding high now."

" Mike," Liz said quietly, " you threw in with Hanna, you're part of his team, and it's blurred your vision. I know what ails you. You can't admit that he might be double-crossing his own financial advisor."

" Ah, come off it. What about Egan? Don't you think Egan must have warned him?"

" What I think is that Robert Egan figured out the smoke screens for this operation. Intuition maybe, whatever, I have a feeling that Signor Niccolò Machiavelli was a cream puff compared to Egan. The man scares me silly."

" I don't like him much myself. But he's smart. And they have some powerful connections in Washington. Could be they feel safe behind that security blanket. If the regulating agencies get too meddlesome, it's barely possible that word may be passed along to cool it."

Liz shook her head. " It wouldn't take. Mr. Gary George Pressman dances to nobody's music but his own. If Fred Hanna's guilty of manipulating the market, and if Pressman nails him, we here at Gregorius & Company had better be as clean and as innocent as the infant Jesus himself."

" We are."

" Maybe. But we're still vulnerable. And I think you know what I mean."

Mike nodded. She did not have to spell it out. The Universal Broadcasting System was the linchpin of Hanna's operation,

E   129

its most consistently profitable division. An FCC hearing on renewal of its license, following charges of corporate malfeasance, could have unpredictable results. Because if the company lost its franchise, with Gregorius heavily in debt in order to carry the UMI account, the brokerage house itself would be skirting disaster.

Liz said, "The maître d' is giving us an evil eye. He has some hungry prospects waiting for a table."

"Tough. At these prices we could have bought the real estate."

"I know. But he makes me uncomfortable. So take me home and I'll buy you a drink."

He accepted at once. She had not permitted him past the building lobby in months.

Her apartment was warm and comfortable. Books and periodicals everywhere, limited-edition lithographs reflecting an eclectic taste. Liz kicked off her shoes and settled into a corner of the sofa, one leg folded under her.

"Where's my drink?" Mike demanded.

She waved. "Help yourself."

He went to the small bar and poured Scotch. "You?"

"No, thanks. I've had my quota."

He sat at the opposite end of the sofa. "So I drink alone. Cheers. What happens if you exceed your quota? It reduces your inhibitions?"

"I have no inhibitions."

"Ha!"

"At least no inhibitions against what I want to do."

"How come you don't want to hold your boss and administer a dose of much-needed comfort? Can't you see the man is feeling low?"

"You? The self-sufficient Michael Ryan?"

"Yes, ma'am."

She moved over, smiling, and tilted her head. Surprized, he held her close, remembering the fragrance and texture of her mouth. After a long interval, she pulled gently away.

"Something wrong?" he asked.

" Your emotional equipment, Mike."

" Elaborate, please."

" You're what—approaching forty? And in all those years you made no commitment to another person."

" Not true."

" Tell me when."

" A long time back. In Toronto."

" Who?"

" My landlady's daughter."

" And?"

" I asked her to marry me. We went off on a trip, Niagara Falls, sort of a shakedown cruise. And I found that I had a very shallow little dish on my hands. So I broke it up and moved to another rooming house."

" How come you missed those qualities before the trip? What blinded you?"

" Glandular turmoil. I was young and impetuous."

She studied him. " Didn't you once have something going with Julie Gregorius?"

" For a while, yes. Don't ask for details."

" She's a beautiful woman."

" I prefer the brainy type."

" Like me?"

" Yes. I find it a more potent brew. I'm keeping it under control. Mixing business with pleasure is not a good idea."

She laughed delightedly. " Now there's a Mike Ryan I can recognize. The ultimate salesman. You find me exciting, but you're not going to let any glandular turmoil affect your perspective. Clever. It challenges the lady. Can she or can she not overcome the man's defenses?"

He gave her an injured look. " You do me an injustice, Liz."

" I do?"

" Yes. I'll prove it. Say goodnight and watch me leave."

" Goodnight, Mike."

He stood, his face lugubrious, and as he headed for the door she sensed his loneliness, and it made her oddly aware of a sudden change in herself.

131

" Hold it right there," she said.

He turned and looked at her, not moving. She got up and went over to him. He gathered her close. She was soft and yielding in his arms, her eyelids heavy. She arched her back. He could feel the pulse in her throat, the slackening of muscles, a surrender so total he began to lose his own identity. He lifted her and carried her in his arms like a bride across the threshold into the bedroom.

She was ready for him at once, crooning his name in a small drugged voice.

*   *   *

In the lassitude of cooling flesh, they stared at each other without speaking.

Finally he said, " How do you feel about your reputation, Liz?"

" Why do you ask?"

" I'm wondering what the doorman will think when we walk out of here tomorrow morning."

" You're planning to stay all night?"

" Unless you throw me out. I haven't the strength to get dressed, and no cabby in his right mind would pick up a naked fare. Besides, if I go home, I won't be able to sleep, thinking about you. And tomorrow is a big day at the office. Please, for the sake of Gregorius & Company—"

" It'll cost you, buster. Night work is extra."

He laughed and then turned serious. " It can never be the same between us, you know."

" I know. Now hush." She walked her fingers down his chest and past his stomach.

" Oh, my God!!' he said.

*   *   *

On Monday morning, when senior staff members of the New York Stock Exchange crossed the marble floor of the executive corridor and gathered in Room 602, their first order of business

132

was a report by Jered Kolbert of the Exchange's Stock Watch.

"I am sorry to say, gentlemen, that up to this point we have made no progress. The short selling of Arcadia shares continues. All of it by nominees in foreign banks. The brokers in question are unable to identify the principals. The entire effort seems extraordinarily well-managed. And I am sure you all know about the extremely negative review of Arcadia's prospects in the *Investor's Newsletter*. It simply fueled the pessimism and the stock continues to fall."

"Do you have any suspicion, Mr. Kolbert, that the review may have been a deliberate plant?"

"Suspicion, yes. Proof, no."

"Should we pursue that line of inquiry?"

"By all means, sir."

"Have you been in touch with the Securities and Exchange Commission?"

"Yes, sir. There has been a considerable duplication of effort. We are both covering the same ground."

"Do they report any progress?"

"Not yet, sir."

The senior members looked grim and determined. "All right, Mr. Kolbert. Carry on."

22

Dan Hedrik did not want to be disturbed. The first third of Logan Stern's screenplay for *The Romanoff File* had been delivered that morning, and he had told his secretary to hold all calls. He was reading with a growing sense of excitement when the girl buzzed him.

"Long distance, Mr. Hedrik. Ross Landry calling from Florida."

"Put him on. Ross?"

"Yes, Dan. I'm still here, sitting on my duff, waiting."

"Waiting for what? Have you spoken to Bendiner yet?"

"Little hitch here, Dan. We should have called first. Bendiner's wife tells me he's in New York."

Hedrik growled one of his rare obscenities. "When does she expect him back?"

"She's not sure. Told me on the phone she'd try to reach him. I'm still waiting."

"We can't waste any more time, Ross. Go over to the man's house and ask to phone Bendiner while you're there. Reimburse her for the toll. Maybe she'll let you talk to him. If not, get his address and fly up to New York, beard him there. Where are you staying."

"At a motel called the Everglades."

"All right. Call me this evening and let me know. I want you back at the studio no later than Thursday. Logan Stern is working overtime. We have the first third of his screenplay."

"How does it read?"

"Marvelous. It'll stand you on your head. We won't have to change a word."

"Have you signed Clyde Elliott?"

"He'll be here this afternoon to sign. He read the book and he's enthusiastic about the part."

"And Kate Rennie?"

"She thought I was kidding when I called her about playing the Grand Duchess."

"Will she come out of retirement?"

"Hell, yes. Soon as we have Elliott's signature on the papers, I'm driving over to Max Klemmer's monstrosity. Kate wants a description of the role."

"Did she say anything about UMI's tender?"

"She turned them down, Ross. She's with us all the way."

"That's good news, Dan. God knows, we need her support."

134

" Amen, Ross. This evening. Don't forget. I'll wait for your call."

*   *   *

The desk clerk at the Kilburne Arms, an apartment-hotel on New York's Madison Avenue, proffered two messages and a letter to the approaching guest, saying, " Pleasant weather, Mr. Bendiner. I hope you're still enjoying your stay here."

" Very much." He took the papers and walked to the elevator.

In his furnished apartment on the seventh floor, he saw that one message was from Julie Gregorius, reminding him of their appointment that evening. The second was from Cora, saying that she would call again later. The letter had apparently been forwarded from Florida, opened by Cora and then resealed. He opened the envelope and glanced first at the signature. Martin Caswell. The name meant nothing. It appeared to be a facsimile letter that had been mailed to all Arcadia stockholders. He read it twice, eyebrows arched.

Dear Fellow Stockholder:

I think you should be in possession of certain information that has come into our possession involving Mr. Dan Hedrik, president and chief executive officer of Arcadia Films.

Mr. Hedrik recently authorised the payment of half a million dollars, plus a percentage of net receipts, to one Logan Stern, an alleged novelist, for the motion picture to a book called *The Romanoff File*.

This unconscionably high sum was negotiated under a secret agreement that provided for a kickback to Mr. Hedrik of $50,000 in cash. At a time when your company's finances are precarious at best, and conservation of capital is essential, such gross malfeasance should bear the closest scrutiny.

Sincerely,
Martin Caswell
Independent Stockholders Committee

He folded the letter, speculating idly on the identity of Caswell. Some stockholder, perhaps, who may have been a

135

former employee of the company, someone with a grudge against Hedrik. He filed the letter in the wastebasket. It did not concern him.

I want no part of a proxy fight, he thought. I owe no loyalty to either combatant. I have no intention of holding on to the shares for any length of time. They are for sale to the highest bidder. I would, in fact, have already sold them had it not been for Ryan's advice to wait a bit.

He smiled, thinking of his talk with the old man, Anson Gregorius. The UMI people must have been breathing down Anson's neck. Now, virtually in retirement, he would have enjoyed locking up the Bendiner shares for delivery to Fred Hanna.

The telephone pealed. Julie, he thought, and reached for the handset. " Hi, darling."

Cora's voice said, " Mental telepathy? How did you know was me?"

He recovered and feigned a quick laugh. " From the way it rang. Sort of sexy. Besides, who else knows this number?"

" When are you coming home?"

" Soon as possible. New York is no bargain, believe me. It's tougher to survive here now than when the settlers first landed. Those Indians were tame compared to the predators roaming these streets."

" Well, give me an approximate date."

" Another week or two at most. It's a matter of timing, trying to get the best price. Anything new down there?"

" That's why I called. There's a visitor here from California. A man named Ross Landry, representing Arcadia Films. He wants to see you. Did you get that letter I forwarded?"

" From some character signing himself Martin Caswell?"

" Yes. Apparently there's going to be some kind of proxy fight. That's what Landry wants to see you about."

" What did you tell him?"

" That you were in New York and I didn't know when you were coming home. I promised to find out and call him back."

" Stall him. I don't think Arcadia is in any position to buy the stock at a premium. And anyway, I'm working on a deal with the opposition."

" You're the doctor."

" Keep that in mind. Matter of fact, I'd like to be playing doctor with you right this minute."

" Any particular speciality?"

" Gynecology."

Cora laughed. " I could use a treatment."

" Happens," he said sadly, " I'm a little out of practise."

" Not to worry, darling. It's like riding a bicycle. Once you know, you never forget— Oh-oh, hold on a minute. Someone's at the door."

He kept the receiver to his ear and yawned. It was indeed time to accelerate the pace here and wind things up. Julie had been a pleasant interval and he expected that she might be flexible enough to take any disappointment in stride.

Cora's voice came back on the line. " It's that Landry man from Arcadia Films. He's waiting for me in the study. I'll call you tomorrow."

* * *

When Cora Bendiner rejoined her visitor, Ross Landry was standing in front of the bookshelves, peering at an autographed snapshot of Ward.

" Interesting shot," Landry said. " Background looks like Mexico. Cuernavaca, isn't it?"

" How can you tell?"

" We shot a picture there once."

" You're right. It is Cuernavaca. We were passing through. I shot it with an Instamatic."

" Nice composition. You should have it enlarged."

She was pleased. This man was in the business. He knew about such things. She had always enjoyed working with cameras. Sexual innovation aside, it was the only creative outlet she had. She gave him one of her special smiles. " Perhaps you can get me a job in Hollywood."

He took her in appreciatively. " In front of the camera, not

behind one. If you're at all photogenic . . . Mrs. Bendiner, get
your husband to agree and I'll arrange a screen test."

" Are you serious?"

" I am indeed."

" Well, Mr. Landry, sit down, please. Let's talk about it."

23

Friday was the maid's day off and the big house seemed
emptier than usual. At eleven o'clock Kate Rennie put on
a bathing suit for her morning swim. Later she would fix a
snack and then rest for her meeting with Dan Hedrik at four.

Kate felt a keen sense of anticipation. The prospect of
emerging from retirement for a juicy character role was most
appealing. She remembered Helen Hayes as the Grand Duchess
in *Anastasia*, a performance that had touched her heart and
filled her eyes. If she could be only half as effective, it would
be a triumphant climax to her career. And of course it would
add spice to a life that had grown increasingly lonely.

She had enjoyed her evening out with Mike Ryan. Amusing
chap. And persuasive too. Had she not been so deeply committed to Arcadia and to Dan Hedrik, he might have pulled it
off. Of course, she didn't really need the money and that had
made a rejection of the tender offer much easier.

She went out to the pool. In the old days she had enjoyed
swimming nude. But Max had put a stop to it when a helicopter
started hovering over the area. An unauthorised photo of Kate
Rennie in the buff would never do, not with the old Will Hays'
office and its tight controls of the film colony's morals. My
God, she thought, how times have changed. In my day even
a decorous kiss had been limited in duration. But now they were

producing hard-core as if the Constitution had been designed to guarantee unbridled license. Lord knows, she told herself, I'm no prude. There had been one or two *caballeros* in my life before Max. And I was tolerant with Davy while he was here. I never said a word about the marijuana stench in his room.

As she tossed her robe over the back of a deck chair, her fingers touched its pocket and felt the envelope. It held the letter from some lying insect named Caswell. She had read it several times and knew it almost verbatim. A damned fabrication. Not a word of it true. Totally out of character. Although it was postmarked New York City, it bore no return address. She had called Information, asking for Martin Caswell's telephone number. There was no listing in the Manhattan directory under that name.

It made her so darn mad. Very few Arcadia stockholders knew Dan Hedrik personally. They had no way to judge the letter's veracity. If Dan agreed, she herself would be willing to sign a statement for publication, denouncing the falsehood and demanding proof.

She descended the tile steps into the pool, clutching the handrail. Her bones were now too brittle to risk slipping. It had been years since she had used the diving board. She swam the length of the pool, a slow dog paddle, breathing hard. She climbed aboard the inflated canvas float, lying supine, drifting, eyes closed against the bright glare of sun, her body absorbing its warmth.

She felt drowsy. Rereading the Logan Stern novel in bed had kept her awake until three A.M. She kept thinking of her role in the new film, playing that imperious old lady of the Romanoff court. Instinct told her that Dan had made a wise move. She agreed completely about the book's cinematic potential.

She thought she heard a sound. The faint bubbling of water beneath her. She started to raise her head, and the canvas float suddenly tilted sideways, sliding her into the water. At the same instant something twisted into her hair with implacable

139

power, pulling her head below the surface before she could take a breath.

Kate's heart lurched painfully. She was confused, disoriented. Everyone knew that she hated practical jokes. Horseplay was for adolescents. And then, in the space of a single heartbeat, she knew with a chilling certainty that this was no joke. Panic numbed her senses. In the magnification of wavering blue-green water her blurred vision caught a flash of some monster creature.

Frail, defenseless, she pulled weakly at the pitiless claws tangled in her hair. Her lungs seemed to collapse. Spots flecked before her eyes. Dizziness pressed close. Her locked throat made whimpering sounds. With veins bulging in her neck, she knew that she could hold out no longer. She was going to die and she could not understand why.

Her mouth opened, an involuntary reflex, gulping for air. There was no air. Only water. It flooded into her lungs. Her ears roared and then, mercifully, darkness engulfed her. Darkness and oblivion. Kate Rennie went flaccid and began to sink.

Al Clinton surfaced for a moment, took a deep breath and followed her down, his palm flat against the victim's skull. Finally he released her, kicked once, and broke into the air again. Below, dappled by sunlight, he saw the lifeless shimmering figure, white hair streaming.

He was satisfied that Kate Rennie was dead. Not a mark on her. No bruises, no contusions. A perfectly executed trashing. He examined his hands and wrists. The skin remained unbroken. They would find no traces of alien tissue under Rennie's fingernails.

He swam to the edge of the pool and pulled himself onto the apron in a single muscular surge. He looked at the woman's towel and shook his head. Too dangerous. They might send it to the lab and find strange hairs. He used his undershirt instead. Not very effective, but good enough. He glanced at his waterproof Rolex. The whole operation had taken less than ten minutes.

Slacks, shirt, and loafers were behind the tall hedge where

he'd left them. He dressed quickly, rolling the wet undershirt into his pocket. He went back to the pool for a last check. He saw that the back of her neck had darkened with purplish blood. What the hell! Old people have problems. She might have suffered a sudden seizure. Or cramps. Or a fainting spell. Maybe even a heart attack He understood vaguely that after a while internally generated gases would float her to the surface.

He clamped a pair of dark aviator glasses to the bridge of his nose, then attached the false moustache and sideburns. He peered through the hedges in all directions, saw no one in sight. He crossed the lawn and walked two blocks to the stolen car.

After driving carefully for several miles, he abandoned the car on a deserted side street. His pulse was even. During the operation it had accelerated only slightly. On his way to a bus stop he discarded the sunglasses and dropped them into a trash basket. Further along, he removed the moustache and sideburns, tossing them into a sewer opening. Crude disguises, he thought, but effective.

Mr. Egan would be pleased with the way he had managed it.

*   *   *

When the Arcadia limousine pulled up under the portico, Dan Hedrik climbed out and said to the driver, "About half an hour, Ben. Maybe a bit longer. Keep it parked here in the shade so you don't cook. Got something to read?"

"I see a copy of *The Romanoff File* on the back shelf there."

"Help yourself. And give me your opinion."

Preoccupied, he rang the doorbell. When nobody answered, he remembered that this was the maid's day off. It was common knowledge that Kate swam every morning at eleven, but the weather had turned hot and humid, and perhaps she had decided on an afternoon dip. He circled the building, passed through the hedge opening, and spotted Kate's robe hanging over the back of a chair, her towel and wide-brimmed straw hat on the table under the candy-striped awning.

141

He turned toward the pool, smiling broadly. His heart stalled and his smile froze. Kate was floating on the surface of the water, face down, arms in front of her. Hedrik stood impaled, his face the colour of sand. Then he was sprinting, howling for Ben at the top of his lungs. He plunged into the water, a flat clumsy dive that brought him to the body. He was nudging it to the pool edge as Ben broke through the hedges. Together they lifted her onto the tiled apron.

" Quick, Ben. Through the back door. Call the police. Tell them it's an emergency, a drowning. We need oxygen and an ambulance."

Hedrik refused to believe his instincts. He saw her face, saw the cyanosis, the blue and swollen lips. Automatically he forced her jaws open and blew his own breath into her mouth. Nothing. His eyes were damp. He pounded a fist under her left breast. He turned the body over, straddling it, barely remembering what he had learned as a boy about artificial resuscitation. His splayed fingers pressed her rib cage, again and again and again.

" Come on, old girl," he whispered. " Breathe. Breathe, god-dammit, Kate, breathe."

He turned her over again, searching for some sign of life. She seemed so small now, so oddly dwindled. He felt helpless. His eyes stung. Suddenly he threw his head back and yelled blasphemously toward the sky. " Why? Why only the good ones? You up there, You know what the hell You're doing?"

Ben had returned. He gripped Hedrik's shoulders, pulling him gently away. " Easy now. It's no use. She's gone."

Dan shook his head, wordless.

They heard the wailing siren then. Brakes squealed, tires spraying gravel on the driveway. Dan Hedrik sat hunched on his heels, feeling cold and empty and oblivious of his soaking clothes and his water-filled shoes.

24

The widely separated tables at the Bankers' Club offered a reassuring measure of privacy. Which was one of the reasons Mike Ryan had selected it for lunch. And of course it was impressive, with its thirty-foot ceilings supported by ornamental columns. He had reserved a window table looking out over the harbour and the city's skyline.

He smiled at his guest and said, "May I suggest the prime ribs, Ward?"

"Fine. Very rare. Do you eat here often, Mike?"

"Only on special occasions."

"Then I'm honored. Does the menu live up to its surroundings?"

"Almost. It sustains life, though it hardly merits total concentration. Martini?"

"Please."

Mike ordered and sat back. He knew that Anson had already discussed the Bendiner holdings in Arcadia and he hoped the old man had not loused up the possibility of an acceptable deal. While Anson enjoyed moments of sharp lucidity, at other times he would lapse into wandering ambiguities. Mike continued to make small talk, watching his guest pack it away, thinking: If he's got something cooking with Julie, he sure as hell needs all the protein he can digest.

Finally, over coffee, Mike got down to business. "I understand Anson spoke to you about your shares in Arcadia."

"Anson thinks I ought to accept UMI's tender. Especially since the stock keeps falling. What's happening to it, Mike?"

"Institutional selling. A portfolio manager gets wind of his

143

colleague's transactions and figures the other chap knows something he doesn't. So he pulls out. That touches off additional selling by individuals, and pretty soon you have a full-scale rout."

" I'm losing money, Mike."

" On paper, yes. Anson was right, you know. You'd be way ahead of the game if you accepted the tender."

" Frankly, I don't think it's enough."

" Then I'm authorised to go even further. Mr. Hanna is prepared to offer you a package of UMI securities worth ten points more than Arcadia's highest price over the past two years."

" Exceeding his official offer to all the other stockholders?"

" Yes, Ward."

" Is it legal?"

" Absolutely. Because it would be a private deal, with the securities coming out of Hanna's personal holdings."

" Mike, that worries me. I'm inclined to look a gift horse in the mouth. Why is he being so generous?"

" Simply because he wants Arcadia Films so badly he can taste it. He is totally and irrevocably committed to this merger. And he's willing to throw every resource he commands into the deal."

" Any restrictions?"

" How do you mean?"

" If I accept this package, can I sell my new securities the next day?"

" Not entirely. Part of the deal involves certain unregistered shares which may not be traded for a specified time. But at the end of that period, if Hanna's record is any indication, you could probably sell the paper at a still higher price."

" Will Gregorius & Company guarantee this in writing?"

Mike chuckled. " I'm afraid not. But there is a chance that Mr. Hanna himself might buy it back."

" When?"

" After the acquisition of Arcadia, when he's in a more liquid position."

There was a long contemplative pause. " Mike, I'd like to

144

accommodate you, but I can't. You're asking me to rely on something that may or may not happen. You're handling my account, Mike. You know that I've been a seller on balance. As I told Anson, the plain fact is, I no longer wish to be in the market at all. I want out. So your Mr. Hanna can have my shares. I'll sell him Arcadia, for cash, and that position is unalterable. Providing, of course, the price is right."

" How much?"

" Twenty dollars a share."

Mike made a quick calculation and whistled. The sum was staggering. Millions. Outside of a large bundle of unregistered paper, almost all of Hanna's personal holdings had already been pledged as collateral, much of it on a margin account with Gregorius.

He said, " That's one hell of a premium, Ward."

" Perhaps. But the current price certainly doesn't reflect the company's true value."

" All I can do is transmit your proposition to Mr. Hanna. Suppose he can't handle it at this time, suppose there's a showdown for control. Would you consider voting your shares for UMI?"

" I'm an Arcadia stockholder, Mike. Part owner of the company. I have to consider its welfare. So I have to weigh all arguments on both sides."

" Fair enough. But the fact is, Ward, you don't owe that company one damn thing. Arcadia's stockholders have been shafted unmercifully by incompetent management over too many years. Executive stock options, unconscionable expense accounts, unwarranted bonuses. Ordinarily, management is entitled to its perquisites. But only if warranted by performance. And Arcadia sure as hell doesn't meet that criterion."

" The new man there, Hedrik, I get favorable vibes. He may be able to do the job on his own."

" That's a possibility, Ward. But it's a gamble. If he blows it, the company is kaput."

There was a pause. " You haven't mentioned the letter accusing Hedrik of accepting a kickback."

" Because it's only an allegation. I don't know if it's true or false. I met Hedrik a few days ago. I was favorably impressed."

" Is it possible that someone at UMI may be trying to discredit him?"

" It's possible, but I won't buy that either. I just don't know." Ryan glanced at his watch. " Ah, well, time to get back to work. I'll talk to Fred Hanna this afternoon. I'll tell him there's no alternative to a cash sale and I'll let him know your terms."

" Thanks for the lunch, Mike."

" My pleasure."

*　　　*　　　*

T. S. Worley, the assistant treasurer of Universal Media Industries, sat on the edge of a chair in the president's office, uneasily watching Fred Hanna and Robert Egan as they scanned his preliminary draft of the company's third-quarter report.

The demeanor of his two superiors did nothing to improve Worley's state of mind. He was a victim of his profession. He suffered from a duodenal ulcer and chronic constipation. Personal problems had exacerbated both conditions. In two months the mortgage on his Westport house matured and he knew that the bank would never renew at the old rate. Double maybe. This fall the twins were entering college, with no chance of scholarships, and where the hell were tuition fees coming from? At dinner last night his blood pressure had skyrocketed when Edith gave him the news. The Park Avenue dentist had botched her mouth and the new man had suggested a complete reconstruction, offering to complete the work for nine thousand, give or take a hundred. And for what? So Edith could chomp her way through an extra Danish at breakfast?

Still, he reflected gloomily, his financial problems were not unique. UMI itself was not entirely free of money problems, suffering from a liquidity problem, despite the cash generated by the new convertible preferreds.

And because the company's chief auditor had been carted off to the hospital yesterday for an emergency appendectomy, T. S.

146

Worley had been elected to face Caesar with this report. Caesar was the nickname tacked onto the boss by most of the company's hirelings. Worley knew that his own nickname, derived from his first two initials, was even less complimentary. T.S. Tough Shit Worley. And not always behind his back either. He'd be willing to bet that nobody ever treated that poet chap Eliot with such disrespect.

Hanna looked up, focusing bleak eyes on the assistant treasurer. "You sure about these figures, Worley?"

"Yes, sir. I ran them through the computer three times."

"When is it scheduled for the printer?"

"Day after tomorrow."

With a gesture of contempt, Hanna slid the report across his desk. It fell into Worley's lap, and dropped to the floor. "Rework the numbers. I want a new report within twenty-four hours."

God, Worley thought miserably, I'll be here all night.

"Something wrong, Worley?"

"I—er—sort of had plans for this evening. My wife—"

"Cancel them."

Worley swallowed. "Yes, sir."

"Do I have to spell it out for you?"

"No, sir. I know what's expected."

"All right. Get cracking."

Hanna waited until the door closed and then turned to Egan. "Think he can handle it, Bob?"

"Worley needs the job and he's a competent juggler."

"Curtis picked one hell of a time to have a gall bladder attack."

"Appendicitis."

"Whatever. When can we expect him back?"

"Couple of weeks at best."

Hanna pondered, tapping a thumb knuckle against his teeth. "Well, we've had liquidity problems before." His telephone buzzed. He reached and depressed a button. He listened, sat erect, eyes suddenly narrowed in speculation. He said, "All right. Try to get more details and call me back." He hung up

147

and stared at Egan. " That was publicity. They just heard a radio bulletin. Kate Rennie is dead."

Egan's face revealed nothing. " How?"

" Heart attack, they think. Dan Hedrik found her floating in the pool." Blunt fingers drummed the desk. " Didn't you tell me her Arcadia stock passes to her nephew?"

" Under Rennie's will, yes."

" Who's the executor?"

" Same man who drew the will. An old fart named Irving Garson, used to be Max Klemmer's lawyer. Semi-retired now."

" Will he probate the will himself?"

" His son, probably. It's a family practise. Garson and Garson."

Hanna studied Egan approvingly. " Rennie's nephew, the boy you mentioned, David Kiser, how does he feel about Arcadia?"

" I gather he has no special loyalty to the company."

" Shouldn't he be approached about a proxy?"

" It's being attended to."

Hanna's face broke into a smile. " Excellent, Robert, excellent. How long before the estate is settled?"

" That depends on Garson. A lawyer can speed up probate or he can stall for months."

" And in the meantime, who has authority to vote Rennie's shares?"

" The executor. Kiser is not the stockholder of record until probate is completed and the stock transfered to his name."

Hanna's smile vanished. " I don't like that, Bob."

" Neither do I. We're exploring remedies."

" Can we light a fire under Garson?"

" We'll sure as hell give it our best shot. I think we should retain outside counsel, some heavy gun with political clout."

" Do it. Today." As Egan rose, Hanna waved him back into the chair. He glanced at his watch. " Ryan is due here any minute. I want you to sit in." He was lost in thought for a moment. " In the meantime, I'd like you to get a signed proxy from Kiser. Just so we have it in hand, as and when required."

148

" It will be done."

" Good."

The intercom spoke, announcing Ryan's arrival. He was brought to the office without delay.

" Have you heard the bulletin?" he asked. " Kate Rennie is dead."

" We heard the bulletin a few minutes ago," Hanna said.

Mike shook his head. " Hard to believe that I had dinner with her only last week. I grew rather fond of the old girl."

Hanna looked properly solemn. " She enjoyed a long life, Mike. If you had succeeded in getting her proxy, it wouldn't be any use to us now anyway."

" Any idea who inherits her shares?"

" Leave that to Egan, Mike. We'll retain some legal talent on the Coast to look into it. How did you make out with Bendiner?"

" He's willing to sell?"

" Under the terms of our tender?"

Ryan shook his head. " He wants cash. He insists on an out-right sale."

" At the current market?" Egan asked.

" I'm afraid not. He's asking for twenty dollars a share."

A rush of blood darkened Hanna's face. " Jesus Christ!" he said thickly. " The man's a lunatic. Arcadia hasn't been up there in years."

" I know. But he's a man of strong convictions. I could not jostle him loose. He thinks that's what his shares are worth."

" What he thinks, friend, is that he has us over a barrel. Those shares are worth what the market says they're worth, not a nickel more."

" Exactly what I told him. He disagrees. He's convinced the current price doesn't represent Arcadia's true value. And he's prepared to hang on until it recovers."

" How about his proxy?"

" It's still up for grabs." Ryan shrugged. " I got the impression that he favors Arcadia's management."

" I thought you had him in your pocket."

149

" I never meant to give that impression."

Hanna turned grimly to Egan. "What do you think, Bob?"

Egan shook his head. "There's no way we could justify UMI's purchase at that price, even if the cash was available. Not when it's selling on the open market for half that amount. We could justify it neither to the board, nor the stockholders, nor the SEC."

"No way his mind can be changed, Mike?"

"I doubt it. And I'm perfectly willing to let you or Mr. Egan have a go at him."

The invitation was ignored. "His position smacks of extortion."

"Extortion?"

"Yes, damnit. Buy my shares at a premium or lose my vote to the opposition. What the hell would you call it?" He swiveled to Egan again. "Suppose I buy those shares personally, with my own funds, for my own account."

"Do you have that kind of money at hand?"

"I know where to get it. What I'm asking is whether my own stockholders could object."

"Probably not, under these circumstances," Egan told him. "Although, conceivably, some dissident stockholder with six lousy shares might hire a shyster to start a class action, claiming you seized a corporate opportunity for your own private gain. For you personally to bag a large block of Arcadia shares at the same time UMI is gearing up for a takeover would certainly raise a lot of eyebrows. And you've got to remember that Pressman over at the SEC has us under constant surveillance."

Hanna gave Pressman the finger. "Up his. Just tell me how to cover myself."

"Call a special meeting of the UMI board. Fill them in. Explain your reasons for acquiring the Bendiner shares for your personal account. Get it on the record, with full board approval."

"Okay. Set it up. And make arrangements for an early flight tomorrow morning. Vegas. Mike, contact Bendiner and tell him I accept. Sew it up." He paused. "I don't expect to borrow the full amount, so I'm buying those shares on margin. Any problem?"

"Post the shares with us, and Gregorius credits you with fifty per cent of the current market value, not what you paid for them. We'll have to raise the balance."

"Can Gregorius handle it?"

"We're not permitted to borrow more than twenty times our net capital. Like everyone else, we're currently borrowed to the hilt. I'll have to brace Anson for additional funds to improve our position. One way or another, we'll manage."

"Will Anson balk?"

"He always balks, and he always comes through."

"Then it's settled. It's not what I wanted, but under the circumstances I suppose it's the best we can do."

Mike nodded. "We'll need a copy of your third-quarter report. When will it be out?"

"It's in the works now. Unfortunately, our chief financial officer is in the hospital for emergency surgery, so there may be a slight delay."

"How does it look."

"Per share earnings up eleven per cent, despite some dilution." Hanna frowned. "Something troubling you, Mike?"

"As a matter of fact, yes. This is a sensitive area, Fred, and I want to meet it head-on. For better or worse, the reputation of Gregorius & Company is now inextricably linked to the welfare of UMI. During my stay on the Coast, a very heavy amount of short selling hit Arcadia Films. It knocked the stock out of bed and started an avalanche. Seems like everybody wanted out at the same time. I came back here to find that investigators from the SEC and from the Exchange were examining our books. Luckily, Gregorius is clean." He looked Hanna squarely in the eye. "Have you any idea who's responsible?"

Hanna's face was stony. "If this is an accusation, I resent it."

"That doesn't answer the question."

"I will not demean myself with a plea of innocence."

Egan moved smoothly into the breach. "We're well aware

151

of what's been happening, Mike, and we're deeply concerned. UMI did not acquire its position in Arcadia just to see our investment go down the drain. They've been auditing our books all week too, and they haven't found one goddamn thing out of line. They've tied up our records and our accounting department. Which is another reason we're late with our third-quarter report. If G. G. Pressman continues this harassment, he's begging for trouble. Mr. Hanna is not without influence in Washington."

Mike shook his head. "That's a bad hand, Egan. Throw it in. No administration would try to discipline Pressman just for doing his job. The man has been around D.C. longer than the President." He glanced at Hanna. "If I've misjudged the situation, Fred, and offended you, I apologize."

Hanna waved his hand magnanimously. "Apology accepted. On second thought, I'm glad you brought it up. Only way to clear the air. Incidentally, there was considerable buying of Arcadia for two days. Did any of that clear through your office?"

"Yes. About ten thousand shares."

"Is it privileged information, or can you tell me who was running against the tide?"

"No secret. Peter Sternbach was on a buying spree for the Croesus Fund. Clearing through other brokers also." Ryan was sharply alert for signs, but Hanna and Egan remained deadpan. No tightening of muscles, not even a flicker of the eye.

Hanna said mildly, "I thought Pete had completed his buying some time ago."

"He had. But at these prices he saw a bargain."

"Smart, smart, he'll clear a packet."

"And he may have bought at the very bottom, too. The price seems to have stabilized." Ryan leaned forward. "There's a point I think should be emphasized, Fred. Once Bendiner's shares are in your account, if Arcadia should drop again, we'll have to call on you for additional margin. With a block that size, you can be hit hard. And Gregorius cannot carry you. The regulations on that are strictly enforced."

152

"I understand, Mike. No problem." He stood up and offered his hand. "Keep Bendiner on ice for me. I'll be back before the end of the week to wrap it up."

Ryan said, "I'll talk to the loan officer at our bank first thing tomorrow morning."

With the sound of the door closing, Hanna's expression suffered a radical change. His smile vanished, a vein bulged in his temple, and he spoke through clenched teeth. "Sternbach! That goddamn miserable conniving opportunistic sonovabitch! He guessed what we were trying to do and he moved in to take advantage. I'll have his balls. So help me, I'll break that bastard if it's the last thing I do."

Egan said placatingly, "Take it easy, Fred. We haven't been hurt too badly. Remember, we had him in here and asked him, as a favour, to use his resources in accumulating Arcadia. We needed his buying power, and ultimately his proxy. We still need it. Only now it's even bigger."

Hanna sat back, eyes narrowed. He locked his fingers and cracked the knuckle joints. A man of mercurial changes, the barracuda smile was back again.

*　　*　　*

In a cab, heading back to his office, Mike Ryan was thinking about the source of Hanna's loan for the Bendiner shares. He'd heard rumours about the Las Vegas connection, that they had supplied Hanna with his initial stake. So he was going back to them again. With their murderous interest rates and all the risks it involved. The syndicate gave you no flexibility, no extensions. Once you were committed, you could neither renege nor disavow. Not even a legal bankruptcy could erase the debt. And the consequences for default were often incurable.

But then, Mike told himself philosophically, Fred Hanna had always been a gambler. And a survivor . . .

153

25

Dan Hedrik's desk was piled high with messages, but his
first priority was a call to Paul Slater, the New York
lawyer retained by Arcadia to block the takeover.

"Been trying to reach you since yesterday," Slater said.

"I know. But I just got back from another session at Police
Headquarters. It's about Kate Rennie, isn't it?"

"Yes. Reports here are sketchy. Fill me in, Dan." Slater
listened to a recap. "Okay. So you found the body. And you say
the cops were skeptical. Skeptical about what?"

"There was a letter in Kate's robe, signed by some character
named Martin Caswell, accusing me of taking a fifty-thousand-
dollar kickback from Logan Stern on the sale of his book."

"*What*?" Incredulity sharpened Slater's voice. "That's bullshit! Who the hell is Caswell?"

"I don't know. I never heard of him. He apparently had the
whole list of Arcadia stockholders and the letter was widely
circulated."

"Are you telling me the cops out there think maybe Rennie
kicked up a fuss about the letter and you took a crack at her?"

"Not in so many words. They were very polite, Paul, but
they have to cover every angle."

"Were there any signs of violence?"

"None visible, not a mark. They're satisfied now. My driver
was with me when I got to Kate's house, and according to the
medical examiner, she had already been dead for several hours.
She may have suffered a cramp or a dizzy spell while swimming.
She was on medication for high blood pressure."

"Now look, Dan, this may not be the right time to discuss

business. I know how you felt about the old lady. But things are moving fast. You have an annual stockholders' meeting coming up. UMI will sure as hell try to capitalize on Rennie's death. She was on our side. So I have to know what happens to her stock."

" It goes to her nephew. Young fellow named Kiser."

" Who's the executor?"

" Kate's lawyer. Irving Garson."

" Jesus! Is he still alive?"

" And kicking. I'll call Garson this afternoon and try to get some details."

" Do that, Dan. It's important. Maybe even vital. Now, how about those Bendiner shares? Did your man Landry get in touch with Bendiner in Florida?"

There was a change in Hedrik's voice, a note of tension. " Landry missed him. It seems Bendiner was in New York on business. I expected a call from Landry two nights ago. The call never came. I tried to reach him this morning, but he didn't answer the phone. I asked the motel people to check his room. It was empty. His bed hadn't been slept in. But his rental car was still parked out front. I don't mind telling you, Paul, I'm worried sick."

" Could he be shacked up with some little pumpkin he found in a local bar?"

" No way." Hedrik was emphatic. " Not Ross Landry. He's a happily married man."

" You're sure of that?"

" Absolutely. I've known Ross for a long time."

" Two days," Slater paused. " I understand your concern, Dan." There was a moment of silence. " I gather this Ocala Beach is a small community with limited law enforcement. Here's what I'm going to do, Dan. I have a connection at the D.A.'s office here. I'll have him call the Attorney General in Tallahassee. A little pressure from the state capitol should get the local law moving. In the meantime, I want you to call the sheriff down there and report a missing person. Where was Landry staying?"

" The Everglades."

" All right. Now let me have a brief profile on Kate Rennie's nephew."

" David Kiser. Formerly out of Haight-Ashbury. Something of a misfit. Kate asked me one time if I could put the boy to work at the studio. I showed him around. But as a card-carrying member of the lost generation, a steady job, application, learning a trade, was the last thing on his mind."

" She had no other relatives?"

" None. The boy's parents are dead."

" Dan, can you take the kid in tow, keep him out of Fred Hanna's hands? I'd hate to see UMI get a lock on those Rennie shares."

" I'll try, Paul. Kiser hasn't been in L.A. for some time. But with all the publicity about Kate's death, we expect him to show up for the funeral. He probably knows he's a legatee and he'll want to claim his rights."

" Naturally. What I want you to do, Dan, and this is important, ask Garson to drag his feet on probate. As executor, he controls that stock until it's legally distributed to the legatee. Would he be sympathetic to our cause?"

" He knows Kate's intentions and he'd do nothing to obstruct them."

" If he puts it on a back burner until after the proxy vote at your annual meeting, we're in clover."

Hedrik sounded dubious. " I know Irving Garson, Paul. The old boy won't go for anything out of line."

" Listen to me, Dan. An estate this size, he can legitimately dawdle for months. The executor has wide responsibilities. He has to assemble assets, have them appraised, notify creditors, and give them plenty of time to file their claims. He may even have to liquidate securities to pay debts. And the IRS needs time to audit transactions for tax purposes. The state people too, reviewing every last item before final distribution is made to the nephew. So if Garson moves with all deliberate caution, it could take us beyond the date of Arcadia's annual meeting and the proxy count."

" Would you talk to him on the phone, Paul?"

" If you want me to. But Garson is an old hand. He knows what's involved and he might resent outside interference."

" Sound him out anyway. I'll do the same. Incidentally, how goes it with our proxy solicitors?"

" We lost some votes because of the stock's recent decline. Otherwise, not bad. But keep your fingers crossed. Stockholders are allowed to change their minds right up to the last minute before a vote is cast. I'm afraid that Caswell letter may hurt us."

" Shit!"

" My sentiments exactly. Listen, this is a long-distance call. I'll keep in touch."

They broke the connection. Hedrik checked his personal directory and dialed a number. Irving Garson's emphysematic voice answered on the second ring.

" Irving? Dan Hedrik. Sorry to bother you at home."

" Where else would I be at this hour? I tried to call you yesterday. Didn't you get my message?"

" It's probably here on my desk. I was delayed by the local constabulary."

" Ah, Dan. Poor Kate. An old cocker like me, what I went through in my life, the people I lost. I cried all night. You found the body, Dan. It must have been terrible. What happened, a heart attack?"

" They don't think so. Leg cramp maybe. It happens to older people."

" I know, I know. My left calf, right now, it's like a knot."

Hedrik pictured the man. Slight, bony, bald as glass, half mummified, nattily dressed, with white tufted eyebrows over a jutting nose, the tired veteran of many courtroom battles, an ancient relic who tottered into his office two days a week to badger his son and goose the stenographers.

" Irving," Hedrik said, " I need some information."

" So ask, my friend. If it doesn't violate a privileged communication, you've got it."

" Kate told me you drew her will."

157

" It's no secret. There were two witnesses."

" I understand her nephew inherits everything, including her Arcadia stock."

" David Kiser, yes."

" Outright? Or in trust?"

" Now you're skirting close to borderline."

" Irving, please. Kate is dead. When you file her will for probate, it becomes a matter of public record."

" What have I got here, an amateur lawyer? You're right, Danny boy. And already I think I know the problem. You're worried about that Fred Hanna, the big-shot gonif. It's coming up a proxy fight, no? You're caught in a bear hug. So Kate's stock is important. Well, my friend, what can I tell you. The boy inherits, lock, stock, and barrel, no strings. I told Kate it was a mistake, but she thought she could straighten him out. And where is he now? In a commune someplace, with the hairy ones and fat little cupcakes, playing house and guitars and smelling like yaks. If he's sealed off from the news, I will maybe have to hire a shamus to locate the momser."

" Don't worry about it, Irving. He'll show up."

" In time for the funeral, I hope. You want I should make the arrangements?"

" The studio will handle it. Unless you have something in mind."

" No, no. Just remember, Max has a nice little mausoleum in Forest Lawn, special accommodations for two. Please let me know about the services, where and when. And have them send all bills to my office."

" Of course. You're Kate's executor."

" Who else? Young Kiser maybe, with the vacuum between his sinus and his scalp?"

" Will you handle probate yourself, or will you retain outside counsel?"

" Outside counsel? In a pig's valise, Danny. What am I, a philanthropist? This is a big estate. Why should we pay legal fees to a stranger? I still have an office. My son Sheldon is a member of the California bar. Almost as smart as his old man, too. And he knows the routine. Even in sorrow a man should be practical."

"Would you do the studio a favor, Irving?"

"First tell me what you want."

"We'd like you to move slowly. Don't shoot this one through probate. Keep it cooking until after the annual stockholders meeting."

Silence. Then a hoarse prolonged cackle. "I know what you have in mind, Danny. For the record, we never hurry. Lawyers charge by the hour. Who gave you this idea? Who's calling the signals for Arcadia?"

"Mr. Paul Slater, Esquire."

"The professor?"

"He teaches classes too."

"You're using your noodle, Danny. You got yourself a good one. Help him along. You see Fred Hanna, keep your back to the wall."

26

When his plane landed at Los Angeles International, Kevin Anthony Duke III went directly to the Avis desk, took delivery of a previously reserved compact, and drove to the Holiday Inn. He unpacked his flight bag, set his alarm clock, stretched out on the bed, and an hour later, fully refreshed, was on his way to the Sherman Oaks residence of Logan Stern.

He had phoned ahead and was expected. The house, a split level on three acres of prime real estate, was part granite, part redwood. For a best-selling novelist, Logan Stern lived comfortably but not luxuriously. He asked for Duke's ID card, inspected it, and led the way to his workroom, a soundproofed studio above the garage. It contained the essential paraphernalia of his trade—electric typewriter, dictating machine, filing cabinets, and floor-to-ceiling reference books.

Stern was a rumpled, ungainly man, crinkle-eyed, with a shock of undisciplined hair.

" What's this all about, Mr. Duke?" he asked.

" May I say first, sir, that I've read several of your novels and enjoyed them immensely. I understand you're now finishing the screenplay of your latest for Arcadia Films, and I'm looking forward to seeing the picture."

Stern sucked on an empty meerschaum pipe. " Okay. That covers the amenities. Now tell me why my working schedule is being interrupted."

Duke smiled amiably at the man's blunt approach. " It concerns Arcadia. You must, of course, be aware of a pending proxy fight for control of the company."

Stern nodded. " I read a number of business publications. But I own no stock in Arcadia, no stock in Universal Media, so the purpose of your visit still eludes me."

" I'm coming to it now, sir. We at the Securities and Exchange Commission are charged with monitoring takeover situations, looking for improprieties."

" Improprieties are not uncommon in the business world, Mr. Duke."

" Exactly. Misconduct is what begat our agency."

" Begat." Stern chuckled. " First time I ever heard that word used outside of a church sermon. All right, Mr. Duke the third, what improprieties are you looking for here?"

" An alleged impropriety, sir. It involves circumstances surrounding the sale of your novel *The Romanoff File* to Arcadia Films."

" I take it you're talking about a letter accusing me of paying Dan Hedrik fifty grand as a cash kickback for negotiating a favorable contract."

" I see you know about that."

" Obviously. A couple of my friends, Arcadia stockholders, received the letter."

160

" It doesn't disturb you?"

" Not in the least," Stern said equably. " It's a fucking lie."

" You will agree, though, that half a million dollars for the screen rights to a single book is a very substantial sum of money."

" For the screen rights, Mr. Duke, plus the additional right to produce, reproduce, exhibit, and transmit the picture by any and all devices which now exist or which through man's infinite ingenuity may be conceived or invented at any time in the future. And that is one hell of a substantial licence. Okay, I'm not complaining. I didn't have to accept the offer. I could have told them to take their money and shove it where the sun never shines. The point is, I could have gotten at least that much from one of the majors. Perhaps more."

" But you did sign with Dan Hedrik."

" Because I know the man's work and I admire it. There was no need for a payoff. Have you met Dan Hedrik?"

" Not yet."

" Then let me tell you something. If I had suggested a kick-back, much as Hedrik wanted the property, he would have walked away from the deal."

" For the record, you deny the accusation."

" Totally, emphatically, categorically. Why should I, a humble struggling author, present fifty thousand dollars to a top corporate executive?"

" A small sum, considering the clause in your purchase agreement giving you a percentage of the film's gross earnings instead of net receipts."

Logan Stern sighed. " I'm not going to argue the economics of this deal. Or its propriety. You think you have a case, you can prove chicanery, go ahead and try."

" We have no doubt about the chicanery, Mr. Stern. Not yours, probably, or Dan Hedrik's. I can't go into details at this time. But we still have to gather evidence. You received a check from Arcadia Films. What did you do with the money?"

" What one usually does with money. I put it in the bank."

" Do you have more than one account?"

"One checking account, three savings."

"Deposits in any foreign banks?"

"The Swiss are now charging negative interest, Mr. Duke. You have to pay *them* to hold *your* money. Not my kind of an arrangement."

"Besides Switzerland?"

"Not likely. I once had an account in Mexico—and they devalued the peso. Bang! Fifty per cent of my equity down the tube. I still have faith in the U.S. A waning faith, but I don't see any alternative."

"Would you object to showing me your bank statements?"

"Strenuously."

"We could arrange for an IRS audit that would compel you to produce all your financial records."

"They audit me every year anyway. Routinely."

"This would not be a routine examination."

Logan Stern stared balefully at his inquisitor, mouth pursed. He reached for the telephone, dialed, and said, "Mr. Brewer, please." He identified himself. "Thurman? There's a little problem here. I'm sitting with a young gent from the Securities and Exchange Commission. His ID checks out. Investigating that kickback crap I mentioned to you last night. He wants a look at my bank records. . . . No, he doesn't have a warrant. Just an exploratory examination. Do I co-operate or not?" He listened, and said, "Wait a minute. I'll ask him." He looked up. "What division are you with?"

"Enforcement Branch."

"The name of your boss?"

"Mr. Gary George Pressman."

Stern repeated the information into the mouthpiece. "Okay, Thurman." He hung up. "My lawyer, Mr. Duke. I pay him for his advice, so I may as well take it. He says I should co-operate." Stern rose, went to one of the filing cabinets, and removed a thick folder.

"It's all here. Statements, stubs, canceled checks, passbooks, everything. All prepared for my accountant. You may use that table in the corner. Spread yourself and have a good time."

Duke sorted papers with a quick, practised eye, reconciling deposits against withdrawals, scratching hieroglyphics, noting dates. When at last he looked up, shuffling the documents into a neat pile, Stern said, "Happy now?"

"Very happy. I like my work."

"You're a lucky man. I can't say the same about writing. Reading is easier. Did you find anything?"

"May we put this on tape?"

"Let's hear the questions first. My answers may nullify the need."

Duke nodded. "You have denied any complicity. Can you support that denial?"

"Why the hell should I? What happened to the principle of presumed innocence?"

Duke remained unruffled. "It still exists, sir."

"Then observe it, or show me why I should continue with this inquisition."

Duke tapped one of the papers. "On August fourteenth of this year, several days after you deposited to your account in the Los Angeles Trust a check from Arcadia Films, you withdrew from the same bank the sum of fifty-four thousand dollars. Would you tell me how those funds were employed?"

Logan Stern looked surprised. He studied Duke with an expression of half-suppressed irony. "Is it the government's contention that I have to account for the way I spend my own money?"

"No, sir. Not after you've paid your taxes. Under the circumstances, however, it might save everyone a lot of bother if you came up with an acceptable explanation."

"An explanation that can be corroborated?"

"Corroboration would help."

Stern sat quietly for a moment, pondering, looking inward. Finally he sighed, then spoke in a carefully controlled voice. "Let me recite a little history for you, Mr. Duke. You may have been too young at the time to appreciate its significance. There was a period some years back when this country of ours was in a malodorous ferment. A sick and shameful time in

163

which our government played a most ignoble role. I am referring to hearings held by the House Un-American Affairs Committee. Stupid, venal, self-serving officials were accepting base-
less accusations by a rancid right-wing organisation known as
Red Channels. Fear was rampant. Industry executives had no
control over their sphincters. Actors, writers, artists, employees
all across the land were being pressured into signing loyalty
oaths.

" I was at the beginning of my career, a young writer full of
ideals. I was not a communist. I was not even a sympathizer.
I loathed everything communism stood for—the regimentation,
the debasement of human dignity, the loss of creative freedom.
But as a matter of principle, I refused to sign. I was blacklisted.
I became an economic pariah. You see, Mr. Duke, I am not a
political animal. All I wanted to do was write. I wrote books
and short stories. But I could not get published. There were
writers, far more gifted than myself, who were unable to support their families. We paid a heavy price for preserving our
self-respect. The point I am making is this, Mr. Duke. I'm
older now. Maybe not wiser, but older. I no longer have the
stomach for controversy, not if it can be decently avoided.
Especially in this case, since you seem to be making an unjustifi-
able assumption about a certain withdrawal of money from my
bank account."

" I think you're being wise, Mr. Stern."

" I don't give a flying fuck what you think, Kevin Duke the
third. I just want to clear the air and get you off my back. And
off the back of Dan Hedrik, too. There's one man who's entitled to a clean slate. Am I clear?"

" You are, sir."

" All right, then. Hear this. I have a hobby. At one time it
was an addiction. Now it's simply a form of recreation. I like
to gamble. High-stakes gin, the crap tables at Las Vegas, sports
contests, whatever. So I decided to celebrate the film sale of
The Romanoff File by spending a weekend at Vegas, indulging
my hobby. I had ten thousand in cash available from a previous
excursion. Net profit. My tax return for last year will show

that it was declared. I lost that ten and then went into the hole for an additional fifty-two. I quit, signed a note, and subsequently withdrew enough money to pay the debt."

" In cash?"

" That's right."

" You withdrew fifty-four. What about the remaining two thousand?"

" Pocket money. Any objections?"

" No, sir. You owed the debt to one specific creditor?"

" The casino at Cinderella's World. There were at least twenty witnesses. Since I never anticipated any problem, I didn't make notes of their names. But I do have receipts from American Express for accommodations at the hotel. Do you want to start over again and put it all down on tape?"

" Not necessary." Duke smiled. " I'm sorry I had to trouble you, Mr. Stern. On behalf of myself and my employers, I'd like to thank you for your co-operation."

" You're doing your job, sonny. It may even be an important job. If you locate this fellow Caswell, the man who wrote the letter, I'd appreciate his address. Are you looking for him?"

" We are."

" Any leads?"

" Not yet."

" That doesn't surprise me. I don't believe the man exists. Will you be calling on Dan Hedrik?"

" Those were my instructions. Although I'm not sure it's necessary now."

" Then you had better make arrangements. God himself couldn't get past the studio gate without a pass."

" If I've said anything at all to offend you, Mr. Stern, I apologize."

" I'm not a sensitive man. No need to apologize."

" Would you shake my hand?"

" Are you carrying a communicable disease?"

" No, sir."

" Then why the hell not." He grinned hospitably and squeezed the young man's palm.

165

27

A solemn-faced David Kiser sat in a front row of the chapel
and listened to Dan Hedrik delivering the eulogy for his
Aunt Kate. Under instructions from Al Clinton, Kiser had submitted to the ministrations of a barber. His hair and beard were
neatly trimmed and he wore a dark suit of conventional cut.

Behind him sat a sprinkling of faded luminaries. Outside,
the morbidly curious had gathered, familiar with Kate Rennie
only through revivals and late-night reruns on television. She
had left specific instructions in her will. She wanted no
valedictory from any cleric who had never known her in life.
And no viewing of the remains. She had requested a simple
service with no cortege to the mausoleum at Forest Lawn. The
studio had arranged for a gathering of friends and associates
at her place of residence.

In some remote and detached way, David Kiser understood
that Aunt Kate's death was a landmark event in his own life.
She had always been a safe haven, warm, concerned, affectionate. Now she, too, was gone, the last of his family, and he was
alone. Suddenly his eyes filled and there was a fullness in his
throat. He was not sure whether these feelings were for himself
or for Kate.

He felt the presence of Al Clinton, seated next to him. He
was not really alone. The thought was instantly comforting. Al
was more than a close friend. Al sustained him. Al was a tower
of strength. And smart too. Al knew all the angles, knew how
to protect his interests. And philosophically compatible. They
believed in the same things.

Since living with Al, there had been no shortage of the stuff that made life bearable. Oh, maybe for a day or two because of money problems. But that was a thing of the past now. With Aunt Kate's inheritance, he could make it easy for both of them.

Hedrik was still talking, but David had lost the thread. He was thinking of the money, trying to adjust to the fact that all of a sudden he was rich. He had no idea how much was involved. Al had said the estate would be much larger if Kate had sold her Arcadia stock years ago.

I'll have to rely on Al for advice, he thought. Al doesn't trust these establishment clowns. Especially Kate's lawyer. Greedy pricks, Al called them, out to grab what they could for themselves. They'll milk the estate dry if we give them half a chance. Instinctively he moved closer to his friend, reassured by the touch of Al's shoulder.

It was Al who had heard about Kate's death and had insisted on decking him out in these junior Chamber of Commerce threads, borrowing the money from somewhere. "You gotta look like a responsible citizen, Davy," Al had said. "Don't give the bastards a chance to pull a fast one."

"A fast one like what, Al?"

"Like saying you're incompetent to handle your own dough. Trying to get a trustee appointed to dole it out in pennies."

"Can they do that?"

"They'll do anything they think they can get away with."

Last night he had slept in his old room at Aunt Kate's, with Al in the nearby guest room. Boy, this gang at the funeral were sure curious about Al, trying to size him up while offering condolences, wondering about their relationship. Especially Hedrik, and that old lawyer fart Garson, so creepy solicitous, all the time prying and snooping. He had played it cool, as if he hadn't heard the questions, following Al's instructions.

He remembered the caterer arriving just before Al and he had left for the chapel. "You see," Al had told him. "The enemy has taken charge already. You're the relative, and they don't consult you about a thing. Just like you're stupid or something. Don't worry, Davy, our time will come."

167

He emerged from his reverie with a start. Hedrik had concluded his eulogy. The services were over and people were shuffling to their feet. Kiser took one last quick look at the casket before Hedrik clasped his arm and started herding him out to one of the limousines. He reached back, hanging on to Al's sleeve, pulling his friend along.

There were four of them in the lead car driving back to the house, he and Al, Hedrik and Garson. The studio had posted a security guard at the gate.

He had talked to Al about the house last night, Al saying it might be a gas to live here for a month or two before selling the joint, just the two of them, rattling around like a pair of lords. They could stash away a lot of horse here. The cops would never raid this joint.

He saw that a number of mourners had already preceded them. Freeloaders lined up at the food table and the bar. Just like it's a party. I could use a blast myself, David thought, but Al says no drinking. Have to stay sober and dignified. He stood in a corner, with Al at his side, accepting expressions of sorrow. And then they were joined by the old mummy again, Kate's executor.

Garson said, "We have a lot to talk about, Davy. Decisions to make. Can you be at my office tomorrow morning, about eleven."

"Sure. I hope you don't mind if I bring Al. Al's sort of my advisor."

"Oh?" Garson studied Al for the hundredth time. "You've had experience in these matters, Mr. Clinton?"

"I read a lot, Counselor. And I use my head."

"Did you know Kate Rennie?"

"No, sir. I understand she was an extraordinary woman."

"That she was. A lovely and fascinating lady. You saw some of her pictures maybe?"

"On television. Look, Mr. Garson, Davy and I have plans. We don't want to hang around L.A. too long. Davy would appreciate it if you would move ahead full steam, wind up the estate fast."

Garson arched his brows, deepening the wrinkles in his fore-head. He spread his hands. "Well now, young fella, this is a very complicated business. Not just a couple of hundred dollars in a local savings bank. There are probate procedures, property appraisals, securities, real estate, debts, creditors, estate taxes, court orders, whatnot. It takes time. It can't be rushed."

Al Clinton smiled, a mechanical smile, square teeth exposed. He jabbed two stiff fingers into Garson's narrow ribs in what was supposed to be a jocular prod. The elderly lawyer reared back with a strangled gasp and steadied himself against a chair.

Clinton said, still smiling, "Don't patronize us, old boy. I know something about lawyers. They like to sit on their hands, making everything into a big deal, so they can boost their fees. Just don't waltz us around, okay?"

Garson faced Kiser, suppressing indignation with an effort. "What's the matter, David? You don't have a tongue of your own? You need a spokesman? This fellow is your guru or something?"

"He's my friend, Mr. Garson. He has my best interests at heart."

"And I don't, Davy? Me? Irving Garson? More than half a century practising law, trusted by my clients, trusted by Kate, never once accused of finagling, and now suddenly I'll shirk my responsibilities? Let me tell you something, Davy. I don't need this. I have half a mind to resign as executor. Except I owe it to your Aunt Kate. She was not only a client, she was my friend." Garson shook his head sadly. "Hardly in her grave and already I'm in an argument about her estate. With a stranger yet. It makes me feel ashamed."

Al Clinton said, "Okay. We get the message. You're a pillar of society. A man of integrity. Over fifty years of experi-ence in the law trade. So tell us why you can't just file the goddamn papers and get the judge's signature and pay off the grocery bill and turn over to Davy whatever belongs to him. All wrapped up in two or three weeks."

Garson exhaled a sigh of infinite patience. "You want a for instance, young fella? I'll give you a for instance. Take this

169

house. Does Davy want to keep it and live here? Of course not. It costs a fortune to maintain. It's a white elephant. So we have to find a buyer. Such a prospect does not walk in off the street. I cannot close out the estate until it's sold. How else would I know how much taxes to pay? And the creditors. They must be given plenty of time to file their claims. The tax people must audit all the transactions. I never found a way to hurry them along."

"There's money in the bank, isn't there?"

"Certainly."

"Save that for the creditors. How about Miss Rennie's securities, her stock in Arcadia Films? Why can't that be turned over to Davy?"

There was a microsecond of comprehension in Garson's eyes, a speculative flicker instantly covered. "You don't understand. We have to go through formalities. The court has to approve my appointment as executor."

"How long should it take?"

"This is not a hundred-yard dash, young fella. It depends on the judge."

"I hear it depends on the court clerk." Al Clinton rubbed the ball of his thumb over an index finger. "A little baksheesh, something under the table, so he'll march into chambers and shove papers under the judge's nose for a signature."

"You want me to offer bribes?"

"Come off it, Counselor. A gratuity, a tip. It's done all the time."

"Not by me." Garson appealed to Kiser. "What's the rush, Davy? You're pressed for cash? You need a loan?"

"I need what belongs to me."

Garson nodded slowly, his eyes hooded. "Let me explain something. As your Aunt Kate's executor, it might be my best judgment to sell all of her securities on the open market."

"Kate Rennie is dead," Clinton said harshly. "Those stocks were left to Davy. He decides what to do with them. You can't ignore his wishes without facing a lawsuit."

Garson surveyed him benignly. "So. You had advice from a lawyer already?"

"We sure as hell can get a lawyer if you make it necessary."

Garson shook his head as if in embarrassment. "Please. This is not the time or the place for an argument. Tomorrow, in my office, we talk about it."

"Sure." Clinton's meaningless smile was back. "No hard feelings, Counselor. Shake."

Irving Garson took the younger man's hand. His answering smile, at first tentative, suddenly turned into a grimace of shock as he tried vainly to withdraw his fingers. He gasped, his face the colour of oatmeal. Al Clinton kept smiling, and after another moment of pressure, he released the old lawyer.

Garson rubbed his knuckles. "Jesus!" he said mildly. "That's some pair of pliers you got there, young fella. You don't know your own strength."

Al Clinton took Kiser's arm. "I'm hungry, Davy. Let's get some food. See you in the morning, Counselor." He nudged Kiser toward the caterer's table.

Garson was still examining his fingers when Dan approached. "What was that all about, Irving?"

"You saw?"

"That's why I came over."

"Come into the study, Daniel. We have to talk. I have some news for you. I don't think you'll like it."

28

After Sheriff Ben Nestor of Palm County, Florida, had finished his inquiries at the motel, he climbed into his patrol car and left Ocala Beach, heading toward the Bendiner lodge out on Route 29. Both calls reporting a missing person had come in earlier that morning. One from a corporate wheel in

Hollywood; the second from the Attorney-General's office in Tallahassee. Nestor did not personally know the assistant A.G., but the man's voice had been crisp, authoritative, and urgent.

Odd, Nestor thought. Nobody down here had mentioned any problem. Man named Landry—Ross Landry. Movie brass. Big executive at Arcadia Films. Visiting Ocala Beach on business. Checked into the Everglades, and two days later he walks out of his motel room and disappears. Hertz rental car still parked outside his unit.

In the motel room Nestor had found Landry's luggage still on the rack, spare suit hanging in the closet, toilet articles neatly arranged on a ledge over the washbasin. No sign of illegal entry or tampering. Nobody at the motel remembered seeing Landry leave or return, but this time of year the place ran less than twenty-per cent occupancy.

The man from Hollywood, obviously concerned, had given the sheriff a detailed description of the missing executive and a brief statement of Landry's mission in Ocala Beach, with the promise of a photograph to be airmailed special delivery. As soon as it arrived, copies would be made and Nestor's deputies could show it around town. In the meantime, he would see what the lady out at The Lodge had to say.

Sheriff Ben Nestor knew most of what was happening in and around Palm County. At least where the locals were concerned. He knew that The Lodge had been vacant for years, that it had been inherited by the owner's son, chap named Ward Bendiner, and that Bendiner's wife had supervized a fairly extensive job of modernization. Bendiner himself stuck pretty close to the place, but Nestor had seen the wife several times, shopping for groceries, and once coming out of Alex Bogart's office. One of the rare ones, spectacular, and generally affordable only by very rich men.

He had mentioned her to Alex once, over coffee at the luncheonette, and learned that Bendiner was a client. Routine matters. A man with Bendiner's interests would occasionally need a local lawyer.

Nestor had been a year ahead of Alex in high school and they had played together on the school baseball team. Then Alex had gone off to college and after that to law school. Nestor admired the way Alex had taken over the judge's practice. The business community here had expected Alex to head north after his father died, join one of the big law firms, or maybe even government service in Washington. But the old judge had left a ready-made practice, almost a legal monopoly, and Alex had settled in comfortably. Able and diligent and generally available, except for off-season vacations. Like now, up in the Great Lakes area, Nestor remembered Alex telling him, and then up into Canada for a couple of weeks. Nestor had no complaints about the way Alex had handled his father-in-law's estate last year, winding it up without a hitch.

He swung the patrol car off the blacktop onto the private road and drove through the gate posted with a No Trespassing sign. He parked in the driveway behind the white Mercedes. The Lodge was surrounded by palm, jacaranda and acacia trees and exuded that special aura of important money.

Nestor lumbered toward the entrance, a tall, lean, leathery man with craggy features, a blade-thin mouth, and clear slate-grey eyes. He hitched his holster off to the side and rang the doorbell. No one answered. Since the car was out front, he kept ringing. Finally he heard a woman's voice: " Okay, coming, coming . . ."

She was wearing a thin silken robe, open at the throat, her face glistening under a light sheen of oil. At the sight of Nestor's uniform and shield, one eyebrow arched inquisitively. With no conscious volition he removed his hat and introduced himself. " Sheriff Ben Nestor, ma'am."

" Sorry I kept you waiting," she said. " I've been sunbathing. Is there something I can do for you, Sheriff?"

Oh, there is, lady, he thought, there sure as hell is. But it better not happen because I might never want to go back to Lottie again. He said, " We have a missing-persons report, ma'am, and I'm making inquiries. A visitor to Ocala Beach, man named Ross Landry. Flew in from California to see your husband."

"Landry? Oh, yes. The man from Arcadia Films. He phoned here several days ago and asked for Ward—my husband. I told him that Mr. Bendiner was in New York on business. He seemed terribly disappointed, but of course he should have made an appointment before traveling all that distance."

"Did he mention the purpose of his visit?"

"Vaguely. Something to do with shares of stock. Ward seldom discusses his business affairs with me." She made a small gesture. "Excuse me, Sheriff. I've forgotten my manners. Please come in."

The room had large windows and a low ceiling with hewn beams. Indoors, she seemed more circumspect, pulling the wrapper tight.

She smiled. "I'd offer you a drink, Sheriff, but policemen never drink on duty, do they?"

"Not supposed to. Thanks anyway. Did Landry give you any indication of his plans?"

"Well, yes. As a matter of fact, he did. He drove out here the following day and asked me to call New York so that he could talk to Ward on the phone. But my husband wasn't at his hotel. I gave Mr. Landry the New York address, and when he left here my understanding was that he would be flying north that evening. Wouldn't that be the place to look for him?"

"No, ma'am. He never checked out of the motel here. His clothes are still in his room and his rental car is parked out front."

"Could he have taken a side trip somewhere—you know, just to kill time?"

"Not without a car. And he failed to make a scheduled call to his boss at Arcadia."

Cora Bendiner shrugged helplessly. "There's really nothing more I can tell you, Sheriff. I imagine he'll turn up in a day or two. People just don't disappear."

Nestor could think of no further inquiry. He thanked the woman and went back to his patrol car. Driving to Ocala Beach, he reviewed the situation. Ross Landry, he had been told, was acting as a corporate emissary. For an executive to travel some

174

three thousand miles in order to discuss a proxy vote with a stockholder underlined the importance of Landry's mission. The sheriff was not unfamiliar with the securities aspect.

Ten years earlier he had courted and married Lottie Spark-man, whose daddy owned the Ocala Beach Hardware Emporium. Tom Sparkman, a widower, owned the building, a two-story structure, with Alex Bogart's law office occupying the upper floor. Four years later, perched atop a ladder while taking inventory, an unsuspected aneurysm suddenly blew, and Tom Sparkman was dead before he toppled to the floor.

Lottie had felt incapable of operating the store. And since Ben Nestor had no inclination for a shopkeeper's career, they sold the business but kept title to the real estate, collecting rent. Nestor was mildly amused by his role as Alex Bogart's landlord.

Alex, of course, had handled the legal details. When the estate was settled, Nestor knew that Lottie's inheritance should be invested. Naïve in money matters, she had told him to do whatever he thought best. A naturally methodical man, he had asked for the appropriate literature from a regional brokerage house up in Naples. After doing his homework he drove up there on his day off, spoke to an account executive, and together they selected a modest list of securities for the Nestor portfolio. At one time he had subscribed to an investment letter, but he soon concluded that its author was a bullshit artist probably earning more money from his advisory service than he had ever made investing for his own account.

Now, back to his office, he called his man at the Naples brokerage house. "Ben Nestor, Frank. What can you tell me about Arcadia Films."

"An interesting situation, Sheriff."

"Is it a good buy?"

"You want an off-the-cuff opinion? For years it lay in the basement, a real bummer. Then lately it started to show some life on news of a takeover by Universal Media. And all of a sudden it's getting murdered by heavy selling. Recently the Croesus Fund began picking it up, and that outfit is run by one very shrewd operator. What's the stock worth? Probably more than it's selling for on the open market. Maybe even a bargain at these prices. But it's strictly a speculation, Sheriff, not your kind of merchandise. You want me to query Research at the home office?"

"Please do. How about Arcadia's management?"

"From available hearsay, the new man, Dan Hedrik, is a solid type. But he still has to prove himself. He's got a hot property in the works now that could be a big money maker."

"The name Ross Landry ring a bell?"

"Yes. He's a producer at Arcadia, been with the studio for years. Had an Oscar nomination back in '72. A Hedrik loyalist."

"Where did you get all this, Frank?"

"I'm in the business, Sheriff. I read all the releases. Look, I'm interested. Is there something in the air I ought to know about?"

"That's a switch." Nestor was amused. "Are you asking *me* for information?"

"Why not? I came down here for the climate. I'm semi-retired. None of my customers are active traders. So commission business stinks. I'm on a fixed income, more or less, and inflation is eating me alive. With a hot tip I might even take a little flier on my own."

"Keep it in the bank, Frank."

"Sure. At five and half per cent, I'm losing money without having any fun."

29

Pete Sternbach walked into the World Trade Centre and took an elevator to the one hundred and seventh floor. His guest, Liz Harmon, had arrived only minutes before. They greeted each other, and he stood back to survey her with open admiration.

"How did you manage to get a reservation at this hash-house?" she asked.

"No problem for a tycoon," he told her. "I was offered a membership when they first opened the joint."

Windows on the World was something of an exaggeration, since in reality the restaurant offered a view of only three states. From their table they could see the western sky where the falling sun had struck a purple bruise across the horizon.

"Ah," murmured Liz, "the privileges of wealth."

"It has its limitations," Pete said. "They refused to seat me last week because I wasn't wearing the proper uniform. How do you like this outfit. Raw silk. A Hong Kong tailor ran it up for thirty-six dollars and ninety-five cents in a single afternoon."

"Three hundred and ninety-five sounds more likely. Anyway, thanks for inviting me. I've been eager to sample the fare in this place. What are you asking in return?"

"The pleasure of your company."

"Don't snow me, Peter. I worked for you once, remember? The general consensus says that Pete Sternbach operates largely from ulterior motives."

He looked aggrieved. "You do me an injustice, Liz. I'm a very ordinary human-type guy."

"Oh, no. Not ordinary, not by a long shot."

"Well," he conceded, looking modestly down his nose, "maybe I have a little talent."

"More than a little."

"And luck."

"That too, of course. Whatever it takes to make money on Wall Street, luck is certainly one of the ingredients. What are you fishing for?"

"A kind word, Liz. Compassion for a lonely bachelor. Approval. Admiration. Whatever you have in stock. Take your time. No hurry. Let's order first." She had come directly from the office and wore a tailored suit, but even so, he found her more desirable than any other female gathered here and bedizined in all the narcissistic paraphernalia of high fashion.

177

Liz relished the ambience, the food, the view, the service. When the waiter finally brought coffee, Sternbach lit a long cigar, handling it with practised panache. She glanced at the discarded label.

"Monte Cristo," she said. "Made in Havana. I thought those things were embargoed. Where do you get them?"

"From one of my investors. A United States senator." He puffed contentedly. "I hear you're on the security analysts' panel at Thursday's luncheon."

"Will you be there, Pete?"

"Wouldn't miss it. I'm eager for your views on the coming bout, Universal Media versus Arcadia Films."

"You'll be disappointed. That's not my topic."

"How can you avoid it? They'll ask questions. I'll raise the subject myself if no one else does."

She studied him. "Something on your mind, Pete? Are you trying to pump me? Don't be bashful. Ask."

He looked innocent. "Just making conversation."

"Pete, Pete. The records show that your Croesus Fund has a very heavy investment in Arcadia Films. If I were to puff the company, extol its management, maybe even applaud a takeover, recommending its purchase to a group of influential security analysts, it might boost the stock. If it does, you could probably close out your position at a very handsome profit."

"Would I try to use you, Liz?"

She smiled sweetly. "Sure you would."

"But why? I really can't lose on the deal, no matter what."

"True. Still, it took courage to buy Arcadia while Fred Hanna was deliberately selling."

"You're sure it was Hanna?"

"Who else accumulated enough stock to sell short against the box on a scale that size?"

"You're guessing, then."

"An educated guess. And I think you reached the same conclusion. But you bought anyway, slowing him down, at least temporarily. Audacious, Peter. Hanna can be as mean as a grizzly with his tassel caught in a trap."

178

"Man talk, Liz? From you?"

"I'm in a man's business. Male-dominated. Doesn't Hanna worry you at all? Or his hatchet man, Egan?"

"Not enough to keep me awake. Peter the Intrepid. That's me. In my racket, investing tens of millions of other people's money, a man needs courage."

"What does it feel like, Pete?"

"All in a day's work, Liz. I worry, but I can't let it interfere with my judgment or I'd never buy anything but American Tel. Let's talk about Arcadia. I know you took a hard look at the company months ago, but you never wrote it up."

"How did you find out? Sternbach Management has an intelligence network?"

"People tell me things," he said smugly.

"I'll have to let Mike know there's a leak at the office." Sternbach laughed. Liz stared at him with dawning comprehension. "My God!" she said. "It was Ryan himself. Ryan told you." She nodded knowingly. "Of course. The Croesus Fund generates sizeable commissions for Gregorius. Part of the deal is information. So you already know that I like Arcadia's prospects under Hedrik's management."

"You see, Liz. I'm not such a devious character, after all."

"Devious enough."

"Then I'll come out in the open. At Thursday's luncheon meeting I'll stand up before our fellow analysts and I'll ask for your considered opinion of Arcadia Films."

"I'll pass, Pete."

"Why?"

"Two reasons. One, Mike's instructions. UMI may want to start buying again at the lowest possible price. Two, with Arcadia shares depressed, more unhappy stockholders may be tempted to accept UMI's tender. Gregorius works for UMI. And I work for Gregorius."

He accepted her decision gracefully. "You win. I won't ask any questions. Where would you like to go now?"

"Home. I'm a working girl, and we're under a lot of pressure at the office these days."

" I've been over the figures several times," Mike Ryan told Anson Gregorius. " Fred Hanna's purchase of the Bendiner shares for his margin account means that Gregorius will have to raise about three point five million."

The old man sat behind his desk in remote isolation, stared at Mike through half-closed eyes and made no comment.

" It's been a profitable transaction, Anson. Commissions from Bendiner on the sale, and commissions from Hanna on the purchase."

" Three point five million. So? Has our bank ever refused us credit?"

He isn't tracking, Mike thought. " The money is available, Anson. I was at the Gotham Trust this morning and Dahl okayed the loan."

" Then it's settled."

" Not quite, Anson."

Apparently the old man had forgotten the 2,000 Per cent Rule. Like most brokers, Gregorius & Company operated largely on borrowed capital. There were, however, definite limits. Stock Exchange regulations prohibited brokers from borrowing more than twenty times their net capital. And Anson knew, if he remembered anything at all, how inflexible the Board of Governors was about strict compliance.

Violating the rule could result in instant suspension. Something a firm like Gregorius could not afford at this particular time, during its takeover negotiations for UMI. Mike had carefully gone over the firm's position with its auditor. The new loan would clearly put them in violation unless Gregorius could generate additional capital. He placed the figures in front of Anson, appealing to the source.

Carefully he refreshed the old man's recollection, adding, " Under the circumstances, Anson, I'm afraid we'll have to lay an additional assessment on members of the firm."

" Which means me."

" Who else?"

" Is there an alternative?"

" Yes. Pull the chain and send Gregorius gurgling down the drain."

Anson grimaced and stroked his closed eyelids. After a moment he said, " I'll sell some bonds. I don't like them anyway." He sighed, reached for the phone, and dialed his son's extension. " Floyd, those UMI debentures in my personal portfolio, plus the telephone bonds. Take them out of the vault and bring them here to my office." His face suddenly tightened and his voice took on a sarcastic edge. "What do I want them for? I'll write you a letter. Now, goddammit, do what you're told."

Mike said, "You sure you don't want to add them to the firm's inventory?"

" No. Sell. I've been locked into that crap long enough. Sell, and credit me with a cash loan."

Mike was familiar with the securities in Anson's portfolio. " That should do it," he said.

*　　*　　*

Janey Spacek saw Floyd Gregorius emerge from his office in a sort of hobbling trot. His jaw hung slack and his face was ashen. She felt a sudden contraction of her scalp. Something was wrong, terribly wrong. She wanted desperately to follow him, to find out if there wasn't something she could do . . .

30

On Tuesday at 3:15 PM Dr. Philip Whitaker, veterinary surgeon, completed his autopsy on Long John.

Long John, a fourteen-foot alligator, had been a recent

acquisition at Sea World, the tourist attraction just south of Naples on the Gulf Coast of western Florida. Despite his massive bulk and the ferocity of his species, Long John had been a disappointment. From the date of his arrival, as he slowly emerged from the tranquiliser, he had been sluggish, apathetic, without appetite. Dr. Whitaker, a specialist in the great lizards, had been summoned for consultation. He examined Long John and diagnosed the problem as a gastrointestinal malady, probably a blockage of the colon. None of the established remedies seemed effective.

Within a week Long John was dead and Sea World ordered an autopsy. The earlier diagnosis proved correct. Dr. Whitaker found a tumorous growth in the colon that blocked proper elimination. He also found a fourteen-carat gold watch, somewhat discolored by digestive juices but still functioning. He removed his rubber gloves and brought his find to the office of Sea World's director.

"Found this in Long John's stomach, Calvin. A quartz chronometer, one of the new ones, still working."

The director, a rotund gentleman with wire-rimmed glasses, looked startled. "Good Lord, Doctor! Are you telling me that Long John dined on one of our citizens before the trappers got him?"

"Not unheard of, though the genus A. mississipiensis is not generally known to attack humans."

"They will if threatened."

"I suppose. The point is, what kind of nut would threaten a fourteen-foot alligator?"

"Not me. But then, it's not likely that I'd go wandering off into those alligator-infested swamps either. On the other hand, if some uninformed tourist chap got lost in there and spotted one of those babies and started thrashing around to put some geography between them, all that frenzied activity might be mistaken for an attack."

"It's a possibility, Calvin. Those old 'gators are not endowed with superior intelligence. They operate mostly on blind instinct."

182

The director cleared his throat before asking with obvious reluctance, "Tell me, Philip, did you—er—find any human remains in the carcass?"

"Nothing identifiable."

"Could they have been digested and passed."

"Under the circumstances, I think not."

The director idly turned the watch over and saw something that caught his interest. He took a magnifying glass from his desk and read an inscription aloud. "*R.L. from M.L.*" He pushed his chair back, frowning in concentration. "Seems to me I read about a missing person, some stranger visiting Ocala Beach . . ."

The swivel chair rocked him forward and he snatched at the telephone, giving instructions to the operator. A moment later he had his party.

"Sheriff Ben Nestor, please. Sheriff? Calvin Rood here at Sea World in Naples. I understand you're making inquiries about a missing person down there. I can't remember the name." He listened and his voice sharpened. "That's it. Landry—Ross Landry. It's possible that I have something here that may interest you."

He quickly recounted his problems with Long John, the alligator's demise, and what had been found at the autopsy. "The battery is still working, Sheriff, so the 'gator may have swallowed it quite recently." Whitaker heard the metallic crackle of a voice at the other end even though he sat three feet away from the director's phone. "Yes, of course," the director said. "I'll hold the watch for you and I'll round up the trappers." He glanced up at the vet. "Can you wait here till he arrives, Philip?" Whitaker nodded.

Calvin Rood broke the connection. His voice was oddly hushed. "The man's wife is named Margaret. *R.L. from M.L.* The initials match. Ross Landry from Margaret Landry. The sheriff is calling California to find out if she gave him a watch like this as a gift."

*　　*　　*

183

Barreling north on U.S. Highway 41, Sheriff Ben Nestor was picked up on radar and would have been cited several times had he not been driving an official car. His face was set in grim lines. The information from California described the timepiece as a twenty-fifth-anniversary gift from Landry's wife. He did not tell the distraught woman where it had been found, and in any event, it was not information to be communicated over the telephone by a stranger.

He made Naples in record time and headed straight for the director's office at Sea World. He greeted Rood and Whitaker, saw the watch, picked it up, and concluded with absolute certainty that it was, or had been, the property of Ross Landry.

He spoke first to Whitaker. The veterinarian thought it unlikely that Ross Landry had provided a repast for Long John, although he could not exclude it as a remote possibility. He conceded, too, that Long John's illness could have made his characteristic reactions to human beings unpredictable.

From Calvin Rood, Nestor learned that the 'gator's lethargic behavior had at first been attributed to the lingering effects of a drug fired by dartgun from the airboat that had captured him. The trappers admitted that because of his size, they had increased the dosage. Neither trapper could explain Landry's presence in the Everglades.

Nestor sat back and extended his legs. He said, "Permit me, if you will, gentlemen, to postulate a hypothesis." He smiled affably at Whitaker, whose expression indicated surprise at such classy rhetoric from a redneck sheriff, encouraging him to continue. "Its validity must of course await further developments. For the time being, let us assume that the missing man is no longer alive. Let us further assume that he met foul play. Why this second assumption? Because of a sentimental attachment to this timepiece, an anniversary gift which precludes any inference that he surrendered it voluntarily. So I am now suggesting that it was removed from his corpse to prevent identification. My question then is this: If Landry's assassin had tossed the watch into those swamps, is it possible that your alligator may have mistaken it for edible nourishment?"

184

Dr. Whitaker bobbed his head. " Why, yes. There is that possibility. Alligators do not have acute vision. If the timepiece came flashing into his vicinity, he most certainly would have considered it some form of marine life and snapped at it instinctively."

" Mr. Rood?"

" Yes. I have seen such reactions."

" Can you spare your trappers for a day or two. I'd like them to show me exactly where they found Long John."

" As long as you need them, Sheriff."

" You're looking for some trace or remnants of the body?" Whitaker asked.

" Yes, Doctor."

" Then Long John's whereabouts at the time of capture may not help. These alligators move around quite a bit. They have been known to roam over rather extensive areas."

" I understand. At the moment my choice of alternatives is limited. And we can cover a lot of swamp in an airboat."

Nestor turned to the two young trappers, who had been sitting quietly in a corner. " All right, fellas, we move out at first light tomorrow morning. Is that agreeable?"

" Yes, sir."

For Nestor, the case so far had been a frustrating one. He and his deputies had shown photographs of Ross Landry to half the population of Ocala Beach, with no results. Now, at last, he had a break, and he sensed with blood-quickening excitement the imminence of some startling revelation. If he did indeed find Landry's body, or any part of it, mauled by alligators, he could expect the media people to descend upon Ocala Beach like a plague of locusts.

Including, of course, some of the brass from Tallahassee. Politicians loved the spotlight.

31

Dan Hedrik stood aside while the technician moved an electronic detector along the underside of Hedrik's desk. Then, methodically, the man brushed his instrument along the wall of photographs, under chairs, the sofa, and over to the windows. Suddenly he paused, head attentively cocked. He mounted the sill and reached under the valance. He tugged and triumphantly exhibited a tiny device.

" Got one," he said.

Dan Hedrik let out his breath. " Sonovabitch!"

" Yes, sir. A little beauty. Japanese. Powerful enough to pick up conversations in any part of this room."

With a visible effort, Hedrik damped down a surge of anger. At the suggestion of counsel, all executive offices at the studio were being swept for electronic bugs. Paul Slater in New York felt that several of his legal maneuvers had been too expertly anticipated by UMI's attorneys.

Because it was his first experience with corporate espionage, Hedrik was curious. " Just how does that thing work?"

" Efficiently, sir. Picks up signals in this room, transmits them to a receiver up to a quarter of a mile away, and records the signals on voice-activated tape. Bingo! No more corporate secrets. Nor personal secrets either, for that matter." He laughed. " Know where I found one last year?"

" Where?"

" Attached to the springs of a bed in the boudoir of a chemical engineer's lady friend. The old goat had set her up in an expensive pad. He was chief researcher for an outfit with top government clearance, working on rocket fuels, very hush-hush.

The lady's employers figured correctly that the couple would be under surveillance, so they avoided personal contact with her and got their information direct via the planted mike."

" What happened to this concupiscent gent and his lady?"

" Conkyou what?"

" Concupiscent. Means horny."

" He sure was, Mr. Hedrik. I was free-lancing for Langley at the time and my work was finished when I delivered the tape. But I understand they put pressure on the man and got him to feed a lot of phony information to the opposition. Trouble is, when he found out he was being used by the woman, he could no longer get it up. So they terminated his clearance and took the lady into custody."

Hedrik looked thoughtful. " Phony information, hey? Might be a good idea for us too. I hope we're not broadcasting on that thing now."

The technician held up his tightly closed fist. " Transmission blocked."

" Good. I want you to leave it with me until I talk to my lawyer."

" Sure. But keep it wrapped in a towel until you need it."

" Would you have any idea how they managed to plant the device?"

" No big deal, Mr. Hedrik. One of your own employees, a cleaning service perhaps, an outside repairman. Even with super-tight security, there are always loopholes for a determined snooper."

Hedrik's jaw rippled. " All right. I want this place swept twice a week until further notice."

" Yes, sir. And we'll also check for a tap on your telephone lines. Ma Bell usually co-operates with us on that."

" You're the expert. Do whatever has to be done."

When the man left, Hedrik summoned his secretary for dictation. He waited until her pencil was poised before speaking.

" To all employees. As you all know, our company is under siege. Universal Media Industries is committing its resources in an attempt to wrest control of Arcadia Films from its present

187

management. Such a takeover, if successful, would be inimical to interests of the company, its employees, and its stockholders. Your officers are resisting with all means at their disposal.

"UMI will stop at nothing. Electronic listening devices have already breached our security. As a consequence, extreme caution must be exercized by everyone. Disloyalty in this struggle will result in a summary discharge without severance, regardless of position." He paused. "Have you got that?"

"Yes, Mr. Hedrik."

"Sign my name. Run it through the duplicator, distribute, and post on all bulletin boards."

She took her steno pad and left. He stared at the telephone with distaste. Damned Judas instrument. He got up and left the executive building. There was a telephone booth in the courtyard. He dialed the operator and charged a call to Paul Slater in New York.

"Paul? I'm talking from a public booth. You were right. My office was bugged."

"Figures," Slater said. "Listen to this, Dan. We had an ad scheduled in this morning's paper, addressed to Arcadia stockholders. And UMI showed up on the following page with arguments attempting to nullify every one of our contentions. So they must have been privy to our last conversation."

"Shouldn't we return the favor?"

"Are you serious?"

"Fire with fire, Paul. Retain one of those big agencies. Pinkerton or Holmes."

"Not a chance, Dan. Those fellows wouldn't touch corporate espionage. It's a shabby business and their regular clients would look with disfavor if they learned about it. Their principal business now is plant security, and it's too lucrative to jeopardise."

"Then how do we fight the bastards?" There was a note of bitter frustration in Hedrik's voice.

"We could publicize the opposition's tactics, providing you understand the risk."

"What risk?"

188

" That sort of thing is an attack *ad hominem*. Hanna would never forgive. If the takeover is successful, you and your people are finished, out of a job."

" He wouldn't have to fire me. I'd quit."

" Well, you wouldn't be unemployed long. I have a group of investors here with seed money. They'd jump at the chance to back you as an independent. Listen, I'm going to work on some maneuvers. We'll feed Hanna a load of bullshit that will confuse the bejesus out of his Wall Street lawyers."

Hedrik perked up. " I was just about to suggest something along those lines."

" Fine. Now, what's the latest on your man Ross Landry?"

Hedrik's voice changed. " Paul, I'm worried sick. Some sheriff down there called Landry's wife and asked for a description of Landry's watch. He didn't say why, but I assume he found it somewhere. I tried to reach him, without success. It sounds ominous. Ross went down there at my request. If anything happened to him, I'm responsible."

" Listen to me, Dan. You can't condemn yourself for lack of omniscience. All you had in mind was a simple business trip. And worrying about it may be premature. Wait until you have the facts."

" It's creating other problems too. I had Ross earmarked as producer of *The Romanoff File*. In the meantime, we have a lot of expensive talent on stand-by."

" Isn't anybody working?"

" The carpenters. Building mock-ups of the Winter Palace and Number Eleven Kropotkin Street."

" Who lives at Number Eleven?"

" The KGB. It's their headquarters. If you're interested come down and watch us shoot. Although I'd rather shoot that prick Hanna. One more item, Paul."

" Yes?"

" We had a visitor from Washington. Chap named Duke— Kevin Anthony Duke III. Sharp young fella. He grilled Logan Stern too, about that alleged fifty-grand kickback. And he checked Stern's bank accounts. He found something."

" What?"

" A cash withdrawal of fifty-four thousand dollars."

" Jesus H. Christ! What the hell, Dan!"

" Grabbed me the same way, Counselor."

" I don't like it."

" Neither do I. And I've got enough on my plate here without it."

" What's Stern's version?"

" He says he owed a gambling debt. It's his form of recreation."

" Can he prove it?"

" Maybe. If the boys at Las Vegas co-operate. Anyway, this Duke wanted to see my bank records too. Polite, but persistent. I gave him a look. What the hell, I have nothing to hide. But of course, only an imbecile would be stupid enough to deposit fifty grand under those circumstances."

" If intelligence is hereditary, this Duke is well-equipped under his scalp. There's a Kevin Anthony Duke II here, a top-notch lawyer. Must be his son. Since it never happened, I doubt if Duke the third will come up with anything incriminating. Who's he working for?"

" Enforcement Branch. SEC."

" That would be G. G. Pressman, an acquaintance of mine."

" Can you talk to him, Paul?"

" Wouldn't do any good. Just keep your fingers crossed. If Fred Hanna gets wind of this little gem, he'll blow it all out of proportion. Too many gullible people abroad, ready to believe anything. We just have to wait and see. Tell me about Kate Rennie's nephew. Have you been able to get a commitment from the boy?"

" Sorry, Paul. That's something else we have to discuss. The news on that is not good. Kiser showed up for the funeral with a friend. Oddball character, older than Davy. Kind of a weird relationship. He's got the boy under his thumb. Watches everything Davy does, thinks for him, talks for him. I sure would like to see Davy's arm for track marks."

" What's the fellow's name?"

" Al Clinton."

" You think he's feeding Kiser drugs?"

" Could be. Anyway, this Clinton is pressuring Garson to probate the Rennie estate fast, before Arcadia's annual meeting."

Slater's voice was urgent. " Dan, I want you to hire a private eye. Today. The best man you can find. Let's get some background on this Clinton. Past employment, personal contacts, source of income, how and where he met Kiser. Strip him naked. I hope to Christ it isn't too late. Without those Rennie shares, we're in deep trouble."

" I know just the man. Did some investigating for us a year ago."

" Put him to work without delay, Dan. It's important."

" Should have thought of it myself. I'm ringing off now, Paul. By tomorrow our phone lines should be cleared, in case you need me."

Hedrik remained in the phone booth, still feeling embattled, no longer safe in his own office. He dropped another coin in the slot, dialed the studio, and asked for Hank Bruno.

When he heard Bruno's voice, he said, " Dan Hedrik, Hank. I'm calling from an outside phone. Give me fifteen minutes and meet me in the projection room. Arrange for a showing of some old chestnut and have the operator turn up the volume. I'll explain when I see you."

" Cloak-and-dagger stuff? Right down my alley. Fifteen minutes, boss."

*   *   *

The director was waiting in an aisle seat. Background music blared deafeningly from the soundtrack. On the screen, with the rosebud lips of a bygone era, a very young Kate Rennie was cavorting in a dated musical with some long-forgotten hoofer. Hank Bruno moved over and made room. He leaned toward Hedrik's ear, using his hands as a megaphone.

" What's this all about, Dan?"

" The whole damn studio is bugged, Hank. Those UMI troglodytes are onto every move we've made. How do you feel?"

"Now there's a *non sequitur* if I ever heard one. How do I feel? For an ageing voluptuary who's losing his hair and his libido, not bad. Why do you ask?"

"Can you handle two jobs?"

"Depends. What are they?"

"*The Romanoff File.* Producer *and* director. On a temporary basis, Hank, until we know what happened to Ross Landry. We just can't afford to waste any more time. Clyde Elliott's contract calls for ten grand a week for every week we run over schedule. In our present condition, that's a lot of tickets."

Hedrik told him about the watch, and Bruno scowled into space. A light flickered on the projection-room phone. Hedrik reached for the handset and covered his other ear. His secretary said, "I know, I know. You told me to hold all calls, but it's Irving Garson and he says it's urgent."

"Put him on. Irving, what's the problem?"

"Young Kiser is the problem. Are you deaf or something. Turn down that radio."

"Never mind the noise. Tell me about Kiser."

"He hired himself a lawyer. I just got served with papers charging dilatory tactics, wasting the estate's assets, and other assorted shenanigans in probating Kate's will. It's all a crock, Dan. But they're gonna force me to speed it up. Any suggestions?"

Hedrik pondered, and then said, almost serious, "Tell you what, Irving. Step outside and start running. Sprint three miles uphill and then have your heart checked. They'll stick you in Cedars of Lebanon for a couple of weeks. With the executor temporarily out of action, no judge is going to push it. The studio will foot the hospital bill."

Garson chuckled. "Don't worry about the bill. I got Medicare. And they wouldn't put me in the hospital. They'd put me in a box. Daniel my boy, you're learning fast. Maybe that Hanna could take a few lessons."

"Irving. Let me get back to you on an outside line. We'll discuss it more fully."

32

Alex Bogart was furious.

"I interrupted my vacation and flew down from Canada just to argue this motion," he said into the telephone. "You objected to my request for a postponement until the end of the month, and I agreed to come back. Okay. I'm here. Now *you* want a postponement. You say you're not prepared. Tough luck, Counselor. I didn't fly over a thousand miles to amuse myself. I'll see you at the county courthouse tomorrow morning at ten, ready or not." He slapped the phone into its cradle before the opposition lawyer could protest.

He looked with distaste at the mail which had accumulated under his door. He picked it up and started sorting, unable to concentrate now on other people's picayune problems. Cora Bendiner knew he was back in Ocala Beach for two days and he expected her momentarily. He could not, of course, drive out to The Lodge.

When he heard the door open he looked up, and there she was, more beautiful than ever. He stood and opened his arms to her headlong rush. They clung tightly.

"I missed you," she whispered. "God, how I missed you!"

He did not speak. He carried her to the old leather sofa and undressed her. As always, there was no tenderness, no murmurs of affection during their initial coupling. In this exorcism of private demons, the ancient ritual became a grotesque distortion.

Later, lying side by side, he sensed her annoyance. "All right," he said. "Tell me about it."

"It's the sheriff," she said.

He turned quickly and stared at her. "Ben Nestor?"

" He's a friend of yours, isn't he?"

" We grew up here in Ocala Beach. Played on the same team at school."

" What kind of man is he?"

" A good man. Incorruptible. And his deputies respect him and toe the line. The state sent him to Washington for some FBI courses, so he knows his trade pretty well. A couple of sharpies came down here a few years back and made the mistake of selling Ben short. Biggest mistake they ever made. Why do you ask?"

" Remember I told you about that man Ross Landry, from Arcadia Films, the one who came down here to see Ward?"

" I remember."

" Well, he's missing from his motel and Sheriff Nestor is asking questions. He came out to The Lodge and I told him that I'd spoken to Landry, explaining that my husband was in New York."

" Ben knew why Landry was here?"

" Yes. The studio called him. They were worried because Landry hadn't been in touch."

" Well, it's no concern of ours. So what's the problem?"

" The problem is your friend Sheriff Nestor. He's making a nuisance of himself. Yesterday I saw him through the window skulking around the grounds. After all, it's private property. I want you to get that man off my back."

He searched her face. " Is there something else I ought to know about?"

" I've told you all I know." She sat up and started getting dressed. " You're my lawyer, aren't you?"

" Strictly speaking, I'm supposed to be your husband's lawyer."

" Same thing. Will you speak to the sheriff?"

" As soon as I can reach him."

" When are you leaving again."

" Tomorrow afternoon. I have to be at the courthouse in the morning." He grinned. " Two more weeks to go on my vacation."

194

" And then?"

" I'll be free. Decide what you'd like to do." He waved at his littered desk. " Let me clean up this mess, honey, And hang loose."

She paused at the door and wiggled her fingers conspiratorially. Bogart dressed quickly and then phoned the sheriff's office. One of the deputies answered.

" Alex Bogart, Tom. Is Ben there?"

" Not at the moment, Counselor. Anything I can do for you."

" No, thanks. Know where I can find him?"

" He's out in the 'Glades with a couple of boys from Sea World. Just south of Ochopee, last I heard."

" The 'Glades? What the hell is he doing—hunting alligators? Doesn't he know that's against the law?"

" He knows. Shall I tell him you called?"

" Please. As soon as he gets back. I'll be at my office here until six. And I'm leaving again tomorrow afternoon."

* * *

An ancient Seminole Indian squatted on a patch of dry land, fashioning mahogany spears for the tourist trade. His anthracite-black eyes looked up as the airboat skimmed past. The seamed face was expressionless and he made no acknowledgment of Ben Nestor's friendly wave.

The airboat bucked and howled through the high saw grass. It had been built by the operator himself. A light skiff driven by a six-foot propeller, powered by an old five-hundred-pound Chrysler V-8 engine, lovingly overhauled. The young man from Sea World sat high on an elevated seat that enabled him to see over the tall growth.

The saw grass worried Nestor. It made him dubious about the success of his mission. A body snagged in this tangled growth would be invisible. And if, on the other hand, it had wound up on one of the raised palmetto hummocks, alligators would long since have sheared it apart, with the circling buzzards swooping in to clean up the debris.

Even so, the effort had to be made, considering the circumstances surrounding the discovery of Landry's watch. But what in Christ's name, he wondered, could have brought a man like that into this dank and alien world? So fraught with danger. Perilous even for a lawman. Some of these backwoods shanties housed out-of-town felons, fugitives ready to cut loose with a blast of buckshot at anyone approaching suspiciously close. And there were botanical dangers too, the manganeel tree whose poison could boil away human flesh like sulphuric acid.

As always, here in the Everglades, Ben Nestor felt anger and a sense of helplessness. Anger at what had happened, and helpless because there wasn't one damn thing he could do to halt the relentless pressures that kept changing the nature of this unique ecological wonder. Road building, canals, dredging by real estate developers, all had altered the natural balance. The original flow of water would never again make its way to its natural outlet at Cape Sable.

It had been a place of infinite wonder, its limestone drainage chutes carved into the earth by the great glaciers thousands of years ago. No similar network of water, plants, and animal life existed anywhere else on the planet. And all of it being ravaged by the greed and blundering handiwork of man.

Perhaps, thought Nestor, this Landry fellow had been some kind of amateur naturalist, with time to kill, wandering the 'Glades for a firsthand look at the area. But then, how in hell did he manage to reach the place without a car?

Another half mile and the roaring machine stutter-stepped alongside a collapsed wooden bridge that ran from an abandoned island to a muddy road. " Here it is, Sheriff. This is where we bagged Long John."

" Did he put up much of a struggle?"

" No, sir. We hit him with the tranquiliser before he could react."

" And you saw nothing else?"

" Only an old bobcat crouching on that branch over there. Evil-looking little bastard."

The actual location of Long John at the time of his capture

meant nothing. He could have traveled a considerable distance since swallowing the watch, or anything else, for that matter. Nevertheless, they nosed slowly through the area for thirty minutes, eyes peeled, before moving on.

" Where to now, Sheriff?"

" Just cruise and keep looking. We damn well want to be out of here before dark."

" Amen to that."

The driver had echoed the sentiment emphatically because at sunset the air would turn thick with mosquitoes, zeroing in greedily on all living creatures. A living hell.

The airboat picked its way between outcrops of limestone. Nestor felt the claustrophobic effect of a low encompassing horizon. Two startled egrets took flight over his head. He kept swiveling from side to side, searching. One of these days, he thought, I'll have to question some of the Swamp Rats, those people who had chosen for private reasons to settle in the 'Glades.

The saw-grass path made a sharp right turn and a flock of buzzards flapped screamingly aloft, perching on branches to watch them with small malevolent eyes.

" *Jesus Holy Christ*!" the operator said in a strangled voice from his elevated seat.

His arm was out, rigid, finger pointing. Nestor stumbled to his feet. This time of day the water level was low. What looked like a body, or part of a body was caught in the tangled growth of a partially submerged palmetto hummock. The boat nudged closer.

Ben Nestor had served as a combat sergeant in Korea. He had seen death in many forms. What the wildlife had done to this victim was no worse than the injuries caused by a fragmentation bomb or a direct hit by a howitzer shell. But this was not war. This was home territory in southwest Florida.

Jaws rigid, nose wrinkled, Nestor said quietly, " We're going to need help." He reached for the portable wireless transmitter. Because of carelessness, perhaps because he had not anticipated finding anything, they had failed to equip themselves with a canvas tarpaulin or sack. What they really needed were gas masks.

33

Floyd Gregorius sat in a state of black despondency, staring numbly into space. His hands hung loosely between his knees. He heard the doorbell again. It had been ringing for some time. A half-empty whisky bottle stood on the lamp table at his side. He had been drinking directly from the bottle, but he did not think there was enough liquor anywhere to obliterate his misery.

The bell stopped ringing and a fist pounded the door. He had the sudden terrifying thought that the police had arrived to take him away. It had never occurred to him that anything like this could happen. It was just plain rotten stinking luck. Those UMI bonds had been tucked away in his father's portfolio for years. Now, without warning, the old man had decided to sell. Now. Right after he, Floyd, had pledged them as collateral for his margin account. Signing Anson's name to a stock power at his broker's request. He hadn't thought of it as forgery at the time, but he knew now there was no other name for it.

He had, of course, intended to return the originals. All he needed was time. Now it was too late. Anson had already sold the counterfeit copies. His imagination painted a picture of himself in prison garb, marching lockstep with felons, thieves, and murderers. Tears of self-pity welled in his eyes. He would be branded for life, an ex-convict, unemployable at the only work he knew, disgraced, shorn of dignity, disavowed by his colleagues. And even worse, Janey might want no part of him.

Janey! His chest constricted painfully. Then the pounding stopped and he heard her voice. " Floyd? Please. I know you're there. I want to talk to you. Please open the door."

198

He sat motionless, wavering. And suddenly he felt a compulsion to talk, to explain, to try to justify. He desperately needed someone to help shoulder the burden. He pushed himself out of the chair and walked unsteadily to the door.

She came in and put her arms around him. She led him to the sofa and sat him down, holding both his hands, searching his face. " I knew something was wrong when you left the office," she said. " You didn't say anything, you didn't even look at me."

" Janey," he blurted. " I did a terrible thing."

" Terrible? You? I don't believe that."

" It's true." And the words came, a rushing torrent, a catharsis. He told her about his speculation in Arcadia Films, the sudden inexplicable reversal, the urgent call for additional margin and his lack of resources. How in desperation he had borrowed his father's bonds, replacing them in the firm's vault with worthless copies. Some of it she already knew, but she did not interrupt.

" It was a loan, Floyd," she said at last. " You'll return the bonds as soon as you get them back from the broker."

" It's too late, Janey." His voice broke.

" Why?"

" Because my father put them up for sale."

" The counterfeits?"

He nodded miserably. " Yes."

She stared at him, biting her bottom lip, her brow crimped in concentration. Suddenly she brightened. " Listen to me, Floyd. It's going to be all right. Suppose your father did sell those bonds. The transfer agent won't even notice that they're copies. He'll just cancel them and issue new bonds to the buyer. Then, when Stoufer, Wingate returns the originals, you simply destroy them. Nobody will ever know."

He blinked, mouth ajar, feeling a glimmer of optimism. Was it possible? My God, yes, he thought, it just might happen that way. With any luck at all, the copies could pass.

" And even if everything went wrong," she said, " you could go to your father and explain. He'll understand."

He shook his head. "I don't think so, Janey. You don't know how it is between us."

"He's your father, Floyd."

"He expected too much of me. I disappointed him. He even picked a stranger to run the company. And there's my sister, Julie—all his affection goes to Julie."

"You'll see," she said soothingly. "Everything is going to be all right."

*　　　*　　　*

Kevin Anthony Duke calculated the time difference and made his call from Las Vegas at 1:45 PM in order to catch Gary Pressman behind his desk at the Securities and Exchange Commission office.

When he had the head of Enforcement on the phone, he said, "Duke reporting from Nevada."

"Let's have it, son."

"These guys out here disgorge information with all the prodigality of a slot machine, Chief. They're very polite, they smile a lot, they seem eager to co-operate, but what you get is something like this." He mimicked the hoarse voice of a boxer who's been hit in the throat too many times. "'Yes, sir. Mr. Logan Stern is a frequent visitor. You can see from the hotel register here that he spent several days with us at the time you mentioned. Whenever he's here, he can be found at the tables. Sometimes he wins, sometimes he loses. On this particular occasion? That's hard to say. It's mostly a cash business. People drop some money and leave. We don't keep individual figures. Wouldn't be practical.'"

Pressman said, "We can apply for a court order to see their records."

"I told them. They don't seem to be worried."

"Two sets of books?"

"It's a possibility."

Gary George Pressman sighed. "They skim the top and it never shows up until it's been sanitized. You reach any conclusions?"

"Yes, sir. I think Logan Stern is on the level. And the one time I spoke to Dan Hedrik, he didn't strike me as a finagler. You want me to keep digging?"

"Negative. We're not going to waste any more time on this. There's no Martin Caswell listed on Arcadia's books. He's not anybody's fellow stockholder. He can't even be found. Catch the next flight east, son."

Duke hesitated. "I have a confession to make."

"To me or to a priest?"

"To you."

"Okay, son. I'm in the booth, behind the curtain. Shoot."

"I'm beginning to take sides. My sympathies lie with Arcadia Films."

"We're supposed to be disinterested and impartial."

"Yes, sir. I know. We're also supposed to look for corporate misconduct and assorted transgressions. I couldn't sleep last night. Jet lag. Tossing in bed, an idea came to me. We know that UMI started buying Arcadia shares in wholesale lots about a year ago."

"So?"

"Wouldn't all that buying be tantamount to a tender without making the requisite disclosure?"

"Appeals courts are still trying to decide that one, son."

"How about state laws limiting acquisitions?"

"Raiders aren't worrying too much about state laws these days. Not since the Fifth Circuit ruled that Idaho's takeover statute was unconstitutional."

"I missed that one, sir. On what grounds?"

"Pre-empting federal legislation and interfering with interstate commerce."

"So the Black Knights ride again."

"With slavering jaws. Only us and the Justice Department to keep 'em in line. Who's paying for this call?"

"The government."

"Have some respect for the taxpayers. Come on home."

201

34

Sheriff Ben Nestor climbed the single flight of stairs with a proprietary air and walked into Alex Bogart's office. The lawyer turned from a filing cabinet and grinned widely.

" Ben. Good to see you."

" Deputy tells me you called."

Bogart was mildly startled by the sheriff's brusqueness. " Same old Ben. Business first, no amenities, even though I've been away."

" Sorry, Alex. Too much on my mind. That was a long vacation. Enjoy yourself?"

Bogart winked. " Got something special waiting for me in Montreal. I'm taking off again tomorrow. No point in being your own boss if you can't goldbrick once in a while. Nothing on the court calendar anyway, except a motion tomorrow morning. Pull up a chair." He canted his head and studied the sheriff, and said belatedly, " Too much on your mind, Ben? We have law-enforcement problems in our peace-loving community?"

" More than usual. This week we're afflicted with a very bad case of the uglies. And you may be involved."

Bogart's chin snapped up. " Me? Involved how?"

" You're the best lawyer in town. Sooner or later, Counselor, when I get a handle on this thing, someone is going to need your help."

" Oh." Bogart relaxed. " Tell me about it."

The sheriff stretched his legs. " First I had a call from the A.G.'s office in Tallahassee about a missing person. Then another call from the head of Arcadia Films in California. One of his VIPs, down here on business, got misplaced. Same individual. Disappeared from his motel."

"Man named Landry?"

"You know about him?"

Bogart nodded. "A client of mine, Mrs. Ward Bendiner, told me you'd been out to The Lodge asking about Landry."

"That's right, Counselor. Seems she was about the only contact he made down here. The A.G. wanted a thorough investigation. I got nowhere for a couple of days until an inscribed wristwatch belonging to Landry turned up."

"Turned up where?"

"In the belly of an alligator up at Sea World, following an autopsy."

"My God, Ben!"

"Yeah. So I got one of the trappers to take me out into the 'Glades on his airboat, and by chance we ran across some human remains."

"Christ, Ben! *Landry?*"

"Who knows? The weather down here is not exactly conducive to the preservation of a dead body, even if the wildlife had ignored it. See what I'm up against? So today I do not feel like anybody's friendly Southern sheriff." Nestor rubbed the side of his jaw. "You called my office, Alex. What's on your mind?"

"Mrs. Bendiner. She tells me you've been prowling around The Lodge and she can't understand why."

"Simple. I have no other leads. Landry went out to see her. Is she claiming harassment?"

"Not at all. Fact is, with her husband away on business, she's alone and it's kind of an isolated place. Having a lawman nearby is a comfort. But she would like to know what's going on."

"How come they don't have a live-in maid?"

"They had two, Ben. Last was a Cuban girl. But Bendiner doesn't like strangers underfoot, so they got rid of her." Bogart frowned. "About that body, Ben, is there no way you can identify it?"

"We're trying. I asked Landry's associates to send us his dental records. We don't have a pathologist here, so the cadaver itself is en route to Miami." Nestor paused. "About Landry's mission here, Alex, can I ask you a question?"

"Go ahead."

"As Bendiner's lawyer, did he ever ask your advice about his Arcadia stock and the takeover?"

Bogart smiled. "Hell, Ben, I'm only a small-town operator. Ward Bendiner needs my advice about money like he needs another nose." The smile faded. "You don't think Landry's disappearance is tied in with the takeover, do you?"

"No idea, Alex. Just looking for a handle." Nestor stood up and offered his hand. "You'll be leaving again tomorrow, then."

"Yep. I want a complete change of climate."

Ben Nestor drove back to the sheriff's office, one hand on the wheel, the other scratching angry welts at the back of his neck. The bug repellent had been only partially effective, and even during daylight, back there in the 'Glades, insects of one kind or another had gotten to him. He was bone-weary and morose. Almost no sleep at all in the last forty-eight hours. He tried not to dwell on the trip back with his ghastly cargo.

Such gruesome chores, admittedly infrequent, made him wonder at times if he had chosen the right line of work. Unlike an apprentice mortician, he had not anticipated these responsibilities when he had first applied as a deputy years ago. The mortician deliberately chose to traffic in death. To Nestor, death was an abomination, a monstrous indignity.

There was a message waiting for him. Call the Attorney General's office in Tallahassee at once. He sighed audibly and reached for the phone, not relishing another conversation with the young assistant.

"Sheriff Ben Nestor at Ocala Beach," he said. "Just got your message."

"About those remains, Sheriff, the A.G. wants your local undertaker to haul them over to Miami."

"The cadaver is already in transit."

" You did that on your own initiative?"

" The only practical solution. Our facilities here are primitive."

" Do you know Dr. Bukantz?"

" The Dade County medical examiner? Not personally. I attended a law-enforcement symposium last year at which he was the principal speaker."

" Best forensic scientist in the state, Sheriff. Spoke to him about an hour ago. The A.G. wants a firsthand report, so we're sending our own pathologist down from the capital to assist. I understand that the body is badly decomposed."

Ben Nestor's eyes suddenly took on a glint of diabolical pleasure. " Yes, sir. It was tangled in some growth on a partly submerged hummock. In addition to the alligators—well, you know what heat and humidity can do to rotting flesh. That swamp area is teeming with rats, snakes, turkey buzzards, and assorted parasites. Flies lay their eggs in the eyes and mouth, and those eggs hatch into maggots that—"

He heard a gagging sound. " Jesus Christ, Sheriff! Please. Spare me the details before I lose my lunch. Just tell me this, is there enough left for identification?"

" The teeth are intact. I've already called California for Landry's dental records."

" Good thinking, Sheriff. Any labels on the clothes, or what's left of them?"

" None we could find. The fabric was badly shredded. Those turkey buzzards have beaks like a linoleum knife and—"

" Sorry I asked. Look, stay on top of this thing, will you? The A.G. himself is interested."

When the line went dead, Ben Nestor sat back and smiled for the first time in two days.

35

For the first time in his life Fred Hanna had been forced to borrow a large sum of money on his own personal note. In past deals he had protected himself under a corporate shield which precluded individual liability. Since he could supply no collateral, the Nevada group had demanded a rate of interest so extortionate he had almost walked away from the deal. It lacked any semblance of sound finance. Nevertheless, his over-riding hunger for the Bendiner shares had canceled prudence and he had accepted their terms.

Now, with those shares locked up, he felt a surge of confidence. Large risks, large rewards. And once Arcadia Films was in his pocket, he could start moving, liquidating some of the company's assets, clean up his debts, and sit back counting his profits. He looked down and saw with surprise that he was dry-washing his hands.

There was a knock and Egan entered. "You wanted to see me, Fred?"

"Yes. What's happening with Rennie's estate?"

"It looks good. Young Kiser is following our suggestions. We've got an attorney representing him out there and he's already started an action against the executor."

"Is he consulting you on strategy?"

"He doesn't need my help. This is a very tough and knowledgeable scrapper. He doesn't usually take cases on a contingency fee, so we agreed on a price. It's depleting my special fund, but he's worth every nickel. I'm hoping old Garson can't stand the pressure."

"You're hoping. Is there any doubt?"

"There's always doubt. I'm not sure how far the courts will go to interfere with Garson's administration of the estate if they find that he's acting in good faith."

"Not good enough, Bob. I want those goddamn Rennie shares wrapped up before the annual stockholders meeting. This legal wonder you hired, just exactly what in hell is he doing to earn his fee?"

"He brought an action against the executor for specific performance, claiming irreparable loss to the estate unless Garson acts with all possible speed. He's alleging that because of Garson's previous connection with the studio, he's biased in favour of management. And he's requesting the court to allow David Kiser, as sole legatee, to vote Rennie's shares at the annual meeting even though final distribution of the estate has not been completed. It's an unconventional approach, but we have no choice."

"We're gambling."

"Yes."

"Then let's change the odds."

"How."

Hanna stared at Egan woodenly. "With money. Buy the goddamn judge, that's how."

"The judge may not be for sale."

"He's a politician. All politicians are for sale. The price has to be right."

"How high can I go?"

"Whatever it takes. You say your special fund is low?"

"Yes. We're running into unexpected expenses."

"Then we'll replenish. I want you to fly out there yourself, Bob, and test the water." Hanna started chewing the inside of his cheek, apparently having second thoughts. "Use your judgment. If it looks too dangerous, drop it." He aimed a finger. "But give it your best shot. I'm in too heavily to let this deal slip away because we were overly cautious."

"I'll leave tonight," Egan said.

*　　*　　*

207

In the Stock Transfer Department of the Gotham Trust, working at a long table, Willie Shafner was checking the serial numbers on a pile of stock and bond certificates, preparing to cancel them and issue new certificates in their place. Shafner was a spindly adenoidal man in his mid-forties. He removed his glasses and wiped them with a tissue. It was late in the day and his eyes were tired. He rested them for a full minute, lids closed, pinching the bridge of his nose.

By some random quirk of chance, his vision no longer blurred, he reached for the next bond on the pile, and a caution signal suddenly flagged his attention. He peered at the certificate, studying it carefully, brows tightly knitted.

Shafner could not immediately identify the problem. But something here seemed wrong, definitely wrong. The color perhaps. Greens brighter than usual. Shafner frequently operated on instinct. He had a good memory. He recalled handling a transfer of UMI bonds less than half an hour earlier. He quickly riffled through his stack of canceled certificates and located the bonds. By coincidence, the serial numbers showed that the questionable certificate had been part of the same printing.

Shafner kept a magnifying glass in his desk. He used it to examine the suspected bond, comparing it with the others, and decided that the colors were off-key, too intense, the texture of the paper not quite the same. He saw that there were four more in his pile awaiting cancellation—just like the first, as phony as a three-dollar bill.

They were all registered in the name of Anson Gregorius.

Oh, boy! thought Shafner. What do we have here? Anson Gregorius is a member of the club. Is it possible the old man is a crook?

Willie Shafner picked up both sets of bonds and brought them to the office of Curtis Dahl, second vice-president in charge of the Corporate Trust Department. He laid the bonds on Dahl's desk, indicated the discrepancies, and waited for a decision.

Curtis Dahl was an austere, flinty man with a low boiling

point. He adjusted the light on his desk and examined the bonds critically, his mouth pinched tighter than usual, his eyes stony.

"Forgeries!" he snapped. "Counterfeits! Registered in the name of Anson Gregorius. The damned old fool! Whatever the hell he's up to, he's not getting away with it. Good work, Willie. Glad you caught it. Who sent the bonds over here?"

"They came with instructions from Meisner & Clark. Bought them for one of their customers from Gregorius & Company. According to our records, we've had Anson Gregorius on the books as the registered owner ever since the bonds were first issued. So the originals must still be in his possession."

Dahl dismissed his employee. He sat, fingertips drumming an angry tattoo on the polished desk. What he should do, he thought, was take the matter directly to the Board of Governors of the New York Stock Exchange. And from there to the District Attorney for prosecution. Although the U.S. Attorney's office here in New York might be more appropriate. His blood cooled a little as he considered the problem and its ramifications. He had a tiger by the tail here. Consequences were unpredictable. The Gotham Trust was Gregorius & Company's principal banker. They held a huge amount of Gregorius paper. In addition, he, Curtis Dahl, had recently approved a new line of credit. Gregorius had already drawn upon it. Millions of dollars were at risk. Ruining the brokerage firm's reputation could endanger those loans. Besides, both old Anson and Mike Ryan kept their personal accounts at the bank, long-time, highly valued customers. At the very least, did he not owe them the courtesy of a warning?

Dahl was torn. A serious crime had been committed. Most assuredly, something had to be done about it. The very foundation of the securities market itself was being jeopardized daily by unsolved fraud. He signaled his secretary and told her to put him through to Michael Ryan at Gregorius & Company.

"Mr. Ryan?" he said. "Curtis Dahl here at the Gotham."

"How are you, sir?"

Dahl ignored the amenities. "We have a problem. More correctly, sir, Gregorius has a problem. Our Transfer Department recently received five certificates representing one hundred UMI bonds registered in the name of Anson Gregorius. These bonds were sold by your firm."

"Yes, sir. I handled the sale myself."

"The bonds are forgeries."

"I don't think I heard you correctly, Mr. Dahl. Would you repeat that, please?"

"The bonds which you delivered to Meisner & Clark, and which they sent to us for transfer, are counterfeits, Mr. Ryan. Not worth the paper they're printed on."

There was a moment of stunned silence. "Are you serious?"

"Dead serious, sir. We are not in the habit of joking about such matters. I wanted to put you on notice that we intend to report this to the proper authorities."

"You're making a serious charge, Mr. Dahl. Those bonds were originally issued to Anson Gregorius. They came to us from your bank as UMI's transfer agent. And they have been locked away in our private vault ever since. So I suggest caution before you do anything rash."

Curtis Dahl was momentarily nonplussed. From accuser, he suddenly found himself on the defensive. "What do you have in mind?"

"A confidential investigation until we can get to the bottom of the problem. May I send a messenger to the bank for those certificates?"

"No, sir. I'm afraid not. The certificates are evidence of fraud."

"Would you let me see them?"

"In my office, yes."

"Thank you, Mr. Dahl. I'm on my way."

*   *   *

One hour later, having verified Dahl's charge, Mike Ryan left the bank, his face stiff with restraint, and returned to Gregorius

& Company. He went directly to Liz Harmon's office and closed the door.

She looked up, saw his expression, and said, "Whatever it is, it can't be that bad."

"It's worse." He pulled up a chair. "For your ears only, Liz. This is strictly confidential. Private. Privileged. Understood?"

"Perfectly."

"First I want to pick your brain. I'm assuming that in all your analytical research you must have picked up several pieces of information. You remember that report you did for us a year ago on Xerox?"

"Of course. A remarkable company. Brilliant research and development, innovative."

"How accurate is their color copier?"

"Frighteningly accurate. Money orders and cashier's cheques are especially vulnerable."

"All right. Let me give you some facts. We closed a deal to buy all of Ward Bendiner's Arcadia shares for Fred Hanna's margin account. A cash sale. To cover Hanna's balance, we had to borrow heavily from our bank. To keep us out of violation, it was necessary to improve our net capital position."

"The 2,000 Per cent Rule."

"Precisely. I appealed to our source. Anson. He offered to sell a bundle of UMI bonds, among other securities, all in his personal portfolio, and to lend the proceeds to Gregorius & Company. The bonds cleared through Meisner & Clark for one of their customers. Delivery was made and the bonds went to the Gotham Trust for transfer. About an hour ago I had a call from the bank. The bonds are counterfeit, worthless."

"Oh, no."

"Yes, Liz. I examined them myself. Curtis Dahl at the bank is convinced they were duplicated on a Xerox 6500. It was only a matter of luck that the substitution was spotted."

Liz was distressed. "We have big, big problems, Mike." She shook her head. "They'll have to restrict access to that machine."

"More to the point, Gregorius & Company is going to have to restrict access to its vault."

She caught his meaning and her eyes widened. "If I remember correctly, only two people have keys. You and Floyd Gregorius."

"That fact," he said dourly, "has not escaped me."

She chewed her lip reflectively. "Like in those detective stories, if we apply the process of elimination, and Mike Ryan is excluded, then who is left?"

Mike nodded grimly.

"But why?" she asked.

"The usual reason, I suppose. Money."

"Could Floyd need money so desperately he'd risk his whole future?"

"That's what I intend to find out."

Liz frowned. "A thought occurs to me. Couple of weeks ago Floyd came to my office. He was trying to appear casual, but I sensed an underlying anxiety, and looking back now, perhaps even agitation. He asked me a lot of questions about Arcadia, about the company's prospects—did I know why the stock was falling, its chances for recovery, the possibility of a successful takeover."

Mike threw his arms up. "Jesus! That's it. The silly bastard took a flier in Arcadia, looking for the jackpot."

"And got in over his head. He must have an account at some other house."

"Stoufer, Wingate. A margin account." Mike consulted his notebook and reached for the phone. He got an outside line and dialed the brokerage firm, asking for the margin clerk. "This is Floyd Gregorius," he said. "I'm checking my current position. Could you tell me, please, how my account stands and should I be prepared for another margin call?"

A voice told him to hold on, please. After a brief pause the voice came back. "Arcadia seems to be holding, Mr. Gregorius. What happens tomorrow or next week is something else. Four more points on the downside and you may have to pony up again."

"I see. Thank you very much." He hung up and said through clenched teeth, "That tears it. Floyd sliced his own throat."

Liz said quietly, "I don't think you should have done that, Mike."

Her disapproval stung him.

"Why? Because I misled the man? Because it was dishonest? Listen to me, Liz. Gregorius has over fifty people working here, supporting families and paying off mortgages. They need their jobs for food and rent and medical bills. And right now I'm responsible for keeping this outfit solvent. So if some brainless idiot puts us in jeopardy, I'm going to fight back. I did not take over from the old man just to let his useless son pull the plug. We can't risk a suspension. Not at this time. I'll do whatever is necessary to keep us afloat. Just spare me from your bleeding-heart righteousness."

Even as he wheeled and strode furiously out of the room, he felt a stab of contrition. He paused and looked back. She was grinning at him. He nodded brusquely, too troubled to smile, then headed for Anson's office.

The old man was mowing grey stubble from his chin with an electric shaver. He saw dark thunderclouds in Mike's expression and clicked off the motor.

"Trouble, Mike?" he asked plaintively. "Can't it wait? Julie's free tonight and we're going out to dinner. Just the two of us. Don't wreck my evening before it starts."

"This can't wait, Anson. We have a problem. A nasty problem. And I'm afraid it affects you personally."

The old man sighed. He settled back. "All right, let's have it."

For a fractional moment Mike hesitated, wondering if he shouldn't spare the old boy and try somehow to solve it himself. No, he decided, not under these circumstances. He got it off his chest in clipped, terse phrases, starting with the call from Curtis Dahl. As the gravity of the situation became clear, Anson's face seemed graven in stone. He sat motionless, his eyes baleful, hands clasped tightly, the knuckles bone-white.

His voice, when he finally spoke, was unusually harsh. "Assuming your conclusions are correct, Mike—do you have any suggestions?"

"Floyd is your son, Anson. The charge is serious. It has long-range implications. The decision is yours."

"And I will make it. Right now I am asking for the benefit of your thinking."

Mike walked to the window and looked out, torn by conflicting emotions. He was the managing partner. He could not shirk his responsibilities. They came with the franchise. If you can't shoulder the load, then it's time to surrender command and take orders from someone else. He turned back to face the old man.

"My thinking, Anson. All right? Let me give you the picture. If the bank insists on filing a complaint, there will be a full investigation. Once that happens, it's out of our hands. A crime has been attempted. Someone will have to pay the price. So it boils down to Floyd. He will be indicted and tried and processed into the slammer. There's been too much fraud on the Street. They won't be lenient. What got Floyd into this mess? There are psychological factors involved. We both know what Floyd was trying to do, and why. He was under pressure. He was trying to prove something, especially to you.

"He thought he had inside information about a merger and he tried to take advantage of it. He bought Arcadia. He went for broke, on a margin account, probably every dime he could spare. Then it all went sour. He got sandbagged by heavy selling. Maybe even stock manipulation, I don't know. At any rate, he got a margin call from Stoufer, Wingate. If he got wiped out, he thought you'd lose what little respect you had for him. So he lost his head. He tried to save himself. He borrowed your bonds. It was foolish. It was stupid. It was reckless.

"But we have to look at it with some compassion. Perhaps neither of us is free from blame. You failed to give him something he needed, as a son and as a man. I thought I had found a slot for him where he couldn't do any harm. For one thing, he should not have had access to the vault. The temptation was

214

too great. For another, I should have given him an opportunity to stretch his talents, whatever they are. I just took it for granted that he was limited.

"Bear this in mind, Anson. Floyd is not a criminal. If you abandon him now, if you throw him to the wolves, if they put him behind bars, I think it'll finish him for good." He paused and met the old man's eyes. "That's it. Where do we go from here?"

The old man stared at his hands, flexing the thickened knuckles. After a moment he looked up. "Will the bank surrender the counterfeit bonds?"

"I don't know," Mike said. "First you'd have to replace them with the originals. Which means we'd have to recover them from Stoufer, Wingate. Will you provide some other form of collateral for Floyd's account? Cash or different securities?"

Anson clamped his jaws. Then he reached for the phone and barked out an order. "Tell my son I want to see him at once."

36

The visiting pathologist from Tallahassee was a stout, irreverent man with a Pekingese face. He emerged from the autopsy lab in Miami and joined Ben Nestor on a bench in the corridor, exuding a faint odor of formaldehyde and bonded whisky.

"Sorry, Sheriff," he said jovially. "You'll have to start all over again at square one. The body you found in the Everglades is not Ross Landry. Landry's dental records do not match the cadaver's bridgework. Not even remotely. And since the remains, such as they are, turned up in your bailiwick, I take it you'll want him identified. So I have some trophies for you."

"Trophies?" Nestor said.

"Yep. A fine clear pictorial record of the deceased's choppers."

"Well now, Doctor, that poses a bit of a problem, doesn't it? Since I don't know who the man is, where he came from, or the name of any dentist who worked on him."

"Cheer up, Sheriff. All is not lost. We managed to lift a nice set of fingerprints for you."

Nestor arched a dubious eyebrow. "From a body in that condition?"

"Yep. We scientists are very clever fellows."

"But I saw the corpse, Doctor. I know its condition. Seems to me that high tide and decomposition destroyed the papillary ridges."

"On the outer surface only, Sheriff. Those ridges can generally be found on the inner portion, where they remain until the skin is totally destroyed. What we do, we cut a flap from the fingertip, the part necessary for classification. We preserve it in formaldehyde and turn it over to the laboratory. The technician attaches it to a piece of cardboard and then photographs it under oblique light, so that the ridges stand out in relief." He proffered an envelope. "It's all here. No charge. And it may do you some good. We like to co-operate with our law-enforcement officials."

Nestor put the envelope in his pocket. "You've forgotten something, Doctor."

"I have? Refresh my recollection, please."

"The cause of death."

"Ah, yes. Well, sir, the evidence points to a cerebrovascular accident. A fatal thrombus in one of the brain arteries. Death was probably instantaneous."

"Then we can write off foul play."

"Foul play. Quaint, Sheriff. Sounds like a Victorian novel. Yes, I am prepared to testify that death was caused by a natural phenomenon, providing we consider it natural for a man to ingest nourishment grossly rich in saturated fats. A prevalent

216

indulgence in our society. People digging graves with their own teeth." He patted his stomach. "Me included." He stifled a yawn. "Right now I need a brandy and transportation to the airport."

"Thanks for your help, Doctor."

"It's my job. The state pays me—neither well nor adequately, I might add."

"You'd make more in private practice."

"God forbid! I prefer to work on cadavers. They don't sneeze in my face or complain about impacted stools." He pushed himself erect. "I'm on my way. Good luck to you, sir."

Nestor drove over to Miami Police Headquarters. An inspector listened to his request and agreed to wire the dead man's fingerprints to Washington and ask for an immediate report, promising to notify Ocala Beach as soon as he had word.

It came the following morning, shortly after Nestor reached his office. Washington had a "make" on the deceased. According to army records, the dead man had been drafted during the Korean affair but had received a medical discharge several weeks later. When he heard the name, Nestor stiffened incredulously. He barely remembered to thank the Miami inspector before hanging up. He sat for a moment, his brain racing behind narrowed eyes, trying to adjust to the new information.

Nestor reached into his desk for the dead man's dental record and put it in his pocket, then strode through the outer office without comment to either of his deputies. When they saw his face they exchanged curious glances. He walked three blocks to the office of Leonard Hager, D.D.S.

Several patients in the waiting-room gave him the blank unsmiling look of people waiting their turn in the dentist's chair. Through the open door he could hear the hum of a high-speed drill. Hager was the only dentist in Ocala Beach, and since his work was well regarded, few of the local residents traveled to larger cities for treatment.

When Hager emerged, ushering out a small boy with a crucified expression, Nestor rose and caught his eye. Hager said, "Problem, Sheriff?"

"Not with my teeth. I need some information."

The dentist beckoned Nestor in and said over his shoulder, "Be with you in a moment, Bonnie." Hager closed the door. "I'm running a little late, Ben."

"This won't take long. Is the name Ward Bendiner familiar?"

"The man out at The Lodge."

"Have you treated him professionally?"

Hager nodded. "Bendiner lost a crown shortly after they moved here. He told me the work had been done in Mexico City, not a very good job. I fitted a new one. It should last as long as he does."

"Anything else?"

"A small amalgam and a prophylaxis. That's all he needed, although I took a set of x-rays to make sure."

"You still have them?"

"Of course."

Nestor reached into his pocket. "In strict confidence, Len, I want you to look at these pictures and tell me if they represent the mouth of the same man."

Hager removed a folder from his files, selected several frames, and aligned both sets of pictures along his viewbox. He snapped on the light, peered closely, and needed only thirty seconds to reach a conclusion.

"Same mouth, Ben. No question. You can see for yourself." He indicated with a pencil. "Here's the crown I installed. Now look at this front cap and the bridgework on these two molars." He turned and looked at the sheriff. "You want to tell me what's going on, Ben?"

"Not now. Later, perhaps. In the meantime I'd like you to initial all your plates for identification and let me lock them away for safe keeping."

Hager blinked. "You gonna need me as a witness, Ben?"

"Could be." Nestor touched his lips. "Not a word to anyone, hear?"

"Jesus, Ben! Sometimes you frighten me."

"Sometimes I frighten myself."

218

Walking back to his office, Ben Nestor uncharacteristically ignored the friendly greetings of passers-by. He was lost in thought, trying to find a semblance of logic in facts so convoluted he needed time to sort them out.

Ward Bendiner was dead. The evidence was incontestable. Fingerprints do not lie. They are as unique as a man's signature. And even more trustworthy as evidence because handwriting can be disguised or forged. Not so those little ridges. Oh, yes, they could be altered and perhaps destroyed, but disfigurement itself was evidence of concealment. And Bendiner's dental records offered additional confirmation.

But the man's wife had told Nestor that her husband was in New York and that she had spoken to him on the telephone at the same time that Bendiner's corpse lay rotting in the Florida 'Glades.

So Mrs. Bendiner was lying. But why? Ward Bendiner had died from natural causes. The autopsy showed a thrombus and heart failure. He decided not to confront the woman until he could find an explanation. He did not think his deputies would be much help. He was on his own.

There were messages from the capital waiting for him. He was still under intense pressure from the brass to fathom the disappearance of Ross Landry.

*   *   *

Floyd Gregorius, knees buckling, stumbled into his father's office with the doomed air of a man entering an execution chamber. Moisture glistened on his forehead. He had not slept over the past few nights and his brain now felt viscous with exhaustion. He saw a grim-faced Mike Ryan seated alongside the old man's desk.

Anson's gaze was stony. In a harsh voice he said, " We had a call from the Gotham Trust. UMI's transfer agent. Do I have to spell it out? So we're onto you, sonny. We know what you tried to pull. Goddammit, don't stand there dithering. Say something."

Floyd moistened his lips. " I'm sorry."

219

" You're sorry. You steal my bonds and you make a worthless substitution and you're sorry. That's all?"

" It was a temporary loan. I intended to return them."

" When? Did it not occur to you that Stoufer, Wingate might sell you out, then liquidate my bonds? That you might lose your own money, and mine too? Or that I might claim your endorsement on my bonds was a forgery and demand a cancellation of the sale? You think Stoufer, Wingate would absorb the loss? In a pig's ass, sonny. And Mr. Floyd Gregorius, the world's prize schmuck, would be up shit creek, indicted as a thief, convicted, imprisoned, disgraced. Not only you. But your family. Where the hell are your brains, sonny?"

Mike Ryan was tempted to leave. If the old man insisted on humiliating his son, it should have been done in private. He started to rise, but Anson waved him back with a peremptory gesture.

" Sit fast, Mike. This involves the firm, too."

Floyd, hangdog eyes fixed on the floor, said in a low voice, " I expected Arcadia to recover. And the bonds were not sold. I only pledged them as collateral."

" That's a piss-poor excuse. You know that Gregorius is acting as dealer-manager for UMI. And you're an officer here, at least you have a title. So you had access to inside information. You've been in the business long enough to know that trading on inside information is illegal. Did that simple thought ever occur to you?"

" No, sir."

" Whose machine did you use to duplicate the bonds."

" I'd prefer not to say."

" You'd prefer not to say," Anson mimicked. " Protecting your confederate, are you?"

" I have no confederate. I just don't want anyone else to pay for my mistake."

Anson arched an eyebrow. " Honor among thieves, hey? Well, it was more than a mistake, sonny. Something scrambled your brains. You'd have more success cracking walnuts with your ass than trying to play the market. And then protecting your position with securities that don't belong to you. Look at me, goddammit."

Floyd lifted his eyes. Surprisingly, he did not flinch.

"So," Anson said. "What do you think we ought to do about it? Should we try to save your ass?"

"The decision is not mine to make."

"You're learning. I talked it over with Ryan. He tells me I should try to bail you out."

Hope flickered. Floyd wanted to say something, but did not trust his own voice.

Anson said, "If we made the effort, sonny, that doesn't mean the banks would go along. Bankers are a sanctimonious clan. It's okay for them to bend the rules, but not anyone else. If they insist on prosecuting, look who's on the spot. Me. Because I sold the bonds and I delivered the fake certificates. Me. Anson Gregorius. Over half a century in this business, respected even by my enemies. So to protect myself, I have to implicate my son. Unless you want me to take the rap and spend my last years behind bars."

"No, sir."

"Thank you. Where is your key to the vault?"

"In my pocket."

"Give it to me." Floyd surrendered the key and Anson handed it to Ryan. "Here, Mike, it's your responsibility now."

Ryan held it for a moment, then offered it to Floyd.

"What the hell are you doing?" the old man asked.

"I'm sharing my responsibility. Take it, Floyd."

Floyd swallowed hugely, made an unintelligible sound, accepted the key, and stumbled hastily from the room.

The grim lines framing Anson's mouth relaxed. "You're quite a man, Michael."

"I just bought Floyd's loyalty and respect, if not his affection."

"Yes, I think you have. What's your next move?"

"The Gotham Trust. I'll arrange a meeting with Loren Harper."

"Right to the top, hey? You want me along?"

221

"Yes. You're still on a first-name basis with the old boy. We work in tandem on this one." As Anson started to rise, Mike added, "Not yet. You'll have to pony up some cash first, or other securities. To cover Floyd's margin account. Something I can exchange at Stoufer, Wingate for the UMI bonds. We'll need the originals before we go to the bank."

Anson grinned. "What the hell would you do here without me?"

37

Pete Sternbach examined the computer print-out. A wide smile stretched his mouth. The Croesus Fund already had a substantial profit on his Arcadia purchase. With the annual meeting drawing close, the short seller, or sellers, had already begun to cover and the stock was moving up. Croesus would beat the opposition hands down this year.

The telephone buzzed and a voice said, "Mr. Fred Hanna on number three. Will you take the call?"

Sternbach exhaled. This one he preferred to dodge. They had not been in touch since he had started buying the stock. At that particular time, in Hanna's view, inexcusable duplicity. Pete did not for a moment delude himself into believing that Hanna was unaware of his transactions. Or that some day the man would not attempt to square accounts. What the hell, Pete thought, smart market strategy called for the exploitation of every opportunity. And Fred Hanna himself had never hesitated to shaft anyone.

Pete said, "Tell him I'm in conference and— Never mind, put him on." He punched a button. "Sternbach."

"Hello, Pete." Hanna's amiable greeting signified that he

was not on the warpath. His voice exuded goodwill, with just a trace of disappointment. " Haven't heard from you in some time. I expected you to keep in touch."

" Busy as all hell here, Mr. Hanna."

" Not busy enough to keep you away from Los Angeles week after next, I hope."

" Los Angeles?"

" Arcadia's annual stockholders' meeting."

" Frankly, I hadn't even thought about it."

" Well now, Pete, your Croesus Fund has a very heavy position in the company. I imagine the outcome of our proxy fight should be a matter of considerable importance. And since UMI hasn't received your proxy, I took it for granted you meant to attend and vote the shares personally."

" As a rule, Mr. Hanna, we try to avoid getting involved in company politics."

" As a rule, yes. But I am going on the assumption that you intend to cash in after the takeover succeeds."

" That would be a fair assumption."

" Then the outcome affects your holdings."

" It certainly does. Thanks for reminding me. Let me have the exact date and I'll mark it down."

" Thursday the fourteenth. Incidentally, Pete, I know you have sources of information. Any idea who was behind that massive selling behind Arcadia."

" Not a clue. The SEC itself drew a blank."

" They tell me you moved in again at the bottom. I thought you had already completed your buying."

" We're always on the lookout for bargains."

" You certainly found one this time. About the annual meeting, Pete, I'll be flying out a day ahead of time. May I give you a lift on the company plane?"

" I appreciate that, Mr. Hanna, but I have a thing about flying. When I'm up there I prefer one of the big ones, like a 747, something with at least four engines."

" As you wish. We'll have a hospitality suite at the Beverly Hills. Drop by for a drink, will you?"

" Free booze I never refuse."

Hanna chuckled. " Well, good luck, Pete. See you in L.A."

Sternbach hung up and stared thoughtfully into space. Then he punched out the Arcadia symbol on his Videomaster. Up seven-eighths. Not bad. The short sellers were covering now at an accelerated pace. Time to start locking in some of his profits. He wanted to be out of the stock completely before the meeting. He reached for the phone again and dialed a number.

" Sternbach," he said. " How many shares of Arcadia can the market absorb without hurting the upward momentum?"

" Give me some numbers, please."

" I'd like to unload about ten thousand this afternoon."

" Then I'd suggest selling in thousand-share lots."

" Use your discretion. Tomorrow find out what the specialist has on his books. We'll start closing out in job lots."

" Yes, sir. And thanks for the business."

" Just remember, pal, we already negotiated your commissions on this one."

" You're cutting me to the bone, Pete."

" I bleed for you. You want the business or not?"

" I want it, I want it."

" Call me back and confirm."

Sternbach hung up and sat back with a feeling of almost orgiastic satisfaction.

*   *   *

We're coming down to the wire, Dan Hedrik thought. We're running out of time. Before his disappearance, Ross Landry had been unable to contact Bendiner. And now the man's shares were in Fred Hanna's pocket. Even worse, the probate court had taken under advisement a motion to compel Irving Garson, as Kate's executor, to vote the Rennie stock in conformance with Kiser's wishes. There was no precedent for granting such a motion, but if the opposition prevailed, Fred Hanna might be fairly close to a victory celebration.

He clamped his jaw and put a call through to Paul Slater in New York, voicing his misgivings.

224

"Don't worry about it, Dan," the lawyer said. "The judge has no choice. He'll have to deny the motion. I don't know why he's sitting on it so long."

"This guy is a political hack, Paul, with a reputation for cronyism. I'm afraid he can be reached."

"Too raw. We'd take it up on appeal and tie the estate into knots for months. So cheer up, friend. We're right on schedule at this end. Our proxy solicitations have brought an encouraging number of votes into camp. And the SEC is still crowding Hanna, checking him six ways from Tuesday. Haven't you noticed the market recovery in Arcadia shares?"

"What does it mean, Paul?"

"Among other things, it means that Dan Hedrik, as chief operating officer, with some hefty stock options in employment contract, is going to enjoy a very affluent retirement some day. Incidentally, Dan, do you have any late bulletins on Ross Landry?"

"Haven't you heard?"

"Heard what?"

"They found a body down there in the Everglades."

"Ah-h, Jesus!"

"We sent them Landry's dental records. It wasn't Ross. So they're still looking. They made some inquiries about an inscription on his watch, but I don't know why."

"I'll try to find out."

"Please. Landry's wife is half out of her mind. She wants to get up an expedition to go down there to look for him."

"Keep her at home, Dan. And let me know the instant you get a decision on that probate matter."

"Of course. About our annual meeting, Paul. When can we expect you in L.A. for the fireworks?"

"At least forty-eight hours before it's scheduled. I've already cleared the decks and two of my people will accompany me."

"No hotel, Paul. You'll stay at my place, you and your staff. I've got the room and the help. And an Arcadia limousine is at your service."

"We accept."

H 225

As usual, any talk with Slater was a shot in the arm. But the moment was short-lived. The instant he hung up, his secretary's voice was on the intercom. " I've been holding a call for you, Mr. Hedrik. Irving Garson is on the line."

Hedrik's heart lurched. He said, " Put him on. Irving? You have a decision on that motion?"

" Not yet. It's Davy Kiser. He's in the hospital."

Hedrik's fingers gripped the instrument. " What happened?"

" They found Kiser on the street, unconscious. In front of a tenement on Alameda, couple of rooms his pal Clinton had sublet. One of the neighbors called the police, and an ambulance took him to L.A. General. They found my card in his pocket and notified me. But tight-lipped, no details. So I got through to an old friend on the hospital staff. He got back to me. An overdose of heroin. Track marks all over the kid's arm. Davy was stoned out of his skull."

Hedrik shook his head. " Sonovabitch! No wonder Clinton had control of the boy. I thought they were living at Kate's place."

" So did I."

" Where in hell is that asshole buddy of his?"

" Nobody knows."

" Can we get in to see Kiser?"

" Not right now. A sergeant working out of Narcotics is in charge and he's posted a guard. They're getting a court order to search Clinton's premises, and if they find any drugs, they take the bastard into custody."

" The studio has some clout in this town. I'll pull a few strings. The boy needs someone."

" Wouldn't help. They've got him in Intensive Care."

" He's that bad?"

" Yes."

" I hope they don't scare Clinton into going underground."

" It's on the sergeant's mind. One of the things I want to talk to you about. He's making no public announcement. He's clamped a lid on it at the hospital. And he's got a stakeout at the Alameda address."

226

" Give me his name, Irving, so I can contact him directly."

*　　*　　*

Sheriff Ben Nestor sat patiently behind the wheel of his patrol car. He was parked off the road behind a huge banyan tree. It was after midnight and his eyes were fixed on the dark shadow of the Bendiner lodge. The air in his patrol car was stale because its windows were wound up tight against marauding insects.

This was the second night of his vigil. Earlier, the flickering shadows of a television set had died and all lights were extinguished. The woman was now safely tucked away for the night. Another hour and he would close up shop and go home.

He heard the night sounds of a tree toad and it brought back another vigil, long-ago, still strikingly vivid. He was crouching in underbrush, watching a group of North Koreans as they squatted around a fire, munching rations. He had been on the point of lobbing a grenade into their midst, and as his hand went back for the cast, he suddenly changed his mind and re-attached the grenade to his belt. He was not sure even now whether he had vetoed the action because the Koreans were teenaged boys or because there might be reinforcements in the area that could overrun his patrol. Nestor had never considered himself expendable.

He snapped to attention, instantly alert. A door in The Lodge had opened. Dim moonlight broke through the cloud cover. He saw an indistinct figure emerge and move toward the carport. A moment later a car door chunked shut and he heard the muffled throb of an engine. Twin beams pierced the night-time darkness and headed out along the driveway to the blacktop. Nestor started his engine and followed.

A mile down the road he picked up the tail-light pattern and faded back. Several times he switched off his own headlamps, turning them on again when an occasional car approached from the opposite direction.

Fifteen miles later he lost her on Route 41. He clicked on the high beams, floored the gas pedal, and sped past Everglades

City, hands gripping the wheel, eyes straining. He muffled an oath, braked the patrol car, and turned back.

When he saw the sign and the arrow he knew why he had lost her. He swung into the circular driveway of the Palms Motel and cruised past the neat bungalows until he spotted the white Mercedes parked alongside a green Mustang. He pulled up and got out. He felt the hoods of both cars. The Mercedes was hot, the Mustang still warm. He did not know Alex Bogart's registration number but he recognized a small diagonal dent in the front left fender.

Nestor took a Polaroid camera from the patrol car and attached a flashbulb. Standing back, he managed to get both cars into focus, together with their license plates and enough of the building to identify its location.

The two occupants of the bungalow were unaware of the sudden bright flash outside their shuttered window. Their eyes were already squeezed tight in an obliterating fog of carnality.

38

Attempting to bribe a member of the judiciary was at best a dubious proposition, and Robert Egan found himself walking on eggs. Nevertheless, by the end of his second day in Los Angeles, Egan had learned enough about Judge Clement Dodge to feel some measure of encouragement.

According to Egan's sources, Dodge had been appointed to the bench by an appreciative governor to complete the term of a recently deceased surrogate. Although heavily involved in the political process, Dodge seemed, on the surface at least, to be a man of decent reputation, good family background, high

Episcopalian, enjoying the prerogatives of office to such an extent that he had decided to make a run for the job on his own when the initial term expired. But, Egan's informant assured him, beneath the polished exterior lurked a character of crass opportunism.

Egan had made an appointment with the senior partner of the firm that handled UMI's legal affairs on the Coast. He approached the subject circuitously, inquiring about the probable outcome of Kiser's motion to compel Kate Rennie's executor to vote her Arcadia shares in conformance with the legatee's wishes.

The lawyer pursed his lips thoughtfully. "Let me tell you something about this particular judge, Mr. Egan. While no one would consider him a heavyweight, he is nevertheless a fairly competent lawyer. I do not believe that he would attempt to dictate estate policy to an executor, not without a showing of fraud, mismanagement, or misconduct. And to the best of my knowledge, Irving Garson is both an able and an honorable man."

"I understand he's over the hill."

"Aged, yes, but far from senile."

"Can the judge be influenced?"

The lawyer lifted an eyebrow and stared at Egan. "Of course Dodge can be influenced."

"By what?"

"By the equities involved. By precedent, if he can find any. Certainly not by any outside agency with a vested interest in the outcome."

"I've heard rumors about Clement Dodge."

"Would you care to be more specific?"

"No."

The lawyer sighed. "I, too, have heard rumors, Mr. Egan. And they may very well be true. But Clement Dodge does not need money. What he wants now is prestige and respectability. He would dearly love to be elected to the bench on his own. Were he to make an unprecedented ruling on that motion, Garson would certainly appeal. And I believe the appellate court

229

would reverse. As you know, reversals do not enhance a judge's reputation."

Egan dropped the subject. There would be no help from this source. Instead he discussed the upcoming stockholders meeting and together they laid out various strategies. An hour later Egan returned to his hotel. He hoped that after a brief nap he might be able to find the right combination to solve his problem.

*   *   *

Approximately two miles from Egan's hotel, two L.A.P.D. plainclothes detectives had been assigned to a stakeout at Al Clinton's apartment. One of them sat in an unmarked car near the garage exit. The other lounged diagonally across the street from the building entrance. Both detectives had studied a photograph of Clinton, enlarged from a snapshot found on the premises.

Something else had been found. Five ounces of pure heroin and half a dozen bottles of various restricted drugs. The detectives were under strict orders not to collar the suspect. It was hoped that under surveillance Clinton might lead them to his connection. The possibility existed, of course, that Clinton himself was a supplier.

David Kiser, they knew, had finally emerged from his coma, disoriented and babbling. They had nevertheless been able to reconstruct a sequence of events. Kiser had been alone at the Rennie house, desperately in need of a fix. He knew that a supply of horse was stashed somewhere in the Alameda apartment. He had gone there and searched until he located Clinton's cache.

Not realizing the stuff was uncut, he had mainlined a blast that racked him up. In panic he had staggered out of the building, probably the smartest move he ever made. Without medical attention his vital functions would probably have suspended operations.

The detective in the unmarked car was bored. Stakeouts were insufferably dull. He scratched the back of his neck and ruminated about the nineteen-year-old heavily bosomed addict he was currently treating with his own brand of therapy. One of the fringe benefits of being a narcotics cop. Then, without warning, his radio crackled into life and the tedium was over.

His partner's voice transmitted from a walkie-talkie said, "Here he comes, Steve. It's him, all right. He's heading for the apartment. About half a block away now and— Oh, shit! One of the residents stopped to greet him. The old fart who saw the super letting us into Clinton's apartment. Sonovabitch! Looks like he's telling him about Kiser. Now he's pointing to an upstairs window. That tears it, man. Clinton changed his plan. He's heading for the garage. Maybe we better pick him up."

"No. Against orders. He thinks we're waiting for him upstairs. Get over here fast."

A couple of minutes later Al Clinton's Volkswagen rolled up the garage ramp and turned west. Unobtrusively, the unmarked police car followed.

"What if he heads for the airport, Steve."

"Then we have no choice. We'll have to take him."

*   *   *

Loren Harper, president of the Gotham Trust, was a heavy-set man with silver hair and a ruddy complexion. He had worked for McNamara at the World Bank before settling in at the Gotham. He rose from behind his ornate desk to greet Anson Gregorius and Mike Ryan with an expression of deep solemnity. Ryan knew that Harper was deeply disappointed in his only son, who lived in a seedy loft, detested the establishment, and composed revolutionary songs.

"Sit down, gentlemen," he said. "We can dispense with the preliminaries. I know why you're here. Curtis Dahl informed me of the situation, but he did not, of course, have all the facts. Anson, how long have I known you? Twenty years? Well, unless there has been some radical alteration of character, I am not prepared to accept this incident at face value."

Anson nodded. "Thank you, Loren."

"Am I entitled to know the facts, exactly what happened and why?"

231

" Tell him, Michael."

Ryan made no attempt to sugar-coat the facts. He laid it all out in a blunt unvarnished statement: Floyd's speculation; the pressure from Stoufer, Wingate; and the attempt to " borrow " his father's bonds, replacing them with copies. And then, at a most unfortunate time, the need for Gregorius & Company to improve its capital position, and Anson's decision to sell his UMI bonds.

Loren Harper sat through the recital with his lips bunched. " Thank you, Mr. Ryan, for omitting any editorial comment. Have you recovered the original bonds from Stoufer, Wingate?"

" Yes, sir. We covered Floyd's account with other securities. The original bonds are now in Mr. Dahl's hands for transfer."

" I take it Floyd made his investment in Arcadia Films without recommendation from your own people?"

" He was acting entirely on his own."

" You've met my son," Anson broke in sourly. " He is not the most astute specimen in our firm."

Harper nodded sympathetically, thinking unhappily of his own son. " Has Floyd's access to the vault been restricted?"

" No, sir," Mike said.

Harper's eyes opened wide. " Then what measures have been taken to avoid a repetition?"

" A system of checks and double-checks, with complete responsibility in my hands."

" Would it not have been wiser to eliminate the temptation altogether?"

" In my judgment, Mr. Harper, Floyd Gregorius was severely traumatized by this incident. The lesson has been indelibly inscribed and I believe guarantees his future integrity. I felt it important to try to help the man by some concrete demonstration that we had not written him off."

The banker nodded slowly. " I am especially vulnerable to such an argument." He smiled meagerly. " And I suspect, Mr. Ryan, that you are not unaware of that fact. But you must understand the bank's position. If we agree to forget this incident, we would be guilty of suppressing evidence about a criminal attempt."

"No one has suffered any loss, Mr. Harper."

"Only because one of our employees was alert. If he had passed those counterfeits . . ." Furrows deepened in the banker's brow.

Mike made no comment.

Harper placed his hands flat on the desk and leaned forward. "I have given the matter considerable thought. I have not discussed it with counsel. And I am not certain that my decision is well-advised. Nevertheless, because of my esteem for Anson Gregorius, because of your prompt action in replacing the counterfeit certificates, and because I cannot see that any useful purpose will be served by pursuing the matter, I am going to put it to rest. The bank will forget that it ever happened."

"And you will so notify Curtis Dahl?"

"Yes. I intend to give him the facts. Do you have any objection?"

"No, sir. I believe the facts are preferable to idle speculation."

Harper punched a sequence of buttons on his telephone. "Curtis, send those counterfeit UMIs to my office. We'll talk about it at lunch." He looked up at Anson. "I'll destroy them in your presence."

"Thank you, Loren."

"May I ask one last question?"

"By all means."

"What is your prediction on the outcome of this proxy fight?"

"As of this moment, the prospects seem to favour Universal Media."

"Is a trade indicated?"

Anson smiled delightedly. "Are you asking me for a stock tip, Loren?"

"I prefer not to label it."

"Then let me be perfectly honest. It's late in the game. Sit this one out."

233

The banker grunted. "A straightforward response in a business known for equivocation. Thank you."

Anson bowed slightly. "Gregorius & Company is indebted to you, Loren."

39

Kevin Anthony Duke III went directly from Dulles International to the SEC offices and presented himself to G. G. Pressman, weary and rumpled. The Enforcement chief puffed on his pipe, its bowl filled with a mixture that burned poorly.

"No recapitulation necessary," Pressman said. "You are convinced that both Hedrik and Stern are on the level. No kickback offered, none received. And I am convinced that the Caswell letter is a fake. Too bad some Arcadia stockholders will be influenced by it. You look tired."

"I've been living out of a suitcase, sir. I'll be fine after a night in my own bed."

"Sorry to deprive you of that luxury, son. You'll be sleeping in New York tonight. Flight reservations are at the front desk. Have you noticed the activity in Arcadia these past few days?"

"No, sir. No quotations available aboard airplanes. But I hear it's on the way up again."

"Yep. In heavy trading."

"Fred Hanna?"

"Probably. Arcadia's annual meeting is coming up fast. Proxies will be counted. So I want you to start checking brokerage houses again."

"We'll get the same runaround."

"Certainly. But if the identical foreign nominees are now

buying again at this particular time, it supports our thesis that Arcadia is being manipulated. I want that information." Pressman tugged at an earlobe. " One of these days I'm hoping we can work out a more liberal exchange of information with those little gnomes in Zurich. And, God willing, the statute of limitations will still be in force."

Duke straightened and gave a mock salute. " I'm on my way."

" You'll be visiting the family, I suppose."

" Yes, sir."

" How long since you've seen K. A. Duke II?"

" Couple of months."

" He still wants you to join that fancy shop of his?"

" He grows starry-eyed at the prospect."

" With fine heavy broadloom underfoot in your office?"

" No, sir. A genuine Bokhara."

" And a partnership?"

" In due course."

" Weekly stipend?"

" Three times what Uncle Sam is paying me."

" And one-third the pleasure."

" One-fifth. I don't think he could pay me enough to compensate for all that boiler-plate crap."

" I'm proud of you, son. Now get on your bicycle and start rolling."

*   *   *

The Cuban community in Ocala Beach was a small one. A handful of refugees, first from Castro and then from Miami. It comprised several domestics and a few shopkeepers, industrious and law-abiding.

Tomás Hernandez operated a fast-food franchise. He greeted Sheriff Ben Nestor with a toothy smile. " Ah, Sheriff, it is many days. I think perhaps you no longer enjoy my Southern fried chicken."

" Very busy, amigo. But today I'm hungry."

Hernandez snapped a finger, and the grinning cook turned

up the fryer and dipped a chicken breast into thick batter Nestor sat at one of the small tables.

" Join me, Tomás. I need your help."

" It is yours, Sheriff."

" You have a *compatriota* here, a young woman who worked as a domestic for some people named Bendiner."

" Ah, yes. Maria Olivera." Hernandez kissed his fingertips. " A most splendid one. But she was dismissed by those people."

" Do you know where I can find her?"

Sudden alarm clouded the dark face. " You think Maria did a bad thing, Sheriff." He shook his head emphatically. " That is not possible. There must be some mistake."

" Slow down, amigo. Nothing like that. I merely need some information about her former employers."

Hernandez breathed a sigh of relief. " What do you wish of me?"

" Her address. Where can I find Miss Olivera?"

" Maria works for the motel here, the Everglades. Part time now because it is not the tourist season."

" Chambermaid?"

" Yes."

" How is her English?"

" Better than mine. She went to school in Miami."

" I don't wish to frighten the girl, Tomás. Will you take me to her and put her at ease? Tell her what a fine fellow I am."

" *Seguramente*. But first enjoy the chicken."

They used the Hernandez car, a four-year-old Buick in mint condition, glittering with chrome accessories. Hernandez sat erect, like the driver of a bus. It was, he told Nestor, Maria's day off. They drove to the Hispanic section at the edge of town. Maria Olivera lived with her parents in a small frame cottage. Nestor, waiting on the porch, heard a rapid-fire volley of Spanish before Hernandez brought her out, an exuberantly healthy young woman, dusky-skinned, smiling tentatively.

" This is Sheriff Ben Nestor, Maria," Hernandez said. " He is my friend. He wishes to ask you some questions."

She looked at Nestor with solemn expectancy.

236

"How do you do, Miss Olivera. I'm told that you once worked for a family named Bendiner."

"That is true, Sheriff."

"How long were you employed there?"

"Almost three months."

"Were they good employers?"

"The gentleman gave me no trouble."

"And the lady?"

"Very bossy, Sheriff, and demanding." *

"Did they get along well?"

"In the beginning they were close. Later, not so much. I do not remember any fighting, but there was strain. And then the gentleman stopped making—" She stopped, and color stained her cheeks.

"Stopped what, Maria?"

"They stopped sleeping with each other."

"How do you know this, Maria?"

"Because there was a convertible sofa in the study and in the morning when I came to work, every morning, I saw that he had slept there."

"No explanation?"

"It was not my place to ask." She hesitated, frowning, on the point of volunteering additional information.

"Yes, Maria?" Nestor prompted. "You were about to tell me something else?"

"I think it was because Señor Bendiner was not well."

"How do you mean?"

She touched her left breast. "He was taking pills for his heart."

"What kind of pills?"

"Nitroglycerin."

Nestor kept his bland and polite expression intact. "And how do you know about such things, Maria?"

She gestured toward the house. "My father is in bed this week. He has suffered from angina attacks for almost a year. That is the same drug our doctor prescribed for him. Tiny white tablets. I myself took the prescription to the pharmacy. And

237

I recognised the bottle when I took things from his bathroom cabinet to clean the shelves."

" When did you leave the Bendiners?"

" About seven weeks ago."

" Who dismissed you?"

" The lady. I had the weekends off and she came here one Sunday after lunch and told me that her husband had been called to New York on business, and that she was going to Miami for a couple of weeks. She gave me cash for the money that was owed me, plus an extra week's wages. She said she would call for me when she got back and maybe if I was still free I could work for them again. But she never got in touch, and anyway, I do not think I would care to work for that one again."

" Why is that, Maria?"

" Because she does not speak the truth. Twice, when she was supposed to be in Miami, I saw her car, the white one, parked at the shopping centre, and I watched until she came out of the supermarket and drove away."

Nestor said gravely, " I am much in your debt, Maria."

" It is nothing."

" I would appreciate one more favor. It is important that you do not discuss our talk with anyone."

" But my parents know you are here. They will ask questions."

" Tell them I am investigating a small disturbance at the restaurant of Señor Hernandez."

" You wish me to speak a lie?"

" A small lie that will harm no one."

A bright smile illuminated her face. " Ah, yes. I was there when it happened. A tourist who had been drinking too much."

" Excellent."

" And in exchange for this small lie that will harm no one, your handsome deputies will not give me any parking tickets."

Tomás Hernandez gave a great roar of laughter. " But, Maria, you have no automobile."

" I know. But one day perhaps some rich *norteamericano* will be generous."

238

Nestor could not repress a grin. "No parking tickets," he said. "But also no speeding, Maria."

"Then we have a deal, Sheriff."

She walked to the car with them and waved as they drove away. Hernandez said, "That one is a treasure, amigo."

"I am beginning to realise that. I think I will have to know Maria much better."

"If I were not married, amigo, you would have competition."

40

It was almost nine in the evening when Robert Egan returned to his room after dining alone in the hotel restaurant. After conferring long-distance with Fred Hanna, it was decided that he should remain in Los Angeles to prepare for next week's annual meeting of Arcadia stockholders.

Hanna had not been pleased at Egan's inability to accelerate the probate of Kate Rennie's will and his decision not to approach the judge. Egan was pouring himself a drink when the telephone rang.

"This is A.C., Mr. Egan." Al Clinton always used his initials.

"Yes."

"There's been some trouble. I need—"

"Hold it!" Egan snapped. "Where are you calling from?"

"A telephone booth."

"Give me the number and I'll call you right back."

He left his suite, notepad in hand, and took an elevator to the lobby. He found a booth and closed the door behind him. He dialed and Al Clinton answered on the first ring.

"All right, Al. What's the problem?"

" Kiser. He went to my apartment, found some horse and overdosed. He passed out in the street and got hauled off to the hospital."

" When?"

" Yesterday. I didn't know about it until this afternoon."

" This afternoon? Where the hell were you all night?"

" Look, I've been nursing Kiser for weeks and I got hungry for a little action."

" You left the boy alone, overnight, an addict, with every chance that he might go back to your place looking for a fix?"

" I had it stashed away pretty good."

Egan suppressed an oath. " All right, Al. It's done. Where do we stand now?"

" Judge for yourself. I was heading back to the apartment this afternoon for a couple of blasts to take back to the Rennie house when I met one of the neighbors. He told me about Kiser. He said the kid was out cold, unconscious. He said the super had opened my apartment for the cops. They had a search warrant. Narc agents probably. Those guys know how to take a place apart. They must have found enough shit to put me back in the slammer. And if Kiser craps out, it's gonna be a lot worse."

" I understand. Keep talking."

" Well, I figured they had a stakeout in the apartment, so I stayed away. I got my car and cut. I've been trying to reach you ever since."

" Do you have a safe place to hole up?"

" Not here."

" Where do you want to go?"

" Mexico. For a couple of months at least. I have a birth certificate and a Social Security number under another name. I can cross over at Laredo. Trouble is, I can't get at my money. I need some cash."

" How much?"

" Twenty grand—for now."

" I'm three thousand miles from company headquarters, Al. The best I can manage right now is about ten thousand."

"Not enough, Mr. Egan. We'd have to be in touch again too soon." Clinton lowered his voice meaningfully. "The risk is too great. And not only for me. They might find out what really happened to the Rennie woman."

After a moment Egan said quietly, "Okay, Al. I'll put the bite on some of our local people. What about the car? It's registered in your name, isn't it?"

"I switched plates earlier this evening. And I'm gonna ditch it anyway, probably tonight. That's why I need the twenty. I want to buy some new wheels at a used-car dealer tomorrow before I take off."

"Where are you now?"

"San Bernardino."

"You're sure no one followed you?"

"Positive. I thought a couple of guys might be tailing me, but I lost them on the freeway. I moved in with a pack, found a hole at the right moment, swung out through an exit, and saw them get swept along in the flow."

"Police car?"

"Unmarked, if it was."

"All right, Al. I'll try to raise the cash. If I can't, I'll wire the balance and it'll be waiting for you in Laredo under your new name."

Clinton sighed. "I don't have much choice, do I?"

"Not at the moment. Where shall we meet?"

"There's a big shopping plaza on Route 66 just east of town. You won't have any trouble finding it. When can I expect you?"

"About eleven o'clock."

"Look for my bug, a tan Volks, at the far end of the lot. There's an ice-cream van parks there every night. I'll be sitting behind the van. The stores are all closed at that hour, except for a Chinese restaurant at the other end, so there won't be many cars in the lot."

"All right, Al. Sit tight and keep a low profile."

"I'll be waiting, Mr. Egan."

241

* * *

The driver of the unmarked police car was an old hand. He knew all the angles. When the tan Volkswagen had slipped into a pack of slower-moving cars, he had instantly surmized Al Clinton's intent and dropped back. He reached for his mike and contacted the backup car behind him.

" I think he's spotted me, Gus. He's gonna try to lose us at the next exit. Get over into the far right lane and follow him off. We'll stick to the freeway until the next exit and then we'll stay out of sight until you need us."

" Got it, Steve. Everything's under control."

* * *

Robert Egan reached the shopping plaza shortly after eleven. He saw the neon sign of the Chinese restaurant and pulled his rental car into one of the parking slots reserved for its patrons. He left the car, carrying his attaché case, and ducked into the restaurant. The characteristic aroma of cooking oils wrinkled his nose. He shook his head at the hatcheck girl and pointed to the telephone booth. He made an elaborate pretence of dropping a coin and dialing a number. He was pantomiming a conversation when a large table of diners, obviously a celebration, came out and headed for the exit. Egan hung up and merged into the group.

As the people headed for their various cars, Egan melted away and blended into the shadow of trees bordering the parking lot. He saw the silhouette of an ice-cream van at the far end. Crouching low, he moved along the shadowed perimeter until he spotted Al Clinton's Volkswagen. When his head suddenly appeared at the side window, Clinton gave a violent start.

Egan gestured and Clinton stretched a hand to release the latch. Egan folded the front seat and climbed into the rear, resting the attaché case on his lap.

" Jesus, Mr. Egan! That was pretty good. I never heard a sound. Where's your car?"

" In the restaurant area."

" Smart. Look, I'm sorry about Kiser. We came close. We almost had it wrapped up."

" Nothing ever runs smoothly, Al. We expect setbacks from time to time. From now on, just stick to the scenario. Okay?"

" You're the boss."

" About this car. I think you ought to abandon it right here. Tonight. Wherever you switched the plates, those people may have spotted it and notified the police. Let's not take any chances."

" Yes, sir. But that kind of restricts my mobility. How will I get around?"

" There's a used-car dealer two miles down the road. To-morrow pick yourself a good late model."

" And sleep where tonight?"

" I'll drive you to a motel close to the dealer's lot."

" I think I know the place. It's a lousy fleabag."

" Can't be helped, Al. One night won't kill you."

" Look, Mr. Egan, I've been listening to the radio. The sky is overcast and they expect rain any minute. You can smell it in the air now. Nobody is gonna stop me with these plates to-night. I'll take off as soon as you leave, and I can be out of the state by daylight. I'll ditch the car first thing in the morning."

" No, Al. You're too valuable to lose. We can't take any chances."

Clinton agreed reluctantly. " Okay. How about the money?"

" I have it right here. Fourteen thousand is the best I could do. The balance will be waiting for you at American Express in Laredo. Give me the name you'll be using."

Clinton produced a slip of paper. " I wrote it down for you. What if the heat up here forces me to stay away longer?"

" No problem, Al. You're on a lifetime pension. UMI appreciates the services you've rendered."

Clinton grinned, showing his square spaced teeth. " Yeah, we been through some hairy jobs together, Mr. Egan."

Egan raised the lid of the attaché case and brought out a heavily packed envelope. " Here's the first instalment. Fourteen thousand. Count it, please."

Clinton faced front and switched on the dim dashboard light. He started thumbing through the bills, intently absorbed, whispering numbers to himself. Egan reached into the case again and quietly removed a .38-calibre Smith & Wesson, its barrel fitted with a custom silencer. At contact range, he shot Al Clinton in the back of the head. The impact sprawled Clinton over the wheel and splattered brain tissue across the windshield.

Egan put the gun away, feeling mild regret. The man had indeed been a valuable asset. He had performed exceptional services. Now, however, he had outlived his usefulness. From the moment young Kiser had overdosed, Clinton's credit at UMI was overdrawn.

Fastidiously avoiding the ruined skull and any trace of blood, Egan leaned over the seat and retrieved the bills. He reached for Clinton's wrist and detected no pulse. Carefully and methodically he wiped all surfaces of the car that he may have touched. Then he opened the door, stepped out, wiped the handles on both sides, and chunked it shut with his elbow. The attaché case was under his arm.

Once again he melted into the tree shadows along the perimeter of the parking lot and worked his way back to the rental car. He started the engine and drove back to his hotel suite in Los Angeles.

*　　*　　*

The unmarked Pontiac was parked at a closed service station across the road from the shopping plaza. The narcotics agent behind the wheel sat waiting. His partner was perched on a stool in the storage room of the Chinese restaurant, night glasses fixed on a segment of the Volkswagen's hood. The rest of the Volks was concealed by an ice-cream van. The agent had been surprized by a sudden fleeting glimpse of a second figure. He guessed that the new arrival had joined Clinton in the bug and he was frustrated by his blocked view. He depressed the transmit button on his walkie-talkie and alerted his partner.

" Somebody's with Clinton now," he said. " Maybe his connection, maybe not. Tricky bastard. I never saw where he came from."

" Shall we take them?"

" Not now. Call Twenty-six and have them block the exit."

They were not quick enough. The man with the night glasses caught another glimpse of the second figure and then lost it again among the trees. Headlights suddenly flashed on in the restaurant parking area. He swung the glasses and noted the registration number of the departing vehicle.

He spoke to his partner again. " The visitor is leaving."

" Which one shall we grab?"

" Let's stick with Clinton. I have the other man's registration. We can get a line on him later and maybe nail a few colleagues."

The Volkswagen had not moved. The agent wondered whether Clinton intended to spend the night there. When the backup car arrived, he decided to have a look. He used the same route taken by Clinton's visitor, approaching from the rear. He drew his gun, crouched low, and moved in. He saw Clinton slumped over the wheel. Damned if the guy wasn't sleeping, after all. He aimed a beam from his pocket torch and sucked in a ragged breath.

" Jeezus!" he whispered and began waving the torch frantically.

41

Two separate dramas were being enacted simultaneously at the Beverly Plaza, one in the thickly packed Grand Ballroom, the other behind the scenes.

From the moment Dan Hedrik had taken his place on the platform to call the annual meeting to order, there had been factional attempts at disruption. Emotions ran high. Arcadia stockholders, primed by UMI's tender offer, kept ignoring Hedrik's gavel to trumpet their grievances. Other stockholders, sympathetic to management, tried to shout them down. They had heard rumors that a slate of directors nominated by Fred Hanna might be elected in sufficient numbers to provide him with a majority on the new board.

Confused ushers, circulating through the aisles with hand microphones, were offering them to dissidents not recognised by the chair. Near-bedlam prevailed.

In a private service area off the Grand Ballroom bonded experts provided by the First California Trust were counting proxies. Two officers of the bank, having filed their statutory oaths, and flanked by their own legal advisers, were seated at a special table, acting as inspectors of election, ruling on the validity of all disputed proxies.

At the moment they were trying to mediate a bitter argument between Michael Ryan and Robert Egan on one side, and Arcadia's counsel Paul Slater on the other. Ryan, waving David Kiser's proxy, argued for its validation even though it represented shares still undistributed by the estate. Paul Slater held a proxy signed by Irving Garson representing the same shares.

Ryan said crisply, " Apparently you don't follow our position, gentlemen. Miss Rennie's estate is still in probate. A motion is on file requesting an adjudication of this point. There seems to be some delay and the surrogate still has it under advisement. At the very least, we insist that any vote on these particular shares be suspended until a decision is reached."

The bank officers looked up at Slater, who shook his head vigorously. The Rennie shares were vital to Arcadia's management. "No delay," he snapped. "We demand a ruling here and now."

The bank spokesman said, " Mr. Ryan, are you asking us to exclude the Rennie shares from our calculations at this meeting?"

246

Egan broke in with cold authority. "Not asking, sir, demanding."

"Can you cite any precedent for such a request."

"I suggest that you set a precedent right now."

"On what grounds?"

"The grounds of equity, sir. David Kiser, as Miss Rennie's sole legatee, is the true owner of these shares and should be empowered to exercise his franchise."

"Our obligation requires us to recognize only holders of record or their legal representatives."

Mike Ryan took up the argument.

At the same time, in the ballroom beyond, Dan Hedrik had managed to restore a semblance of order. His corporate officers sat behind him at a long table, with a stenotypist alongside to record the proceedings.

A number of seats in the front row had been reserved for Fred Hanna and his UMI associates. A messenger scurried back and forth to whisper bulletins on Ryan's progress in the other room. The proxies from Hanna's offshore nominees had been counted and the news was encouraging. Hanna's huge investment in the Bendiner shares was paying off handsomely. And if Ryan succeeded in validating the Kiser proxy, the battle would be won. He turned his attention back to the platform.

Over the public address system, Hedrik's voice was now clearly audible. "I believe most of the stockholders here are acquainted with the issues. I want to remind you that as stockholders you are the true owners of Arcadia Films. And that under the law you are entitled to change your vote at this meeting even though you have previously sent your vote by mail."

Fred Hanna smiled. Even if every stockholder in the ballroom, impressed by Dan Hedrik's air of integrity, decided now to support management, it would not affect the outcome. Most of Arcadia's stockholders were dispersed across the country and only a small percentage had appeared in California for the meeting.

Hedrik had offered Hanna a chance to address the meeting,

247

but Hanna had decided to forgo the opportunity. With victory almost in sight, there was no point, he felt, in exposing himself to a small group of dissidents.

Hedrik had continued speaking. "You have all been informed of management's plans for the company and what we hope to accomplish in the future. I can assure you that—" He broke off, staring in blank astonishment at the door to the service area.

Eyes turned and a sudden profound hush fell over the ballroom. Fred Hanna craned his head and shock froze his stomach and his reflexes. He could not believe his eyes. Robert Egan had just emerged through the folding doors, his face white and angular. Two bulky men had fastened a grip on each arm above Egan's elbows, pulling him along the side aisle toward the exit. Hanna saw that Egan's wrists were handcuffed behind his back.

For the space of a single heartbeat Fred Hanna suffered a total paralysis. Then, abruptly, he lunged to his feet and was moving. He caught up with the three men at the bank of elevators, closing in with that air of command which had often terrified his underlings.

"I'm Fred Hanna," he said brusquely. "President of Universal Media Industries. Mr. Egan is an officer of my company. Where are you taking him?"

The two men eyed him, impassive and unimpressed. "Police Headquarters," one of them said. "He's under arrest."

"On what charge?"

"Suspicion of murder."

"Do you have a warrant?"

The elevator door opened. Without responding to Hanna's last question, the two men shouldered Egan into the car and blocked Hanna from following.

Fred Hanna wheeled and stalked back to the ballroom, down the side aisle and into the service area. He saw Mike Ryan conferring in a corner with UMI's local attorneys, all of them looking stunned.

Hanna approached and said, "What the hell happened here, Mike? What's this all about?"

"I don't know. They marched in here without warning, shook Egan down, cuffed him, read him his rights, and took him away."

Hanna turned to one of the lawyers. "Get on the telephone and find out what's happening."

"I'll try, Mr. Hanna. But you may be disappointed in the results. My firm has no experience in these matters. Our practise is limited to corporate law. We have no contacts in either the police department or the prosecutor's office."

Hanna concentrated a blue glare. Anger and frustration reverberated in the suddenly high nasal pitch of his voice. "Christ! We spend a fortune on lawyers and they don't know what the hell to do in an emergency." Before the man could frame a reply, Hanna was stalking over to Arcadia's counsel.

"Mr. Slater?"

"Yes."

"You saw what happened here?"

Slater nodded shortly. "Mr. Egan was standing next to me when the police appeared."

"I know your reputation, sir. I remember that case you handled in New York. We're on opposing teams here, but I do not think there would be any conflict of interest if you were to offer some advice. Mr. Egan is, after all, a member of the New York bar. He appears to be in grave trouble. Would you care to make a suggestion?"

Paul Slater was surprised. Despite Hanna's hubris, his eyes betrayed a vestige of uncertainty, as if he had lost his right arm. The man, Slater judged, was under severe strain, perhaps even a bit derailed, appealing to me, of all people. Slater said, "Those cops mentioned a homicide charge. They would not have arrested Egan without convincing evidence. What he needs is the best damn criminal defence lawyer you can find. Preferably a local man. Los Angeles is a big city. There must be dozens of them here. Your counsel should be able to—"

Slater broke off as one of the messengers approached. "Long-distance call, Mr. Slater. Your office in New York. They say it's urgent."

249

Slater excused himself and hurried to the special lines that had been installed for the use of company officers.

"Paul?" a familiar voice said. "Jim Sloane here. Listen, all hell just broke loose. We thought you should be notified at once. The facts are confusing and we have no specific details. Something about Ward Bendiner. Seems the man has been dead for over a month. So how in hell could he have sold those shares to Fred Hanna?"

Slater's mind raced, absorbing implications. "My God, Jim, that spins this whole election right off the spool. Now look, time is of the essence, pull strings, get the facts, and call me back as soon as possible. Contact Nicoletti in the D.A.'s office. In view of the proxy fight out here, he may open the bag for you."

"Right. Can you keep this line open?"

"Yes."

"How's it going?"

"Touch and go, until a couple of minutes ago. Talk about all hell breaking loose, listen to this: a couple of cops walked in here and put the arm on UMI counsel Bob Egan. Suspicion of murder."

Jim Sloane whistled. "Are you serious?"

"The man is in handcuffs and on his way to Police Headquarters. And get a load of this, Fred Hanna just came over to me and asked for my advice."

Sloane laughed. "By God, that's rich! Must be something in the water supply out there. Or else Hanna is half out of his wits."

"Probably a little of both. All right, Jim, I can't talk any longer. I'm about to throw a bomb into the annual meeting of Arcadia stockholders. We may have to adjourn the proceedings until some of the smoke clears."

42

Three thousand miles across the continent from the Arcadia meeting, on the morning of that same day, Sheriff Ben Nestor landed at Kennedy Airport on an early-bird flight from Florida, and rode a Carey limousine into Manhattan.

On his two previous visits to New York, Nestor had found it a city of prodigal attractions. He was beguiled by its energy, its glitter, and its cultural profusions. At the same time he took a jaundiced view of its cynical opulence and its intemperate commercialism.

The A.G. in Tallahassee had already phoned the police brass to explain his mission. He spent thirty minutes with a local commander, clarifying his visit, informing the man that at this time it was no more than a fishing expedition.

Now, in civilian garb, he stood looking up at the Kilburne Arms, feeling a hollowness in his stomach and a quickening of his blood. He checked again the small .22-calibre handgun tucked into the waistband of his trousers. Not much of a piece but lethal enough at close range. Nestor knew that he would feel no compunction at firing a mortal shot if his own life were at stake, nor for that matter any pleasure either.

He reflected on the events that had brought him to this city and to this address. After divulging his findings to the Palm County prosecutor, it was decided that Bendiner's Ocala Beach telephone should be tapped. A court order was granted and one of Nestor's men had monitored the line from Saturday through Sunday. Several calls had been made to New York, answered by a switchboard operator saying, " Kilburne Arms," then ringing the requested suite and adding, " Sorry. Mr. Bendiner does

251

not answer." Cora Bendiner had left her name, but the calls had not been returned.

"What I would like to know," the prosecutor had said, "is how in hell it is possible for the woman to keep calling a man in New York who's been identified as a corpse in Florida. Talk it over with the A.G., Ben. They may want you to fly up there and check it out."

Entering the Kilburne lobby, Nestor by-passed the desk and went directly to the self-service elevator. He knew the suite number and ascended to the seventh floor, stopping in front of apartment 7-A. He listened for a moment, heard movement inside the apartment, and rang the bell.

A tall black woman, holding a dustcloth, opened the door. She stared at him without expression. "Yes?"

"I'm looking for Mr. Ward Bendiner."

"The gentleman," she said, emphasizing the word, "is not here."

"Do you know when he'll be back?"

"Sometime today, I guess. The housekeeper told me he was away for the weekend."

"May I come in and wait?"

She frowned. "That's against the rules."

"Perhaps you could bend the rules a little for a lawman." He showed her his shield.

"Why don't you ask at the desk?"

"Because I want to surprize Mr. Bendiner and I expect the clerk would tell him I'm here."

She looked dubious. "Let me see that badge again."

He held it up. "I'm from Mr. Bendiner's hometown in Florida."

"Thought I recognized your accent. Where in Florida?"

"Palm County, Ocala Beach."

"Hey! I'm from Tampa myself." The dark eyes changed, narrowing suspiciously. "It says Sheriff on that thing, doesn't it? You one of them cracker lawmen gets his jollies beating up on us woolly heads?"

"No, ma'am. Not now, or ever."

" How many deputies you got?"

" Three."

" How many blacks?"

" Thirty-three and a third per cent."

" Fair enough." She stared at him. " He your token nigra to butter up the black vote?"

Nestor consulted his watch. " Isaac is on duty now. I'll give you the number. Call collect and ask him yourself."

She flashed a white smile. " Can't put my finger on it, Sheriff. Could be your eyes. For some reason, I kind of believe you. Come on in." She stood aside and then closed the door behind them. " This Bendiner in some sort of trouble?"

" That's what I'm here to find out."

" Well, I hope you give him a hard time."

" I take it you don't like the man."

" That's the truth, Sheriff. He made a pass and I blocked it. I don't like being pawed by the man because I'm stacked pretty good and he thinks maybe I'll peddle it for a couple of bucks or a pat on the head. Tell me, what's my protection if I let you wait here?"

" The question won't come up. If it does, I'll tell them I used a passkey. Or picked the lock."

" Okay. Set. I'll be finished here in a couple of minutes and out of your way."

He watched her vacuum the carpets. She held up crossed fingers and left. Nestor went into the bedroom and examined the closets, then the bureau drawers. He found a package of brokerage statements and confirmation slips from Gregorius & Company. He was tempted to pocket them, but resisted the impulse. It would be a violation of the constitutional protection against illegal search and seizure, and he wanted to provide no escape hatch.

There was a small pantry. He pulled up a stool and sat behind the partially open door. It gave him an angled view of the apartment entrance. Time passed slowly. He found himself staring at the refrigerator and realised that his stomach was rumbling with hunger. He reached over and found a packet of cheese, reasonably fresh. He peeled off several slices and began to chew methodically.

He had lost track of time when he heard the foyer door open. He held his breath and peered through the hinged opening between door and wall. He heard footsteps and the shuffling of paper. Probably messages picked up at the front desk. He could not see the arrival. Then he heard the man's voice at the telephone, asking the operator to get him a long-distance number. Nestor recognised the Ocala Beach area code.

Within moments the call was completed and the voice said, "Cora baby, it's me."

All that education, Nestor thought irrelevantly, and his grammar is shot to hell. Nestor longed to hear the other end of the conversation, but he could not risk the telltale click of an extension phone on the pantry wall.

"I was out of town for the weekend," the voice said, "Just got back and found your messages. Anything new down there?" There was a long pause. "Well, don't worry about it. Relax, baby. I'll be finished here in a few days. Then you can close The Lodge and we're off. Sure, miss you too, baby." The handset dropped into its cradle.

Ben Nestor walked quietly into the living-room and said, "Hello, Alex."

Bogart wheeled. Color drained from his face and his jaw sagged. His mouth stretched into a ghastly smile. "Ben?" he whispered.

"Your old school chum from Ocala Beach, Counselor. Where is he?"

"Where is who?"

"Your client. The man who's supposed to be living here. Ward Bendiner."

Perspiration broke out on Bogart's forehead. "I—I don't know."

"Don't shit me, Alex. Bendiner is dead and you know it. Maybe you even helped the lady haul the body off to the 'Glades, where you hoped it would disappear forever. We found him, Alex, and we have a positive make. Fingerprints, dental

254

records, the works. And his widow is acting as though he were alive and staying here in New York, at this hotel, in this apartment." Nestor raised his hand. " Save it, Alex. Don't waste my time. The staff here can testify that you're passing yourself off as Bendiner. And so can the people at Gregorius & Company."

" It was a natural death, Ben. He died in bed."

" And you carted his corpse off to the Everglades."

" A misdemeanor, Ben. Transporting a dead body."

" Well, thank you, Counselor. We're making progress. What I'm trying to understand is why you concealed the fact. Why you're masquerading as the dead man."

" Nothing terrible, Ben. Just trying to expedite the estate."

" Expedite? That's a dry hole, Alex. Looks more like a conspiracy to strip the estate clean. Tell me why. The woman was married to Bendiner. If he died from natural causes, it's all hers anyway. So why this elaborate charade? Or did Bendiner find out that somebody was pronging the lady and decided to change his will? Did he come to you, Counselor? Did he make a new will, cutting his wife off? Is that why you kept his death a secret? To circumvent the will? To fleece the estate?"

Bogart clasped his hands in supplication. " Ben, please, you—"

" Don't weasel on me, Alex. I want the truth. All of it. I know you were banging Cora Bendiner. I have a late-night snapshot of your car parked alongside her Mercedes at a local motel. Sure, she's something special. So you lost your head over a piece of ass. But your moral compass, Alex? How did she cross your wires and turn you into a crook?"

Nestor saw it coming. As a lawman he had witnessed such breakdowns in the past. Disintegration from the shock of sudden exposure. An attempt to wipe the slate clean by confession, words tumbling out in a catharsis of guilt.

" I was hypnotized, Ben. My God, I'd have done anything she asked. Bendiner did make a new will. She had signed a prenuptial agreement, and he left everything to some charitable foundation in Vermont. We couldn't destroy the will and have

255

him declared intestate because he'd sent it to the foundation for safekeeping. So she had to keep his death a secret."

" You told her about the will?"

" Yes."

" Whose idea was it to loot the estate?"

" Hers. She phoned me one morning and asked me to drive out there. She said it was important."

" And you found Bendiner dead?"

" Later. First she . . . she . . ."

" Took you to bed, Alex?"

He nodded miserably. " Yes. She told me Ward had gone to Miami for a few days and she led me to her bedroom."

" With her husband lying dead in his study, where he'd been sleeping. Like a damned alley cat. And after she had you nicely mellowed, she showed you the body?"

" Not yet. She told me about the money. She said there were millions, just for the taking. And she knew how to get her hands on it. She said we could live anywhere in the world, like royalty. I thought I knew what she was leading up to. I thought she wanted me to help her get rid of Bendiner. I told her no, count me out."

" And that's when she told you that he was already dead?"

" Yes. She took my hand and led me into the study. My God, Ben, we stood there naked, looking at him. She told me she found him when he failed to get up for breakfast. She said it was a heart attack and I believed her."

" And on the spur of the moment she decided to keep it a secret."

" Yes. Because she knew Bendiner's will disinherited her and she had some vague ideas about his money."

" Tell me about her ideas, Alex."

" She had a power of attorney for Bendiner's safe-deposit box. I drew it myself at his request. She would have no problem getting his securities. And if we got rid of the body, nobody would know he was dead. He had no friends in town. Nobody would miss him. There was a Cuban girl, a maid, and she went to see the girl at home and discharged her. She said she would tell people that Ward had gone to New York on business. And later, after we had the money, she would close the house, saying she was going to join him."

" She had already hatched up this little scheme about opening a brokerage account in Bendiner's name?"

" Most of it. She told me how easy it would be if I came to New York and set up an identity as Ward Bendiner. Nobody here knew him or what he looked like. I could even use his Social Security number. We decided that I should buy some stocks at first, paying promptly, establishing myself as a responsible customer. And after a while I would start to sell, delivering Bendiner's securities."

" And you figured it would work."

" It did work, Ben. And we weren't really stealing from anyone. Cora was Bendiner's wife. She was entitled to his estate."

" You were stealing from the foundation."

But Bogart, Nestor saw, had anesthetised himself, contriving his own rationalisation.

" Why should they get all that money, Ben? They hadn't lived with Bendiner, slept with him, nursed him." He added plaintively, " Where did we go wrong? What put you onto us?"

" Murder," Nestor said.

" Ah, Ben, I told you it was a heart attack."

" Not Bendiner, Alex. Someone else. The man Arcadia Films sent to Ocala Beach to see Bendiner. Ross Landry."

Bogart stared. " I never met Landry."

" That's right. Cora Bendiner prevented it."

" But why, Ben?"

" Because we know that Landry went out to the Bendiner lodge. I've been there myself. There's an autographed snapshot of Ward Bendiner on a shelf. Landry saw it—he must have seen it. And he told Cora he couldn't wait any longer, he'd have to fly to New York and face the man there. She couldn't let that happen. If Landry found you instead of the man in the photograph, he'd blow the whistle. This whole charade would collapse. The planning, the conniving, the scheming, all for nothing. Instead of the money and the luxury, she'd wind up in a cell, in a cotton smock, eating jailhouse food. What's left of her youth wasted. And she's getting a little long in the tooth anyway. She had no time to plan. She had to make a quick decision. So Landry never got out of that house alive."

Bogart said in a rusty voice, "My God, Ben, I . . . I can't believe that."

"Sure you can, Alex. There's no other explanation for his disappearance. Think about it. She's a strong woman. Does her calisthenics regularly. She has the strength and capability of carting him off. Probably into the 'Glades. And why not? It had worked, she thought, with Bendiner. She stripped Landry of identification, threw his wristwatch out into the saw grass. We found the watch, Alex. And we'll find Landry too, one way or another. She made too many mistakes. She drove Landry's car back to his motel, late at night probably, and took a cab back to The Lodge. We can check that out easily enough. She should have left Landry's car out in the Everglades, as if he'd driven it there himself. But you were in New York, and she was acting alone this time, and she had nobody to bring her back."

"Then you haven't found the body, Ben. You have no proof he's really dead."

"Don't worry about it, Alex. We'll find him. She may even have buried him on the grounds, getting rid of anything that might identify the body out at the 'Glades. We've got some pretty good dogs down there. The hounds will clue us. And I have an idea your lady will melt under heat, after you turn state's evidence."

Bogart instinctively recoiled. His throat was clogged and he kept shaking his head.

"You have no choice, Alex. It's the only way you can save your neck."

Bogart swallowed and stood nibbling the corner of a thumb-nail, his eyes half closed in remote speculation. He said very softly, "There is another way, Ben."

"Tell me."

258

"The money. More than Cora and I will ever need. More than enough for the three of us."

"You're offering me a deal?"

"Yes."

"How much?"

"One million. Cash. With no tax liability. In a numbered account it can bring you an income for the rest of your life."

Nestor shook his head sadly. "You won't ever learn, will you, Alex? Even if I could be bribed, it's too late. We have a tap on the Bendiner phone. You called Cora a little while ago and your voice is on tape. Easily identified. And the Attorney General knows I'm here to check out the occupant of this apartment. I'm taking you in, Counselor."

"You have no authority here."

"The New York cops have a John Doe warrant and they're waiting for my call. Of course Florida may have to wait for extradition if New York wants first crack at you for forgery and fraud in this state."

"Ben, Ben, don't *do* this to me."

"You did it to yourself, Alex."

"Suppose I walked out of here, would you shoot me?"

The small handgun suddenly materialised in Nestor's hand. "Don't try it, Alex."

Bogart's eyes were suddenly bankrupt. He held clenched fists close to his chest and started to shake. Then he dropped his head and covered his face with his hands. Nestor felt a twinge of compassion, instantly suppressed. He went to the telephone and put a call through to his office in Ocala Beach.

When he had one of his deputies on the line, he said, "Ben here, Isaac. Drive out to the Bendiner place and take the woman into custody."

He watched Alex Bogart for a moment and then called the commander of the local precinct.

43

Additional clarification about the events in New York reached Paul Slater at the Beverly Plaza while he was still conferring privately with the attorneys for the inspectors of election.

Mike Ryan, still mystified by the arrest of Robert Egan, unable to evaluate its effect upon the meeting, was waiting at the table with the two bank officials when Slater approached.

"May I have everyone's attention," Slater said. "An important announcement that will vitally affect these proceedings. An impostor masquerading as Ward Bendiner has just been apprehended in New York. The death of Mr. Bendiner himself was unreported and kept secret. Under Bendiner's name and signature, the impostor sold a significant block of Arcadia shares to Fred Hanna. Since that sale was fraudulent, those shares were improperly registered on the books of the corporation, and may not at this time be legally voted. Arcadia Films demands their immediate invalidation, which should drastically alter the present figures. I would—"

Slater broke off at an angry explosion of voices. The bank officials threw their hands up in helpless consternation. Mike Ryan, his voice carrying over the bedlam, shouted, "Nonsense! Absolute nonsense! This is hearsay. Where is your corroboration, your proof?"

"It will be presented as soon as available. There should be a radio bulletin any moment. In the meantime, Arcadia requests a postponement of these proceedings."

"No, sir. Universal Media strenuously objects to any delay."

Paul Slater wheeled toward the inspectors. "You just saw

260

Robert Egan, UMI's counsel, being taken into custody. At this time the full implications of that arrest are unknown. When the nature of the charges against him has been disclosed, other votes may have to be invalidated. On behalf of Arcadia Films, I am now lodging a formal protest against the Bendiner shares until clarification of their authenticity."

Slater lowered his voice and aimed his finger. "Unless that vote is set aside, Arcadia will commence a legal action that may result in a judgment far exceeding your bonded protection. You gentlemen, personally, and your bank may find yourselves financially hobbled for years. We're talking here about control of a company with net assets worth many millions of dollars."

The bank officials visibly paled. They huddled with their advisors, whispering, gesticulating, casting anxious glances at Slater. They came back to the table, and the spokesman cleared his throat.

"We have no precedent to guide us, Counselor. However, if Mr. Hedrik, as president of Arcadia Films, chairing these proceedings, is disposed to adjourn the meeting, then we are prepared to suspend all tabulation of votes and proxies."

"Would you direct him to do so?"

"We would prefer Mr. Hedrik to exercise that authority at his own discretion."

A banker's normal caution, Slater thought, always hedging their bets. "Do you care to suggest any specific language for the stockholders?"

"We leave the phrasing in your competent hands, sir."

"How about this? Unforeseen developments of critical importance to the welfare of the company and its stockholders compel us to adjourn this meeting until further notice. We deeply regret the inconvenience, and further information will be forthcoming at the earliest possible moment."

Ryan's voice was gritty with effort. "UMI's objection still stands."

"Yes, Mr. Ryan, but under the circumstances we see no alternative. Preliminary calculations assured Mr. Hanna of at least three seats on the new board. The validity of those seats are now in contention. Mr. Slater has every right to challenge. We are unable to resolve the issue until the facts are established. Mr. Hedrik is presiding over this meeting and has the legal authority to adjourn."

" Not without putting it to a vote," Ryan snapped.

" Your voting power, Mr. Ryan, is precisely the point in dispute."

The banker, his colleague, and his advisors gathered their papers and marched out. Paul Slater made a few notes on the adjournment announcement and took them out to the Grand Ballroom for Dan Hedrik to read over the microphone.

*　　*　　*

The senior partner of UMI's California law firm had finally managed to uncover some information about Robert Egan's arrest. The attorney, his face weathered to a look of distinction, remembered that only a week earlier he had discussed Judge Clement Dodge with Universal Media's counsel.

He looked across his desk at Fred Hanna and said, " The situation is serious. I enlisted the help of a former associate who is acquainted with the Commissioner."

" Did you get me the name of a criminal lawyer?"

" Yes. But hear me out first. You may decide to save your money. Egan is charged with first-degree homicide in the death of a character named Albert Clinton."

" On what evidence?"

" Clinton was a suspected drug dealer, under surveillance by narcotics agents. On Wednesday the twenty-fifth he held a late-night rendezvous in the deserted parking area of a shopping plaza with a man in a light-blue Pontiac. The driver of the second car joined the suspect in Clinton's Volkswagen, spent about fifteen minutes with him and then left. The Volkswagen stayed put. One of the agents shadowing Clinton approached to investigate. He found Clinton dead, shot in the back of the head."

" No shots were heard?"

" Apparently a silencer had been used."

262

"And how do they fit Egan into this picture?"

"Albert Clinton was young Kiser's inseparable companion. Kiser, as you know, inherits Kate Rennie's stock in Arcadia Films."

Hanna stared at the lawyer, his face inscrutable. "I see. However, that is not what I meant. How do they connect Egan with the homicide?"

"The agents had the number of the Pontiac, a rental car. Vehicle Registrations provided the name of the company. They checked with Hertz and learned that the car had been leased to the holder of an American Express credit card. American Express informed them that the card had been issued to Universal Media Industries for the use of Robert Egan. A call to UMI headquarters in New York revealed that Egan was here in Los Angeles for the stockholders meeting of Arcadia Films. Egan's signature is on the Hertz rental agreement. They knew where Egan was staying. They had him under observation for several days and then obtained a warrant to search his hotel suite. In a bundle of soiled laundry locked up in Egan's suitcase they found a .38-caliber Smith & Wesson revolver. Ballistics tests conclusively prove it to be the same weapon that fired the fatal bullet into Albert Clinton's brain." The lawyer opened his hands. "There you have it. They expect an early indictment."

Hanna lapsed into silence, his lips tightly compressed. He said finally, "I want Egan out on bail."

"That may not be possible, Mr. Hanna. In any event, you will have to discuss it with a lawyer versed in these matters. I have already contacted such a man and he's agreed to handle the case."

"I want to speak to him personally. Arrange a meeting immediately."

The lawyer spoke into his telephone, made some notes, broke the connection, and looked up. "In one hour. His office is only three blocks from here." He handed his notes to Hanna.

"Then we have enough time to discuss another matter. The Bendiner shares. If the sale to me was fraudulent and subject to cancelation, what is my remedy?"

"You're entitled to a refund. Providing, of course, that the money can be found."

"Just what the hell does that mean?"

"Mr. Hanna, I very much doubt that this alleged impostor deposited the fruits of his crime in some local bank account for any length of time. In all probability, that money is already out of the country."

It changed the shape of Hanna's mouth, twisting it into a pained grimace. He said hoarsely, "How about Gregorius & Company. They negotiated the transaction."

"Gregorius will have to share responsibility. It's a member firm of the New York Stock Exchange and you relied on its representations. In arranging the transfer of that stock to your name, there was an implicit guarantee of authenticity."

"Can I compel restitution?"

"I think so, yes, even if it forces Gregorius into bankruptcy."

44

In his suite at the Beverly Plaza, ten floors above the scene of the recent setback at the Arcadia meeting, Mike Ryan paced the floor restlessly, plagued by misgivings, his brain dull with exhaustion. First, Egan's arrest, and the likelihood that young Kiser, after learning about Egan's role in the death of his friend, would switch allegiance from Universal Media to Arcadia, withdrawing his lawsuit and allowing Rennie's executor to vote the Rennie shares for the film company's management.

But worse, far worse, was the exposure in New York of Ward Bendiner's impostor, with its cataclysmic implications for

Gregorius & Company. Mike paused in front of a mirror and studied himself with unimpressed derision. The upwardly mobile Michael Ryan, finally perched at the summit, caught now in a tangled web of his own creation and teetering precariously on the brink.

His mood suddenly altered, shading into anger. No, he thought, not my own creation. Others had played a role. Hanna, with his overweening ambition and duplicity. The greed and larceny of Bendiner's impostor. Bob Egan, guilty of sins still unknown. Ryan's jaw clamped tightly. He had not fought and clawed his way up the ladder to be toppled without a fight.

He headed for the telephone, but it started to ring before he could pick it up. " Ryan," he growled.

"Don't bite my head off," Liz Harmon said. "I'm not responsible."

"Don't say it, Liz."

"Don't say what?"

"Don't say I told you so. Don't tell me you disapproved of Fred Hanna from the beginning."

"You underrate me, friend. I am not gloating. I'm suffering."

He was instantly contrite. "Liz, I'm sorry."

"I tried to reach you several times. Don't they take messages at that place?"

"Not the hotel's fault. I was too preoccupied to stop off at the desk. Fact is, I was on the point of calling you when the phone rang."

"Preoccupied, Mike? Rather a mild reaction, isn't it?"

"In a state of shock, if you want the truth. Stunned. Rocked to my heels. By God, Liz, this Bendiner caper—after all these years in the business, to be ripped off by a bunco artist. We're getting it piecemeal out here. Who is this Bogart character, anyway?"

"Alex Bogart, a lawyer from Bendiner's hometown in Florida. Apparently working this scam with Bendiner's widow. A scheme of some kind to circumvent her husband's will."

"Any clues up there regarding Bogart's disposition of all that money?"

" Not yet."

" Gregorius is vulnerable, Liz. Not only on those Arcadia shares, but on all the guy's transactions, the whole goddamn Bendiner portfolio."

" I know," she said. " We're beleaguered here, besieged by calls from a dozen brokerage houses and their lawyers."

Mike groaned. " How's the old man taking it?"

" Anson Gregorius is resting comfortably."

" Resting?"

" In Manhattan General."

" *What*!" Mike was gripping the handset. " What happened, Liz?"

" Cardiac arrest. But not until he threw his weight around to get us some information about Bogart's arrest, so I could pass it on to you. He was briefing me when he suddenly turned chalk-white and slumped over his desk. I called for an ambulance and I called Floyd, and a cardiac unit was here within minutes."

" Oh, Jesus! What's the prognosis?"

" It was a fairly mild attack, but how many more of these can he take? Right now he's hooked up to one of those oxygen contraptions and driving his nurse out of her tree. Julie's in the adjoining room."

" Staying close to the old boy?"

" Not quite. Touch of hysteria. She drank herself into a stupor when she heard about Bendiner."

Anguish clotted Mike's throat.

" She's a flexible lady," Liz said. " She'll get over it. When are you coming back?"

" I'll leave tomorrow morning. Nothing to keep me here now."

" Do you have any marching orders for me?"

" Yes. Take a look at the canceled checks we gave this Bogart character. They should tell us where he deposited the money. Get in touch with our lawyers and have them slap an attachment on the Bendiner-Bogart account. One way or another I want that money tied up here in the States."

266

"He was out of the city for a couple of days last week, Mike, remember? Maybe he transfered the loot already. What do we do if the money is no longer in his account?"

"I hope to God it can be traced. No one moves sums that size in cash. And he may want to make a deal with the authorities, restitution in exchange for leniency. It's our best hope. Where is the sonovabitch now?"

"Everybody is claiming jurisdiction—the Feds, the Manhattan D. A., the State of Florida."

"Florida?"

"Something about a murder conspiracy down there. Right now he's in the Federal House of Detention, remanded by a U.S. magistrate. Bail was set at half a million."

"Half a million!" Mike's voice scaled high in frustration. "That's insane! With the money he stole, he'll make bail, forfeit, and disappear into one of the banana republics."

"I doubt it, Mike. He's in custody. How can he get his hands on the money. Whom can he trust? And so far, no bail bondsman is willing to take the risk. Look, I have some questions too. What's all this about Bob Egan?"

"Beats me. We'll know soon enough, I guess."

"How is Fred Hanna reacting?"

"Haven't seen Hanna since they hauled Egan away. And after that Bendiner bombshell, I'm not looking forward to it, either."

"Mike, a swindle like that could have happened to any outfit on the Street. Regardless of regulations, how much identification does any brokerage house demand from a new account? We're all hungry for business. Sometimes registered reps never even meet the client. They send a customer's agreement by mail, the prospect signs and mails it back, and they start trading for him."

She was right, of course, and he told her so, though it hardly diminished his own feeling of culpability. "Doesn't stop me from feeling like a horse's ass," he added.

"I have confidence in you, Mike. You're a survivor. To quote a tired old aphorism : Time heals all wounds."

" I like it better the other way around, Liz. Time wounds all heels."

" Are you referring to Fred Hanna?"

" Who else? I'm convinced now that Hanna was responsible all along for the manipulation in Arcadia stock. They may never nail him for it, but he's bound to suffer some repercussions from the Egan affair. It's a terrible kick in the ass for UMI."

Liz remained oddly silent.

" Something else on your mind?" he asked.

" Not now. You've had enough for one day. I'll tell you when you get back."

" No. Let me have it now, Liz. While I'm still half numb with shock."

" Are you sitting down?"

" That bad, is it?"

" Bad enough. While I was in Anson's office, he had a call from a lawyer representing some charitable foundation. His client is the chief beneficiary under Ward Bendiner's will. The foundation had possession of the will, they knew its contents, and when they heard about Bendiner's death and the fraudulent sale of his stock, they got in touch with their lawyer. And he wanted Anson to know that he's holding Gregorius & Company responsible for recovering every single penny."

Mike's voice took on a fresh vigor, as if the additional adversity had nourished his determination. " So they're coming at us from all directions, are they. All right, Liz. I'll switch my reservation and fly back tonight."

" Michael?"

" Yes."

" I miss you."

" Then I'll come straight to your place. Will you stay up?"

" Wake me."

45

At 6:45 A.M. Kevin Anthony Duke III was awakened by the hotel telephone. He groped for the instrument, mumbled hoarsely, and heard the familiar voice of Gary George Pressman.

"Banker's hours, son? Get your tail up to Room 2110 pronto." There was a click and the line went dead.

Duke sat up, wide awake. The boss was in New York, staying at the same hotel. It was not unusual for the Enforcement chief to take a personal hand in cases where knavery was so unprincipled he could no longer guide its unraveling from behind a desk. Duke skipped his morning shower, dressed, ran the electric razor over his face, and within fifteen minutes was knocking at Pressman's door.

G.G. snapped the button on his stopwatch. "Good boy. You shaved nineteen seconds off your record. We'll eat here. I've already ordered breakfast."

"When did you leave Washington, sir?"

"Last shuttle out of Dulles International last night. What have you got for me?"

"Not much," Duke said. "Same problem. Foreign nominees covering their short sales."

"How about Gregorius?"

"Only Arcadia stock they cleared were those Bendiner shares transferred to Fred Hanna. Sale negotiated by Mike Ryan."

"You spoke to him?"

"He was in L.A. They expect him back today."

"Did you meet Elizabeth Harmon?"

"Yes, sir."

"Special, no?"

269

" All the way up to the furnishings on the top floor. I think she suspected manipulation in Arcadia, but skirted any direct comment."

" Naturally. The chief suspect is a Gregorius client."

" Outside of lax procedures on that Bendiner swindle, their books seem to be in order. Do you think they'll survive, sir?"

Pressman shrugged. " They're going to be hit with lawsuits from twelve different directions. Depends on how much they can recover from the Bogart operation."

" The firm was thoroughly jobbed, sir. They're still in a state of shock. It put old man Gregorius in the hospital."

There was a knock on the door. Room service had arrived. Kevin Duke goggled at the heavily laden cart.

" What the hell!" Pressman said with a Teddy Roosevelt grin. " If we stick within our per diem allowance, we'll wind up with two acorns apiece. We got a big day ahead of us and we need the energy. Sit, son, and partake. I know you were trained not to talk with your mouth full. In the Bronx, we were not quite so fastidious, all seven of us ate and talked at the same time. Today you will forgo etiquette. Try the sausage first, the bacon next. I'm asking if you heard any rumors here." G.G. poured syrup over his pancakes. " I know for a fact that Fred Hanna was stretched thin. Where did he raise enough cash for the Bendiner stock?"

Duke stabbed a poached egg and watched the yoke bleed over a slice of bacon. He said, " Nobody at Gregorius had a notion. None of their business. But we do know that Hanna flew to Vegas and came back with enough money for his margin account."

" Syndicate dough? He must have been hungry for those shares. And he buys the stock for his own personal account at the same time UMI is angling for control. Kind of dodgy, no? The woods are loaded with legal talent itching to rake up class action lawsuits. To say nothing about trouble from the SEC."

Duke swallowed a piece of toast and poured more coffee. " How?"

" Think, son. Think hard."

" Ten B-five, sir."

" Give the man a cigar. Ten B-five. Correct. A violation of the Securities Act. Failure to disclose insider trading."

" But the law applies only to holders of ten per cent of a company's stock. Does Hanna fit?"

" Universal Media fits. And Fred Hanna is the largest single stockholder of UMI. Seems fair to say that he is the constructive owner of Arcadia shares within the meaning of the statute."

Duke grinned. " They always make some little mistake, don't they?"

" Well, son, the man's got a lot on his mind. Especially since the arrest of his UMI counsel. Let's take a look at that little development. California's charging Egan with homicide. He was at the scene of the crime, he had possession of the murder weapon. Opportunity and means. Now, how about motive? I've been mulling it over. Yesterday I phoned the prosecutor out there and we gave each other an earful. I provided the man with some fascinating assumptions and he told me the known facts. Fair exchange. Are you interested?"

" Enthralled, sir." Duke pointed. " Aren't you having any sausages?"

" Pork sausages, son? My dear old grandmother would turn over in her grave."

" But you're eating bacon."

" There you have it. A vivid demonstration of man's inconsistencies. You may have my share of the sausage. All right now if I proceed with the case of UMI's counsel?"

" Yes, sir."

" Egan's victim was a man named Al Clinton. From available evidence, a very shoddy piece of goods. Mercenary, pederast, narcotics pusher, and quite possibly murderer. In short, not a very nice person. So, I ask myself, and you too, what is the connection between this vermin and the distinguished general counsel for Universal Media Industries. What is the link?"

" Kate Rennie's nephew David Kiser."

" You're clicking today, son. Now, according to the prosecutor, young Kiser is a very frail reed, impressionable,

271

exploitable. And somehow this Clinton becomes Kiser's guru, his protector, his asshole buddy. In no time at all, Kiser is dependent on Clinton—dependent emotionally, probably sexually, certainly for a regular supply of happy powder. Are you with me so far?"

" All the way, sir."

" Good. Then we can move on, from Kiser to Rennie to Max Klemmer to Arcadia Films. Which last is Fred Hanna's target. We are talking about a block of Arcadia stock that may possibly spell success or failure in a takeover effort. So he seeks Rennie's support. Without success. Not even Mike Ryan, the super-salesman, can sell her a bill of goods. Rennie's loyalties are with the company and the people running it, her friends. The conglomerateur's bear hug is repulsed. So Egan moves in." Pressman paused and narrowed his eyes at the younger man. " Get my drift?"

" I think so. Please continue."

" So what happens next? Kate Rennie drowns in her own swimming pool. Conveniently—on her maid's day off. David Kiser inherits her Arcadia stock, which he immediately tries to vote in favour of UMI. Doesn't even wait for distribution from the estate. Applies heavy pressure, including a lawsuit, on Rennie's executor. Here is a kid doesn't know his ass from third base about corporate takeovers suddenly becoming aggressively involved in the UMI-Arcadia struggle. Most unusual, wouldn't you say? Piques your curiosity, doesn't it? You have to ask how come. Who provoked him into this action?"

" Al Clinton?"

" Right. And who was the moving force behind Clinton?"

" Robert Egan."

" Considering subsequent events, a logical assumption. Listen to this. In addition to the murder weapon in Egan's hotel room, they also found ten thousand dollars cash money. And on some of those bills they were able to bring out a few latents that matched Clinton's fingerprints. First time in fourteen years, they tell me, that they got a set of prints they can use at a trial."

Duke leaned intently forward. "A payoff from Egan to Clinton for services rendered. Getaway money perhaps?"

"Precisely. Not only to avoid a narcotics charge, but the possibility of more damaging revelations."

"Such as the death of Kate Rennie."

"They found a diving mask in Clinton's Volkswagen. Evidence? To a devout believer like myself, yes. Well, Clinton got away, all right, into the next world, with a slight assist from Robert Egan. Clinton must have been counting the money when Egan squeezed one off. Clinton had become a liability. He knew too much. He was untrustworthy. He could blow it all."

"And Egan," Duke said quietly, "leads us directly to his employer, Mr. Fred Hanna."

G. G. Pressman nodded. "President and chairman of the board of Universal Media Industries. Does it shock you, son? A man in his position? Me, too. But it happens more often than you'd expect. Hell, look at the record. The Pakistanis executed a former Prime Minister for complicity in the murder of a political rival. The head of a powerful trade union is in prison for hiring a couple of goons to assassinate an opponent. I don't know if Fred Hanna gave specific orders, but he told Egan his goals, he permitted the man to plan strategy, and he provided the funds."

Kevin Duke whistled softly.

"Finish your coffee," Pressman said, "and let's get the hell out of here. The government is entitled to a day's work for a day's pay."

46

Cora Bendiner lay motionless on a cot in the holding cell of the sheriff's office in Ocala Beach. She felt soiled and damp. The white linen slacks were rumpled and the green silk waist clung to her skin. Blisters of perspiration glistened on her upper lip. She was slowly emerging from a lethargic haze when she heard a key grating in the lock.

She sat up and stared with icy hostility at the black deputy. He was the same man who had taken her into custody at The Lodge. He had been polite, but firm, showing her his papers and indicating the patrol car. In the sheriff's office she had been allowed to use the telephone, but had been unable to reach Alex in New York.

She said in a tight voice, " This place stinks, Mr. Deputy, and so does the food. It's a violation of my rights and I'm going to—"

He cut her off. " I just follow orders, ma'am. The sheriff is here now."

He led her along the dank corridor. Ben Nestor sat behind his desk, flanked by two men. One of them she recognized from local newscasts. Walter Kleeburg, the Palm County prosecutor, carp-faced and florid. The third man, formal in manner and attire, with pale eyes and sandy lashes, projected an air of monastic sterility. He was thin-lipped, unsmiling, unmistakably in charge.

" This is Mr. Matthew Maulder," Nestor said. " From the Attorney General's office in Tallahassee."

She turned to him at once, chin high. " These people have kept me here overnight, Mr. Maulder. Under the most unspeakable conditions. Without charging me, or filing any complaint."

" Were you given an opportunity to contact anyone?"

274

Maulder's voice was flat, uninflected, with no trace of any regional accent.

" Yes. I tried to reach my husband in New York, but I couldn't get through to him."

Maulder deliberately pushed the telephone across the desk. " You may try again now, if you wish."

She frowned, hesitated, and shook her head. " He's never in his hotel room at this hour."

" Do you have an attorney?"

" Yes. Mr. Alex Bogart. But I believe he's on vacation somewhere in Canada."

" Mrs. Bendiner, let me state our position. Then you can make up your mind whether you wish to co-operate. We are trying to establish what happened to Ross Landry of Arcadia Films. He came to Ocala Beach to see your husband on a corporate mission. So far as we know, you are the only individual he spoke to at any length. Shortly afterwards he dropped out of sight. He is not the kind of man who would disappear of his own free will. No accident has been reported. There has been no attempt by kidnappers to contact his family. We now believe that he may have been the victim of a crime, possibly murder."

Her frown deepened. " Murder? Have you found the man's body?"

" We do not need the actual corpse to prove homicide, Mrs. Bendiner. The words ' corpus delicti ' mean the body of the crime, not the body of the victim."

She mustered a patronizing smile. " Seems to me, Mr. Maulder, that you're drawing unwarranted conclusions."

" No, ma'am. Sheriff Nestor found Landry's watch under highly suspicious circumstances." He opened an envelope and thoughtfully inspected the gold timepiece for a moment.

Cora's expression was unfathomable. " I still don't understand how you would like me to co-operate."

" We're hoping Mr. Landry may have said something to you that could aid us in this investigation. Under the laws of this state we have asked for and received a court order empowering us to hold you in protective custody until a duly convened

275

Grand Jury decides whether or not you should appear to testify and give evidence during their deliberations. Of course you may not wish to speak to us at all. That is your privilege."

" I have nothing to hide."

" Then you agree to co-operate of your own free will?"

" For whatever it's worth, yes."

Maulder reached into his briefcase and removed a portable tape recorder. He activated the mechanism and adjusted the sound level.

" Is that thing necessary?" Cora asked.

" For your protection as well as ours, Mrs. Bendiner. Since Alex Bogart is not available you may wish to consult with some other attorney. I'm sure Sheriff Nestor could supply the name of a competent man in this area."

She flipped her hand in a dismissive gesture. " I'd like to get this over with as soon as possible, Mr. Maulder. Ask your questions."

He leaned toward the microphone and stated names, place and date. " Now, Mrs. Bendiner," he continued, " would you tell us in detail about the several conversations you had with Ross Landry during his visits to your home?"

" I've already told everything I know to Sheriff Nestor."

" Repeat it, please, for the record."

She sat back, nibbling a thumb knuckle, collecting her thoughts, and then, in a bored monotone, she recited almost verbatim her previous statements.

Maulder nodded. " Thank you, Mrs. Bendiner. You say that after Landry's second visit you never saw him again?"

" Never. He told me that he was leaving immediately to fly north and see my husband in New York."

" And you were under the impression that he had left Ocala Beach?"

" Yes."

" Did you phone your husband and tell him that he should expect a visit from Landry."

" Of course."

" Landry never approached him?"

" That is my understanding."

" When was the last time you spoke to your husband?"

" I called him yesterday, at about two in the afternoon."

" That would be September the fourth?"

" Yes."

" You had a housekeeper working for you here, a young girl named Maria Olivera. But you dismissed her."

" She was neither very diligent nor very bright."

" You made no effort to replace her?"

" That's right. My husband and I are planning on an extended trip abroad."

" Your husband doesn't socialize with the people here. Any reason for that?"

" He's a very private person, Mr. Maulder." She paused and stared carefully at all three men in turn, her brow furrowed, resting an elbow in the palm of her hand. " I'm afraid I don't understand this line of questioning, Mr. Maulder. How does it relate to Landry's disappearance?"

The thin lips smiled minimally and without humor. " That, Mrs. Bendiner, seems to be the jackpot question."

Her mouth tightened. " Well then, I don't think I care to go any further. Not until I've spoken to my lawyer. We'll just have to wait until Mr. Bogart returns."

Maulder said with a cold and deadly emphasis, " That might take anywhere from ten to twenty years, madam. Possibly longer."

Ben Nestor, watching the woman closely, saw the expression of startled puzzlement, a fleeting instant of comprehension, followed then by a look of cold hostility. " What are you saying?"

" I'm saying that Alex Bogart will not be back here for a long, long time. And even then he wouldn't be any help to you. The commission of a felony, Mrs. Bendiner, generally results in disbarment."

Her eyes were guarded. " A felony? Alex Bogart? I don't believe you."

" It should be in your local paper tomorrow morning. Bogart

was arrested in New York yesterday on a charge of conspiracy to defraud. He's been selling large amounts of corporate securities that do not belong to him."

His words changed the shape of her mouth, distorting it. She swiveled toward Nestor. "You've known Alex all his life, Sheriff. He's lying, isn't he?" Her voice was loud, strident.

"I brought him in myself, Mrs. Bendiner," Nestor said. "I found him in New York, masquerading as your husband, forging your husband's signature on stock certificates, depositing the proceeds in a fraudulent bank account. The U.S. Attorney up North expects to indict him within a week. And after he gets out of a federal prison, the state of Florida will extradite Bogart to face charges here. He may even walk out of a cell some day, if he lives long enough."

A spasm passed over her, head to foot. Her eyes squeezed shut. It was over, finished. Alex had failed, made some stupid mistake. Her brain whirled, seeking alternatives, wondering desperately how much could be salvaged. She opened her eyes, looked at them pleadingly, and said in a thin, wailing voice, "Where is Ward? Oh, my God, what did Alex do with my husband?"

Matthew Maulder at last showed some expression. His thin lips curled in sour contempt. "You just told us your husband was in New York, Mrs. Bendiner. You said you called him there and spoke to him only yesterday."

She glared defiantly. "I thought it was Ward."

"I see. Would you have any idea how Bogart came into possession of your husband's securities?"

"No. Ward never consulted me about his business affairs."

"Consulted? You're using the past tense, Mrs. Bendiner. Is your husband dead?"

"I . . . I don't know. I'm confused. I don't know anything any more."

"The bank here tells us that your husband signed a power of attorney giving you access to his safe-deposit box. It was notarized by Bogart. Did you remove your husband's securities and pass them along to Bogart?"

278

She gave him a look of vast indignation. " I certainly did not."

" What was your relationship with Alex Bogart?"

" Purely professional. He was our attorney."

" Were you at any time intimate with him?"

Her face flushed. " What do you think I am?"

" My opinion, Mrs. Bendiner, would not be admissible in a court of law. And in any event, it's irrelevant." Maulder reached into his briefcase for an envelope. He held up an enlargement of the snapshot taken by Sheriff Nestor's Polaroid. " Here is a photograph taken late at night in the parking area of a motel located just north of Everglades City. It shows two automobiles. The registration numbers are clearly visible. One of these cars is your Mercedes, the other belongs to Alex Bogart."

She seemed mesmerized by the picture. She gave him a warped smile. " Sometimes Ward borrowed my car."

Maulder gave her a pitying look. " That's a dry hole, Mrs. Bendiner. Don't drill yourself into it any deeper. Sheriff Nestor can identify you as the driver that night, and also the date of the assignation."

She glared at Nestor. " Is that how you spend your time, Sheriff? Is that the sort of thing that interests you?"

" Not as a hobby, ma'am. Only when it completes the picture of a crime. Because when the wife of a very rich man takes a lover, she automatically becomes a suspect when her husband is murdered."

Her palms flew to her throat. " *Murdered?*"

" Yes, Mrs. Bendiner. We found your husband's body in the Everglades. He has been positively identified by fingerprints and his dental record."

Cora Bendiner went rigid. She threw her head back, neck muscles straining, and said in a high, shrill voice, " Nobody touched him. He died of a heart attack. He—" She caught herself and clapped a hand over her mouth, staring at them, eyes wide and dismayed.

The three men returned her stare in cold unblinking silence.

Cora came up out of her chair, disorganized, confused, and started for the door at a hobbling trot. Ben Nestor rose and brought her back. She sank into the chair. Very slowly the tension around her mouth relaxed and her face took on the brave, consecrated look of a martyr.

"You tricked me," she said in a small childlike voice. "Not that it's going to do you much good. Ward died from natural causes. Why don't you have an autopsy performed?"

"We did," Nestor said. "The report shows cardiac arrest as the cause of death."

She blinked at him. "You see? I told you. Then you don't really need me any more. May I go home now?"

Maulder said, "Mrs. Bendiner, you don't seem to be tracking well. Obviously your husband didn't go wandering off into the Everglades after he died. Somebody transported the body. The purpose, of course, was to keep his death a secret in order to loot the estate. Bogart has already implicated you in that conspiracy."

"Oh, Alex is a terrible liar. I don't know anything about it."

Maulder sighed patiently. "We had a tap on your telephone, Mrs. Bendiner. You called Bogart in New York. We have a recording of that conversation. Both voices are recognizable, and for courtroom purposes can be conclusively identified through a spectographic voiceprint."

Tears glistened in her eyes. "Ward was my husband. Why would I steal from his estate?"

"Because you had signed away your rights in a prenuptial agreement and he had made a will cutting you off completely. We have evidence that he moved out of your bed into his study."

"Maria Olivera told you that, but she's mistaken."

Maulder waved a stern finger. "You promised to co-operate with us, Mrs. Bendiner, but you keep inventing new lies."

"No," she said in a little-girl voice, her eyes remote. "I don't think I care to co-operate any longer. You listened to my telephone and you're not supposed to do that. It's against the law. You people are not to be trusted." She brooded at him petulantly, thumb in her mouth, and said in a querulous voice, " I don't want to stay here any longer. I don't like it here. You're supposed to take me before a judge so I can ask for bail." She smiled and fell into a reverie.

To Ben Nestor, the woman's statements were rational enough, even shrewd, but her words were inconsistent with her bearing. Her eyes were glazed and she seemed disconnected from the scene, as if they were talking about someone else. Maulder must have had the same impression because he snapped his fingers to recapture her attention.

" Mrs. Bendiner, we have reason to believe that Ross Landry must have seen a picture of your husband at The Lodge. If our assumption is correct you could not of course permit him to leave Ocala Beach for New York. So he had to be eliminated. At this moment, the sheriff's deputies and a number of other men are on their way to search your property and the surrounding area for the body of Ross Landry. We do not think you took him out to the 'Glades by yourself, only some of his possessions. You were working alone and probably did not bury Landry deeply enough."

Maulder shook his head with grudging admiration. " You almost pulled this off. If your husband had not owned stock in Arcadia Films, if Ross Landry had not come here to Ocala Beach, it might have succeeded. Alex Bogart played his role well, hoodwinking the brokerage firm and even starting a torrid affair with the broker's daughter."

She came alive, furious, eyes suddenly burning. " That's a lie! A damned dirty lie!"

" Tough to swallow, isn't it, Mrs. Bendiner? Alex Bogart is a born chaser, a womanizer. He couldn't even stay faithful to you for a couple of weeks."

Her jaw worked spasmodically. She took a raw sucking breath and choked back a cry of despair. She turned with sudden irrationality to glare at Kleeburg, the Palm County prosecutor. " You!" she fumed. " You fat red-faced baldheaded prick, sitting there all this time with that stupid grin—don't you have anything to say?"

Kleeburg looked startled, but she forgot him instantly. She started to laugh, cut it short, and broke into gravely sounds of weeping.

Maulder looked at the sheriff. "Jesus!" he said softly " Unpredictable as a barracuda."

Ben Nestor shrugged, feeling no sense of satisfaction.

47

On a clear, crisp day in late October, Anson Gregorius sat in the VIP lounge at Kennedy Airport. He looked fragile and waxy, but a trace of the old tenacity still lingered in his eyes. He was chafing irritably as Julie tightened the long knitted scarf around his neck.

" Dammit!" he said. " That's enough. Let me be. You don't have to baby me because your boyfriend gave Gregorius a royal shafting."

" Now, Daddy, I thought we agreed not to talk about Alex."

" You did, girl. I never agreed to anything. And it gives me pleasure."

" He was hypnotized by that terrible woman. He didn't know what he was doing."

" He knew damn well what he was doing. You keep defending that lousy whoremaster, I don't need you in St. Kitts for two weeks."

" He told them where to find the money, didn't he?"

" He made a deal to save his neck. Fine. Pin a medal on him. That woman in Florida killed a man. They might have implicated him in that if he hadn't turned state's evidence."

" You're ticked off because you were gullible too."

" Not me. He was Mike's customer."

" You met him and you liked him."

" All con men are likable. Otherwise they'd have to find another trade. I don't want to talk about the bum any more."

" Suits me, Daddy. You brought it up, remember?" She waved as she saw Floyd enter the lounge. He joined them and handed Julie tickets, luggage stubs, and boarding passes.

" All set," Floyd said. " You're checked straight through."

Julie gave Anson a quick look, narrowing her eyes, moving her lips silently.

Anson cleared his throat. " Thank you, Floyd. Will you do me one more favor?"

" Name it," Floyd said, nodding.

" Don't hang around here till flight time. Go back to the office. Pick up that girl of yours and drive her down to the Municipal Building. Get a license and have the clerk marry you. Take the day off and start making babies. For Christ's sake, I want to see my grandson before they plant me."

" Hey!" Julie said. " Not so fast. That clerk business is a little impersonal. Maybe there ought to be something a little more elaborate."

" Like your first wedding, girl? The freeloaders at the Plaza and the musicians and the bishop himself presiding, and the divorce lawyer three months later? A fancy ceremony is no guarantee—"

" For Janey's sake, Daddy. She's entitled to—"

" No," Floyd broke in. " Janey doesn't need any window dressing. The clerk will do fine."

Anson looked dubious. " If Floyd agrees, I'm not so sure—"

" Knock it off, Daddy," Julie said. " Do they have your blessing?"

" They have my blessing."

Floyd said quietly, " I was planning on this whether we had anyone's blessing or not."

The old man stared, and suddenly his dentures were gleaming in a broad grin. " You're improving, sonny. Got a little starch now, have you? Because you finally made a couple of bucks on that Arcadia stock. Just remember who pulled your chestnuts

283

out of the fire. Okay. Take your lady away for a couple of weeks. The honeymoon is on me. Anywhere but St. Kitts. This is no goddamn family reunion. I'm supposed to be convalescing." He offered his hand. "Don't squeeze. And stay the fuck away from the market. You'll sleep better."

They shook hands awkwardly in what seemed to be an altering relationship. Floyd said, "I have some news for you."

Anson eyed him warily. "Yes?"

"Janey saw a doctor last week. She's pregnant."

"*Sonovagun!*" The old man beamed delightedly. He looked at Julie and laughed. "We got one in the oven already. The Gregorius family is back in business."

Julie gave her brother a hug and then Floyd headed quickly for the exit. A moment later the door opened again as Mike Ryan and Liz Harmon came hurrying into the lounge. Mike presented Anson with a gaudily decorated package.

"Southern Comfort," Mike said. "Use sparingly."

"Who the hell is minding the store?" Anson demanded.

"We have fifty-eight employees," Mike reminded him. "With an office manager and six department heads. Somebody steals a couple of pencils, we'll buy more." He turned. "Take care of him, Julie."

"Hello, Mike," she said. "Miss Harmon. We weren't expecting a send-off. Thanks for coming."

Anson looked at Liz. "You're happy to see me out of there, hey? Nobody to futz around with your syntax."

"Listen," she said, "come back soon and I promise not to complain even if you put it into Swahili."

"Oh, I'll be back," Anson said. "Count on it." He turned to Mike. "Didn't think you'd make it to the airport. What happened at the hearing this morning?"

"Every member on the Exchange board knows about the difficulties in certifying new customers. It's a continuing problem. They read me a bill of particulars, and they're formulating new rules. We'll all have to tighten procedures. What saved us, I suppose, was recovery of the money. Otherwise we'd be out of business, and Sipic, too, would have taken a loss."

"Sipic?" Julie asked. "Who is Sipic?"

"Not who, what," Mike explained. "SIPC. Security Investors Protection Corporation. Covers customers of defunct brokerage firms for certain losses up to a hundred grand."

Anson sighed. "Couple of years from now it'll be a bad memory. I hear Fred Hanna dropped out of sight while I was in the hospital."

"He's been seen in Rio. UMI has some interests down there. I guess he wants to keep a low profile until he sees what happens at Egan's trial. In the meantime, they can't lay a glove on him because we have no extradition treaty with Brazil."

The loudspeaker crackled and a voice said, "Flight 36 is now ready for boarding. Please report to Gate 21."

Anson leaned on Julie's arm. "Anything down there you want me to bring back?"

"Yes," Liz Harmon said. "Yourself."

*   *   *

In the taxi on their way back to Manhattan, Liz said, "Do you think we'll ever see him back at the office again?"

"Probably not." Mike felt a sense of guilt tinged with sadness. Guilt because several times in the past year he had been forced into conflicting positions with the old man. Sadness because now that full retirement seemed inevitable, he was touched with a sense of profound loss. Anson Gregorius had played a vital, even a parental, role in his life.

"You'll miss him, won't you?"

"Yes."

"So where does Gregorius & Company go from here?"

"We'll have to retrench, Liz. Operate on a much smaller scale until memories of the Bendiner fiasco fades."

"Fewer employees?"

He nodded morosely. "It'll have to be done if we're going to survive."

"You want me to resign and make it easy for you?"

He brandished a fist under her nose. "Don't tempt me, Liz.

I don't know my own strength. From here on I expect you to play a key role. Especially when expansion plans impair my judgment. Together we may be the only husband-and-wife team running an important investment house."

She sat erect. " Are you proposing to me, Michael?"

" If you'll have me, yes."

She turned and studied him carefully, holding her chin, lips pursed, feigning a critical appraisal. " The notion has possibilities," she said at last. " You're reasonably young, reasonably virile, moderately bright, almost presentable, with fairly decent prospects."

" What do you mean, almost presentable?" he asked with mock indignation.

" Look in a mirror. See for yourself. But then, I've always been partial to rough-hewn villainous types. You may kiss me, if you're in the mood."

" Later. Our driver has a rear-vision mirror. It's unseemly for important executives to be seen necking in taxicabs."

" But this is the only proposal I've had this week."

" Did you have any last week?"

" One."

" From who?"

" Watch your syntax. Whom. From Pete Sternbach. Although I'm not quite sure whether it was a proposal or a proposition."

" Sternbach? I thought he was only interested in money."

" Money first, romance second."

" Pete is very rich."

" I know."

" And he cleaned up on his Arcadia speculation. His Croesus Fund will rank number one this year."

" Then he'll be happy without me. He can fondle his balance sheet every night."

Mike laughed. " Did you see the paper this morning?"

" This morning I was studying figures on our gross national product. Something I missed?"

" Several things. G. G. Pressman made an interesting observation. Every time something goes radically wrong, it reveals

286

a fracture point in the system, which gives the SEC a shot at remedial legislation. Preventing future grief."

"I like his attitude. Anything else?"

"Yes. There seems to be some medical evidence that Ross Landry was still alive after Mrs. Bendiner brained him and planted the body among the scrub trees on the family grounds."

"Oh, dear God, no!" Liz said in a shocked voice. "How awful. The woman is a monster."

"Right now she's a zombie. Doesn't respond or talk to anyone, not even her lawyer. Just sits and rocks. Almost catatonic."

"Too bad. Makes my eyes sting a little." Liz was silent for a moment. "And Bob Egan? Will he implicate his boss?"

"He may try. But so far there's no evidence that Hanna knew about Egan's machinations. In any event, the California prosecutor is holding firm on first-degree homicide."

"Wouldn't it be nice, Mike, if all the predators in the world canceled each other out?"

"You're full of surprises today."

"I know. I'm a woman of many facets. Happens also I'm a dutiful daughter. Look. My dad is conducting seminars at Cambridge this semester. Let's drive out so he can meet his future son-in-law."

"Fine. Now how about setting a date for the big event?"

She appeared lost in profound contemplation. Suddenly she brightened. "Tomorrow?"

"Perfect."

"Do we have time for a honeymoon?"

"We'll make time. The hell with executive dignity. Come here."

The driver, watching them in the rear-vision mirror, was impressed.

287

48

High-intensity beams slanted across the night-time sky above Hollywood. Television crews had installed their equipment beyond the glittering theatre marquee. Movie fans strained against the ropes to ogle and applaud as limousines lined up to discharge celebrities for the gala premiere of Arcadia Films' *The Romanoff File*.

Dan Hedrik arrived in a company car with three guests: Logan Stern, Paul Slater, and David Kiser, hustling them past the master of ceremonies. For Hedrik, this was the moment of truth. He had labored long hours with the director and film editor on the final print. He had personally supervized the dubbing of background music. And two weeks ago he had arranged a private screening for a noted critic, who, when the curtain fell, had sat in silence, enraptured, before awarding the picture his ultimate accolade in a single eloquent word: " *Wow!* "

So Dan Hedrik now felt reasonably confident. As he shepherded his guests into the theatre he heard squealing and then a burst of applause, and he knew that his star, Clyde Elliott, had stepped out of the next car in line, accompanied by a sumptuously endowed young actress who had played a minor role in the film. Hedrik was certain that Logan Stern's screenplay and Elliott's performance would be honored by the Academy.

The auditorium filled rapidly. There was electricity in the air, an undercurrent of excitement, of anticipation. But even now Dan Hedrik kept thinking how much more he would have relished this moment if only Kate Rennie and Ross Landry were at his side to share the triumph.